Main

BURNT RIVER

ALSO BY KARIN SALVALAGGIO

Bone Dust White

BURNT RIVER

Karin Salvalaggio

MINOTAUR BOOKS

NEW YORK

BURNT RIVER. Copyright © 2015 by Karin Salvalaggio Ltd. All rights reserved. Printed in the United States of America. For information, address St. Martin's Press, 175 Fifth Avenue, New York, N.Y. 10010.

www.minotaurbooks.com

The Library of Congress Cataloging-in-Publication Data is available upon request.

ISBN 978-1-250-04619-2 (hardcover)
ISBN 978-1-4668-4633-3 (e-book)

Minotaur books may be purchased for educational, business, or promotional use. For information on bulk purchases, please contact the Macmillan Corporate and Premium Sales Department at 1-800-221-7945, extension 5442, or write to specialmarkets@macmillan.com.

First Edition: May 2015

10 9 8 7 6 5 4 3 2 1

For my parents,
Karin and Graham Breck

Acknowledgments

Thank you, Deborah Crombie, Felicity Blunt, Kari Stuart, and Elizabeth Lacks for all your support and encouragement. It's a real comfort knowing you guys have my back. I'm also grateful to my lovely network of friends and family but especially for my wonderful children, Matteo and Daniela, who are always there for me. Lynn Tabb Noyce, Kevin J. Pusey Jr., Nick Campbell, Katherine Mozzone, and Rebecca Hurst—thank you for taking the time to answer questions of a more technical nature. Finally I'd like to give a very special thanks to my father, Graham King Breck, Chief Master Sergeant, U.S. Air Force (Ret.). My childhood may have been nomadic, but it has inspired me in unforeseen ways.

Between the wish and the thing the world lies waiting.

—CORMAC MCCARTHY,
All the Pretty Horses

BURNT
RIVER

The woman fell to her knees at the base of a tall pine and prayed for the third time that day. The smoke was so thick she could barely breathe. She squinted, trying to find a way out, but there was nothing she could call a path. The forest burned in spiraling pyres that rose up into an exploding canopy. The scream of splitting trees filled her ears. Covering her mouth with a shirtsleeve, she stood and ran toward the only opening she could see. Hot cinders dropped down on her hair and clothes; her eyes stung and her skin blistered. Silver-leafed shrubs scraped against her bare legs. She followed a narrow path that ended at the top of a cliff. Far below there was a rocky streambed; toward the east, a hint of blue sky. Taking hold of exposed tree roots, she lowered herself over the side. Her left shoulder ached and her hands were covered with sweat and blood. Halfway down she slipped. Her body glanced off the sharp rocks as she fell. She woke up in a shallow pool, eyes closed, but still breathing. Slowly the world regained its shape. Nearby she could hear water rushing over rocks. Closer still, her heartbeat vibrated through her body like the low notes of a double bass. She opened her eyes. That hint of blue sky was gone. Black smoke amassed as the fire razed everything in its path. Flames leapt across the narrow canyon. Along the shoreline, cottonwoods lit up one by one and wildflowers withered and turned to dust. Her arms and legs were motionless beneath the waterline. Her cries for help were lost on the fire.

1

The sun crept above the low hills, marking the eastern slopes of the wide valley. Granite boulders the size of houses glowed ghostly white and steam rose from the forested hills of monochrome pine. The Flathead River ran silver in the half-light, narrowing where it should have widened, a trickle where there should have been a flood. It was late July and no end to the heat wave was in sight. The big sky was shrouded in an acrid haze and further along the valley, the latest wildfire sent plumes of smoke nearly three hundred feet up into the air.

Dylan Reed rode his chestnut mare at an easy trot, picking his way along a narrow path that skirted the riverbank. With every sway of the saddle, his lips hardened into a grimace. He held the reins with one hand and massaged his thigh with the other. Six months earlier he'd been shot while doing house-to-house searches with his platoon in Afghanistan. He knew he was lucky. He could have just as easily come home in a box. He leaned out from the saddle to spit before pulling back his hat and focusing his green eyes on the escarpment. It was still a half-hour ride to where the cliffs overlooked the northern shore of Darby Lake. Overhead he heard the steady hum of an airplane's twin engines. Water tankers were using the lake as a fill station. They circled round the valley before skimming along the surface to fill their floats with water. With so many fires, they'd been flying nonstop all summer. He gave his mare a flick with the tail end of his reins, urging her forward at a faster pace.

Up ahead, Route 93 rested in the quiet cool of morning, but above him dark lines of tautly strung power cables buzzed and popped. He headed toward a heavy steel bridge spanning the Flathead River. The horse's hooves struck at the asphalt like hammers on an anvil, disturbing the starlings nesting high in the arches of the bridge. A roar went up and the flock rose in a swarm before darting back down between the metal girders. They flew low over the stony riverbank before disappearing into a stand of cottonwood trees that grew farther along the bend.

A rusted gate sagged across a road that had once led up to a scenic overlook. His friends John and Tyler had agreed to meet him there at six, but there was no sign of them. He guided his horse through the woods before rejoining the track some twenty yards farther on, and followed a series of tight switchbacks. In places the ground had cracked wide open and dry golden grasses grew in patches and hardened up like razor stubble. As he climbed, a view of the valley opened up. The low hills to the east were completely in shadow, but long fingers of light struck through the mist clinging to the river. A neat grid of streets marked the town of Wilmington Creek. The trees were so densely planted he could barely make out the rooftops. A patrol car was speeding along Route 93, its lights flashing. It entered Wilmington Creek from the south but did not leave.

At the final switchback, he struck out across the open face of the wide escarpment, coming close enough to the steep cliffs to catch glimpses of the still, dark waters of Darby Lake. The road ended at an unpaved turning circle that had once served as a parking lot for the scenic overview. Faded plastic bags fluttered in the trees and beer cans and whiskey bottles grew like wildflowers amongst the dwarf pines and scattered boulders. The safety railing had collapsed years earlier when a chunk of earth the size of a bus fell down into the lake. Warning signs were posted everywhere. The whole area was considered unstable. Dylan dismounted about twenty feet from the cliff's edge and rested his leg. It was numb from knee to hip, but the pain would come back soon enough. He dug his military-issue binoculars out of the saddlebag. Between him and the cliff's edge there were deep cracks in the rocky soil, some running in a solid arc that stretched into the undergrowth. Staying low, he inched his way across the bare earth. In places he could see the lake through the fissures. He hung his head over a drop of more than fifty feet and debris clattered down onto the exposed rocks that spilled like dice along the northern shore. He eased the strap of the binoculars around his neck and prayed the cliff would hold. The waterline had receded since he last checked. It was now possible to make out the contours of the lakebed. The dark rectangular shape stood out amongst a group of boulders. It was only a matter of time before one of the tanker pilots saw Ethan Green's pickup truck. Dylan rested his cheek against the warm earth and listened to the slow shifting of the overhanging cliff beneath him. A wolf howled and he turned the binoculars to the lake's eastern shore. It took a few minutes to spot the pack. A couple miles off, they emerged from the pine forest next to the picnic area before fanning out along the shore. In all there were six adults and three pups. He tracked their progress until they once again vanished in the trees.

Dylan returned to stable ground and sat against a boulder that faced the rising sun. He'd not gone to bed until one and had been on his horse by five. His stomach felt raw and his head hurt. Out of habit he patted his shirt pockets for his cigarettes, folding his hands across his lap when he remembered he'd quit. He closed his eyes and wished he'd kept his promise to stop drinking, too. The sun glowed warm and orange on his eyelids. He concentrated hard, picking out sounds both distant and close by. The land crackled in the growing light. It wasn't long before a shudder ran through his body and his head lolled to one side. He breathed deeply, his chest rising with each inhalation. His legs kicked out in front of him, his heels scratching at the earth as he muttered in his sleep. Another plane passed overhead and his eyes fluttered open but then shut just as quickly. His breathing slowed, his legs sprawled outward, one bent, the other dead straight.

A familiar voice cut right through his dreams. "Wake up, you lazy son of a bitch."

Dylan made a grab for the rifle that should have been lying across his lap and panicked when it wasn't there. He held his hands up, but could see nothing beyond a blinding light shining straight into his eyes. A shadow stepped between him and the rising sun and he blinked into a face he'd known since childhood.

Tyler's mouth was twisted into a smile of sorts. "Rise and shine, asshole."

Dylan kicked at him with his good leg. "Tyler, that was so fucked up."

Tyler stood with his hands in his pockets, watching his friend. He was shorter, but twice as wide. His thick arms were covered in tattoos and scars from where he'd been badly burned. His bald head was peppered with so many tiny bits of shrapnel that his skull looked like a speckled egg. He squatted down in front of Dylan and took a drag of his cigarette.

"I really shouldn't do that sort of shit to you."

Dylan couldn't disguise the tremor in his voice. "No, you shouldn't." He looked around. "Where's John?"

Another draw followed a steady gaze. "I was hoping he was with you."

"He's probably still asleep." Dylan tucked his chin in and crossed his arms. He wasn't cold, but he couldn't stop shaking. "Did you see what I meant about the water level?"

"Yeah, I'd say we're in trouble. How long do you reckon we've got?"

"Less than a week before it's visible from the air." He stood with difficulty and pointed up at the sky. A tanker plane was coming straight at them. It circled above the escarpment before dipping down toward the lake's surface. "One of these pilots might call it in."

"Not necessarily. I'm sure it's not the first truck that's been dumped in the lake. It could have been there for years."

"I don't think we should take that chance."

"It's supposed to rain."

"They've been saying that for weeks."

Tyler hurled a stone out toward the lake. "I knew this shit would come back to haunt us."

"Only bad choices."

"I don't recall being given much of a choice." Tyler teased a bit of tobacco out from between his teeth before walking toward the cliff. He stood with the tips of his boots over the edge. For a second he almost looked as if he might jump. "John is right. We're going to have to blow the rest of the cliff." He sprang up and down on the balls of his feet like he was testing how much weight it could take. "A few well-placed charges along these cracks and we could bury our problem forever."

"They'll hear it miles away."

"So what? It's not like they're going to dig up the lake." He stopped talking and set his eyes on Dylan. "And then there's Jessie."

"What about her?"

"You've got to talk to her. Find out what she's gonna say if all this blows up in our faces."

"Jessie was wasted that night. She doesn't know anything."

Tyler walked up to Dylan so their noses were just inches apart. "I never bought that. I think she was playing games. She knew how her father would feel if he found out she was hanging out with Ethan." He took a long drag off his cigarette. "We've got to make sure she stays quiet no matter how much pressure is put on her."

"John said she won't talk about it."

"John's full of shit. He doesn't want to upset her."

"You can't blame Jessie for wanting to put it all behind her."

Tyler grabbed Dylan by the collar. "Look, I really don't give a damn about what she has or hasn't been through," he said, holding on tight when Dylan struggled against him. "Either you sort her out, or I will."

Dylan broke away. "If you touch Jessie . . ."

"Struck a nerve, did I?"

"Fuck off."

Tyler cupped his hands against the breeze and lit another cigarette. "I always wondered whether you might have taken advantage of the state she was in that night. She stayed at your place, slept in your bed." He blew a thin stream of smoke in Dylan's direction. "John's not here. You can tell me, bro."

Dylan limped over to his horse and pulled a bottle of water out of his saddlebag. "You've got a sick mind, you know that?"

Tyler walked to the ledge again. "Calm down, little man. I'm just fucking with you. Whether John likes it or not, we've got to make her understand what's going on here. If someone spots the truck, she's got more to lose than anyone else."

"I know."

"She's not a child anymore."

"I guess."

"So you'll go speak to her."

Dylan leaned his forehead against the saddle. "I will."

"Good. By the way, I called my buddy Wayne."

"The ski patrol guy?"

"Yeah, he owes me big time. He'll give me what we need to blow the cliff. Been squirreling away explosives for years."

"How'd he manage that?"

"He's on avalanche patrol. No one seems to keep track of how much they use when they're out on the slopes."

"It has to happen this week."

"That goes without saying."

"You can trust him to keep his mouth shut?"

"Relax. I own his ass. He won't say a word."

Dylan untied his horse and struggled back into the saddle. "I'm heading home. You coming?"

"Yeah," Tyler said, his eyes never leaving the heavy plumes of smoke that blighted the southern sky. "I'll be along in a minute."

2

Police Chief Aiden Marsh stood on the sidewalk outside the Wilmington Creek Bar and Grill with his hat in his hands. At five foot eleven and without an ounce of spare flesh, he had an air of efficiency about him. He was so focused on his conversation with an older gentleman, he failed to notice Detective Macy Greeley's state-issue SUV gliding into the parking space right behind him. She sat in the driver's seat with the windows open, sipping her coffee. The two men kept their voices low, but once Macy cut the engine she could hear every word.

"Jeremy, I just want you to know how sorry I am."

The man Macy guessed to be Jeremy Dalton leaned his considerable bulk against the doorframe and smoothed his closely clipped gray beard with a meaty paw. Eyes in shadow, he had a ball cap pulled down tight on his head. His long gray hair fell past his shoulders.

"Aiden, with all due respect, I don't want your sympathy. I want answers."

"And I promise I'm going to get those answers for you."

Swallowing hard, the older man fought for control. "I just can't believe my boy is gone."

"Detective Macy Greeley should be here soon. Once she's had a chance to look things over I'll bring her in to talk to you."

"It doesn't seem right that they're sending a woman."

"Greeley is very good at what she does."

"You know her?"

Aiden picked his words carefully. "I've met her but we've never worked together. She was in Collier when they had all that trouble a couple of years ago."

"I hope you don't feel like I overstepped by calling the governor. I just thought he'd give you more men. I didn't realize they would send an investigator up from Helena to take over."

Aiden squeezed Jeremy's shoulder. "It's okay, Jeremy. I'm grateful for the help. I want to make sure we get this right."

Jeremy's chin barely moved. "Don't be too much longer. I've got to get home. I don't want Annie and the girls finding out from someone else."

The door closed and Aiden walked a few paces along the raised wooden walkway. He stood for a long time staring across the street. Macy had met him five years earlier at a law enforcement convention in Las Vegas, but their paths hadn't crossed since. During his seven-year tenure as Wilmington Creek's police chief, there'd been virtually no crime. Macy's colleagues in Helena were impressed, but she was keeping an open mind. She was too much of a cynic to believe such idyllic places existed anymore. Unlike most law enforcement personnel in Montana, Aiden kept his hair fairly long, but she couldn't find any fault with his uniform. It was immaculately pressed. He wore sunglasses, so she couldn't see his eyes in the fragmented reflections that scrolled across the mirrored lenses. From experience she already knew they were a pleasing baby blue.

Macy took a sip of her coffee and sank down farther in the seat. Since leaving home, she'd been plagued by the beginnings of a headache. She blamed the third glass of red wine she'd had last night instead of dinner. She'd been nibbling on a bagel for a couple hours, but really needed something more substantial if she was going to make it through the day. The first telephone call from the head of the state police had come at around two in the morning. When she answered, she thought Ray Davidson was calling her for personal reasons; it had been three weeks since they'd last spent time together. She should have known better. A half hour later she was leaving the home she shared with her mother, Ellen, and one-and-a-half-year-old son, Luke. She had a small suitcase tucked in the back of her vehicle and the state police captain's words ringing in her ear.

Macy, the governor called me personally. There's going to be a lot of pressure to get this right. I need you to get up to Wilmington Creek immediately.

Everything else she knew about the case had come in over the speakerphone as she drove north on Route 93. John Dalton had left the army right before Christmas on an honorable discharge and returned to his childhood home. He was twenty-six years of age and a highly decorated war veteran who'd survived three deployments in some of the most dangerous places in the world. According to witnesses, he'd stopped at a bar called The Whitefish to buy cigarettes at quarter past one in the morning. A half hour later he was found dead in the alleyway. There was a single gunshot wound to the back of his head and two in his upper back. The medical examiner was a cautious woman, so it surprised Macy she was already saying that it looked like an execution.

Macy followed Aiden Marsh's gaze. A group of patrol officers were gathered in the alleyway between The Whitefish and Flathead Valley Savings and Loan. Somewhere beyond a low screen that had been erected, John Dalton was lying facedown in the gravel.

There was a tap on the car window and Macy put her coffee to one side. Aiden stood a few feet from the door. He'd removed his sunglasses and was staring down at the pavement. It was only when he raised his chin that she saw he was trying not to cry. Macy grabbed her bag and stepped out of her vehicle. Her long red hair was secured in a ponytail and the only thing on her face was an ever-thickening layer of freckles. It was colder than she'd expected, but the tops of the east-facing shop windows were already ablaze in the reflected light of dawn. By midmorning, temperatures would be in the eighties. By noon they'd reach one hundred.

They shook hands, but did not smile. "Good to see you again, Detective Greeley. I just wish it were under better circumstances."

"You and me both. I take it you knew the victim and his family."

Aiden tilted his head toward the restaurant and spoke in short bursts. "I've known the Daltons for years. John's father, Jeremy, is waiting inside. Telling him about John . . . well, that was the hardest thing I've ever done."

They walked across Main Street side by side. Wilmington Creek was well kept. Low-lying buildings struck out in even intervals in both directions. Mature trees shaded the sidewalks. Houses stood back while their wide green lawns stepped forward. White picket fences framed colorful borders. Three blocks to the west, Route 93 followed the rambling course of the Flathead River. During the drive up from Helena, Macy had passed hay fields as finely sewn as gossamer. They rolled off for miles before butting up against the foothills. The view ended there. Wildfire haze obscured the Whitefish Range. There'd been three fires in the area in the past two months. The latest was southwest of town.

Macy slipped on a pair of protective shoe coverings and pulled her sunglasses back on her head. The officers who'd been keeping watch over John parted as she and Aiden drew near. Not one of them looked up.

"Tell me about the family."

"The victim's father, Jeremy Dalton, owns one of the biggest ranches in the valley. John has been working there since he was discharged from the military."

"What about his mother? I heard she was unwell."

"Annie's been suffering from early onset dementia for quite a few years now."

"Any siblings?"

"A twin sister named Jessie, although you wouldn't know it if you met her. They look nothing alike." Aiden pulled up the crime scene tape and Macy ducked underneath as she slipped on a pair of latex gloves. "The family is well connected."

"I kind of figured that, given the number of phone calls I received in the middle of the night."

"Jeremy and the governor go way back. Hunting, fishing, that sort of thing."

"When will the forensics team be here?"

"They're on their way. The medical examiner and the photographer finished about an hour ago." He handed Macy an evidence bag containing a wallet. "We found the wallet in his back pocket. It's full of cash. This wasn't a robbery."

"What about his cell phone?"

"On the ground next to him. It's been smashed up a bit. Already sent it down to Helena."

Macy walked toward the front entrance of the saloon. "If it's okay with you, I'd like to start over here."

Aiden pointed out the two security cameras located along the roofline. "They're directed toward the entrance. There's nothing covering the alleyway or the parking lot."

Macy peered through the glass door. Only a single lamp above the bar was illuminated. There weren't any windows that she could see. She thought of going in, but changed her mind.

"I'm guessing you didn't find anything on the security tapes."

"Nothing so far. The bank next door and a couple shops further along have cameras. We'll check them all."

She turned toward the alleyway and tried to steady her nerves. There was no avoiding the inevitable. "Shall we?"

The sunlight slicing between the buildings glanced off the pale gravel. Macy lowered her sunglasses. The employee entrance was propped open with a cinder block. There were muted voices she recognized from the same talk-radio program she'd been listening to on the drive. Farther along, an access road that serviced the businesses along the eastern side of Main Street ran perpendicular to the alleyway. Beyond the road, there was a low white bungalow with a bright green lawn and a screened-in side porch. She could see the silhouette of a man seated inside. He was bolt upright in his chair and seemed to be staring straight at her.

Macy pointed at the house. "I'll want to talk to the guy hanging out on his screen porch. He may have seen something."

Aiden shielded his eyes from the glare. "That would be Mr. Walker. I'll send over a couple of officers to speak to him, but don't get too excited, he's almost blind."

Macy slid the plastic sheeting away. The dark entry wound on the back of John Dalton's skull was clearly visible. A pool of blood soaked into the loose gravel beneath his head and she was relieved she couldn't see the exit wound on his face. Even if she hadn't been told ahead of time, she would have guessed he was ex-military. His hair was clipped short and there was something about the details of his dress that spoke of years of discipline. A bloodstained T-shirt stretched across his wide shoulders; two bullet wounds spaced a few inches apart cut into his right shoulder. No tattoos or distinctive markings were visible on his arms. There were no abrasions to his hands and his wrists were free of ligature marks. He wore faded blue jeans, but his boots appeared to be brand new. Macy pulled his wallet out of the evidence bag and flipped through it. There was a driver's license and military identification card along with several photos, a couple of credit cards, and more than a hundred dollars in cash. A frayed business card for a therapist with offices in Collier was tucked into a recess.

Macy picked up a flashlight lying on the ground next to the body and read the label. *Property of The Whitefish* was scrawled in black marker across a piece of masking tape.

"Did the people inside know the victim?"

"Yes, but at that hour there was only one customer left and he's still drunk. According to the manager, John spent most of the time he was inside speaking to his on-again off-again girlfriend, Lana Clark."

She held up the flashlight. "So they heard shots fired and came out to investigate?"

"They heard something that sounded like a gunshot, but with the music on inside they didn't think much of it. Thought it might be a car backfiring or kids screwing around. The manager found the body when he came out to smoke a cigarette."

On the concrete steps leading to the employee entrance, tiny shards of broken glass glittered amongst the piles of discarded cigarette butts. The light fixture above the door was broken. "Any idea when that happened?"

"According to the manager, it must have happened last night."

"A blind spot, a broken bulb, and no sign of robbery. This doesn't feel random."

"That was my thinking."

"Three tours of duty in Afghanistan and he's gunned down in his hometown."

"It doesn't seem right."

Macy checked her notes. "This woman in the bar, Lana Clark? She's an on/off girlfriend?"

"That's the story that's going around."

"Where is she now?"

"Patrol car took her home to pick up a few things. She's pretty shaken up."

"When's she coming back?"

"It will be another hour. She lives pretty far out of town."

"Did you find John Dalton's car keys?"

"They were in his pocket."

"Do you have them? I'd like to have a look in his truck."

"No need. It wasn't locked."

John Dalton's pickup truck had six inches of dried mud haloing the wheel wells and looked like it had been rolled at least once. The windshield was dotted with divots and a fine web of cracks. On the door a panel read *Dalton Ranch—proudly raising quality livestock since 1863*. Inside, a single rifle was locked in a gun rack. Empty food containers and Coke bottles were scattered about on the floor. Everything was covered in dust and dog hair. It smelled like a farmyard.

"It looks like he lived in his car."

"Given the size of the ranch, this is probably where he spent most of his time."

"So what's the deal with Lana Clark?"

"Since he returned home there's been a lot of confusion concerning John's relationship status. There have been two girls in particular. Lana was one, and Tanya Rose was the other."

"You do know the Daltons well."

"It's a small town and people like to talk. Apparently, Tanya broke up with John because of Lana. Word has it that he has been trying to get her back ever since."

"I'll need to speak to her too."

"I'll let her know."

"Any idea who John Dalton was with earlier in the evening?"

"A couple of friends. We're calling them in for interviews."

"Is it possible he came across something he wasn't supposed to see? Do drug dealers use this parking lot?"

"It's a rural community. You go a few miles north or south and we wouldn't notice if you set off a bomb. There are better places to deal drugs."

"How do you think he was adjusting to being back home? Three tours of duty can take their toll." Macy poked through the glove compartment and came up with a semiautomatic pistol. She slid the chamber open and found it was loaded. She held it up. "He may have gone looking for trouble."

"According to his dad, he's been working pretty long hours. Really focused."

"This is a man who was dating two women. Seems like he had plenty of time for trouble."

Aiden shrugged. "We should probably go speak to Jeremy. He's anxious to get home to his family before they wake up and turn on the news."

Macy slipped the handgun into an evidence bag and shut the car door. "Once they've done a preliminary, I want the truck towed down to Helena for further processing."

Macy suspected that Jeremy Dalton kept his heavily calloused hands folded on the table so no one would realize how much they were shaking. His deeply tanned face was lined with fine creases. Like on a map, the contours changed depending on the depth of his expression. Out on the street there was a flurry of activity as the forensics team pulled up to the alleyway. His eyes shot up, but his hands stayed clenched. For a long time he stared, the valleys of his face sagging as the seconds passed.

Macy pulled a slim black notebook out of her bag. "Mr. Dalton, my name is Detective Macy Greeley. The chief of the state police, Ray Davidson, has personally requested that I handle this case. I'm normally based down in Helena, but I've worked up here in the Flathead Valley before."

Jeremy cleared his throat. "I was just on the phone with Sheriff Warren Mayfield. He speaks highly of you. Said he liked the way you handled things when they had that trouble in Collier."

"I'll have to thank him." Macy pushed her business card across the surface of the table with her index finger. "First let me say that I will do whatever it takes to bring your son's killer to justice."

Jeremy smoothed his beard. He didn't wear a wedding ring and his eyes were pale and red-rimmed. "When John was in Afghanistan, I stayed up a lot of nights worrying. Since he came back home for good, I've been sleeping like a baby."

Macy waited.

"He had other options but he enlisted anyway. Felt it was his duty."

"From what I've heard, he was a fine soldier. You must have been very proud of him. Did you serve in the military?"

"I was too young for Vietnam and too old for the next one." His voice shook. "I guess I got lucky."

There was an older gentleman sitting a couple booths away. He was dressed in a dusty pair of jeans, a long-sleeved shirt, and work boots. His white hair was cut close to his scalp and his dark eyes hadn't left Macy since she walked in the restaurant. Other than Jeremy, he was the only person there who wasn't law enforcement.

Macy returned the older man's stare. "Did you come on your own, Mr. Dalton?"

Jeremy took off his hat and twisted it in his hands. "I woke up my foreman, Wade, when I got the call. He drove."

"Do you mind if he sits in on our conversation?"

"Wade Larkin is like family."

Macy wrote Wade's name down in her notebook. "When was the last time you saw John?"

"Supper yesterday evening. We ate around six. He said he was going to see friends."

"Anyone in particular?"

"I expect it was the same ones as usual." He glanced over at Aiden before rattling off a list. "Dylan Reed, Tyler Locke, Chase Lane. Beyond that I'm not really sure."

"Did John often stay out late on a weeknight?"

"Not normally. Today was supposed to be his day off."

"Can you think of anyone who would have wanted to harm your son?"

19

"If there was a problem, he never mentioned it."

Macy thought back on what she knew about the Daltons. "What about your family's ranch? Have there ever been any disputes that have turned ugly?"

"We've been in business a long time. We've had disgruntled employees. We've been sued more than once, but there's been nothing in the past few years."

"Any issues with the local militias? There's been some friction in other parts of the state. Some of the big landowners have been targeted."

Jeremy looked down at his hands. "It's just a few crazy libertarians that are making things difficult. If you ask me, they're pushing their luck with their latest demands."

"How do you figure that?"

"They don't believe in private ownership of productive land. That's not going to go over well with anyone in this state. Like I'd just roll over and give up my ranch to a bunch of misfits that have nothing better to do than play at being soldiers."

"Have you been threatened?"

"Nothing more than a couple of late-night phone calls."

"Did you inform the police?"

"I can't bring myself to take those idiots seriously." He paused. "There's a woman who's been researching the militia groups in the valley. I think her name was Patricia Dune. You should ask her if you want to know more. In my opinion she seems a little too well informed."

Macy glanced up at Aiden. "Do you know about this?"

"She interviewed me a couple of months ago. She's doing research for her doctoral thesis. It all seems aboveboard but there's been some talk."

"What kind of talk?"

"People think she's stirring things up unnecessarily. They're worried—"

Jeremy interrupted him. "She came out to interview me a month ago. Kept asking about Ethan Green. I had to ask her to leave."

Macy frowned. Ethan Green was a name she knew well. He'd formed one of the state's first private militias. "I thought Ethan Green skipped town after a warrant was issued for his arrest."

Aiden spoke again. "He's wanted for questioning in relation to a sexual assault that occurred last year in Collier. No one has seen him since."

Macy made some notes before asking Jeremy the next question. "Why do you think Patricia Dune is so interested in Green?"

"I have no idea. You'll have to ask her."

"Do you know if Green believed in public ownership of productive land?"

"He did at one time. I'm not sure what he believes now. His manifesto was subject to change."

"Could he have been the person who called you?"

"It wasn't him."

"You seem very sure."

"That's because I am. I've known Ethan all my life."

"Is it possible that John came into contact with him?"

"My kids knew to stay clear. There's no way they'd have gone anywhere near him."

"This friction between you and Green. Do you think it could have become violent?"

"Our argument dates back to before my children were born. I doubt either of us gives it much thought these days."

"This is going to be difficult for your family, but we'll need to interview each of them, and anyone your son John worked with. He may have confided in someone."

Jeremy stumbled over his words. "I have to get home. I have no idea how I'm going to tell them . . ."

He pressed the base of his palms into his eyes and wept. Macy was the only one who didn't look away. This man had lost his only son. She fought hard not to imagine how that must feel. Her son Luke seemed so far away. She had the sudden urge to escape the diner and drive straight home. She had no idea how she could protect him if she was never there. Macy handed Jeremy a tissue from a box someone had placed on the table, and signaled Wade Larkin to come over.

"Mr. Dalton, a couple of officers are going to escort you home. There's a victims support officer here from Helena. Her name is Sue Barnet, and she is going to make sure you have everything you need. I've left you my business card. You should feel free to call me any time. There might be something you remember. It may not seem important, but I want you to tell me anyway."

Macy gathered her bag and slipped the thick strap over her shoulder. "I'll come out to see you and your family this afternoon. Mr. Dalton, it's important that I speak to anyone who was close to John."

He picked up her card and slipped it into his shirt pocket before pushing his chair away from the table. His legs buckled as he rose from his seat, but Wade was there to catch him. In the silence that followed, the cell phone that had been sitting on the table next to him rang.

3

essie Dalton rubbed the sleep out of her eyes and rolled over to check the time. It was a little after six in the morning and the bedroom was still dark. She fell back on the pillows and stared at the low ceiling. She'd spent most of the night making lists in her head and now she'd be too tired to get anything done. She put her hand on her chest. Her heart was still beating. At times she felt it was all she had to remind her that she was alive. A floorboard creaked and she sat up.

"Who's there?"

Her mother, Annie, passed through the narrow strip of light cutting through the gap in the curtains. She wore a flowered dressing gown and her long gray hair swayed like a skirt from a perfect parting. She clutched one of her hands to her throat.

"Did I wake you?"

Jessie watched her mother, trying to judge her mood. Not that it mattered. Annie's temperament was difficult to pin down. Like a stray bullet, its direction could shift in unexpected ways.

Annie sat on the edge of Jessie's bed and poked at the thin quilt with her index finger, making patterns in the folds. Her words landed in perfect time with her finger. "Your. Brother. John. Is. Dead."

Jessie waited for the flustered explanations that usually followed her mother's more outrageous statements, but they didn't come. Jessie spoke to her mother the same way she spoke to her daughter—a lift at the end of each line and a smile on her face, even when she wanted to cry.

"John is home from Afghanistan now. You don't have to worry anymore."

Annie held up her cell phone. Her nails were shredded and her knuckles were swollen like ripened fruit ready to split. She brought the screen within inches of her eyes and scrunched up her face.

"I can't make sense of it. If he is dead, how could he send me a message?"

Jessie pictured Annie ten years younger and forty pounds heavier. The woman sitting in front of her was an imposter. Too tired to play their usual game, Jessie changed her tone. The smile was gone.

"It must be some sort of a joke."

"John was the serious one in the family. He wouldn't have joked about something like this."

"Quit talking about him in the past tense."

Annie inspected her reflection in the mirror above the dresser. She ran her fingers through her hair and frowned. "I can't count how many times I imagined him dying. Every time the doorbell rang I thought it would be soldiers coming to tell us he was gone. It got so bad I ripped it out of the wall."

"Nobody blames you. We were all worried." Jessie reached for the phone. "Let me see the message."

Annie snatched it away and pressed it to her chest. "How do I know you won't read my other messages? They're private. I don't want you seeing them."

"I promise that I'll just read the one John sent."

"John is dead. He couldn't have sent it."

"Can I have the phone?"

"You've lied to me before."

"I've never lied to you."

"Now I know you're lying."

"Mom, I'm trying to help. I don't want you to be upset. I'm sure John is asleep at his place."

"His bed's not been slept in. He never came home last night."

John lived in a mobile home out near the stables. Jessie checked the time again. It was just coming up to six thirty. As a rule, her mother wasn't supposed to leave the main house. They worried she'd wander off and get lost in the deep canyons that bordered the ranch, or worse, head for the Flathead River. She'd succeeded in getting out twice. Both times they found her contemplating the drop at Bridger Falls.

"He probably stayed at Tyler's place. Did you speak to Dad?"

"Jeremy's not here either." Her long fingers fluttered through the air before landing on her chin. "Probably out with that woman. I told you it would happen eventually. Give Jeremy time and he'll tire of me. I hear him whispering to my doctor. I know he's going to have me put in an institution."

"I promise not to read the other messages. I just want to see the one you received from John."

"Maybe he'd still be alive if I heard it ring, but I've been sleeping so soundly. It's all those pills the doctor makes me take. I'm surprised I can still dream."

"Mom, the phone."

"You'll give it right back?"

"Of course I will."

She started to hand it over. "You realize he's gone now. Nothing you do will change that."

"Stop saying he's dead. You're scaring me."

Annie dropped the phone on Jessie's lap and turned to the window. "You should be scared."

The phone was warm from being held so tightly in her mother's hands. Jessie turned it over and read what was on the screen.

I'm sorry, Annie. John gave me no choice. He had to die.

Jessie reread the words to herself several times before whispering them aloud. In the otherwise silent room they sounded like a prayer. Annie slapped at the air in front of her, trying to catch a mosquito. Everyone in Wilmington Creek knew Annie was unwell. She'd been diagnosed with bipolar disorder in her teens and had been living on a changing cocktail of medication ever since. But it was the early onset of dementia that took everyone by surprise. Not that anything could have been done if they had realized what was going on. In an attempt to hold on to reality, Annie began to obsess over writing down every thought that came into her head. Jessie remembered the look on her father's face when he came across the stacks of notebooks hidden in the back of the cupboard under the stairs. They'd pored through them together while Annie pounded at the locked office door. She remembered events from more than fifty years earlier like they happened yesterday. The only thing she ever wanted from the store was writing pens and paper. Three years on, and her fingers were stained black and her eyes ruined.

Jessie tried phoning her brother, but there was no response.

"This is just a sick joke," she repeated.

Annie ripped into her cuticles with her teeth. "I have to decide what to wear to John's funeral. Everything I have is so big now. I want to look nice."

"There isn't going to be a funeral. John is alive."

Annie grabbed her daughter's chin and twisted it upward so their eyes met. "Why don't you just believe me this once? It's not a competition. You and Jeremy don't have to be right all the time."

Jessie tore her mother's hand away. "John isn't dead."

"Call Jeremy if you don't believe me. He always seems to know what's going on around here."

Jessie poked at the keypad absentmindedly. Doubt crept through the curtains with daylight. Jessie worked hard to hold it back. John was alive. He was home now. He was finally safe.

Annie paced in front of the backlit curtains. "Come on now. Call Jeremy. What are you afraid of?"

Jeremy answered on the first ring. "Hi, sweetheart," he said softly, swallowing back something.

There was an eruption in the pit of Jessie's stomach. Jeremy's voice was wrong. It was soft. Jeremy was never soft. Jeremy was like a bull. He didn't so much enter rooms as crash into them. He didn't so much talk to people as bully them. Jessie closed her eyes. She already knew her mother was right. Jeremy never called her *sweetheart*.

"Where are you?" she asked.

"In town. There's been some trouble."

"It's John, isn't it? Something has happened."

"I'll be home shortly. I'll tell you everything then."

"Is he really dead?"

Jeremy's voice cracked. "I'm sorry you heard from someone else. I should have been the one . . ."

Jessie let out a sharp cry. "When?"

"In the middle of the night."

"Someone texted Mom using John's phone."

"Christ. How's Annie?"

Jessie lowered her voice. "She's in my room."

"What's she doing?"

"Pacing. She's real upset."

"I'm coming straight home."

"Why is this happening?"

"I don't know, Jessie. I honestly don't know."

Annie Dalton took hold of the curtains and laughed. "I told you I was right about John."

Jessie read the message again. It felt like her heart was being wrung dry. She couldn't breathe, let alone speak. She had no words. Her mother swung upward and pulled the drapes wide. As if caught in stage lights, she opened her arms to the rising sun.

"It's a good day to die. Don't you think?"

"Shut up."

"Come on, look at that amazing view. Who could be sad on a day like today?"

Jessie jumped out of bed and shoved Annie against the closet, slapping her before grabbing her long face. The bones were there for everyone to see. If Jessie knew anything about anatomy she could have labeled them all.

"I told you to shut up."

A smile played on Annie's lips. "And I told you your brother was dead."

Jessie was screaming. "Not another word. I'm tired of this. We all are."

Annie sank down to the floor and curved her ink-stained fingers around her skull. Jessie couldn't stop shaking. She crawled back into bed and curled up in a ball beneath the blankets. There was a crude tattoo of a rose on the back of her hand. She always scratched at it when she was upset. She had no memory of the night she visited the tattoo parlor in Reno. Her daughter had been conceived in that same fog. Tara was now six years old. It had been a year since Jessie'd had her last drink, four years since she last used meth. The fog was finally starting to lift.

Somewhere in the house a door sighed on its hinges. Tara was awake. John had promised to take her riding. He'd mentioned something about going to see a pony a friend was selling. Jessie checked the time. It was still early. There was no rush. Then she remembered that John wasn't taking Tara anywhere. She dug her nails into the rose tattoo and felt the skin break.

Annie spoke slowly. "John was my only son. I loved him more than anything."

"I'm sorry. I shouldn't have hit you."

"You're not the first. You won't be the last."

"You're not well. None of this is your fault."

'When I couldn't get pregnant, Jeremy said I was to blame, but he was the one with the problem." She lowered her voice. "You and your brother proved that. You saved me."

"I've never saved anyone."

Annie rose to her feet and brushed herself off. The downstairs television had been switched on. Tara always watched it with the volume turned up high. Jessie and her brother John had done the same thing when they were young. It drowned out the sound of their parents arguing.

"I wanted to shout the truth from the rooftops, but by then I'd learned to keep my mouth shut. You were the one thing Jeremy couldn't take from me."

Jessie got out of bed and picked through the clothes she'd dropped on the floor the night before. "Tara is awake. I have to get dressed."

"You let her watch too much television. She'll turn out to be nothing if you're not careful."

Jessie was thinking she might let Tara spend the rest of the day in front of the television. She wouldn't notice time passing. She wouldn't remember promises made and broken. She had an entire life ahead of her to feel pain. It didn't have to be today.

"Leave Tara alone. She's fine where she is."

Annie stared out the window. Her eyes were clear. For the first time in ages she sounded completely lucid. "We've got company coming. I better go and make some coffee. It's going to be a difficult day for all of us."

Her mother slammed the door shut as she left the bedroom. Jessie turned to the window and watched four vehicles make their way up the long driveway. From a distance it looked as if they were coupled like train carriages. Lights flashed. Dust kicked up in their wake. They were coming whether they were welcome or not. Jessie felt like she was on the cusp of waking but still caught in a dream. John couldn't really be dead. He was her twin, her best friend and her protector. He was a foot taller than her and could throw her over his shoulder and run for miles if he wanted to. His hands were freakishly large. He used to palm her head like a basketball.

The cars pulled into the driveway and the flashing lights went out. She watched her father walk across the gravel drive, hitching up his trousers as he went. Seconds later his voice filled the house. He called out Jessie's name with a sense of resignation that left her cold. She hesitated in her bedroom, her fingers hovering above the door handle. Jeremy barely tolerated having her in the house. It had always been John who stood up for her, encouraged their father to be more patient, to show more forgiveness. Jessie stepped away from the door. She was still wearing the T-shirt she'd slept in. Her dark, unwashed hair fell across her face. She couldn't go downstairs looking like this. Her father called for her again and she reached for a pair of shorts hanging off the back of a chair. Her mother started screaming before Jessie had a chance to put them on. She bolted from the room, banging her hip hard against the doorframe as she cut the corner. She caught glimpses of her parents through the banister as she made her way downstairs. Annie had Jeremy by the throat. Wade had hold of Jeremy's right arm as her father's left struck out blindly at Annie, knocking a bronze statue of a horse from where it sat on a shelf.

"Because of you, Jeremy. My son is dead because of you."

A uniformed officer grabbed hold of Annie and she swung an elbow back, hitting him hard on the cheek. Another officer locked his arms around her so tightly she could barely move. She kicked at Jeremy as he lunged toward her, striking him hard in the breastbone with her bare foot. At that point there was little they could do to subdue him. He was a bull. Two officers piled on top of him while Wade begged both him and Annie to calm down.

Jessie took the rest of the stairs two at a time. The living room was empty and the television turned off. Jessie opened all the cupboards, looking for her daughter. The lilt in her voice had returned.

"It's okay, Tara. You can come out now."

Aiden Marsh appeared at the door. "Tara's being looked after outside. If it's any comfort, I don't think she saw any of it."

Jessie bit her lip. She couldn't keep her hands still. She let out a sharp cry and leaned against the back of the sofa. She felt winded.

Aiden put a hand on her shoulder. "Just take a second to calm yourself down."

She covered her ears. There was a constant roar. Her father and mother were trading insults through the closed door that separated the entryway from the kitchen. Wade was trying his best to talk sense into Jeremy, but it wasn't working.

Jessie shook her head. "I don't have a second."

"Tara is all that really matters right now, and she's fine. You take that second."

Jessie felt flushed and hot. She dragged her hair away from her face. It stuck to her damp palms like cobwebs. "I'm sorry. Annie isn't herself."

"It's nobody's fault."

A patrol officer entered the room. Jessie recognized the face, but forgot the name. His right cheek was swelling from where he'd been caught by Annie's sharp elbow.

"Something's wrong with Jeremy. He's out cold."

Jessie was unsteady on her feet. She thought she'd never make it to the door. In the kitchen, her mother was shouting out instructions for making a pot of coffee. At some point she must have memorized the manual. Her father's long legs stretched out across the front hallway. She was surprised she'd not heard him hit the floor. It should have sounded like thunder.

Wade Larkin was on the floor next to Jeremy, speaking to him in a low voice. Jessie knelt down and placed her hand on her father's heaving chest. His heart was pumping like a piston. His eyes were wide and searching. Jessie stared. She'd never seen him look vulnerable. She could put a pillow to his face, and he wouldn't be able to struggle against her. The thought was oddly comforting. Wade's voice was in her ear. He smelled of coffee and cattle. Another sort of comfort.

"Jessie's here now. Everything is going to be okay."

She put a hand on her father's forehead. There was a fine layer of sweat, but the skin was chilled. He didn't feel human anymore.

"Jeremy, you have to let us take care of you now."

Aiden stood above them. "There was a mountain rescue helicopter in the air already. They should be here in less than five minutes."

The door leading to the kitchen opened. Annie was no longer shouting. They'd put her in handcuffs. As she was led to the front door she stumbled on the hem of her dressing gown. Jessie looked down at her hand. Jeremy was squeezing it tight. Like John's, his hands were large. She couldn't remember the last time he'd touched her. She blinked and her mother was gone.

Jeremy's voice was forced. "I don't need a fucking helicopter. I need that woman out of my house."

Jessie snatched her hand back and Jeremy's fingers slid away like scales. "What you need to do is calm down."

Wade's knees creaked as he shifted his weight. "It wouldn't hurt for a doctor to take a look."

Jessie noticed the knife lying on the floor next to the skirting board and picked it up. It was from a set in the kitchen. "What is this doing here?"

Jeremy tried to sit up. "Your mother threatened me."

Jessie handed the knife to Aiden. "Please take it."

Her father was still trying to get up. "Lots of witnesses this time."

Jessie closed her eyes. Over the years she and John had had ring-side seats. "There have always been witnesses."

The windows rattled. A helicopter was setting down somewhere nearby. The front door was wide open and warm dust blew straight into the house. Paramedics soon followed. Jessie leaned against the wall with her T-shirt pulled down over her knees. She didn't realize she was crying until Aiden handed her a tissue.

"Where are you taking my mother?"

"I've called the psychiatric ward at Collier County Hospital. We're lucky they have a bed available." He took hold of her arm. "You need some fresh air."

"I have to get dressed."

"I'll wait outside your room."

Jessie struggled with the buttons on her shirt, pulling it off and grabbing another when she couldn't get her hands to stop shaking. She stuck her head out the open window and took a deep breath. Through the trees she could see her daughter moving back and forth in a graceful arc. The rope swing hung from one of the oak trees on the western side of the house. Tara's long black hair flowed behind her like a cape and her mouth was wide with laughter. Jessie didn't recognize the redheaded woman pushing her. She called Aiden into her room.

"Who's with Tara?" she said, pulling on a pair of shorts. She was so thin, her hip bones protruded like stones.

"She's the special investigator the state sent up from Helena. She seems okay."

"Seems?"

"I don't really know her that well so I'm mostly going by what I hear. She's good at her job."

"Why has someone come all the way from Helena?"

"Your father called the governor."

"That's just like him."

"He means well."

Jessie tied her dark hair in a tight ponytail and sat down on the edge of the bed. She couldn't think what she was supposed to do next. In a matter of hours her world had tilted on its axis. She swallowed back the sick that kept building in her throat.

"It's too much. I can't do this."

Aiden sat next to her. "If anyone can do this, it's you. If it helps, think of Tara. Stay strong for her."

Jessie covered her face in her hands. "Why John?"

"We're trying to figure that out."

"He was home. He was safe."

"I want you to think very carefully, Jessie. Do you know of any reason why someone would do this?"

Jessie inhaled like she was taking a hit. The imaginary smoke curled through the contours of her lungs like birds riding a slipstream. She wanted to vanish into the horizons that usually followed.

"You and John were close. He would have told you if something wasn't right."

She held her breath. She wasn't ready to let go of her need just yet.

Aiden shook her. "Keep that up and you're going to pass out."

Her vision blurred. She felt light-headed. She exhaled.

"Think, Jessie."

She focused in on John's photo and felt his pale eyes on her.

"He's been different since he got back."

"Different how?"

"He never talked to me about it. He never said why. I thought it would be okay given time, but now there's no time. I tried to discuss it with Jeremy but you know what he's like. He said I was just trying to get attention. After the shit I've pulled, I can't blame him."

"Stop beating yourself up. You're clean now. And you worked damn hard to get that way. No backsliding."

She leaned her head on his shoulder. "I'm scared."

"We all are."

"I don't want you to take my mother away."

"I'm sorry, but I really don't have a choice."

4

Tara Dalton's bare feet brushed against the low tree branches. She twisted in the swing and asked Macy to push her higher. Too tired to argue, Macy obliged. She'd felt ill on the drive up to the ranch. Aiden's easy manner was reassuring, but his long, drawn-out way of talking left her feeling trapped. She had to stop herself from finishing his sentences. She was worried he would bring up the night they met in Las Vegas five years earlier, but he'd not referenced it once. That made her anxious for other reasons. They'd both been attending the same law enforcement training conference and had met at a bar. There'd been a misunderstanding. She hadn't realized he was married, but he hadn't exactly advertised it either. She'd been indignant. Fast-forward five years and now she was the one in a questionable relationship with the truth. After eight months of repeatedly saying he was separated, Ray Davidson didn't seem any closer to ending his marriage. Macy was beginning to think he was lying to her.

Macy had held tight to the handle above the door as Aiden swung the patrol car onto the long drive leading up to the ranch. They'd found Tara Dalton crying on the front porch of the main house.

Granny is mad at me, she'd said.

Jeremy Dalton hadn't taken much notice of his granddaughter. He'd brushed his fingers through her hair like it was nothing more than seed heads on a crop of barley. His wife Annie had stood in the door leading to the kitchen. After calling for his daughter, Jessie, a couple of times, Jeremy walked toward Annie, hitching up his trousers as he went. Her features had sharpened as he approached. A knife's blade glinted in her hand. Macy hadn't waited to see what would happen next. She'd yelled a warning, grabbed the kid, and walked away.

Macy had introduced herself to Jeremy's granddaughter and let her hold her badge.

I'm one of the good guys.

Tara Dalton wouldn't believe anything Macy said until she saw her gun. Macy had unloaded the pistol before placing it on the table between them.

Now do you believe me?

Tara had inspected it like a pro. *My uncle John has the same one.*

Macy hadn't said that she already knew all about her uncle John's gun. She'd just reloaded her own and returned it to its holster. There were muffled shouts coming from the house, but Tara hadn't seemed to notice. She'd gone about making an imaginary breakfast using a selection of expensive broken crockery that Macy imagined had once been used as weapons. Macy had been trying to get her bearings. She'd had to admit she was thrown. She'd expected the Daltons to be the quintessential all-American family. She should have known better. It made her think she was losing her touch. Motherhood was making her soft. She'd opened her eyes a little wider and taken a good look around.

From its raised position, the ranch house had sweeping vistas across the northern Flathead Valley. The Daltons had fifteen thousand head of cattle on twenty thousand acres of land. This wasn't a family home. It was a business. She wondered if the property was still in Jeremy's name. His marriage to Annie might have been financially motivated. According to what Aiden had told her on the drive, Annie came from a wealthy East Coast family. She'd been drawn to Montana from what she saw in films and on television, and ended up falling in love with a rancher. Annie Dalton would have found the reality of life in Montana tough. It wasn't all horse-whispering and fly-fishing. The ranch was miles from town, and as an outsider, Annie would have found it difficult to make friends. She'd attended Harvard and had a Ph.D. in English literature. Macy had glanced up at the house again. It was so isolated. There was such a thing as having too much time to read.

The tennis court was missing its net. Someone had been using it as a shooting range. Smashed beer bottles glistened on the pavement and weeds grew up through the cracks. The court was less than fifty feet from the house. The noise would have been deafening. An old sofa sat next to the swimming pool, and someone had pulled an oversized barbecue right up to the edge. An inflated alligator floated on the surface. Pink flamingos dotted the lawn. A few had bullet holes. Some of the heads were blown clean off.

Several horses had gathered near the fence surrounding the paddock. They'd seemed to be watching her. Macy had closed her eyes. On average these days she slept less than five hours a night, and it was starting to take its toll. She couldn't focus. Everything ached. Tara's voice had prattled on, making her miss her son even more. She didn't want to be in the Flathead Valley. She wanted to be back at home. Macy had scrolled through photos of Luke on her phone until she found one of him sitting on the front porch. Sometimes he'd wait there for Macy to come home from work. She often found him asleep with his head on his grandmother's lap.

Tara's voice had been in her ear. She'd pointed at the phone. Her fingers were stubby. She smelled of soap.

Who's that?

My son.

37

What's his name?

Luke.

Tara had taken Macy's hand in hers and inspected her ring finger. *You're not married.*

Nope.

Just like my mommy.

I suppose we have that in common.

Tara had held a few strands of Macy's hair so she could look at the color in the sunlight. *I like your hair. It's like fire.*

I like yours too.

I don't.

Macy had raised her teacup so Tara could pour. *Why wouldn't your granny let you watch television?*

Tara had bit her lip. *She said Uncle John was dead and it wasn't right to watch TV when people die.*

Oh, I don't think it can hurt. Do you?

She'd shrugged. *John liked TV.*

Were you good buddies?

He used to take me for drives in his truck.

Where did you go?

Lots of places. He said we'd drive until we had to go home.

Sounds like fun.

She had a singsong voice but breathed through her mouth. *We used to do things like have ice cream for dinner. He said to keep that secret from my mommy because she'd be angry.*

Did he tell you to keep other secrets?

Her chin had bobbed up and down. *Once there was a man.*

Go on?

A shrug. *He and John didn't like each other much. He called my mommy bad names.*

When was this?

It was a long time ago. I think when I was still five. She'd grabbed Macy's arm and dragged her toward the swing. *Can you push me?*

Macy had watched a helicopter approach from the northwest. Even from a distance, she'd recognized the markings. Apparently, someone in the house needed rescuing. The helicopter landed on the far side of the building, but Tara hadn't been interested in going to see it. She'd pointed at the swing.

John built it for me.

So Macy had pushed the swing and Tara had been swept up to the sky, her bare feet pointed into the blue. She'd grinned from ear to ear. Macy was just about to go looking for Aiden when he appeared on the back porch with a young woman. She was about Macy's height, but unlike Jeremy and John, who were fair, she had dark eyes and thick black hair. She was also far thinner. Her limbs were as substantial as kindling. She wore loops of bracelets around her wrists, a pair of tiny cutoff shorts, and a T-shirt with a band's logo on the front. Although she looked nothing like her twin brother, Macy guessed that the woman was Jessie Dalton.

Tara tried to stop the swing by dragging her feet on the ground. Macy took hold of the ropes and the girl slid from the seat and ran toward her mother.

Macy brushed off her hands and went over to say hello. Jessie had lifted Tara onto a hip. Jessie might have been slim, but she was far from emaciated. Braided muscle ran down the length of her arms. There was a crude tattoo of a rose on the back of her hand. It looked like it was bleeding.

Tara cupped her hands around her mouth and whispered something in her mother's ear. Jessie's voice wavered.

"Yes, I can see that," said Jessie, glancing past Macy toward the table. "Was it a nice breakfast?"

Tara nodded her head vigorously.

"I hope you saved some for me. I'm starving."

Tara took her mother's hand and led her away. Macy couldn't help but think Jessie looked relieved to be going.

Macy watched them. "What happened in there?"

"You missed a good show."

"I'm sure it was nothing I haven't seen before. I just want to know if anyone else died."

"Thankfully, Annie dropped the knife before she could do any harm. It got pretty physical though. Luckily, they're both still breathing."

"Why the helicopter?"

"Jeremy is a big man with a bad heart. They're flying him over to Collier County Hospital."

"What about the wife?"

"She's going by car. She's being admitted to the psychiatric ward for evaluation. It's up to the doctors to decide what happens next. As you can imagine, Jessie is in a bit of a state."

"Do you have her mother's phone?"

Aiden handed it to Macy. "I spoke to Jessie. She doesn't seem to know anything. Apparently John has been very distant since he returned from Afghanistan. They barely talked. She has no idea why anyone would want to harm him."

"How long has she been clean?"

"Is it that obvious?"

"Are you kidding? She could be a poster child." She paused. "It may be relevant. Maybe she's gotten mixed up with someone she shouldn't have."

"Long shot. She's been off meth for four years and everything else for at least three. Gave up drinking last summer."

"And what about the kid? Is there a dad?"

"Jessie has no idea who he is. She did just about anything to get drugs. From what I hear, she was passed around a lot."

"Not exactly your all-American girl."

"It's not exactly your all-American family."

"It's not what I expected." She glanced over at the rolling hay fields. "All this going for them and they seem as fucked up as any of us." She read the text message Annie had received. *"I'm sorry, Annie. John gave me no choice. He had to die."*

"Whoever sent the message was showing remorse."

"I've never seen something like this. Why would the killer take the time to send a text? It makes me think they must know the family."

Aiden pulled off his sunglasses and rubbed his eyes. "Or it could just be someone who's done their homework. The Daltons have a high profile. It wouldn't have been difficult to get information on them."

Macy scrolled through the calls and messages. "We really should have a court order before we look at this thing."

"That won't be a problem. What were you doing out here all this time anyway? You kind of ran off."

"Someone had to get the kid out of there. Has Annie Dalton always been violent, or is this a symptom of dementia?"

"There have been incidents over the years, but nothing this extreme. If you ask me, I'd say Jeremy and Annie being together was never a good idea."

"I asked Tara about her uncle."

"You want a court order for the phone, but you interviewed a child without permission?"

"I've never been known for consistency."

"I'm getting that. Did you learn anything?"

"It could be nothing, but one time when she was out with her uncle, they met a man. Tara said the man was saying stuff about Jessie that made John very upset. John told her to never tell anyone about it."

"Was this recent?"

"Hard to tell. She said it was a long time ago when she was five."

"Well, I think she only just turned six, so it could have been recent. Anything else?"

"She volunteered that much. It didn't feel right to press her. She needs to be interviewed by a specialist. I put in a call. They're sending someone up from Kalispell."

"We should get back to town. The tech guy wants to walk us through the security video, and John's friends are coming in."

"And Lana Clark?"

"She's on her way as well."

Aiden pointed out the two-story building that housed the Wilmington Creek Police Department. It was only a block away from The Whitefish. He backed into a spot and pulled up the parking brake.

Macy judged the distance to the murder scene to be less than a hundred yards.

"Pretty bold to shoot a man within shouting distance of the sheriff's office."

"I have to agree with you on that one. It's the first time something like this has happened in Wilmington Creek. I'm afraid it will change things around here forever."

"Did you grow up here?"

He scrolled through the messages on his phone. "I'm not sure I'm officially a grown-up so I don't know how to answer that."

"Seriously, have you always lived here?"

"Born and bred." He pointed to the east. "My parents live about four blocks away."

"I couldn't imagine it."

"Then try not to."

"It's not that it's not pretty."

He laughed. "You don't need to apologize. I get it. Even I have my bad days."

"What do you do on your bad days?"

"Drink a bit too much, look up job openings on the Internet. Contemplate applying. Fall asleep."

"Sounds like my typical Saturday night."

"At least in Helena you have options. You should get out more."

Macy reached for the door handle. "You sound like my mother."

"Don't knock mothers. They're usually right about these things."

"My life is complicated."

42

"A guy?"

"Isn't it always?"

"If it's complicated it's not worth it."

"Sometimes it's just a matter of being patient."

"I've heard my sister say that. It seems to be code for *he's married.*"

Macy's expression darkened. She'd had enough sharing for one day. She walked toward the entrance. The sun was high in the sky. Heat reflected off every surface. Main Street was an oven.

"We should go watch those security tapes."

Sarah, the video technician, had set up her computer in a far corner of the office, next to a microwave oven dating back to the early 1980s. She took her time scrolling through the video footage. "According to the time code, John Dalton pulls into a parking space at three minutes past one. He spends thirty-six seconds in the cab before walking to the front door."

Macy leaned in to get a better view. "He looks sober."

"He's inside for exactly fourteen minutes and thirty-three seconds. He finally leaves at one eighteen A.M." She searched again until she found what she was looking for. "I'm just getting to the part where John Dalton leaves the bar."

"No other cars pull up while he's inside?"

"I watched it five times. There's nothing more exciting than a plastic bag blowing across the pavement." Sarah pointed at the screen. "Here we go. John comes out and walks directly to the alleyway. From this angle it's impossible to tell if he's speaking."

Aiden's voice was right in Macy's ear. "He may have heard something."

Macy asked for the clip to be played again. "There's no hesitation. If someone called his name, you'd expect him to look up."

"We'll send the files down to Helena and see if we can clean them up, but I don't think they're going to tell us much more."

"Send them anyway. Everything goes through Helena."

"Will do."

Macy looked up at Aiden. "What time is it?"

"Just past eleven."

"Any word from the officers you sent out to canvas the area?"

"So far we have nothing other than the guy in the screened-in porch."

"You said he couldn't see."

"True, Phil Walker is nearly blind. He's been sleeping on the porch because it's been so hot. He heard a car at around one in the morning. Twenty minutes later he heard gunfire."

"What about the car? Can he tell us anything about it?"

"He says it was probably a V8 in need of a tune-up."

"I want to talk to him, but I have to make a couple of phone calls first. Do you have a desk I can use?"

"I'm afraid we're a bit short on space, so you'll have to share my office."

Macy sat down at the small desk wedged in the corner and pushed the door shut with her foot. She pinched open the window blinds. Two patrol cars were parked outside The Whitefish. Traffic slowed as it passed the crime scene. A few people mingled across the street. There were bouquets of flowers stacked up in the forecourt. The officer on duty took a bunch someone handed through the window of a passing vehicle and put it next to the others.

Macy's mother sounded like she'd had to run to answer the phone. "How long will you be away?"

"A few days at least. The governor has gotten involved. Apparently, he's a family friend."

Ellen's voice was sharp. "Layton Phillips is nobody's friend. All he cares about is getting reelected."

"Well, like it or not, he pays my salary. How's Luke?"

"Don't worry about a thing. He's fine."

"I'm not worried. I just miss him."

"Then try to come down over the weekend."

"I'll do what I can. I should know more by the end of the day."

"You look after yourself."

There was a knock at the door. "Mom, I have to go. I'll call you later, when I've checked into the motel."

Aiden held up two Diet Cokes. He had a brown bag wedged beneath one arm.

"I wasn't sure if you had time to eat."

Macy took the can he offered. "I managed to grab a bagel at a gas station on the drive up, but it's been awhile."

He handed her the bag. "Another bagel, I'm afraid."

She talked between bites. "Has anyone spoken to John Dalton's friends?"

"They'd gone out riding early this morning. John was supposed to meet them. They were out of cell phone range, otherwise we'd have heard from them sooner."

"When are they coming in?"

"They'll be half an hour or so."

"I'm going to go have a word with Mr. Walker."

"You want me to tag along?"

"Nah, I think you've got your hands full here. You'll need to set up an incident room. Have someone notify the press that we'll make a statement tomorrow morning at ten. Until then nobody talks to reporters. And get hold of that officer who took Lana home. I want her here by the time I come back."

"Oh, just so you know. I've put in a few calls to Patricia Dune, the doctoral student researching militia groups. She's not picking up."

"Keep trying," Macy said, reaching for the door handle. "I shouldn't be too long."

Macy was unprepared for the sudden change in temperature. A sign above the bank registered 102 degrees. She wavered. It would be just as easy to send someone to collect Mr. Walker. It was the hottest time of day and the town should have been empty, but a small crowd had gathered across the street in front of The Whitefish. Young people clung to one another; some were on their knees reading the cards that had been left for John Dalton. A reporter Macy knew stood in front of a tripod-mounted camera pointed toward the alley, but stopped talking when she spotted Macy. Macy kept her eyes on the pavement and headed up Charlotte Street without acknowledging her.

She entered Mr. Walker's yard through the front gate. The grass was going yellow in the areas where it was most exposed to the sun. Beneath the trees a mound of earth marked a freshly dug grave. A dog collar hung from a cross.

She leaned against the screen door and yelled, "Mr. Walker, it's the police. I'd like to speak to you about last night."

"Hold your horses, young lady. I'm blind, not deaf."

His fingertips brushed along the walls as he made his way. Clean-shaven and well dressed, he was like his house, compact and perfectly formed. There was a photo of a younger Mr. Walker on the mantel, arm in arm with a woman Macy guessed to be his deceased wife. After offering her a cold beverage, he led Macy to the screened porch where he'd slept the previous night. A gray cat dozed on the camp bed with one eye open. A fan hummed in the corner, raising the hair on its back with every oscillation.

Macy looked out at the alleyway. Even though John Dalton's body was on its way to the coroner's office in Helena, the barriers were still set up at either end. The forensics crew moved about the crime scene. She recognized Ryan Marshall and a few others she knew. The employee entrance to the bar was still propped open, and she thought she could hear music.

Mr. Walker leaned against the windowsill. "It's a shame my eyesight isn't what it once was, otherwise I might have seen something that could be of use to you."

"Do you often sleep out here?"

"When it's hot like this summer, I do. In the winter I use it as a freezer, it's so cold out here."

"I imagine it would be. Tell me about last night."

"I turned in early. I had to bury my dog yesterday so I was pretty tired."

"I'm sorry to hear that."

"She just collapsed. I think it might have been the heat. Anyway, with her gone it was a very quiet night. I'd woken up to go to the bathroom, otherwise I don't think I would have heard the car at all. Polly would have woke up the whole neighborhood had she been here when the car drove up. She had a tendency to bark."

"Do you remember the time?"

"It was a little past one. The car was coming up the service road behind the shops. It was traveling slowly. To tell you the truth, it was kind of spooky the way it crept up the road with its headlights off."

"Are you sure about the headlights?"

"If they were on, I'd have seen them. Light and dark I can see just fine. It's details I have problems with."

"You said it was a late-model V8."

"It had that big-engine sound. You know that low growling you used to get when you barely put your foot on the gas? Might have been something like a Pontiac GTO or a Chevy Chevelle."

"You seem to know your cars."

"I used to be a mechanic, and like I said, there's nothing wrong with my hearing."

"What else did you hear?"

"A voice. I couldn't make out the words, but there was something about it that seemed familiar."

"Try me."

"Nearest that I can say, it was like someone was delivering a lecture. It had that tone to it."

"Did you hear the gunshots?"

"Yes, I did. After all that quiet it was like cannons going off. The car left pretty quick after that, sprayed gravel all over my window screens. The next time that guy comes creeping up the alleyway I'll know to call the police. I'd always thought it was kids sneaking home after curfew so they kept the lights off."

"You'd heard the car before?"

"Three, maybe four times in the past month. Always late at night. Always had the lights off."

Aiden was leaning back in his desk chair with his phone propped under his chin. "I want you to come find me as soon as you get her here." He hung up and cursed.

Macy dropped her bag on her desk. "What's wrong? Did we lose our only witness?"

"No, they're on their way. They're just taking their sweet time. Apparently, Lana needed to do a few things around her house. What news from Mr. Walker?"

"He thinks he's heard the car on at least four occasions in the past few weeks. Every time it came down the service road it had its headlights off."

"Then this could have been a chance encounter. John may have been in the wrong place at the wrong time."

"Possibly. It also might be that someone has been following him. I'm sure this wasn't the first time John has stopped in at The Whitefish to see Lana Clark. By the way, has anything significant ever happened in that alleyway before this?"

"Nothing I can think of. A few fights over the years. Can't think of any that John was involved in."

"It was a big risk pulling off something like this in such a public location. The location may be important."

"I'll have the guys go through the records."

"Also check with dispatch. They might not keep records of all the calls that come in, but it's a small enough town that someone might remember something that wasn't logged."

"Fair enough." Aiden held up some papers. "This came through from the coroner. It's only preliminary."

"Any surprises?"

"Nothing of note. He took the shot to the head first, and was shot twice in the back after he fell."

"Caliber?"

"It was a nine-millimeter."

Macy stood reading. "Did you see this bit about the gravel embedded in his right knee? His jeans had a hole in them."

"Yeah, it looks like John was on his knees for quite a while."

"Either that or he fell."

"No abrasions to his hands, so I doubt it. The kneeling works if we're considering this an execution. Although the two bullets in his back seem like overkill."

"The one part that's random is John's movements. The killer had no way of knowing that he would be showing up there at one in the morning."

"Unless someone told the killer where he was, or he was being followed."

"It could have been someone in the bar or one of the guys he was out with."

"We already checked Lana's phone and the phone at the bar. No outgoing calls or texts between the time John arrived and was found dead in the alleyway."

"What about John Dalton's phone? Anything yet?"

"No prints. It was wiped clean. There are texts between him and his friends, making arrangements to meet earlier in the evening. All very aboveboard. By the way, Dylan Reed and Tyler Locke are in the diner where we met Jeremy."

"Is that where we do all the interviews?"

"Nah, but it's gotten pretty crowded in the office. I thought it would be better to park them there until we were ready for them."

"What can you tell me about them?"

"Tyler Locke was John Dalton's platoon sergeant, but they've known each other for years. He's done six deployments, but has been home on extended leave from Afghanistan because his grandmother passed. He normally lives down at Fort Benning, Georgia. He's thirty-two and has a stellar service record, but got into the service on a criminal waiver."

"He has priors?"

"He went off the rails during his teens but found his feet again. The Daltons took him under their wing and really straightened him out. Sadly, it turned out he was stealing from them. He was pulled over for speeding and the arresting officer found two hundred pounds of ammonium nitrate in the back of his truck."

"Fertilizer?"

"Yeah, but I doubt he was intending to use it that way. Jeremy said it was stolen but Annie said it was a misunderstanding. He got two years' probation." He held up a file. "Aside from the stuff when he was a teenager, it's in here."

"What do you think? Was it a misunderstanding?"

"Hard to say. It's been more than ten years and he's not put a foot wrong since. I'd like to give him the benefit of the doubt."

"I'll keep that in mind."

Aiden nodded. "You should know that he's pretty beat up. Got a little too close to an IED and was sprayed with shrapnel. He has burns on his arms from trying to rescue someone in his unit from a Humvee that got hit by a roadside bomb. He's kind of scary to look at and can be abrasive, but I've never heard anyone say a word against him."

"What's Dylan Reed's story?"

"Dylan is the same age as John and they've been friends pretty much since birth. They enlisted at the same time, but Dylan went to train in San Antonio as a combat medic after completing his basic training at Fort Benning. He was shot in the thigh five months into his fourth deployment. From what I hear, he's lucky to still have a leg."

There was a knock at the door and they both looked up. A uniformed officer handed Aiden a printout. "This just came through. It's Tyler Locke's army service record."

Aiden took a quick look before handing it to Macy. "That was fast. Anything on Dylan Reed yet?"

"Not that I've seen."

"Okay, keep me posted."

Macy flipped open Tyler's file and started reading. "How do you want to do this? I'm beginning to think you're a little too close to some of the witnesses."

"I won't be offended if you question them on your own. I'll ob-serve."

"Are you sure? This is your town. I don't want to overstep."

"Don't worry, I'll let you know if you do."

5

Dylan felt anxious standing in the entryway of the restaurant. He was about to tell Tyler he was leaving when a waitress, who looked vaguely familiar, took him by the arm and smiled sympathetically. She seated them in a booth next to the front windows and leaned in to set out the cutlery. He didn't know what to do when she handed him the menu. He sat rigid in the cushioned seat, but his eyes moved across the restaurant like mine sweepers. He could actually taste the acrid smoke. Red dust was gritty in his mouth. He tasted blood too. It was that day again. He was out on patrol with his platoon. Hot white light reflected off buildings. One minute he was walking. The next he was falling. They dragged him into a nearby school. The high windows were cracked, the broken sky blue. Dark-eyed children cowered under desks. Their teacher begged the soldiers to leave. All that chaos. All that noise. The medic was calm, though. He never stopped talking to Dylan.

You're going home now. You're safe. Just focus on that.

Dylan glanced from one diner to another, but found no sign of home. Every spoken word was a warning. Every noise reverberated in his head at ten times its natural volume. Perspiration beaded on his skin. He clenched his fist and the blue veins on his forearm swelled like rivers. He reached for the knife only to have someone snatch it away.

The man sitting across from him spoke in a low voice. His disjointed words floated through the air. Dylan tried to put them in an order he understood, but nothing made sense. A big round head with searching eyes leaned toward him.

"Dylan, what's wrong? Are you okay?"

Dylan flinched at the sound of his name. He opened his mouth to speak, but his plea for help rolled back on his tongue like a sucking tide. He swallowed. There was pressure on his hand. It was being squeezed. The knife was gone. The fork too.

"Dylan, it's okay."

Dylan glanced down at his arm and watched the veins swell. *It is not okay.*

"Do you need to get out of here?"

He might have said *yes*.

There was no way they could leave through the front door. There were too many people. He'd never make it. The round face was no longer across from him. A voice whispered in his ear.

"Come with me. Let's get you outside."

The man pulled him by the arm and he stumbled from the booth. A woman looked up from her newspaper and stared. Another held a phone to her ear. He could hear every word. There was a squeal and a small child was lifted high. It floated through the air from one set of hands to another. A bell chimed and the front door opened. More people crowded in. They wore work clothes and were strangers to him.

Dylan let himself be led. They went out the back way. He dragged his fingertips along the wall as he tripped down a narrow passage that took him past the kitchen. His shirt was damp with sweat but his mouth was as dry as ash. A door swung open and he was thrust out into sunlight. It bounced off the whitewashed wall of the building opposite. He staggered toward it, only to be wheeled round again.

"Dylan, I want you to listen to me. You're home. You're safe. No one is going to hurt you again. Do you hear me, Dylan?"

Dylan understood everything this time. He buried his head in Tyler's shoulder and wept.

They sat in the front seat of Tyler's Suburban, staring out at the people gathering in front of The Whitefish. Despite the heat, Dylan was shivering. He pulled his sweatshirt's hood over his head and closed his eyes. Now that it was over he only wanted to sleep.

Tyler spoke through a cloud of cigarette smoke. "I don't suppose you want to talk about what just happened in there."

"I've got it under control."

"No, you don't. You've got some serious shit going on in your head. How long has this been going on?"

"I'm not sure. It started slowly and just got worse."

"You taking anything for it?"

"Zoloft, Remeron, Xanax, morphine, prazosin . . . I could go on."

"Shit, Dylan. Why didn't you tell me?"

"It's not something I like to tell."

"You shouldn't go through this kind of shit on your own."

"I said that I have it under control."

"Not from where I'm sitting."

"It's worse when I'm stressed."

Tyler pointed his cigarette at the police station. "In a few minutes' time they're going to want to put you in a small room and interview you. Given your state of mind, you've got no business going through something like that. Aiden will understand. Just let me tell him what's going on with you."

"That won't be necessary. I'm fine now."

"Dylan, you've got to learn to accept help when it's offered."

"I don't want to talk about it."

"If you guys would just listen. I'm here for you."

"What's that? You think I'm not listening? I hear everything, Tyler. Everything."

"Let's just drop it."

Dylan picked up Tyler's lighter and flicked the flame on and off. "So, what do you think happened last night?"

"I don't know. A robbery that went wrong?"

"That's what I'm thinking."

"John wouldn't have gone down easily."

"I was so pissed off at him this morning. I feel like shit. I should have been there for him."

"Don't be so hard on yourself. I've been having the same thoughts."

Dylan rubbed his face. "We should go see Jeremy. Pay our respects."

"Tomorrow will be soon enough. I imagine they've got their hands full today."

"When was the last time you saw Annie?"

"Christ, Annie. I forgot about Annie. It's been more than two years now."

"A few months back, I went up to see Jeremy about a job and she came into the kitchen. She walked past him like he wasn't there. She's so thin now."

"I hear she dresses like a witch."

"I guess you could call it that."

"Did she say anything?"

"She said plenty. It just didn't make much sense." Dylan lowered his voice. "She kept trying to touch me. It got a little awkward. Jeremy had to ask me to leave."

"She's crazy. She should be put away."

"People might say I'm crazy too. You going to put me away?"

"Nah, it's different with you. You've earned your crazy. After everything you've seen . . ."

"You're fine. John *was* fine. Why me?"

"Well, for starters, we didn't get shot up like you did. It makes a difference. You live with it every day. I respect you for keeping a lid on it. It's tough."

"It's almost worse being back here. I worry too much about Ethan's truck. Every time the phone rings I think it's someone calling to say they've found his body. I really didn't give it much thought until I came back."

"It's too quiet here," said Tyler, stubbing out his latest cigarette. "Suddenly, there's too much time to think. If we're given time to imagine the worst, that's just what we'll do."

"I can't get my head around this. John should have outlived us all."

"I suppose he must have gone to see Lana."

"He told me he was going to drop her."

Tyler raised his voice. "Well, he lied, didn't he?"

"What do you suppose was going on with him?"

"Hard to say. A walk on the wild side, I guess."

"Lana's not that wild."

"Yeah, tell me another one."

"If you took the time to talk to her you'd realize she's smart."

"If she was smart she'd still be back in Georgia, not living here and working at that dive."

"I don't think she had much choice but to leave."

"So she says. All I know is that John had a choice last night and he chose wrong. If he'd gone home or to Tanya's place, he'd probably still be alive now."

"You think Lana had something to do with it?"

"Maybe."

"You'll have to do better than maybe."

Tyler's phone rang. He looked at the screen before shutting it off. "It's Aiden. Are you sure you're ready for this?"

"Yeah, I'll be fine."

"Just so you know, I'm here for you. You need someone to talk to, you come to me." He grabbed Dylan's shoulder. "You hear me?"

Dylan reached for the door handle. "Yeah, I hear everything."

6

Macy thought Dylan Reed was far too thin. He had birdlike wrists and cheekbones that looked sharp enough to cut glass. Unlike John Dalton, he didn't look as if he'd ever been in the army. His brown hair fell across his face and an oversized hooded sweatshirt hung off his narrow shoulders. He unfolded from his seat like a jackknife and held out his hand. Macy introduced herself and he spoke softly, stating his name and telling her he'd do whatever he could to help.

He took his time easing into the chair, his lips hardening into a line once he was settled. Macy's heart went out to him in ways she didn't expect.

"You don't look like you eat," she said.

"Ask my friends, they'll set you straight."

"How bad is it?" she said, gesturing to his leg. He'd slung it out to the side like a piece of excess baggage.

"I'm lucky to have it, so I can't complain."

"I imagine it's going to take some time to heal properly."

"They tell me it's as healed as it's going to get."

"You still seem to be in a lot of pain."

"There are metal plates holding my leg together. They tell me I'll always be in pain."

Macy glanced down at her notes. "You enlisted with John?"

"Yeah, we went over to Billings together. I was still drunk from the night before, otherwise I don't think I could have gone through with it."

"Sounds like you're the reluctant hero."

"Really, it was John who wanted to join. I guess I came along for the ride."

"Did you always follow John's lead?"

"Pretty much."

"What are you going to do now?"

He lowered his voice to a whisper. "I've got no idea."

"How was John settling into life back here in Wilmington Creek? Having been away for so many years it must have been difficult to adjust to being home full time. It's pretty quiet here compared to Afghanistan."

"Compared to anywhere it would seem quiet here."

"True."

"I really have no idea if John was happy, whatever that means. I will say that he was focused. Aside from his girlfriend, Tanya, he seemed to pick up where he left off. He worked hard. He spent time with his family and friends. He was thinking of going into politics."

"Tanya is his ex-girlfriend?"

"I wouldn't say she was an ex. They'd been seeing each other again, but it wasn't the same as before. They were both being very cautious." He hesitated. "All things considered, Tanya's been very patient. During his first two deployments she stayed at Fort Benning, but the last time he was on leave he spent more time out with his friends than at home with her. She was lonely so she came back here."

"Were there hard feelings?"

"I can't speak for her, but John felt pretty shitty about how he behaved. He'd always fooled around, but this time she found out. Someone posted something on the Internet."

"Did this have anything to do with Lana Clark?"

"Yeah, she's the one John was seeing, although she wasn't the one who rubbed it in Tanya's face. I don't think John knew what hit him when he met Lana. She's smart in a way the girls around here aren't. She's lived a lot of places. Sees things differently. Meanwhile, Tanya is this girl from a small town. I don't think John knew what he wanted. He'd be out partying with Lana on Saturday night but then he'd meet Tanya at church on Sunday morning. Those two women couldn't be more different."

"John had just had a big change in his life. It's understandable that he'd be conflicted about how he wanted to spend the rest of it."

"That's what I thought, and to tell you the truth, I'd say Tanya was sympathetic to what he was going through. Lana less so. Lately I got the impression she could take it or leave it. I think she wanted more, but she wasn't willing to play those sorts of games."

"Where were you yesterday evening?"

"Tyler Locke's house."

"Who else was there?"

"It was only Chase Lane, Tyler, me, and John. We played some video games, drank beer. That sort of thing. It was going to be an early start so I left around eleven."

"Were you the first to leave?"

"Yeah, but Chase was on his way out as well. He works for John's family. The foreman up there doesn't like it when you're late."

"I've met Wade Larkin. He's kind of intimidating."

"I spent a couple of summers working for him. Credit to him, he treated John the same as the rest of us. After working for Wade, basic training seemed easy."

"Did John seem distracted last night?"

"I didn't notice anything."

"Was it normal for him to stop in at The Whitefish on his way home?"

"That's probably a question for Lana."

"Do you often go for early-morning rides?"

"Not as often as I'd like to." He put his hand on his leg.

"Where'd you go this morning?"

"Up near Darby Lake."

"Seems too hot to ride."

"It was cold when I started out this morning."

"What time was that?"

"Around five. I had to cover a lot of ground and I'm slower than I used to be."

"Have you had difficulty adjusting to being back home?"

"I'm sure Aiden has told you all about my problems."

"Actually, he hasn't."

"Well, that's awkward."

"So what are your problems, Mr. Reed?"

Dylan looked down at his hands. "When I came home from the VA hospital in Denver, I really couldn't be on my own, so I moved in with my mom. She made the mistake of coming into my room to wake me up. Sometimes I get confused as to where I am. I don't remember hitting her."

"Is she okay?"

"Not really. She locks her bedroom door and tries her best not to jump every time I lift a finger."

"That doesn't sound good."

"We're working on it."

"What were the other incidents?"

"Nothing major. A couple of fights. I got my ass kicked, so no harm done."

"Did you have any issues with John?"

"No, we got on fine. Other than Tyler, John was the only person around here who really understood what I've been through."

"I found a card in John's wallet for a therapist in Collier. Do you know anything about that?"

"Yeah, I gave it to him. It's a woman I see."

"Why did John need a therapist? You said he seemed well adjusted."

Dylan hesitated. "It doesn't seem right sharing what he told me in confidence."

"I need to understand his state of mind. If he was struggling with adjusting to civilian life I'd like to know."

"It was nothing like that. This was about family. The stress of living with his mom was really starting to get to him. She was telling him some shit about Jeremy not being his real father. Apparently she was pretty convincing. The poor guy felt guilty for even thinking it might be true. Hence the therapist."

"Did his mother say who this man was?"

"Not that I know of. At some point John decided to drop it."

"Did his sister know?"

"He asked me never to speak to Jessie about it."

"Do you think it could be true?"

He shook his head slowly. "I always told him it was his mother's illness talking. If you spent any time with Jeremy and John you could see they were father and son."

"And you're sure Jessie never knew about it?"

"She's never mentioned it. I was a little surprised John was so worried about her finding out. Given how difficult her relationship is with Jeremy, I imagine she'd have been relieved to learn there was a possibility they weren't related."

"That bad?"

"She hasn't made it easy for him."

"Can you think of anyone who would want to hurt John?"

Dylan sat quietly for a few moments. "There's the usual shit that goes on when we're out. Maybe it's been a little worse lately, but I can't think of any particular time when John has caused offense. Compared to Tyler and me, he's pretty tame."

"Could John have been seeing someone who was married or in a relationship?"

"That would have been hard to pull off without Tyler and me finding out."

"You'd be surprised at what people keep hidden."

"That's not the John I know."

"But John may have changed."

"I suppose so."

Macy put her notes aside. "Thank you for coming in. It may not seem like it, but you've been very helpful."

"I wish I could do more."

Macy shook Dylan's hand. "Please contact myself or Police Chief Marsh if you think of anything else that may be helpful in our investigation."

Tyler Locke rocked his chair on its back legs and stared at Macy. Jumbled with third-degree burns, ruined tattoos ran down his arms, and his scalp was pocked with shrapnel wounds. She fought the desire to look away. Unlike Dylan, Tyler challenged her with every word and gesture. Every time he moved, she flinched.

Macy got up and went over to the window.

"Do you mind if I open this? It's a bit stuffy in here."

Tyler leveled his gaze at her. "Suit yourself. It's your show."

"Well, it's mine for now."

She pulled up the blinds and the room brightened, but the window was jammed shut. She tugged at the latch a couple of times and it didn't budge. She didn't hear Tyler get up from his chair. One second he was sitting and the next he was right next to her. She jumped and this time he noticed.

"Here, let me try," he said.

Once she was seated Macy put her hands on her lap so he couldn't see that they were shaking. She nodded her approval when he managed to force the window open.

"Thank you, that's better."

Tyler stayed where he was, his eyes fixed on something outside. "I hate air-conditioning. The hum drives me mad."

"I suspect there's not much air-conditioning in Afghanistan."

"You'd be surprised."

"Maybe you should enlighten me."

He returned to the table. "Maybe another time."

"What can you tell me about John's experience over there? I understand you were in the same unit."

"I suppose you want the *Reader's Digest* version like everyone else?"

"John was one of your best friends. You and Dylan were closer to him than anyone. I need to know if there might be a connection between his military service and his death here in Wilmington Creek. If he was struggling, I need to know it. It's important to understand his state of mind. He may have been doing things he shouldn't have been doing, putting himself in danger unnecessarily."

"I know what you mean, but I don't think John had it in him. Don't get me wrong, in the beginning John was as ready to mix it up as anyone."

"And in the end?"

Tyler hesitated. "In the end, John lost his nerve. He'd been solid since day one and then he was scared shitless every time he left the compound. I guess we all have our tipping point."

"What do you suppose changed?"

He rubbed a palm across his peppered scalp. "He saw what happened to me, and we lost a few other guys. I guess he decided his number was up. We're all pretty superstitious but in that last month John took it to another level. There were all these little rituals he had to perform before he went out on patrol. He'd try to hide it, but I saw what was going on. And then one night, it wasn't enough. I had to really push to get him in the Humvee."

"So he came home."

"No. I kept him going. Nothing was ever put in his record. There was never a mark against him. Last summer he had an option to continue on, but he took an honorable discharge instead. No shame in that."

"Then why are you telling me?"

"Because last night he was doing the kind of shit he used to do before he was going out on patrol. To tell you the truth, I don't even think he realized it."

"Could he have been doing it all along? You've only been on leave for a few weeks."

"I was worried how he was adjusting so I was keeping a close eye on him. I'm telling you now. He was different last night. Dylan might have noticed too, but he left a good hour before John, so he didn't see it."

"Did you say something to John?"

"I tried to, but Connor was hanging all over him so I didn't get a chance."

Macy looked at her notes. "Who's Connor?"

"I was looking after my nephew last night. He stays over sometimes when I'm in town. He idolizes John. This is gonna break his heart."

"I think it's going to break a lot of hearts."

"Connor is only six. He won't understand much. I guess that makes it easier."

"Did John often stop at the bar?"

"Maybe. It's the only thing open around here after ten at night."

"What about the woman who works there, Lana Clark? I hear they were in a relationship."

Tyler snorted. "I guess you could call it that. I think John was trying to take a walk on the wild side. Lana wasn't good for him."

"Why's that?"

"Well, for starters she's a class-A mind fuck."

"Would you care to elaborate?"

"John didn't see her for what she really is. Big hair, big tits, big ass.

What's not to like? But believe me when I say the woman is a total bitch." He took out a pack of cigarettes and tapped them on the table. "John was a great friend. I only wanted what was best for him."

"How well did you actually know her?"

"I knew her back in Georgia. We all did. She lived near Fort Benning. We all used to hang out together. She knew he was with Tanya but that wasn't stopping her. I could tell she had her eye on him."

"Did John know you disapproved of Lana?"

"I'm not one to keep things to myself."

"I'm getting that."

"John wasn't happy with what I had to say, but it didn't go both ways. It wasn't like I was angry at him for making an ass out of himself with Lana. I figured he'd figure it out eventually all on his own, so I let it drop."

Macy checked the time. "I read in your file that you're due to join your unit again soon."

"Two weeks from today."

"Afghanistan?"

"I put in a request for Hawaii but they had other ideas."

"Given your battalion is still in Afghanistan I'm surprised you were granted extended leave."

"I'd accrued a lot of time off. If I didn't use it, I'd lose it. I took a chance and requested an extension." He looked her in the eye. "I guess they were feeling generous."

"I'm sorry but I need to ask about the two hundred pounds of ammonium nitrate that were found in the back of your truck ten years ago."

He stared at her for a few seconds before answering. "Never apologize for doing your job."

"You testified that you had no idea how it got there."

"That is correct."

"The judge didn't believe you. You were sentenced to two years' probation."

"He remembered me from when I was going through the juvenile courts. He wasn't about to give me the benefit of the doubt."

"Neither was Jeremy Dalton."

"I made my peace with Jeremy years ago. He made a mistake but I decided to forgive him."

"So no hard feelings?"

"None. My time in the army has been the best years of my life. No regrets."

She slid her card across the table. "I want you to contact me or Aiden if you think of anything that could be helpful."

"This wasn't a robbery, was it?"

"I'm not at liberty to discuss the details of the case."

"I'm right though. I can tell from the questions you're asking me. It doesn't add up."

Macy leaned back in her chair. "Mr. Locke."

"Call me Tyler."

"I really appreciate you coming in to speak to me, but I'm afraid I can't give you any more information. I may want to speak to you again, and I'm counting on your cooperation."

Tyler pushed his chair back. "Well, you'd better hurry. When you're due to ship out, two weeks goes by pretty quickly."

Macy waited until Tyler had left the room before putting her head in her hands. She rubbed her eyes. Her day wasn't even half over. She held up a piece of white paper and waved at Aiden through the one-way mirror. Tyler Locke was made of much stronger stuff than Dylan Reed. One of them had adapted. The other had been defeated. How John Dalton had been shaped by his time in the military was still a mystery. She looked through her notebook for the contact details for the therapist in Collier and picked up her phone.

7

Dylan sat on the sofa in the living room of his childhood home and waited for the painkillers to kick in. Across the room, Tyler leaned against the breakfast bar, scrolling through his text messages. Dylan closed his eyes. The interview had been exhausting. Macy Greeley may have meant well, but he resented her for feeling sorry for him. He didn't want people's sympathy. He wanted their respect. He shifted his weight, but it was no good. His leg was throbbing. It was as if every nerve ending in his body was knotted up in his thigh. Sometimes he imagined taking a gun and blowing another hole right through it. He slowed his breathing. Another five minutes, ten tops, and the edge would be worn down to a dull blade. His doctor wanted him to learn to manage the pain without drugs. He'd handed Dylan pamphlets on alternative medicine and the healing power of meditation. Dylan had driven all the way to the VA hospital in Helena for that little gem. He couldn't help but resent his doctor too.

Tyler stretched out his back. "John's parents have been taken to the hospital."

Dylan wasn't sure he'd heard right. "Pardon?"

"Annie attacked Jeremy."

"You're shitting me."

"Check your phone. Everyone seems to know."

"Are they okay?"

"Far as I can tell. Jeremy's there as a precaution, and Annie's in the psych ward."

"I'll call Jessie."

"I just got a text. She wants us to meet her at Collier County Hospital in about an hour." He looked at the clock on the wall. "I'm driving down to Kalispell to see Wayne, so you're going to have to go without me."

"There's no way I can drive now."

"You'll be fine once you eat something." He walked over, picked up Dylan's medication and shook the bottle. "You shouldn't take that shit without something in your stomach."

"Sometimes you're such a mom."

"Someone has to do it."

"You need to come with me to the hospital. We have to be there for John's family."

Tyler returned to the kitchen and spoke with his head in the open refrigerator. "Yeah, and by going down to see Wayne that's just what I'm doing. With or without John, we've gotta bury that truck."

"What's this about a truck?"

Dylan's mother, Sarah Reed, stood in the doorway holding a bag of groceries. Her blond hair was swept back in a ponytail and her eyes were swollen from crying. She placed the bag on the counter and pulled Tyler into a hug. "I heard about John. It's just awful . . ." She started sobbing and Tyler held her, mouthing *what the fuck* to Dylan, who stared at them from the sofa.

Tyler eased her grip. "I was just making us some lunch."

She shook her head. "No, you sit down and I'll do it. It's better if I stay busy." She raised her voice. "Dylan, do you mind taking your feet off the coffee table?"

Dylan eased his leg down, but instead of staying put he rose unsteadily to his feet. "I have to go meet Jessie in Collier. I'll get something to eat on the way."

Sarah put a hand on Tyler's arm. "Don't tell me you're going too. I really don't want to be alone right now."

Dylan grabbed his car keys from a row of hooks on the wall in the kitchen. "Tyler, I'll call you later."

Dylan pulled into the hospital's parking lot and sat with the engine idling. It was the first time he'd been back since his father passed away a few years earlier. It was supposed to be a routine operation but his father had succumbed to an infection and was dead within a week. Dylan circled the crowded parking lot a few times before finally giving up and pulling into a handicapped space. He dug his badge out of the glove compartment and threw it on the dashboard. It was nearly five in the afternoon and the sun was still in full bloom. The air was clearer than it had been in weeks. In the distance a vague outline of the mountains was visible. According to the news, the wind had shifted and the authorities were hopeful that the latest wildfire was finally under control.

Jessie was sitting on a bench outside the front entrance. She had her legs tucked under her and was using an empty Diet Coke can as an ashtray. For a while they sat side by side without saying a word. He closed his eyes and let the smoke drift over him. Jessie held up the pack.

"Want one?"

"No thanks, I quit."

"Seems the wrong time to quit."

"Is there ever a right time?"

"Guess not." She paused. "Thank you."

Dylan closed his eyes again. "For what?"

Her shoulders bounced. "For coming. I didn't think you would."

"Now you're just talking shit."

"What did you tell that detective?"

"I told her everything I know, which isn't much."

"So you're talking shit too."

"I didn't lie."

"Did she ask you if you knew of any reason someone would want to kill John?"

"I didn't lie."

Jessie leaned in close and whispered. "I killed Ethan Green and John hid his body. That seems as good a reason as any."

"That has nothing to do with what happened to John. Nobody knows about that night except for you, me, and Tyler, and we're not talking. Besides, Ethan's gone. It's not like he rose from the dead."

"He may not have, but something sure did. All it would take is one of Ethan's people finding out and we'd all be dead." She looked past him toward the parking lot. "Where's Tyler?"

"He's sorry. He really wanted to be here for you." Dylan remembered that look of longing in his mother's eyes and closed his own. She and Tyler had been sleeping together for years. It had started when Dylan was still in his teens. Like with most things, Dylan found it easier if he just pretended it wasn't happening.

"What could be more important than this?"

"He had to go meet someone about some explosives. He's going to blow the rest of the cliff. Bury Ethan's truck forever."

"He talks a good talk."

"I think he means it. He's getting what he needs from his friend Wayne."

"It's not a good idea to drag anyone else into this. The fewer people who know, the better."

"Don't worry. Tyler's got it covered."

Jessie looked him full in the face. Her eyes were bloodshot and swollen from crying. "Everyone is always telling me not to worry. We wouldn't be in this mess in the first place if I'd called the cops instead of listening to John. If it comes out, I could go to prison for the rest of my life."

"It was self-defense. He attacked you."

"Don't you think I know that? But we covered it up, didn't we? Now you and Tyler could go to jail as well. And John. I don't know. I don't know. Something in my gut tells me what happened to John is related."

"That's only because that night is always on your mind."

"Not just me."

"Yeah, it's on my mind too. It's good that Tyler is dealing with it. He's solid."

She waved her cigarette and ash drifted onto her bare legs. "There's all this shit swirling around my family. If I try to think about it all at once, I freeze."

He sighed. "I know what you mean. How's Jeremy?"

"Unfortunately, he's fine." She blew on the lit end of her cigarette. "Should be coming home tomorrow."

"And your mom."

"She's been admitted. I think they'll keep her for a while this time."

"It would give you a break."

"Did the police give you any details about what happened to John?"

"No, but Tyler made a few calls. It's kind of crazy how much those cops talk."

"Don't I know it." She stubbed out her cigarette and slipped it into the can. "Everyone's pointing fingers at Lana, but I don't think she had anything to do with it."

"That sounds like Tyler's doing. He's got all these conspiracy theories. So many that I don't really listen anymore. How about you? Still clean?"

Jessie lit another cigarette. "I've not touched a drop since that night on Darby Lake."

"I think it's time you told me everything."

"Why?"

"Because the whole thing was fucked, that's why. Why were you hanging out with that asshole in the first place? You knew damn well he was bad news. If I'm laying everything on the line for you, I think I deserve to know why."

"That's more than John ever asked for."

"John was family. He couldn't see through you like I can."

"What's that supposed to mean?"

Dylan thought about this for a few seconds. Jessie was one of the few people in the world he felt he knew better than himself. He'd watched her for years. During the four years she was away, he'd imagined the worst, and he hadn't been far off. He'd seen the scars on her wrists. He'd peeled back the bracelets when she was too wasted to notice. He leaned in and looked her in the eye. More than anything now, he needed the truth.

"I think you were playing games. You knew hanging out with Ethan would piss Jeremy off so you went and did it."

"You've got it all wrong."

"I'm here to learn."

"I was sitting in my car at The Whitefish. I couldn't drive. If I'd gotten another DUI, Jeremy would have kicked me out of the house and taken custody of Tara again. What's fucked is that I don't even remember meeting Ethan, but he must have offered me a ride. One minute I'm sitting there, contemplating sleeping it off, and the next I'm in his pickup truck pulling into the Darby Lake picnic area, laughing my head off. It was that same way I always get. I can't see where the line is but I can sure as hell cross it every time. One minute I'm okay, the next I'm not. In the morning I couldn't remember much of anything."

"Come on. There has to be something you remember."

"I remember taking a swing at him and waking up half naked with my face in the dirt. Ethan was dead and I was still drunk. I had bruises so deep they lasted for weeks." She closed her eyes. "He must have beaten the crap out of me."

"I know what you looked like. You were out at my place for three days And for the record, you were a total bitch."

"I don't even know who that girl is anymore. If I met her on the street I swear I'd slap her."

"I came close a few times."

"Which brings me back to what I said earlier. I'm surprised you came."

Dylan plucked one of the cigarettes out of her pack and held it in his lips, leaving it unlit.

"I mean, look around. It's not like my friends are coming to see me."

"That's bull. You've got plenty of friends. Monica would come in a heartbeat. You just haven't called her. Which brings me to my next question. Why did you want me here?"

"You're John's best friend. You know everything."

Dylan pulled the unlit cigarette out from his lips and put it back in the pack. It wasn't exactly what he wanted to hear but it would do for now. "I can't believe he's really gone."

"I can't stop crying."

For a few minutes they said nothing.

"Did Annie really attack Jeremy?"

"I don't think she really meant to hurt him. She was just upset."

"Jessie, I hear she threatened him with a knife."

"Aiden says she never so much as pointed it in Jeremy's direction." She pressed a tissue to her eyes. "Anyway, I shouldn't have let her out of my sight. The things she was saying . . ."

"You can't let it get to you. She's not well."

"That's the thing. She actually sounded pretty lucid."

"Still."

"It wasn't her usual crap. It made me miss her even more." She lowered her voice. "How's your mom? Any better between you?"

"She's fine, but we're not." He checked the time. With any luck his mother would be pulling a night shift working out at the diner at the truck stop. "Do you need a ride anywhere?"

She stood up and stared out past the parking lot toward the Flathead River, where a thin thread of silver wove through the trees. "I wish I could go for a ride. I wouldn't stop until I was anywhere but here."

"Play your cards right and I'll take you there someday."

She placed her hand on his forearm before standing. "I need to go see about Jeremy."

"Do you want me to wait?"

"Nah, it's okay. Aiden said he'd make sure someone gave me a ride home."

Dylan gripped her elbow and pulled her toward him. They were both unsteady on their feet. He hugged her close but she stood with her arms inert by her sides. He held his lips to her forehead for a second too long. When he finally walked away she wouldn't look him in the eye.

"I'll come check on you later," he said, cursing under his breath for never knowing when to let go.

8

Macy held up Dylan's and Tyler's DMV photos. "What do you think?"

Aiden plucked Tyler's photo from her hand and hung it on the wall of the incident room. "I think Tyler is a very angry man."

"While Dylan is a very broken man." Macy stared at Dylan Reed's face. He'd aged considerably since the photo was taken. She checked the date. It was only two years old.

"Unless you count Tyler's six-year-old nephew Connor, neither one of them has an alibi for last night."

"True, but I'm not seeing a motive either. Do either of them drive a late-model V8?"

"Tyler drives a Suburban. As far as we can tell, it's the only vehicle registered to him."

"And Dylan?"

"Like pretty much everyone else in the state, he's got an F-150 pickup truck. And just so you know, I don't see Dylan or Tyler doing something like this."

She put his photo to one side. "I don't either, but we should check anyway."

"Fair enough."

"There's the militia angle that still needs looking into."

"With such a surge in memberships in those groups over the last few years, I don't even know where to begin."

"The state's database should tell us who's active in the area. Anything on Patricia Dune? She may have learned something we can use."

"Nothing yet."

Macy looked around expectantly. "Where's Lana Clark? I'm beginning to think she doesn't exist."

"She's waiting for us over at The Whitefish. I figured she could walk us through everything that happened."

"Oh, by the way, I spoke to the therapist in Collier. She confirmed that she met with John Dalton six times."

"Is she willing to talk to us?"

"Yes, but she won't compromise patient-doctor confidentiality."

"What good is that, then?"

"She's willing to discuss John's general state of mind. She's assuming we'll be discreet."

"Well, at least we know why he was seeing her in the first place. Once she realizes that, maybe she'll loosen up."

"That's what I'm hoping." She gathered her things. "I'll head over to Collier tomorrow morning. You feel like coming along?"

"Providing everything is under control here, I don't see why not."

"What's your opinion on what Annie was telling John about his father?"

"I'm with Dylan on that one. I don't believe it."

"Why do you suppose John thought it was a possibility?"

He followed Macy out the door. "I wish I knew."

Macy stood in the entrance to The Whitefish and waited for her eyes to adjust. It wasn't much more than a cave carved out of cinder block. A horseshoe-shaped bar was set toward the back of the room. Dimly lit booths ran along the sides. Everything was clad in darkly stained pine and smelled of stale beer and sweat. In the middle of this sat a young woman with skin so pale it glowed. She wore a flowered sundress and heavily tooled cowboy boots that had never been near a horse. A patrol officer hovered close to her, one hand resting on the back of her chair. Aiden cleared his throat and when the officer turned toward them he had a grin on his face. The smile quickly faded.

"Dean, I think you've had enough time with Lana for one day. I need you to head over to Waldo Canyon. They found a burnt-out vehicle. Go see if you can get a registration number off it."

Macy couldn't help but notice that Lana Clark was beautiful. It was midsummer, yet she didn't have a single freckle, mole, or blemish. She wore deep red lipstick, and thick lashes framed her acid blue eyes. Auburn hair was piled on top of her head in a complicated series of knots. Macy took the vacant seat across from Lana and held out her hand.

"Lana, I'm Detective Macy Greeley. I apologize if we've kept you waiting."

"It's no trouble," she said, sniffing into a wadded-up tissue. Her voice was husky and low and she spoke with an accent that was difficult to pin down. "I'm not sure how I can help though. I already told Aiden everything I know."

Macy opened her notebook. "That's what I'm here to find out. Would you like something to drink or eat before we get started?"

"No, thank you, we stopped for something on the way back into town." She clutched her hands between her legs and swiveled toward Aiden, who had positioned himself on a barstool. "I wouldn't mind something stronger, though. Is that allowed?"

"Lana, you need to have a clear head."

"It would calm me down."

Macy thought a drink would be very welcome, but knew it would have to wait until later, when she planned on having a very large glass of red wine. She looked up and Lana was staring at her.

"Lana, once we're finished here you can drink all you want, but right now I need you to focus. As far as we know, you were the last person to see John Dalton alive."

"But I was inside when the gun went off. I didn't have anything to do with it."

"I want you to walk me through what happened. Nothing more, nothing less."

"Me and the manager, Jean, were cashing out. We thought it was a car backfiring, but then Marty raised his head off the bar for the first time in about a week and announced it was gunfire. He was in Vietnam so I guess he knew what he was talking about after all. At the time we thought he was full of shit, so we ignored him."

"How long after that did you find the body?"

"Maybe fifteen minutes. Jean came running in and yelled at me to call the police."

"Did you go outside?"

"I wanted to, but Jean told me to stay where I was." She pressed the tissue to her eyes. "I didn't know it was John. Jean wouldn't tell me anything."

"Were you expecting John last night?"

"We hadn't made any plans, if that's what you mean. In fact, I was kinda surprised to see him at all. He'd been pretty distant in the past couple of weeks."

"How serious were you about the relationship?"

"I was as serious as I needed to be. He'd changed his mind so many times about what he wanted, I'd given up on trying to get it right."

"How do you mean?"

"Just like last night. He shows up out of the blue and expects me to act like everything was cool between us."

"And how did you act?"

"I acted like everything was okay. No matter how much of a dick he was being, there was no way I was going to let him know how much it hurt."

"So you thought John was being a dick?"

"Yeah, news flash—Mr. Holier-Than-Thou Dalton could be a bit of an asshole." She paused. "I don't think he meant to. He had his life all planned out. He didn't know how to fit me into the puzzle. I was worried what his parents would think of me. I think he was as well."

"Why's that?"

She shrugged. "I'm a complete unknown. Tanya comes from a good family. She's local. They've known her forever."

"How long had you been seeing each other?"

"On and off since I moved up here in March. We went out for a couple of months pretty steadily and he was already talking about marriage. It kind of freaked me out. John wanted a wife to live out on that ranch with him. Anyway, I told him I needed more time to think it through, but he didn't seem to want to wait. He started seeing Tanya again. I began to think I was the person he came to when he was bored. Tell you the truth, I think he found life here a little too insular after having been away for so long, and no offense, but Tanya isn't exactly worldly."

"Care to elaborate?"

"John and I would talk about the world outside the valley. He wanted to get involved. Make a difference for war veterans. There are only a few people around here like that to talk to. It's like the rest of the world doesn't exist."

"The Flathead Valley is certainly a long way from Georgia."

"I'm not saying it was any better there. You can live in the middle of New York and not give a shit about the wider world. It's a state of mind. John was different. I think his time in the army really opened his eyes."

"I understand you met John when he was stationed at Fort Benning. Did you come here to be with him?"

"No, it wasn't like that. People are saying that we were messing around, but all we did was go out a few times before he came back here for good. I met him and Dylan when they were doing basic training. Tyler was in charge of John's platoon. We all kept in touch. When things got weird in Georgia, John suggested I come up here. He found me this job and a place to live."

"What happened in Georgia?"

"An ex-boyfriend was harassing me, so I had to have a restraining order issued. There were a few incidents, but nothing could be proven so he was released after they'd questioned him. Things got worse after that."

"Moving two thousand miles away seems an extreme reaction."

"I was pretty freaked out, and no offense to you, Aiden, but the police there were useless." She let out a nervous laugh. "They actually suggested I get a dog and then shrugged when I said I already had one. My car was vandalized and I know he was following me. Sometimes he'd call and just hang on the line not saying a word. One night he even set fire to my front porch."

"Is this when you left town?"

"I managed to hang on another week but then he poisoned my dog. I couldn't stay after that. I figured I was next. I was so upset I don't even remember packing my stuff. I drove up here in late February. Wilmington Creek seemed so quaint." Her voice broke. "John said it was the safest place in the world."

"Any chance your ex-boyfriend figured out where you live now?"

"I've been careful about who I communicate with back home. I don't give anyone my address, but I guess there's always a way of finding out. My friends say Charlie dropped out of sight a couple of months after I left."

"No word from him since?"

She blinked. "Nothing, it's like he vanished."

"I'm going to need his full name."

"Charlie Lott."

"And you have no idea where we might find him?"

"After I kicked him out he moved in with some friends. You can contact the case officer. He'll tell you everything you need to know."

"I'll do that." Macy went through her notes. "Was Charlie friends with John as well?"

"Yeah, we all used to hang out together. At one point he was giving John guitar lessons."

"Was he aware that you had formed a relationship with John?"

"I don't see how. Like I said, we really only went out in Georgia as friends."

"So were you pleased to see John last night?"

"I had mixed feelings. I got the impression he expected me to be grateful."

"You sound bitter."

"More like disappointed. When I first started seeing John, he seemed like a really great guy. On our third date he took me to dinner and to see a live band." She clasped her hands together and placed them under her chin. "He didn't want to let go of my hand when he was driving. He couldn't stop smiling. I really thought I meant something to him. Fast-forward five months and everything had changed."

'How so?"

'Well, just like last night. I'm pretty sure he wanted to split up with me again. Do you know how many times we've done that? I really couldn't go through it again."

"Are you sure that's what he wanted to talk about?"

"He didn't say it outright, but that was what I was expecting. I told him to go around back and wait for me."

'Did you go meet him?"

'No, I was really pissed off at the way he was treating me so I decided to leave him out there looking like a fool. Last laugh, so to speak."

'And now John is dead."

Lana looked down at her hands. "And no one is laughing."

"I want you to think carefully. Have you noticed anyone suspicious hanging out at the bar over the past couple of months?"

"It's mostly regulars here. We're off the highway so we don't get many people who are just passing through."

"Your manager mentioned that some guy named Nick has been harassing you."

"That was nothing."

"I'd rather be the one to decide that."

"Since the fires started we've had some guys from the crews coming in. Nick was one of them."

"The manager said he overheard him telling you that you should be grateful some men are still willing to pay for it. Apparently, he was very insistent."

Her cheeks reddened. "He seemed to think women who tend bar double as prostitutes. It's nothing I haven't come across before, but Jean happened to overhear it that time so he kicked Nick and his friend out. I don't know his surname and I have no idea what the friend's name was. He mostly just sat there and stared at me."

"Did this guy Nick know you were dating John?"

"Never had the reason to tell him, but I guess he might have seen us together."

"Anyone come in specifically asking about John?"

"Aside from the usual snide remarks coming from Tanya's friends, no one spoke to me directly about John except for Dylan. He's a real sweetheart."

"I interviewed him this morning."

"It breaks my heart to see how low he is."

"What about Tyler?"

She put her hands palm down on the table and took a deep breath. "God knows why, but Tyler hates me. As far as I know, I've not done a damn thing to cross the guy except go on a few dates with his friend."

"You said that your relationship with John had become on and off lately. Were you seeing anyone else?"

"Is this really necessary?"

"We're interviewing a lot of people, Lana. If there's something I need to know, I'd rather find out from you."

"But it's none of your business. In fact it's nobody's business."

"If you withhold information that becomes important to the investigation later on, I could charge you with obstruction."

Lana looked up at Aiden. "No offense, but the opportunities around here are slim and few."

Macy tried again. "That doesn't answer my question."

"I don't want to get anyone into trouble."

"I take it he's married."

"Four kids and another one on the way. He keeps saying he's going to leave his wife but I ignore him. A guy who cheats on his wife. I'd have to be an idiot to believe him."

Macy frowned. "I need a name."

"You'll be discreet?"

"I'll do my best."

"Bob Crawley."

Aiden finally spoke. "Shit, Lana. That's wrong on so many levels."

"I never said I was a saint."

Macy tapped her notebook with her pen. "Have you ever known him to be jealous?"

"To tell you the truth, he's really mellow. Plus, he's married. It would be out of line if he expected me to be faithful to him."

"She's right about that," said Aiden. "The guy is mellow."

"We'll still need to know his whereabouts last night." She circled his name a couple of times. "Lana, what is your take on how John was adjusting to civilian life? Would you say he was changed by his experiences in Afghanistan?"

"You mean like Dylan?"

Macy nodded.

'As far as I could tell he seemed fine."

'Did he get on okay with his family?"

Lana pursed her lips. "For the most part I'd say yes. He did seem to be at odds with his sister. I asked him about it and he just said it was nothing she'd done."

9

iden held up his phone and apologized before taking the call. "It's the officer I sent over to check on the house Patricia Dune is renting."

Macy reached across her empty dinner plate and poured another glass of wine. The headache was finally gone and a pleasant buzz was beginning to settle in. Her smile came quicker and the laughter that followed almost sounded genuine. She warned herself to slow down. Even though Aiden was becoming more entertaining as the evening went on, getting drunk would not be a good idea. She put her wine to one side and thought about what her mother had said over the phone when they spoke earlier. By the time Macy had managed to make the call, Luke was already asleep. Not that it mattered. It wasn't like he could carry on a conversation. It was Ellen who always filled Macy in with all the details of his day. There'd been a doctor's appointment, a trip to the local pool, and a visit from the neighbor's cat. As long as Luke stayed perfectly still, it would come sit next to him.

I've never seen him sit still for so long.

Macy had laughed. *Nice trick. We should have that cat visit more often.*

Oh, I almost forgot. I have to drive up to Kalispell tomorrow to pick up a chair I've had restored. Can you meet us in the afternoon? There's a park just across the street from where I'm going.

I'll try my best to get there. Do you have an address?

Aiden placed his phone on the table and picked up his knife and fork.

"Given the contents of her mailbox, it looks like Patricia Dune hasn't been home for a few days. There's no car in the garage and the lights are all off."

"She may have gone out of town."

"Hard to say at this point. Tomorrow we'll try to track down someone at her university who can tell us where she may have gone."

Macy reached for her water glass. "The text message that was sent to Annie is a game changer. I'm struggling to see how John's murder could have something to do with the local militias. This feels personal."

"I know what you mean, but the killer could have done it to throw us off." He wiped his mouth with his napkin and took a sip of his beer.

"They're not usually that clever. Who else have we got on our list?"

"Bob Crawley, for starters. He should be easy enough to sort out. I don't feel like being discreet though."

"What does a girl like Lana see in a married man with four kids and another one on the way?"

"You mean aside from his dot-com money?"

Macy leaned in and whispered, "He's loaded?"

He lowered his voice even more. "Plus I hear he's rather well endowed."

She fell back in the chair and laughed. "That's funny."

"Well, it's what the ladies around here are saying."

"Lana isn't his first, then."

"Nor the last. I suspect he's having too good a time to stop now."

"There's also Tyler Locke and Dylan Reed."

"I think you're reaching with them."

"Am I? Dylan is pretty messed up. Don't get me wrong, I feel for the guy, but I'm not going to strike him off my list just yet. He has blackouts. And then there's Tyler. I think I want to rattle his cage just as a matter of principle. Either of them could have followed John to The Whitefish."

"Yeah, I get your point. I just think it's a waste of time. Besides, you seem to forget that Tyler's nephew Connor was staying at his place."

"Connor is only six, not exactly a reliable witness. Given the pressure we're under to get this right, I say we have to follow every lead."

"That leaves Lana Clark's ex, a firefighter named Nick, and a dotcom millionaire named Bob Crawley."

"I'm liking Charlie Lott for this. It is troubling that he's dropped out of sight. What has he been doing all this time? Living out of his car?"

"Obsession is a very powerful motivator. Lana is a beautiful woman."

"She is."

"But there is a slight problem. Why would Charlie Lott send a text message to John's mother?"

"He and John were friends back in Georgia."

"I doubt they were that close."

Macy sipped her wine. The restaurant had emptied, leaving just the two of them. She looked out the window. Her motel was right across the street. She'd checked in but had yet to see her room. The façade was classic 1950s. It didn't look promising. Her room was on the upper floor and the door practically opened onto Main Street.

She swallowed back some more wine. "I suspect you work every day."

"You suspect right."

She looked down at his hand and noticed he still wasn't wearing a wedding ring. "So how's the wife?"

"We've been divorced for three years."

"Sorry."

"Me too."

"Does she live around here?"

"No, she's over in Billings. Figured it would be better if she had a fresh start. We kept running into each other. It was too easy to slide back into something neither of us wanted anymore." He looked up from his plate of food. "I hear you have a kid."

"Yes. I managed to do something right."

"How's that working out? Your hours aren't exactly child friendly."

"We live with my mom. She can't believe her luck."

"You never got married?"

"It doesn't seem to be in the cards."

He pushed his plate away and picked up his beer. "Look, I'm sorry for the comment I made about married men earlier today. It was out of line. Like I said, I barely know you."

"Don't worry, it's nothing I don't tell myself on a regular basis."

"You seem like a nice lady. You deserve better."

She finished off what was left in her glass and reached for the bottle again. "We all do."

The waitress put another beer in front of him and he tilted his glass toward Macy. "Here's to that."

"And anyway, it's not like I planned it. You slide into these situations. You have all these ideas of what your life will look like, but then you make do."

"You don't have to talk about it if you don't want to."

"I want to explain myself. I don't want you to judge me."

"I'm in no position to do anything of the sort."

"It's complicated. He's the father of my child."

He peeled the label from his beer bottle and smiled. "Now you're going to have to explain."

Macy took a deep breath and tried to focus. If she was going to overshare she wanted to make sure she was making sense.

'The first time he and his wife separated they lived apart for nearly two years. I started seeing him a few months after they split up. Unfortunately, they ended up getting back together again."

"And you ended up pregnant."

"I don't regret it. Luke is the best thing that's ever happened to me. Anyway, the man in question recently announced that he was leaving his wife and wished to resume our relationship, but after eight months he's not moved out of the family home and lately I hardly see him."

"You must realize what it looks like from the outside."

"No matter what I do, I end up feeling guilty."

"Did you ever think that maybe he's only saying these things so he can get close to his son?"

"It has crossed my mind. I've been trying to distance myself, but it's tricky. He's the father of my child. A part of me really wants this to work." She paused. "Why do you think we're attracted to people who can hurt us?"

"I don't know, Macy. I suppose it has something to do with actually wanting to feel something. I guess it would be easier to be with someone who lets you glide along the surface, but who wants to live that way? The problem with your situation is that there is no balance."

"All I know for sure is that I'm tired of hurting." Macy leaned back and stifled a yawn. If she wasn't careful, she'd fall asleep. Aiden looked deep in thought.

"Sorry," she said. "I got a little serious there, didn't I?"

"You did indeed." He rapped the table with his knuckles. "If you're going to get serious, I'm going to order a serious drink. You want something?"

Macy swirled the wine in her glass and admitted that she did.

They walked back to her motel together, occasionally bumping shoulders when they misstepped. Both had their hands dug deeply into their pockets. He helped collect her bag from her vehicle, which she'd parked around back. She pointed to the enclosed stairwell.

"I think I can make it from here."

"Too risky. You might get lost."

Macy wasn't sure who started it. One second, they were walking side by side, and the next they were midgrope, backed up against a wall at the base of the stairwell.

"This is a bad idea," he said, fumbling with the buttons on her shirt.

"Exceptionally bad," she said, kissing him harder.

He slid his hand up her shirt. "But it is nice."

"Very."

His cell phone vibrated in his pocket and his hand stopped moving. He put his forehead against her shoulder. "That would be my conscience calling."

"I'm sorry to hear you have one."

"I should go."

She held him a little tighter. "Probably a good idea."

He kissed her on the shoulder and groaned before backing away. He nearly tripped on the stairs.

Macy laughed. "You're not driving, are you?"

His finger waved in a northerly direction. "I live a block that way. It's 23 Sutter Street, in case you have a change of heart."

She saluted him. "Duly noted."

"Tomorrow, can we pretend this never happened?"

"That's probably for the best. Sleep well, Aiden Marsh."

"You too, Macy Greeley."

Macy peeled away from the wall and gripped the handrail tightly as she made her way up the stairs. She passed by her door twice before seeing the room number. No doubt Aiden was laughing at her from across the street. She had to admit she liked the sound of his laugh.

"Good kisser too," she said, closing the door behind her.

The room was a time capsule from the 1950s. Everything from the curtains to the wallpaper to the furniture was retro, but it was clean and didn't smell of the former occupants. She sank down on her bed and slid her phone out of the pocket of her jeans. The text messages from Ray had become more insistent as the evening wore on. She looked at the time. It was only just coming up to ten o'clock. With any luck she'd get eight hours of sleep. She took a deep breath and typed, checking the message twice to make sure she had it right.

I'm finally in my motel room. Call me. We need to talk.

She hit Send with a flourish and went to the bathroom to brush her teeth and down a couple of ibuprofen, stripping off her clothes and leaving them rumpled on the floor. There was a text from Ray waiting for her when she climbed into bed.

Sorry, no can do. How was your day?

Macy squinted at the phone and threw it to one side. Just as she closed her eyes the phone buzzed again.

Macy? You still awake?

She sat up and the room started spinning. *Yeah, I'm still here.*

What's wrong?

I'm surprised you care.

Come on.

It's wrong that you can't pick up the phone and call me. That's what's wrong. Don't even get me started on the rest of my list.

It's too late to get into this. I'll call you tomorrow.

Why not now?

I can't and you know it.

Your wife knows you're leaving so what's stopping you? You live in a five-bedroom house FFS. Go downstairs to the kitchen. I need to talk to you.

I'm really sorry. I promise I'll call tomorrow.

Now.

I have to go.

Then go already.

We're okay though?

I don't know.

Macy turned off the lights and pulled the covers over her head. She didn't feel drunk anymore. She only felt angry. She closed her eyes and sank farther into the pillows, rolling over onto her stomach and burrowing in deeper when the phone buzzed again. This time she ignored it.

10

Jessie stood in the front window and watched Wade make his way across the yard toward the bungalow he'd been living in since his farm had failed twenty-eight years earlier. He stooped with difficulty to pick up a stick to throw to the dogs. Five Labradors were running circles around his legs, almost tripping him up. They were usually locked up at night, but Wade had thought it best that they were set loose. *Someone comes up here causing trouble and they'll get chased off.* He'd also thought it best that he sleep on the sofa, but Jessie had told him she'd be fine on her own. She double-checked all the doors and windows before heading upstairs. By the time she reached the first landing she was shaking. Two steps farther on and she could barely breathe. She crawled up the remaining stairs and lay marooned in the hallway outside the family bathroom. For a long time she pressed her cheek into a carpet that smelled of bare feet and was coated with a fine layer of dust. She cried properly for the first time since she had heard the news about John. She imagined him a hundred different ways. Memories tumbled on top of each other, some bringing her joy, others compounding her pain. There was no beginning and no end. Thoughts of Tara brought Jessie to her feet. She stumbled down the hall. A trail of discarded toys led her straight to her daughter's bedroom.

A fan sat next to a large east-facing window, drawing in fresh air. The outside lighting cast erratic shadows across the property. The dogs emerged from beneath a spiderweb of tree branches and fanned out across the lawn. In the distance the swimming pool glowed greenish blue. One of the dogs bent to drink while another barked at the inflated alligator as it drifted across the deep end. Jessie removed the flashlight from Tara's bed, its pinpoint bulb dimming. A frayed copy of an old comic book rested on the girl's chest, rising and falling with each breath. Jessie placed the book on the nightstand before shutting the door behind her and stepping into her own bedroom across the hall. She peeled off her shirt and threw it in the clothes hamper with the rest of her things, but by the time she'd brushed her teeth she'd changed her mind about going to bed. It might be a long time before she had another chance to look through her mother's things. The doctors at the hospital had given Jessie all of Annie's personal belongings, including the key to her bedroom door. Jessie padded down the hallway, wearing only a T-shirt and boxer shorts. Annie's room was nearest the stairs, and as usual the door was locked. For the past few years Jeremy had been sleeping downstairs in his office.

With its single bed and writer's desk, the bedroom was as austere as a monk's cell. The closet no longer had a door and there were very few items of clothing, since Annie had burned most of her belongings in a bonfire two years earlier. The walls were bare, aside from drawings that Tara slid under the door. The barred window had Plexiglas panes instead of glass. During a particularly heated encounter with Jeremy, Annie had smashed the original window with her bare hands. At the hospital, she had told the doctors that Jeremy was trying to kill her. When pressed, she had to admit that she had been speaking metaphorically, but it was too late. Jeremy had already been brought in for questioning. He moved a bed into his office that very same day.

Most of Annie's journals were kept on a bookshelf. Jessie picked up the one that was sitting open on the desk. Although the pages were undated, Jessie assumed it was recent, as it wasn't yet filled. The handwriting was small and tightly controlled. The sentences were well structured. The vocabulary was rich and the prose refined. Once again Jessie was struck by how coherent her mother seemed. In one section Annie described her childhood home in Connecticut in intimate detail, beginning at the front door and working her way through all sixteen rooms until she finished up at the back door. The house was nothing like the home Jessie had visited during the summers she went back east with Annie and John. By then her grandparents had moved south to a retirement village in Florida. There was nothing for the children to do aside from hang out at a local shopping mall or watch television with the sound turned down low. When their funerals came in quick succession, John had joked that their grandparents must have died of boredom.

Jessie moved to the next section of the journal, which was also undated. At some point her mother had visited some hot springs about twenty miles north of town near a tributary that ran west from the Whitefish Range. She'd gone in late spring when *leaves were at their brightest and the world was full of promise.* There was a tree filled with offerings left by visitors. They *twinkled under a sky crystalized by starlight.* Bathing in the springs was meant to make you feel reborn. Dying there would grant you immortality. *I left an offering and held my head under but He said it wasn't my time. He wrapped me in cotton towels and I returned home to face a slow death here instead.* Annie drew a map pinpointing the exact spot. Jessie closed the journal and stood staring into space. She had no idea who *He* might be.

She skimmed the pages of the other journals, looking for further references. In one passage Annie referred to his thick dark hair and in another to his friendship with Jeremy. At times the writing was so rich in erotic detail that Jessie skipped entire sections. Jessie went back through the journals one at a time, trying to establish a timeframe, but it was impossible to say whether the affair had happened recently or years ago. It was also impossible to say whether or not the whole thing was a figment of Annie's imagination. Jessie dropped the final journal on the bed and walked over to the window. The Plexiglas was filmed with dried breath and fingerprints. She wiped it with a tissue dampened with spit and stared out across the expanse of lawn toward a low grouping of outbuildings. Every light in Wade's house was on. Jessie waited. She didn't see Wade, but had the feeling that his eyes were on her. Wade had always been there for them. He'd often acted as a liaison between Jeremy and Annie. Maybe Annie had built up an entire fantasy world around Wade while she stood looking out the same window. Then again, maybe there was more to Wade than Jessie realized.

Jessie couldn't remember what he had looked like when he was younger and had a full head of hair. All that was left now was a narrow ring of white, which he kept clipped close to his scalp. He was in his late sixties, and she couldn't imagine that he'd ever been attractive enough to turn Annie's head. They'd always called him Wade; never Uncle Wade like had been suggested on occasion.

Jessie went downstairs to the living room, where the photo albums were stored in a cupboard. She flipped through the earlier ones and the plastic-coated pages creaked with age. The old photos were burnt orange and lemon yellow, losing color and definition. In some of the albums, photos were missing from almost every page. All that was left were shadows where they had once been, and crossed-out captions. Always wearing a hat, Wade stood on the periphery of family photos, arms crossed and smiling stiffly. She picked up another album and a photo slipped from the pages. Jeremy stood between two men, one of which she thought might be Wade. Jessie flipped it over. Her paternal grandmother had excellent penmanship. She'd written the date and the names in long, careful lines. Thirty-two years earlier Jeremy had gone hunting with Wade Larkin and Layton Phillips, now the governor of Montana. Back then Layton still had a shock of red hair, which now everyone suspected was dyed, as it was the color of salmon past its sell-by date. Wade's hair was jet-black and he was quite good-looking.

Jessie slipped the photo between the pages and went down the hall to her father's office. The employment records were kept in a tall filing cabinet. She switched on the overhead lights and flipped through the name tabs. Wade's file included his original letter to Jeremy asking if he'd be willing to take him on. It was dated July 1982. The bank had just foreclosed on his farm. He wrote that nothing had been the same since he lost his wife, Alice, in a fire a few years earlier—that his luck had gone from bad to worse. Jessie pushed the file drawer shut and looked around the office. There was a small drawer below the desk where Jeremy kept his personal files. It was locked but she found the key in the bowl full of spare change. Her heart froze over before she even had a chance to start looking. There was a file on Ethan Green. She pulled it out and set it down on the desk. No one in the family or in Jeremy's employment was allowed to mention Ethan by name. They'd fallen out over a business matter when she was only a baby. She opened the file and sifted through a pile of correspondence between her father and a lawyer named Giles Newton who had an office in Collier. He was acting on behalf of Ethan Green. None of the letters mentioned the dispute. They were haggling over a sum that was to be paid to Ethan. Ethan's lawyer called it restitution, while Jeremy referred to it as extortion. The language was terse and the letters went on for three months. In the end, Ethan agreed on the sum of thirty thousand dollars. In return for payment, he was to sever all ties with the Dalton family. The money was transferred to a private account at the Flathead Savings and Loan five months after Jessie and her brother were born.

Jessie copied down the name and address of the lawyer in Collier before returning the file to the drawer and locking it away. Upstairs she gathered the rest of her mother's journals. Once he was home, Jeremy would probably read them, and there'd be no way Annie would ever be allowed to come home again if that happened. Jessie put the journals under the loose floorboards in her bedroom and crawled into bed. The backlit curtains glowed ghost white, and outside, the occasional dog barked. There wasn't a hint of a breeze. She kicked the sheets away and lay sweating in the darkness. Her parents had been together for nearly thirty years, but the fact they were married seemed to matter little to either of them. Jeremy spent most nights in town with his girlfriend Natalie and Annie spent all her time fixated on events that may have happened before her children were born. Jessie closed her eyes and felt her body soften. Although she doubted he would tell her why Ethan and Jeremy fell out, she would contact the lawyer in Collier in the morning. If that didn't work, she'd go speak to her mother.

Sleep, when it finally came, was deep and haunted. Ethan grabbed her and dragged her underwater as she swam near the picnic area at Darby Lake. His thick black hair floated around his pale face and his mouth gaped open greedily. Jessie sat bolt upright and gasped. She'd been holding her breath. There'd been a sharp crack that sounded like gunfire. She listened, and seconds later it happened again. She scrambled out of bed, her ankle catching in the tangled sheets. She fell to the floor and the loose floorboards rattled like teeth. She peered down the hallway before jumping across and opening the opposite door. Tara was still sound asleep. A thin film of sweat shone on her skin. Jessie closed the door as quietly as she could and returned to her room.

Wade answered his cell phone on the second try.

"Wade. What's going on?"

He was winded. "It's nothing, go back to sleep."

"What do you mean nothing? You scared the shit out of me."

Wade yelled something, but his hand was over the mouthpiece so she couldn't make out the words.

"Who's out there with you?"

"A few of us decided it would be a good idea to keep an eye on things tonight. Tyler and Dylan are here as well."

"What are you shooting at?"

"Tyler thought he saw someone moving along the southern boundary. I'm not so sure. The man seems pretty trigger-happy. He's packing enough ammo to take out half of Wilmington Creek. I'm worried I'm going to find some dead heifers in the morning."

"He means well."

"I'll try to keep that in mind."

Jessie held tight to the flashlight as she walked the length of the corridor. She tried the wall switch, but nothing happened.

She could barely speak. "Wade, you need to get back up here. The power's been shut off."

"Get in Tara's room and lock the door. We'll be right up."

Jessie returned to her daughter's room and stood at the window, straining her ears. The house was so quiet when the power went off. The outdoor lights were still on. It could be that the fuse had blown. It happened sometimes. The house was old and not particularly well cared for. Birds nested in the eaves and mice lived beneath floor-boards. They ate through everything, including wiring. Jessie tapped the flashlight and the bulb brightened. The fuse box was in a cup-board in the utility room.

She walked downstairs on tiptoe, stopping every so often to listen. The tile floor in the kitchen was gritty and cool. Tree branches tapped against the windows. Outside, she heard dogs barking and the hum of ATVs. They must have reached the stables. The sink faucet rattled and a thin stream of water drained out into the empty sink. Jessie swung the flashlight around, hitting all the dark corners. The room was empty. The utility room had a door that led out to the backyard. Inside the room it was pitch black and smelled strongly of laundry detergent and dogs. She focused the beam of light on the outside door. It was shut and the keys were in the lock where she had left them. Clutching the flashlight in her armpit, she opened the cup-board. The main circuit breaker was down. She flicked it and the room brightened instantly. Behind her the hot water heater ticked into life. Above her the lighting hummed. She switched off the flashlight before bending down to pick up a stray sock. There was a knock at the door and she screamed.

. . .

"I decided it was probably a blown fuse and I was right. I'm fine. Tara's fine. That's what's important." Jessie lowered her mug of coffee and returned Tyler's stare. She'd already had one argument with Wade about not waiting in Tara's room, and she was quite willing to mix it up with Tyler as well.

Dylan stepped between them and grabbed an apple from a bowl on the kitchen table. "Well, no harm done. We've checked the whole house. No one seems to have been here."

Wade grumbled. "That fuse blows all the time. One of these days this whole house is going to go up in flames."

Jessie placed her cup on the counter. "I'm going to go check on Tara."

Dylan opened the door for her. "I'll go with you."

"You don't need to."

He picked up the rifle leaning against the wall. "Yeah, I do."

"You're not bringing that in my daughter's room."

"I wasn't planning on it."

They stood in the doorway and watched her sleep.

Jessie leaned her head on the frame. "Have you ever heard of some hot springs about twenty miles north of town?"

"No, why?"

"Something I read in my mother's journals."

"Is that what you've been doing all night?"

"Pretty much."

"No offense, but do you really think you can believe everything your mother says?"

"She drew a map."

"Show me."

He didn't ask why she'd hidden the journals under the floorboards. He traced his finger over the crude drawing. "There are some landmarks here that I recognize. Have you asked Wade? He'd know."

"I can't."

"Why's that?"

"I think my mother was having an affair. I'm pretty sure it was a long time ago but there's a possibility it was with Wade. There's no way I can say anything to him."

He held the map up to the light and inspected it more closely. "Well, we can drive up there if you like. Have a poke around. Why are you so interested?"

"I want to know if she's telling the truth. If this place exists, maybe the other stuff she wrote about happened too."

"Makes sense, I guess."

Jessie woke up in Tara's bed. Her daughter was braiding her hair. Jessie smiled when she heard Tara humming. She smelled like milk and bread dough. She breathed through her open mouth.

"Hi, Mommy."

"Hi, baby girl."

"Why is Uncle Wade sleeping on the sofa?"

Jessie tried to sit up, but Tara still had hold of her hair.

"You've been downstairs?"

"Hold still. You're ruining it."

Jessie settled back onto the pillow.

"Someone left you a present."

"Pardon?"

"It was on the front porch."

"Did you open it?"

She shook her head vigorously. "That would be cheating."

"Where is it?"

Tara slid off the bed and skipped across the room to the dresser. She returned, holding a small box. "See, it has your name on it."

Jessie shook it very gently. It hardly weighed anything. She peeled off the card and turned it over. There was no message.

Tara was breathing in her ear. "Why did you get a present? It's not your birthday."

Jessie peeled back the paper. "There are lots of reasons people give presents. Sometimes you give presents because you want to make someone feel better."

Tara smoothed a tear that had slid down her mother's cheek. "I love you, Mommy."

Jessie held her breath for a few seconds. "I love you too. Can you hand me a tissue?"

Tara plucked one from the box on the nightstand and gave it to her mother. "We're going to be sad for a long time, aren't we?"

"We are."

"So do you think someone gave you this so you'd be less sad?"

Jessie removed the lid and emptied the contents into her palm. "I think so."

Tara reached over and picked up the necklace. "It's pretty."

Jessie remained silent.

Tara studied it carefully. "The thingy that closes it is broken."

Jessie tried to keep her voice steady. "Here, let me have a look?"

The heart-shaped locket felt heavy in her palm. It was plain silver and had no markings of any sort.

"Is there a picture inside?"

Jessie flinched when Tara reached over to open it. "Let Mommy do it, sweetheart."

Jessie dug her thumbnail in the groove and the locket popped open.

"Mommy, is that me?"

"Yes, it is."

"How old was I?"

Jessie almost choked. "I think you were four."

"Are you less sad now?"

Jessie nodded again

"Then why are you crying?"

11

Macy crossed through the industrial end of Collier without much more than a sideways glance. The road going through town had been improved since the winter her son was born at the nearby hospital. Route 93 now bypassed the entire length of Main Street, leaving the residents in peace. Macy parked near the town square and stepped out into the heat. The eighteen-wheelers may have gone, but the black soot they left behind had yet to be washed off the sidewalks and buildings. Cracks snaked across the sidewalks and ran up walls. A couple of buildings had been repainted, but for the most part the storefronts were as colorless as the sky. The smoky haze had thickened overnight. Visibility had been poor on the drive up from Wilmington Creek, and several emergency vehicles had passed her heading south.

It was ten in the morning and the tarmac was already baking. Eager to reach the next bit of shade, Macy struck out across Main Street. A car swerved onto the road from a side street and bore down on her at speed. The horn sounded as the car came to a stop a few feet away. Macy took her time checking the license plate while the driver gesticulated wildly from the other side of the windshield. From the twist of his mouth Macy could tell he wasn't wishing her well. She flashed a weak smile and waved apologetically. When he rolled down his window and called her a stupid bitch, she took out her badge.

"Are we finished now?" she said, holding it in his face. "Because we could spend the whole day discussing what an idiot I was just then. How I'd had a temporary lapse in judgment as I went about my otherwise flawless day. But you of course never make any mistakes, do you? I can tell you're a perfect citizen just by looking at the expired plates on your car. Maybe we should discuss those."

The man started to roll up his window, but Macy stopped him.

"Maybe the next time our paths cross I'll be the one speeding in a thirty-mile-an-hour zone." She raised her voice. "You'll know it's me because I won't bother to stop."

She felt nauseous. She'd woken up at three in the morning with all the lights in her room on. After taking some more ibuprofen she'd stumbled back to bed and slept through her alarm. When she finally surfaced there were several missed calls from Ray, but no messages. She'd read through the texts they'd exchanged the night before, and her mood soured further. Even in her advanced stages of denial she could see it wasn't a healthy situation. She made yet another solemn vow to stop drinking, give up on Ray, and get a grip. She couldn't believe how she'd behaved the night before. She'd been so embarrassed she'd not checked in with Aiden before heading to Collier. She tried to sound natural when she picked up the phone and dialed his number, but she wasn't fooling anyone.

"Hey, Aiden."

He seemed to be in a rush. There were sirens in the background. "Hey to you too. Thought I'd have heard from you by now."

"I had a late start so I thought I'd better head straight to Collier."

"Just as well. I've got my hands full. The wind shifted overnight and that fire south of town tried to jump Route 93. Quite a few early-morning evacuations."

"No casualties, I hope."

"Fingers crossed. Nothing reported so far."

Macy relaxed. "How's your head?"

"Tender. Yours?"

"Same." She paused, then sputtered, "About last night. We're okay, right?"

He laughed. "I'm a little frustrated but I'll get over it."

"Always a bridesmaid but never a bride."

"Something like that."

A silence followed.

"So, I'll check in with you once I've spoken to John's therapist."

"I might be out of range for a while. I'm heading south on 93 now."

"Okay. Talk later then."

In her late forties, the therapist, Janet Flute, had pale eyes, bloodless lips, and a boy's haircut. Small in stature and stripped of ornamentation, she was someone who'd blend into any background. Her expression varied little and she was so considered in her answers that in the intervening silences Macy found herself spouting out all sorts of unsolicited information. Within the first few minutes, she admitted to being hungover, stressed out, and disappointed with the state of her love life. Janet blinked, which Macy suspected was her way of expressing shock.

"Christ," said Macy, gathering herself. "That wasn't very professional."

Janet only tilted her head as if she was inviting Macy to continue.

"I guess you get that a lot. People confessing."

She almost smiled. "That's generally the idea with therapy, although some people respond better than others. Do you have a therapist?" She reached for a business card and passed it to Macy. "Perhaps."

Macy stared at the card. Unlike the one in John Dalton's wallet, this one was crisp and white. She pocketed it and focused on the task at hand.

"I'd like to thank you for speaking to me today. I can only assure you that anything you tell me will be kept in strict confidence."

"I want to help. John Dalton was a very decent young man. It's a terrible loss for the community. I think he would have gone far in life if given the chance."

"You said on the phone that you were willing to discuss his visits."

She opened a thin file. "John only came to see me half a dozen times, so what I have here is a fairly limited impression of him. It may not even be accurate. It sometimes takes awhile to get to the core of a person's issues. Perhaps you could tell me what you're looking for."

"Was he traumatized by his time in Afghanistan? Was he exhibiting behavior that could have put him in harm's way?"

"Recently there has been a lot of bad press about war veterans. All the headlines seem to be about those that are having problems, but very little has been written about the vast majority who've adjusted well to civilian life."

"I suppose in my line of work I only come across the folks that are struggling, so I may have developed some misconceptions. Domestic violence, drug abuse, and suicide seem to top the list of the problems we're seeing. I need to know if John was someone we should have been worried about."

Instead of answering right away, Janet glanced down at her notes. "I'm sorry, I just want to make sure I get this right. I don't want to confuse matters."

Macy sat back in her chair and fought the urge to check her phone. "Please take your time."

"In my opinion, John Dalton was adapting to civilian life well. Like many young men and women who go into service with a strong sense of patriotic duty and a steadfast faith in the military structure, he was well equipped to endure the hardships he faced in Afghanistan. He chose to enlist. He wasn't forced by economic reasons or peer pressure. It was John's way of striking out on his own and proving himself. Considering how much action he saw, I'd say he was lucky to come away unscathed both emotionally and physically. He wasn't displaying any signs of self-destructive behavior or post-traumatic stress. In fact you could say that his coming here of his own volition to sort out issues of, shall we say, a more existential nature, was a sign that he was in a rather sound state of mind."

"That contradicts what someone close to him was saying about his behavior."

"I can only go by what's in front of me."

"You should know that I interviewed Dylan Reed. He told me that he recommended that John come see you."

"Did he tell you why?"

Macy nodded. "According to Dylan, John was finding his relationship with his mother increasingly stressful. Amongst other things, Annie told him that Jeremy wasn't his real father."

"As you may know, John's mother, Annie, has been suffering from early onset dementia for some time now."

Macy waited.

"She's prone to outbursts, flights of fantasy. It's difficult to tell whether she's telling the truth or only saying things that she believes to be true. John had difficulty believing what his mother told him, but as he looked back on the problems his parents have had over the years, things started to make sense. But John loved Jeremy as a father. He felt disloyal because he was becoming increasingly interested with finding out the truth as to who his real father might be. Add to this the recent changes in his life—leaving the military, the return home, and the breakup of a long-term relationship—he was feeling a little lost. He came to me because he wanted someone to speak to in confidence."

"I take it Annie gave no indication as to who his real father was."

"If, indeed, Jeremy isn't his real father in the first place. Annie isn't well. A difficult marriage doesn't necessarily mean it was an unfaithful one."

"And these revelations were recent?"

"Yes, since he was discharged from the army in December."

"It could explain why he has been distant with his sister."

"He'd found out something that could be devastating for her to know. It would make sense."

"You met with John last week?"

"Yes."

"How did you leave it? Was he in a good state of mind?"

"He'd made his peace. Jeremy may not have been related to him by blood, but he'd been there for John his entire life. In John's eyes, Jeremy was his real father."

"So he gave up trying to find out who his mother was referring to?"

"He didn't say as much, but I was under the impression that he'd figured out who it was some time ago. He'd just been unwilling to let go and move on."

"He didn't confide in you?"

"No, I'm sorry. I can't help you there. I will say that the last time he was here he seemed adamant about closing this chapter in his life. He was a very determined young man; I have no doubt he would have succeeded."

Macy closed her eyes for a second. "Did John ever speak about his relationships outside his family?"

"I don't think I'm revealing much that isn't in the public domain by saying that he was at a crossroads romantically. I think the revelations about his parents really shook him up. Made him question the validity of long-term commitment. I saw his relationship with Lana as an act of rebellion, but also a way of reaching beyond the borders of his upbringing. Intellectually, she challenged him. It was a refreshing change."

"And what about his friends? Dylan, for instance."

"Dylan is my patient so I'm not at liberty to speak about him directly. I will say that John admired him greatly. Loved him like a brother."

"What about Tyler Locke?"

"Tyler was both John's close friend and his platoon sergeant. There was a great deal of mutual respect. He really looked up to Tyler, but he also worried about him."

"Did he say why?"

"He didn't go into detail. I imagine they depended on each other a great deal during their deployments. It would make sense for that interdependence to carry over into civilian life. Plus, Tyler was still in harm's way and John was no longer there to protect him."

Macy started to gather her things. "Do you know if John spoke to his sister about what Annie told him?"

"As far as I know she wasn't told." She paused. "I hope something you learned today was helpful. The news of John's murder has been quite a shock."

"As I said, we've had some conflicting information about John's state of mind. Given the source, it has to be taken seriously, so I'll need to follow that line of enquiry further. At this point I have no idea whether the question of John's parentage played a factor in his death, but it may yet come up."

"You will keep me posted?"

"Absolutely. And again I apologize for earlier. Sometimes my mouth runs ahead of my head."

"I get the impression you're very stressed."

"I'm a single parent, I work long hours, and the governor is a close friend of Jeremy Dalton. The pressure to get this right is enormous."

"You just have to let go of the stuff you can't control. Who takes care of your son when you can't be there for him? Do you feel he's in good hands?"

"Yes, that's all fine. He's well looked after."

"And your love life?"

"I wasn't joking. It's a disaster."

"What about the drinking? Working in law enforcement is very stressful. You wouldn't be the first one to drink one too many glasses of wine."

Macy rubbed her eyes. "More like whiskey."

"I think you should make a real effort to cut back. It will just exacerbate any problems you're having, both at work and in your personal life."

Macy almost said that the two were the same thing, but kept her thoughts to herself. She stood up and held out her hand. "You're right, of course. I'll try."

Janet smiled for the first time. "Good to hear."

Macy sat in Aiden's office, going through her notes. It made no difference that the door was closed. Every sound, no matter how slight, set off a painful vibration in her skull. What she wanted more than anything was to go home to Helena and sleep for three days straight. She checked the time. She'd been assured that John Dalton's commanding officer would be available to take her call. She'd already reviewed John's service record and there was nothing to indicate that he had had any sort of breakdown. She took a sip of water and waited to be put through. Lieutenant Colonel Paul McDonald's battalion was stationed at Bagram Air Base in eastern Afghanistan. She'd been expecting him to be full of bravado and bark down the phone like a character from a war movie. He was nothing of the sort. Once he heard the news about John it took him a long while to regain his composure. Macy was not prepared to hear a thrice-decorated soldier cry on the other end of the line.

She tapped her notebook with her pen. "Perhaps I should call back later. This has been a big shock for everyone involved."

"No, no. That won't be necessary. Just give me a sec."

Macy flipped through John's service record. John had served under Paul McDonald for three years. She'd wait.

He spoke softly. "In a way, everyone out here is like family, but John stood out. He was like a son."

"Considering where you spend most of your time, it must be difficult to stay emotionally detached."

"I breathe a sigh of relief whenever they head home unharmed. Can you tell me what happened? Was it an accident?"

"Early yesterday morning John suffered a single gunshot wound to his head and two to his back. Death was instantaneous."

"A robbery."

"Nothing was taken."

"Christ."

"I'm interviewing everyone who was close to John. I'm not only trying to piece together his movements, I'm also trying to understand his state of mind. I've had some conflicting information in that regard, and I was hoping you could set me straight. I've read his service record, and there's nothing to indicate he was having any difficulties during his time in Afghanistan."

"That's because he wasn't."

"There were never any incidents when he was fearful of going out on patrol, any indications that he had some sort of breakdown?"

"I have an entire battalion under my command. Nearly eight hundred soldiers. I can do some checking but I'm telling you right now that John Dalton was of sound mind when he left here. How he reacted to being back home is another matter. Not everyone adjusts to civilian life. They live under constant strain here. We train them to be on guard to any threat, no matter how slight. I'm not going to apologize. It's what keeps them alive. But what's right for a war zone doesn't always set well back home. I've seen some cases where these kids just snap. I don't blame them. What they're facing over here isn't natural. Thankfully, the vast majority of our soldiers make the adjustment without difficulty."

"Did John have any worries about returning home? Did he ever mention any specific issues?"

"I would have remembered something like that. I come from a family of ranchers as well. We used to drive everyone nuts talking about it. He seemed to really miss working with his father. He did mention his sister a lot. I think she was his twin."

"Yes, that's right. Her name is Jessie."

"There was some kind of problem. Drugs, as I recall."

"She's clean now."

"Well, that's good."

"Who was John closest to in his platoon?"

"That's an easy one to answer. It was always Tyler Locke. They grew up together."

"I've met Tyler."

"Yes, I understand he's back home now as well."

"Is there anyone else besides Tyler who I can speak to?"

"Hmmm. There are a couple of guys, but at the moment his platoon is stationed at the advanced command outpost."

"Any idea when they'll be back?"

"That's classified."

"I'd like you to put them through to me as soon as you can."

"That might be a problem. I'll get a message to them. One way or another I'll make sure you get the information you need."

"I'm reaching here, but could something have happened over there that may have followed John back to Wilmington Creek? I don't know. A friendly fire incident? A disagreement with one of the other men? I can't believe they're weren't any disputes."

"I'm telling you now that John was more of a peacemaker. I will ask the guys though. Someone may have heard something."

"I'd appreciate that."

Just as she was hanging up, Aiden walked in, smelling of wood smoke. He collapsed in his chair and threw his hat on the desk before gesturing to a small refrigerator in the corner. "Can you check if there's anything to drink in there? I'm dying over here."

Macy raised a 7 Up and he nodded his approval. "That will do nicely."

She handed it to him and he drained it in a single shot.

"You want another?"

"Yes, please. Christ, it's hot out there." He dragged his hands across his face, leaving dark smudges.

Macy gave him a tissue, along with another soft drink. "You have soot all over your face."

He mopped up. "I'm not surprised. It was hell down there. The crews only just managed to stop the fire from jumping Route 93. Ten homes were lost." He tapped his desk with his knuckles. "So far no one has died."

"You've had three fires in quick succession. Have you considered the possibility that it might be arson?"

"We've considered it, but so far we've got zilch. People are under the misconception that arsonists are stupid, but that's because it's only the stupid ones that get caught. How was your morning?"

"I've just printed out Lana Clark's case report. The officer handling her harassment case is supposed to call me after lunch."

"What about the therapist?"

"Janet Flute confirmed that John was seeing her because he was having difficulty coming to terms with what Annie told him."

"Did she have any insight as to why John would believe Annie in the first place?"

Macy got up and shut the door. "Janet advised John to be cautious, but apparently there were reasons for him to believe there was a possibility it was true. Janet wouldn't go into detail, but did say that John had made his peace. He was loyal to Jeremy. Nothing his mother said would change that."

"Did he ever figure out who Annie might be talking about?"

"The therapist was under the impression that John had figured it out some time ago, but he didn't reveal any more details."

"Anyway, I'm not sure it's relevant unless the father was someone who didn't want to be found, and how likely is that?"

"My thoughts exactly. Anyway, she didn't corroborate what Tyler told us, but she only had six sessions with John and admits it's impossible to develop a reliable picture of someone in such a short time. However, John's former commander in Afghanistan also swears John wasn't having any issues, but is putting me in touch with some of the guys that were closest to him. He did say that John and Tyler were exceptionally tight and that there was no telling how well a soldier would adapt to civilian life."

"So we're still thinking Tyler would be best equipped to give us an accurate picture of John's state of mind."

"Yes, but where does that really get us? Say John was stressed. That doesn't explain why someone put a bullet in his head and then sent a message to his mother apologizing."

"You got another copy of Lana's case report?"

"It's on the desk in front of you."

He yawned into his closed fist as he rose from the chair. "I'm gonna get some coffee. You want to join me?"

"No thanks. I reached my daily limit a few hours ago."

"Okay, suit yourself. I'll be back in a half hour or so." He picked up the file and left without shutting the door.

Macy stared at the open door. She had no idea if Aiden was offended or not. He seemed as hungover as she was, maybe a bit more irritable, but that was understandable considering the morning he'd had. She kicked the door shut with her foot and returned to her desk, where she sat facing the corner. Even though she'd done nothing wrong it always felt as if she was the one being punished. She'd spent the last three years being loyal to Ray Davidson, but he didn't seem to be any closer to moving on from his marriage than he was when they started seeing each other the first time he and his wife separated. The only promising thing he'd done recently was to acknowledge that Luke was his son, but the way he'd gone about it only frustrated Macy further. He wanted Luke to have his surname and was surprised Macy didn't jump at the chance to change the birth certificate. Ray had seen Luke only four times since he was born. The first occasion had been when Macy ran into him and his wife at a barbecue. Luke was eight months old and anyone who was looking could see how much he resembled Ray. His wife hesitated before offering her congratulations. Macy knew she was doing the math. She was a smart lady. She would have figured out then and there that Luke was conceived while she and Ray were still separated. Since Ray had asked about changing the birth certificate, Macy had also been doing some math. In the nineteen months since Luke was born, Ray had had less than four hours of actual contact. There was no way her son would ever be Luke Davidson. Macy looked over her shoulder at the closed door. She'd lied to Aiden. She was actually desperate for another cup of coffee. She slipped Lana's case report in her bag and went to find him.

12

The home Tyler had inherited from his grandmother was located close to where Tucker Road came to a dead end on the eastern shores of the Flathead River. It stood on a windswept lot guarded by chain-link fencing and warning signs. It had been closed up since his grandmother went into the hospital seven months earlier, and no matter how long Tyler left the windows open, the smell of her last year in residence wouldn't be shifted. His mother liked to say that she'd been too stubborn to leave the place in peace. Tyler liked to say his grandmother had been too stubborn to change her colostomy bag.

Dylan knocked a couple of times before easing open the screen door.

"Hey, Tyler. You here?"

The television was frozen on the image from a video game. Blankets were strewn across the sofa, and the ashtray on the floor next to it overflowed with cigarette butts. Porn magazines, video games, and empty beer bottles covered the coffee table. Dylan went into the kitchen and felt the coffeepot with the back of his hand. It was still warm so he poured some into a cup. Thinking Tyler may have gone back to bed, he wandered down the hallway.

"Tyler, I got your message."

The bedroom door was ajar, the unmade bed clearly visible. He knocked but there was no answer. He eased the door open further. The floor was covered in dirty laundry. A military kit bag was thrown in the corner, its contents spilling out. He heard music coming from the direction of the garage. He shifted the curtains and looked outside. The side door to the one-story building was open. Dylan went back into the living room and found a scribbled note on the sliding glass doors telling him to come around back to the garage. He stepped out onto the porch. A backhoe was parked above a deep pit. Cinder blocks were stacked on wooden pallets along the back fence.

Dylan knocked loud enough to be heard over the music and waited by the door. Tyler was sitting on a stool at the workbench, wearing only a pair of boxer shorts and flip-flops; his wide tattooed back was damp with sweat. He adjusted the position of a lamp that was attached to the wall before reaching up to lower the volume on a pair of portable speakers.

"Hey, Dylan."

"Hey."

"You manage to get any sleep?"

"A bit. You?"

"Not really."

Dylan leaned against the open door where it was marginally cooler. Self-conscious about the scars that roped his thigh, he hadn't worn shorts in public since he was wounded. Compared to the glaring sunlit sky outside, the garage was dark and his eyes were slow to adjust. Every tool Tyler's grandfather had ever owned was carefully displayed along one of the walls. Fishing and hunting gear took up the other. There were two deep freezers humming along the back wall. Above them Tyler had taped the blueprints for a nuclear fallout shelter he was digging in his backyard. Dylan and John had laughed when Tyler told them about the plans he'd downloaded from a survivalist's Web site. He'd glared at them.

We'll see who has the last laugh.

Tyler uncoiled orange det cord from spools and cut it into equal lengths. There were eight three-pound Pentolite explosive cylinders and a single electronic detonator stowed in a box on the floor. Dylan walked over and picked up the detonator. It was the same type they used in the army.

"I see Wayne isn't the only one stealing stuff from work."

Tyler shrugged. "It's not like they're going to give me a gold watch."

"You have everything you need?"

Tyler picked up an explosive cylinder and peered down the hole bored through its length. "You should see Wayne's place. He's gonna get caught if he keeps taking this stuff."

"Is there any way it can be traced back to him?"

"If they blow like they're supposed to do, that won't be a problem we have to worry about."

"And if they don't?"

"I'll make sure they're clean." Tyler threaded det cord through the cylinder and tied off the end before wrapping the cord in loops and securing it with black electrical tape. He put the bundle to one side and started the next one.

"This seems like too much."

"We only have one shot at it so I'm going for overkill."

"Wade called this morning."

Tyler frowned. "Did anything happen after we left?"

"No. He just wanted to thank us for helping out."

"And so he should."

"He went out early this morning to have a look around. You'll be relieved to know you didn't shoot any livestock."

"I wasn't imagining things. I saw something out there."

"I'm not doubting you."

He pointed. "Hand me those wire strippers."

"How long did you make the detonator cords?"

"Fifty feet."

"Is that enough?"

"It's adequate. There are plenty of places to take cover up there. Plus, I have to pack all this shit in."

"I'll help you."

"No offense, Dylan, but I'm going in on foot. You'd slow me down."

"When are you going?"

"If all goes well I'll set off early tomorrow morning. I've got a friend who has a place south of Darby Lake. I'll hike in from there."

"Oh yeah, who's this?"

"Guy named Lacey I met in Iraq. He's running a training course for a militia on the Mexico-Arizona border for the next month and wanted me to keep an eye on things. I figured I'd kill two birds with one stone."

"I didn't know anyone lived down that way. It's pretty remote."

"It's a sweet setup. Completely off the grid. Only access is a logging road." He shot Dylan a quick glance. "How are you holding up? Better than yesterday?"

"Yeah, I guess. I'm sorry about being a dick. I know you were just trying to help."

"You don't need to be sorry about anything. Just don't shut me out. I'm here for you."

"I know. It's just been hard. John has had my back all this time. Now he's gone and you're leaving."

"One more deployment and I'm coming home."

"Really? I thought you'd never call time."

"I've had enough. Maybe I'll become a consultant like Lacey. He gets paid a shitload of money."

"It would be nice to have you around."

"In the meantime, you've got to dig deep. I know you've got it in you. You're a strong person, Dylan. You've just lost sight of that. You find it again and you'll be fine." He paused. "And quit taking all those meds. It can't be right."

"That's harder than you think."

"I've heard of guys that are taking so much junk they've accidentally overdosed."

"That's one way to look at it."

"What do you mean by that?"

"They could have done it on purpose. There's a lot of that going around."

"Don't even think it, Dylan."

"I'm not."

"Good to hear."

"How are you holding up?"

"I'm a little worried about being called in again for questioning. Aiden's cool, but that detective from Helena isn't going to like that I have a criminal record."

"That was years ago."

"Well, as far as I know they don't have squat aside from Lana's ex and some guy from a fire crew. They'll be checking anyone who was close to John."

"I heard through the grapevine that they are going to interview Bob Crawley."

"Why would they do that?"

"Lana's been seeing him."

Tyler stopped stripping the ends of the det cord and stretched out his back. He stared straight ahead when he spoke. "She kept that quiet."

"It's not something she'd want to advertise. He's married."

"Hand me that detonator."

"I thought for sure you'd go for a fertilizer bomb."

"Hiking in with fifty pounds of ampho on my back didn't sound like my idea of fun."

"You've done worse."

"Yeah, but that was because I was taking orders. No one carries that stuff on their back if they have a choice." He held up a cylinder. "These bad boys weigh less and are a hell of a lot more reliable. Plus

I can slip them right down in the existing cracks in the cliff. No need to drill bore holes."

"You ever heard of some hot springs about twenty miles north of town?"

"That's a new one on me. Why?"

"Jessie found a map in her mother's room."

"Seems like Jessie has more important things to think about."

"That's what I said."

"What's your read on her?"

"She's going through hell."

"Did you ask her about Ethan?"

"Yeah, but she's still saying she doesn't remember anything."

"At this point I just want to know that she's going to keep her mouth shut."

"That's not a problem. She doesn't want to drag us down with her. I get the impression she'll be relieved once the cliff is blown."

"You seeing her today?"

"Yeah, I think half of Wilmington Creek is heading up to the ranch. You coming?"

"My mom wants us to go as a family, so I'll wait until my dad gets off work."

"How's Connor taking it?"

"I have no idea. He's gone quiet like he's thinking it over. I'm not sure how much he understands."

13

Aiden yawned. "Hey, you want more coffee?"

Macy threw Charlie Lott's photo on the table. He was heavy-set, with long dark hair that was parted in the middle. A beard covered half his face. There was really no telling what he looked like without it.

"At this point the only thing that's going to help is going back to sleep."

"Sorry. The whiskey was my idea."

"It's not like I needed much convincing." She looked at her phone. "I'm surprised there's been no word on the DNA."

"Given the state of John's truck and number of cigarette butts in that alleyway, I'd say they've got their hands full. It might be a few days yet."

Macy flipped through the case file again. "Lana wasn't exaggerating."

"I have to admit that I was dubious, but it seems she had just cause to be alarmed."

"I might be reaching here but I've just had a thought. Mr. Walker's dog died the day John was murdered. He said it had a tendency to bark."

"You're thinking it could have been poisoned, too?"

"If Charlie Lott was willing to poison his girlfriend's dog, it stands to reason he wouldn't hesitate to kill one he had no attachment to. It's buried in the side yard."

"Are you thinking we should dig it up and run some tests?"

"I'm not sure. Dogs die all the time from natural causes. It doesn't seem right to distress Mr. Walker unless we have more reason to believe it's related."

"Well, let's say you're right about the dogs. There are no other parallels. No one got shot in Georgia."

"Lana wasn't seeing anyone new then, so maybe Charlie was content with following her and leaving little gifts so she knew she was being watched."

"But then it suddenly escalates. Within a week of vandalizing her car and setting fire to her porch, he poisons her dog. No wonder she ran. That's some scary shit."

"She's probably still scared. That sort of fear never really goes away."

He tapped the photo of Charlie Lott. "We need to find him."

Macy pushed her chair away from the table. "You know, looking through these reports, I'm kind of surprised she was granted a restraining order. There's nothing in these files that ties her ex-boyfriend directly to the incidents. The night her house was set on fire, his friends say he was out with them."

"All the more reason to track him down and eliminate him as a possibility. When is your phone call with Lana's case officer?"

Macy checked the time. "In ten minutes. I'll take it back at the office. Do you mind giving the lab a shout? You'll want to speak to Priscilla Jones. She may have something preliminary to tell us. Also chase up the sketch artist. Robert's been with Jean and Lana for the past hour."

"Will do."

"Has the state sent over a list of firefighters who've been working in the area?"

"A preliminary one. There are a few guys named Nick. Given the number of fires, there's been a lot of influx from other states. They're compiling various lists."

She stood. "When I've finished on the phone I want to talk to Bob Crawley."

"I spoke to him this morning. He has an alibi for the night John was killed. A certain Ms. Angela Hutton will vouch for his whereabouts."

"That needs to be followed up. Given his resources he can afford to create a pretty sound alibi."

"His wife and kids are out of town, so I said we'd come see him up at his place."

"And here I was thinking you were going to haul him downtown and be tough on him."

"I'm telling you now he's not our guy."

"You might miss something important if you don't keep an open mind."

He picked up his hat and slid it back on his head. "I could say the same thing about you."

Aiden offered to drive and Macy let him have his way. He was the local police chief. Traveling in the passenger seat probably didn't suit his image, but she balked when he tried to open the door for her.

"Seriously, it feels like the 1950s around here."

"Nothing wrong with good manners."

"How long is the drive?"

"It's about a half hour east of town."

It was over a hundred degrees in the interior of his car. Macy started pushing buttons on the dashboard. "Which one of these turns on the air conditioner?"

Aiden reached over and adjusted a dial. "It will cool off in a few minutes. Quit acting like a child."

"If that were the case I'd report you to social services. I could die in here."

"Keep it up and I'll make you walk."

"So, now you're all tough."

He shuffled through some papers on the seat between them. "I tracked down the sketch artist. His handiwork is somewhere in this mess."

Macy held up the composite sketch of the firefighter who'd been harassing Lana. "I need to speak to Robert. Lately he's making all my suspects look like evil geniuses. Beady-eyed, bald, and sporting a goatee. Hardly original."

"I sent a PDF over to the Forestry Service. He should be easy to pick out."

"Any luck with the lab?"

"Nothing so far. That woman Priscilla practically bit my head off."

"That's why I had you call. Any idea when she'll get back to us?"

"She was pretty stressed. I didn't want to press her."

"Anything on ballistics?"

"They didn't return my call."

Macy adjusted the vent to the air conditioner so it was blowing away from her. "Great, now it's freezing."

"How was the phone call with Lana's case officer back in Georgia?"

"Brief."

"Why's that?"

"There wasn't much to say that wasn't in the report. When I pressed him he did agree that the evidence on the ex-boyfriend was flimsy, but given that Lott had publically threatened Lana in the past they had just cause to suspect it was him. Just so you know, there's also a history of prescription drug abuse."

"That's no surprise. It seems to be the scourge of rural America at the moment. Did he give you any ideas as to where we might find Mr. Lott?"

"It turns out he has a paternal grandmother who lives out near Spokane. A few years back he listed her as an emergency contact on an employment application."

"That's only a couple hours' drive."

"It does bring him within a comfortable range. I still find it weird that he's been off the radar for so long. Lana's case officer did a quick follow-up. No one has been in contact with him for a couple of months."

"Time to call Granny."

"I tried. There was no answer. I've contacted the authorities in Spokane. They're sending over a couple of uniforms."

"Very efficient use of your time." He pointed out the front window. "You see that lake down there?"

"Yep, what am I looking at?"

"Well, Bob Crawley owns it and pretty much everything else between here and the Idaho border."

"Lots of places to hide a body down there."

"Well, I guess that's one way to look at a beautiful view."

A restored railroad car served as a gatehouse at the entrance of the Crawley property. Three security cameras were visible and there were two guards on duty. A long, poplar-lined driveway led to a house designed to blend into the sage green hills behind it. Hazy reflections of the Whitefish Range were reflected in the three-story front windows. In places Macy could see straight through to the swimming pool in the backyard. Unlike the rest of the landscape it sparkled an unnatural emerald blue. Bob Crawley answered the door in a pair of swimming trunks and a T-shirt. Slim and surprisingly young-looking considering he was fifty-six, he had bare feet and he held tight to the collar of a large yellow mastiff that tried to jump up on Aiden.

He shook Aiden's hand. "I think Buster must have taken a liking to you when you came out to the barbecue last month."

"May have been that hamburger I fed him."

"That will do the trick."

"Bob, this is Detective Macy Greeley. She's been put in charge of the homicide investigation."

"Pleasure to meet you, Detective Greeley. I'm just sorry it wasn't under better circumstances."

"We appreciate your cooperation." Macy looked past him toward the pool. A woman was sunbathing topless in one of the deck chairs. "Is that Ms. Hutton?"

"The one and only. She's an old family friend."

"We need to speak to her as well."

"She's leaving for New York in the morning so you'll have to be quick."

"Aiden, do you mind?"

Aiden slipped his sunglasses back on and headed for the sliding glass doors with Buster trailing behind him. "Not at all."

"You and Ms. Hutton were together on Thursday night?"

"Yes, we had dinner here. I never left the property that evening. I'll make sure my assistant gives you access to the security tapes."

"That's very helpful. As you can imagine, we need to follow every lead. Is there somewhere we can talk?"

"We'll go to my office."

Bob Crawley had a youthful complexion and a mane of blond hair that he was constantly flipping back with one hand, yet he had both the money and the manners of someone considerably older. She took a chair opposite him and tried not to be distracted by the beautiful view and the exquisite furnishings. She'd spotted a Picasso as they walked in. She doubted it was a print.

"Mr. Crawley—"

He held up a hand. "My father is Mr. Crawley Please just call me Bob."

"I understand you've been in a extramarital relationship with Lana Clark since April of this year."

"Am I really a suspect? I can prove that I was here."

"You have resources most people can only dream of. I have to consider it's a possibility, regardless of how remote, that you arranged John's murder."

"Money, yes. Motive, no. My relationship with Lana wasn't serious. She's a beautiful girl who likes to have a good time. End of story. Ask Lana if you don't believe me."

"I did ask Lana."

"So you know."

"Maybe you grew a little too fond of her?"

Bob Crawley stared at Macy from the other side of the desk. The ready-made smile slid south, along with his youthful features. He suddenly looked very tired. There was strain in his eyes she hadn't noticed before.

"I had nothing to do with John Dalton's death. I admired the man. I was hoping he'd run in the upcoming election. Shake things up a bit."

"I'm sure you of all people will appreciate that it's my job to check everything thoroughly. I need to look at the security footage and speak to your staff."

"Do whatever it takes. I just want this to be cleared up as soon as possible."

"We'll arrange for a video technician to come up this afternoon. We can interview your staff today as well. Do you keep guns on the property?"

"Yes, but they're under lock and key. To my knowledge, none have been fired for months. You are welcome to have a look."

"Thank you for cooperating. What are your security arrangements?"

"Aside from the alarm and video surveillance, I always have someone on site. Why?"

"If John Dalton was murdered because of his involvement with Lana, it follows that you may be a target as well."

"But we've been very discreet."

"I'm sure you have, but like it or not your name is out there now. It worries me. Therefore it should worry you."

He rubbed his temples. "And I thought I just had my wife to deal with."

"I'm afraid it might not be that easy."

"You've never met my wife."

Macy paused. "Do you mind if I ask you a personal question? I mean no disrespect and it's completely off the record. Feel free to tell me to go to hell."

"Shoot."

"If you're so unhappy why don't you just end your marriage? I'm sure there are plenty of other girls like Lana out there."

"Do you want the long answer or the short answer?"

"The short answer is fine."

"I love my wife. I'd be lost without her."

"And yet you're willing to risk losing her by seeing other women."

"If I really believed there was a risk I'd never take it."

"So, she'll forgive you?"

"It's bumpy for a bit but she always comes around."

"You're a lucky man."

"I know I am." He paused. "But having an affair doesn't make me a murderer."

Macy fiddled with her pen. "When are your wife and children returning home?"

"On Saturday."

"Can they prolong their trip until this is cleared up?"

"Yes, I'm sure that's possible."

"In the meantime you may also want to take extra security precautions."

"Of course."

"Have you noticed anything unusual? It could be as simple as feeling like you're being followed."

He sat back and folded his hands in his lap. "There may have been an attempted break-in a couple weeks back."

"Aiden didn't mention it."

"It wasn't reported."

"Tell me what happened?"

"It was about three in the morning. The dog started barking before the alarm went off. It was either a fault in the system, or someone tried to force one of the basement windows open. We can't be sure."

"Nothing was picked up on the cameras?"

"No footprints either. The area beneath the window is paved."

Aiden stood at the open door. "Macy, could I speak to you a second?"

"We're just finishing up." Macy stood up and held out her hand. "Mr. Crawley, it was a pleasure meeting you. We'll be sending up a team to interview your staff and review the security tapes this afternoon."

"Ms. Hutton was very convincing."

"As was Mr. Crawley." Macy walked across the shaded driveway. The patrol car was parked in a carport. Someone had washed it. "What did you need to tell me?"

"I got a call from Spokane. Charlie Lott hasn't been seen for a few weeks. His grandmother said it wasn't unusual for him to take off. They checked his room above the garage. No sign he's been there recently. A few months ago he bought a new car."

"A late-model V8?"

"A dark blue Chevy Chevelle, no less. Mr. Walker nailed it."

"Release Charlie Lott's photo to the press along with the details about his car. It should be easy to spot."

"It's a classic."

"I hear there's a gathering up at the Dalton Ranch."

"Yeah, I'm going."

"Let me know if something comes up. I'm driving down to Kalispell. My mother is there on an errand. We're going to try to meet up for a couple of hours."

"Sounds nice. I take it she's bringing Luke."

Macy smiled. "Yes. I feel a little guilty though. It's a long drive for them."

"By the way, we still haven't found anyone who can tell us Patricia Dune's whereabouts. Most of the staff at the university seem to be on vacation."

"Summers off. Must be nice to be an academic."

"That's just what I was thinking."

Macy walked beneath the mature trees shading the downtown Kalispell park with her phone pressed to her ear. Video footage indicated that Bob Crawley was home the evening of John Dalton's murder. She thanked Aiden for letting her know and said good-bye. Her mother sat on a picnic blanket near a small pond that was surrounded by a low brick wall. Luke was hopping up and down as he laughed at the ducks that had gathered in front of him. He seemed more intent on eating the piece of bread he held than sharing it.

Macy ran up behind Luke and scooped him up in her arms. "How's my favorite boy?"

She kissed him on the cheeks and smoothed his hair out of his eyes while he giggled and squirmed in her arms. He held a piece of bread to her lips before popping it in his own mouth and laughing all over again.

Ellen had been keeping one eye on her grandson as she flipped through a magazine. "Do you remember this park?"

Macy pulled Luke up onto her shoulders and spun around. "Should I?"

Ellen pointed to a softball pitch in the far corner. "You pitched your first no-hitter here when you were fourteen."

Macy took a second to look around. "They should have erected a statue in my honor. I'm going to have to complain."

She sat Luke on the picnic blanket and plopped down next to him. Seconds later he made a beeline for the duck pond.

"I'm going to come here again," said Ellen. "Those ducks have kept him entertained for the past hour."

"I'm sorry I'm late."

"I'm sure you did your best. How's Wilmington Creek?"

"Baking."

"There was an article on John Dalton on the front page of the Helena paper this morning. He survives three tours in Afghanistan and ends up getting murdered in his hometown. Wilmington Creek doesn't seem like the sort of place this kind of thing happens."

"You're right about that. People are worried it's going to change things forever."

"I overheard you talking to Ray on the phone yesterday morning. What has he got to do with all of this?"

A few months after Luke was born, Macy had relented and told her mother about her two-year relationship with Ray, the sudden breakup, and the unexpected pregnancy that followed. Ellen wasn't pleased when they started seeing each other again. As far as she was concerned, Ray wasn't to be trusted. For months she'd hated him on Macy's behalf.

"It was nothing personal. Ray is my boss. He was doing his job."

"It just seems that every time he says *jump*, you say *how high*."

Macy poured herself some orange juice. "Mom, this is an important case. I'll jump through as many hoops as I have to."

"Last week you told me you were thinking of ending it."

"I still am. It's just that I see so little of Ray that I haven't even been able to speak to him about how I've been feeling lately."

"You could write him a Dear John letter."

"How quaint."

"It worked for me."

"How many Dear John letters have you written?"

"Enough to keep the mailman employed."

Macy unwrapped a sandwich her mother had prepared. "You were such a heartbreaker."

"Your father used to write to me. They were the most beautiful letters." She glanced up at Luke and smiled. "He would have loved Luke. It's so sad that they never got to know each other."

Macy touched her mother's knee. "It's been two years."

"Almost to the day."

"You've done well."

"Luke is keeping me busy. That's a good thing." She paused. "Macy, I know you have this idea in your head about Luke having a father figure in his life, but you must realize that Luke will be fine as long as he's surrounded by people who love him. It doesn't have to be with his real father."

"I know." Macy stretched out on the blanket and shut her eyes. "I just look at what you and Dad had together and I want the same thing."

"Meanwhile your brother and his wife are ripping their family apart. She's asked for full custody. Apparently, she wants to move to Virginia so she can be closer to her boyfriend."

"That's unreasonable."

"Tom is distraught. He's already upset about how little he sees the girls."

"Is he still dating his personal trainer?"

"He's obsessed with fitness. Keeps telling me about his BMI number, whatever that means."

"Remind me never to have a midlife crisis."

"All I'm trying to say is that it's not such a bad thing, having Luke all to yourself." She reached out and squeezed her daughter's hand. "Nobody will ever be able to take him away from you."

14

Jessie waited outside her father's hospital room while staff and patients drifted past. On the way to see her father she'd gone by the building where Giles Newton once had an office, but an insurance salesman had taken over the lease six years earlier. He suggested she check with the chamber of commerce. Jessie thanked him and left with a leaflet on life insurance that she threw in the first garbage can she came across. At the hospital she took the elevator up to the sixth floor with a patient in a wheelchair. Chin up, his mouth hung open as he followed the elevator's progress. He didn't move when the doors opened in front of him. A thin stream of drool escaped the corner of his mouth. His skull was cracked like an egg, and a scar snaked from the top of his head to his nose. An orderly came in and wheeled him away.

Natalie was in the room with Jeremy, helping him fill out some paperwork. Aside from being her father's girlfriend, she was also a hospital administrator. Jessie cleared her throat so they'd know she'd arrived. Jeremy raised his bloodshot eyes, but said nothing. It was Natalie who turned and smiled warmly before pulling Jessie into a long hug. She'd organized Jessie's drug rehabilitation program, working wonders with insurance forms and getting Jeremy to pay the excess. She'd also been there when Jessie relapsed. By all accounts she was a wonderful woman. Her only blind spot seemed to be Jeremy Dalton. Jessie couldn't understand why she liked her father so much, when she herself could barely tolerate being in the same room with him.

"You're late," said Jeremy.

Natalie kept her voice low. "Jessie, be patient with him. He's really upset."

"So am I."

"I know, but you're the grown-up in this relationship. Remember that."

"Natalie," said Jeremy. "You're going to suffocate the girl if you keep holding on to her like that."

Natalie led Jessie over to the bed, where Jeremy sat back against the pillows, fully dressed. "You two need each other more than ever now, so you've got to find a way to get along. I'm going to get these papers signed by your doctor so you can go. They'll send a wheelchair up for you."

"I don't need a wheelchair."

She kissed him on the forehead. "You don't have a choice. It's hospital policy."

Natalie left the room, and for a few minutes Jessie stood next to her father's bed, staring out the window toward the parking lot. She listened to Jeremy's steady breathing. Despite what the doctors kept saying about his weak heart, she was pretty sure he'd outlive them all. When he raised his voice to speak, there wasn't any of the vulnerability she'd detected the day before.

"I hear one of Lana Clark's ex-boyfriends is a suspect. Some guy called Charlie Lott."

"John told me she came up here from Georgia to get away from him."

"John should have never gotten involved with her."

"He couldn't have known her ex would do something like this."

135

"Then she should have warned him."

"We both know John wouldn't have listened. I saw Tanya this morning. They're worried she might do something stupid and hurt herself. She's been sedated."

"She should have stayed out in Georgia and waited for John to come home."

"John was gone for nine months at a stretch. His last deployment was fifteen months. She was lonely."

"I still think she should have stayed put. He was coming home to her. He needed to believe she was waiting for him."

"I tried to go see Mom, but they said she wasn't allowed any visitors."

Jeremy twisted his hands in his lap. "We can't have her living with us anymore. She's not going to get any better."

Jessie sat down in a chair next to the bed. Jeremy wouldn't meet her eye. "It sounds like it's already been decided."

"It has. There's a facility in Helena."

"That's too far."

"Jessie, what in the hell am I supposed to do?"

She didn't answer.

"Come on, tell me. You always seem to have an answer for everything."

"I don't know."

"John saw how difficult things had become since the last time he was home. He's the one who asked Natalie to look into it."

"He'd never do that."

"Ask Natalie if you think I'm lying."

There was a knock at the door and Jessie looked up. Wade had worn a good shirt. He pushed a wheelchair into the room with an apologetic look on his face.

"Come on, Jeremy. Let's get you home where you belong."

"There's no way in hell I'm getting in that thing."

"It's only to the exit."

Jeremy jumped off the bed and grabbed his bag. "Fuck that."

He slipped past Jessie without a word and disappeared into the corridor.

Wade frowned. "Jessie, do you need a ride back to the ranch?"

"No thank you. I drove."

"Don't be too late coming home. A lot of family are showing up this afternoon. Quite a few friends as well. I've got Anita keeping an eye on things, and plenty of people have offered to help."

"It's too soon."

"A lot of people loved John. They want to show their support."

Jessie closed her eyes. More than anything she wanted to be alone, and as much as she hated her father, she was pretty sure he felt the same way.

"Do you need me to pick up anything?"

"Don't worry yourself about that. It's all taken care of."

"Wade, I need to ask you something."

Wade glanced out in the corridor. "I don't want to keep Jeremy waiting too long. You know how he gets."

Jessie shook her head. "You're right. It can wait."

He touched her shoulder. "Are you sure?"

"Yeah, I'm sure. You go on home. I'll be there soon."

Trying her best to make herself invisible, Jessie wandered the downstairs rooms of the ranch house. Friends and relations mingled over plates of food. Warm, heavily cushioned bodies smelling of perfume and sweat pulled her into lingering hugs. Thick arms dragged her into corners for quiet confidences. For a while Tara had stayed close, tugging at the hem of her mother's pale blue dress, and whispering in her ear when she wanted something, but then she'd gone outside to play with her friends. Her absence left Jessie feeling untethered. Beneath her feet, floorboards creaked like on an old ship. The pastor from their church wanted to speak to her in private. He squeezed Jessie's hand and spoke fiercely, firing off one overused platitude after another. It was like being assaulted by a greeting card company. Jessie focused on his hair. It was dark brown in color, but gray at the roots. She pictured him in the bathroom rubbing dye into his scalp and remembered what Jeremy had once said about him. *How can you trust a man who lies about his hair?*

Monica arrived with her two children in tow. She still wore her hair in the same high ponytail she had sported since high school. She took Jessie to one side and sat her down before sending her eldest off to fetch a glass of orange juice.

"Jessie, you look pale. You need to drink this."

Jessie did as she was told.

"You're getting thinner by the minute. Are you eating?"

Through the bay windows Jessie could see Tara running across the front lawn. Someone had given her a Popsicle. She held it aloft like a sword.

Jessie picked up a potato chip from the bowl in Monica's hand and popped it into her mouth. "Where's Patrick?"

"He stayed home with the baby. She's been colicky. None of us are getting much sleep."

"Are you sure having Tara stay a couple of days won't be too much?"

"Don't be silly. We'd love to have her. Did you pack her bag?"

Jessie started to get up. "It's in her room."

Monica looked at her eldest child again. "You go on up to Tara's room and fetch her bag. And hurry. We need to get going."

Jessie's voice went up an octave. "You only just got here."

"I have to get back with the car. Our truck is in for repairs, so Patrick needs to use the minivan to drive to work. I promise I'll call you later." She hugged Jessie before taking a quick glance around the room. "Besides, it looks like you've got your hands full here."

Jeremy was camped out on the drawing room sofa with Natalie right by his side. As far as Jessie knew, it was the first time they'd been seen together in such an open way. Jessie caught glimpses of him as she passed in and out of the room. His watery eyes darted like fireflies, but his face was immobile. They both looked up at the sound of a sudden outburst. John's ex-girlfriend Tanya had arrived in tears and was immediately swallowed up by mourners. She was passed from one pair of open arms to another. Her face was blotched and red. Thick drops of mascara rolled down her cheeks. Jessie edged toward the nearest exit. She had her own way of dealing with grief, and at the moment it was threatening to boil over in the back of her throat. She ducked from the room with her hands over her mouth. She was choking on it.

She slipped through the kitchen, where a group of women were busy decanting potato salad, macaroni salad, and slices of cold roast beef onto platters. They were all speaking at once and moved with the restless energy of overheated atoms. They didn't see Jessie stumble out into the backyard where the grass was warm and the air was even warmer. The sofa next to the pool was gone and someone had arranged the deck chairs in a neat row and plucked the bullet-riddled pink flamingos from the lawn. A group of boys stood at the pool's edge, daring each other to jump in. As Jessie turned to the west, there was a splash, followed by laughter.

You're so dead.

Jessie picked a point on the horizon and started walking. Soon the tall grasses were brushing the hem of her dress. Dying light drifted across the seed heads and dust flew upward like ocean spray. In another hour the sun would disappear over the ridgeline and the land would lie in cool hands until dawn. She'd caught sight of Dylan rounding the back porch just as she stepped outside. He was following her, but she didn't turn to greet him. She laced her fingers through the dry grass and twisted it. She blinked into the hard-slanting sun and imagined she was beautiful. The field dipped and rolled toward a low, wooded area where a shallow stream bled through the rocks. She kept walking and he kept following. She lost him when she entered the wood. The path was narrow and steep and even though she took her time he could not keep up.

"I'm here," she said. She was perched on a flat rock face that slanted down to the stream. She'd taken off her sandals. The water was like ice. She curled up her toes and wrapped her arms around her knees so she could pull them in close.

Dylan leaned against a nearby boulder and stared at the water. He'd worn a button-down shirt of light cotton and a pair of freshly pressed chinos. They must have been new, because they didn't hang loose on him like most of his other clothing. He cracked his knuckles one by one. A freight train rumbled along the tracks that skirted the western boundary of the property. It was heading north toward Canada. Horseflies the size of walnuts ricocheted through the trees. He brushed one away when it flew too close to his head.

He opened his mouth to speak and Jessie threw him a warning glance.

"I didn't come down here to talk."

He pulled himself up onto the boulder and sat with his legs stretched out in front of him.

They glanced at each other every few minutes, and each time Jessie shook her head. The shadows thickened and the silence grew deeper. She scooted farther up the rock and pressed her feet into the warm surface.

"Crowds make me nervous."

"You don't need to explain why you're down here."

Jessie tossed a stone into the water. "I'm not doing too well." She put her palm to her chest. "There's so much pressure inside it hurts."

"Apparently it helps if you talk about it."

"I do talk. At least I try, but it's like there's this buffer between me and everyone else. I feel so numb sometimes I wonder if I'm still alive."

Jessie glanced back up toward the house. She could just make out the roofline. Sun was catching in the surrounding treetops. They looked like they were on fire.

Dylan threw a pebble in the water. "At least you can be in a room with other people. I can't even do that."

"You're not missing much. Take it from me, the *room* is overrated."

"John would always tell me that it was going to get better. I just had to give it time."

"Did you believe him?"

"I've seen too much shit to believe in much of anything anymore. If I learned anything in the army it's that there are too many ways to hurt a man. A lot of them you can't see."

"I dream about Ethan sometimes. I wake up trying to fight him off."

"I'm not going to lie. It may never get better."

Jessie picked her way over the boulders in her bare feet and sat down next to Dylan.

"I'm going to tell you something and I need to know that you're going to be understanding because it's a little crazy."

"I'm listening."

"It's about Ethan," she whispered, suddenly afraid that saying it aloud might make it true.

"Go on."

"What if he's still alive?"

"Is that what you're thinking?"

She dipped her head and her face was lost behind a veil of hair. She'd wanted to stay strong but she was crying again.

Dylan touched her lightly on the arm. "You're letting all those voices in your head get to you. Ethan is dead."

"What if we got it wrong? What if Ethan was still alive when the truck went in the lake?" Her voice cracked. "He could have gotten out."

"Why are you torturing yourself? He attacked you. You defended yourself. He's dead."

Jessie fished the necklace out of the pocket of her dress. She'd been worrying the chain like prayer beads as she wandered through the crowds up at the house. It was tangled in knots.

"You see this?" she said, holding it and watching the heart-shaped locket spin. "It was left gift-wrapped on the front porch this morning. There was a card with my name on it and nothing else. I thought I lost it in Ethan's truck." She opened the heart. "There's a picture of Tara inside. It was the only thing that could tie me to Ethan's death."

"Maybe someone found it in the picnic area."

"Then why not just give it back to me then? Why leave it on the porch while I was sleeping? Why not put their name on the card?"

"I can't answer that."

"You can't answer it because it doesn't make any sense. I might be right. He could be alive."

"Where has he been all this time then? He would have been hurt. He couldn't have walked away from something like that."

"Maybe he's spent the last year recovering. He'd want revenge. John, me, you, Tyler. We'd all be on his list."

"You've been watching too many movies. Between them, John and Tyler have done eight deployments in Afghanistan and Iraq. They know when someone's dead."

"But you didn't see Ethan, did you? By the time you arrived they'd already put him in the bed of the truck. You're the medic. You're the one person who would have known for sure."

"You need to put this out of your mind. Ethan didn't kill John. Someone else did."

She held up the necklace again. "Then explain this."

15

Macy was lying in bed with her eyes closed. She'd thought she heard her son crying, but woke up to silence. She buried her face in the pillow. The fabric was rough and smelled like cigarettes. Her head throbbed. She was too warm. She kicked the blankets away and pried her eyes open. In the dim light she picked out grainy images. A framed print of a farmhouse and a flat-screen television hung side by side on the far wall. She wouldn't have heard her son if he screamed. He was in Helena, and Macy was still several hundred miles away in a motel room in Wilmington Creek.

She rolled onto her back. The bathroom door was ajar. Steam billowed into the room. Ray must have been very quiet getting out of bed. According to the digital clock on top of the minibar it was coming up to one in the morning. Macy searched the bedside table for her phone and found his instead. She scrolled through his messages and missed phone calls. Frowning, she threw the phone to one side and buried her face in the pillow again.

Ray had appeared unannounced at her motel room door a little after ten. She'd been getting ready for bed and was in no mood for company. For a few seconds a security chain was all that had separated them. He'd smiled and she'd tried to do the same. As happy as she was to see him, there'd also been a familiar sinking feeling. No matter how good it would be to have him there, pain would surely follow.

What are you doing here?

I felt bad that I couldn't talk last night. I needed to see you. I had to make sure everything was okay between us.

"Need" is an interesting word choice.

It's been a long drive and I'm tired. I have to admit it's all I've got.

What about when I need you? It never seems to work both ways.

He'd held up a bottle of wine. *You can't turn me away. I've brought a friend.*

I'm trying to spend less time with your friends.

Now you're talking nonsense.

Ray, you can't just pop into my life whenever you like. It's not okay.

Oh, come on. I'm in full view of Main Street. How long are you going to make me wait before you let me in?

She had unhooked the chain, but shrugged away when he tried to kiss her. *I keep hoping that someday I'll be able to tell you to go to hell.*

Why do you say that?

Because it's true.

I've missed you.

I've missed you too. It doesn't change anything.

I'll leave if you want me to.

I wish it were that easy.

Aren't you the one who said, "If it's too easy it's not worth the trouble"?

She'd lowered her voice to a whisper. *You really should go to hell.*

He'd pulled her down onto the bed. *Only if you promise to come with me.*

Ray stepped out of the bathroom and dressed with his back turned to her. Water seeped from his wet hair onto the collar of his dress shirt, leaving a thin, dark line along the edge.

"I went to see an apartment yesterday."

"I'd say you could move in with me but I don't think my mother would approve."

"How's she finding looking after Luke full time?"

Macy almost told Ray about her impromptu trip down to Kalispell to see her mother and Luke but kept it to herself.

"Ellen loves it."

"But it must wear her down. You work pretty long hours."

"Don't worry, Luke is well cared for."

"I'm not suggesting otherwise. I just wonder whether she's getting enough support."

"We can't all be stay-at-home moms. Someone has to pay the bills."

"I'm sorry."

"I'm not."

"Have you given any more thought to amending the birth certificate?"

"I don't think this is the right time to discuss it."

"It's a simple court order. I thought you wanted Luke to have my last name."

"I never agreed to that."

"I don't see why you're so against it."

"Being alone in that delivery room may have something to do with it."

"How many times do I have to say sorry?"

"How about I let you know when you get there?"

He sat on the edge of the bed and Macy scooted forward so she could hold him from behind.

"Don't go," she whispered.

He kissed the inside of her wrist. "You know I don't have a choice. Please don't ask me again."

"It's what I want. I'm not going to quit asking."

Ray mumbled a response as he bent forward to slip on his shoes. "Then don't get upset when you don't like the answer."

Macy got up and peeked through a narrow gap in the curtains. A

145

man sat by himself at the end of the diving board with his legs dangling above the motel's kidney-shaped swimming pool. It was too dark to make out his features. He drank what was left of his beer before standing. He bounced several times and the board creaked so loudly that Macy thought it might snap in two. He steadied it before turning his gaze toward her. Macy drew the curtains shut and shrank back into the room.

She closed her eyes and tried to feel her way into the questions that always needed asking. "You said you spoke to your wife again. She hasn't changed her mind about the separation."

Ray was standing, his silhouette backlit by the light coming from the bathroom. Beyond him she could see the fogged-over mirror.

"That was the easy part," he said, his eyes tightening. "Now, we have to tell the girls."

Macy crawled across the bed and handed him his phone. "Your wife has been trying to call you for the past three hours."

Ray held the phone up and squinted. "Don't exaggerate. These aren't all from her."

"But quite a few of them are."

"She's the mother of my three children. There will always be something we need to discuss."

"I can't forget what happened last time."

Ray put a hand on Macy's knee and held it there. "Macy, you have to believe me. My wife and I are never getting back together again. It's over."

Macy watched Ray's eyes trace over the lines of text as he continued to read his messages. In the past few months he'd lost weight, and his hair, which was once graying at the temples, was now completely silver.

"You haven't told me what you think of Aiden Marsh. I hear he can be difficult."

"That's not my experience so far." She almost smiled. "He's been very accommodating."

"Well, he might not be for much longer."

"Why? Has something happened?"

"It's hard to say. It may be related."

"Tell me."

"We've got someone working undercover in Wilmington Creek."

"What the fuck, Ray? If you've got someone on the ground here then I need to know about it. What do you think would happen if we bumped into each other in town? Do I even know them?"

"You're familiar with Lindsay Moore."

"Great. That's just wonderful."

"I get it. She's not your favorite person."

"As far as I can tell, she's nobody's favorite person."

"That's out of line."

"Don't you dare lecture me about what constitutes being out of line. What is she doing here, anyway?"

"For the past six months, she's been posing as a doctoral student doing research on the dramatic rise in militia groups since the last presidential election."

"Lindsay Moore is Patricia Dune?"

"How do you know the name she's been using?"

"I know the name because it's come up in the investigation. We've been looking for her. We want to know if she's heard anything that might be related to the case. Jeremy Dalton has received a couple of threats. People think she's been stirring things up with the militia groups with all her questions."

"She's trying to get information on Ethan Green."

"I thought he was long gone."

"We did too, but remember that highway patrol officer in Missoula who got shot last summer? An informant identified Green as the shooter. The FBI are also saying they've got good intelligence that he's re-forming his militia."

"Ray, sometimes you have a very short memory. You assigned me to the special task force set up to investigate that shooting. My name is on the report. We found no evidence that any of the militia groups were involved."

"Well, there have been some developments."

"Can you trust this informant of yours?"

"We've used him before. He's never let us down. When I sent Lindsay up here I was hoping she'd be able to flush Green out."

"Do you think he may have something to do with John Dalton's murder?"

"I heard there's some bad blood between Green and Jeremy Dalton. Whether it became violent remains to be seen."

"What does Lindsay have to say about it? She's on the ground here. As I recall, she usually has an opinion."

"That's just it. Two days ago she dropped out of sight."

"When did you last speak to her?"

"I guess it's been a week since we last spoke, although I did get a message from her a few days ago. She said she had some new information, but didn't go into details."

"You're worried?"

"I am. It's not like her to be out of touch." He handed Macy a set of keys and an address. "Tomorrow I want you to go by her place and have a look around."

"Why me?"

"You're here already."

"I'm in the middle of something else."

"Look, this is probably nothing, but please just do this for me. I need to know whether I should be worried."

Macy closed her hand over the keys. The week Lindsay transferred to the Helena office, Macy had come across her and Ray speaking in low voices outside the elevator. Their heads were bent in conversation and they were laughing at some private joke. There was an awkward silence as the three of them rode the elevator down to the lobby. In those few minutes, Macy's mind had gone into overdrive. Ray and Macy had just started seeing each other again and she was paranoid. She'd glanced up at Lindsay's reflection in the mirror. At nearly five foot ten and wearing heels, she was as tall as Ray. It didn't help that she had ice blond hair and perfect posture. Macy had felt like a child standing next to them.

Ray brushed the hair out of Macy's eyes. "I don't deserve you."

"True."

"I am sorry I have to leave."

"It kind of goes with the territory. You're a married man."

"Separated."

"When you've moved out I'll start believing that."

"There's going to be some serious fallout."

"You need to move out and spend a year pretending to be on your own. It's the only way this is going to work."

"Could you really handle that?"

"I don't feel we have a choice."

Through a gap in the curtains, Macy watched Ray drive away. She shifted her gaze to the swimming pool, but the man on the diving board was gone. In the bathroom she stared into her image in the mirror. Other than the state of her hair there was little to indicate she'd been with Ray all evening. She stepped into the shower. The sense of vertigo she felt when he left her to go back to his wife and children always took her breath away. She was still light-headed when she shut the door to the motel room and went to find her car.

Outside the air was cold, and overhead a haze of wood smoke blocked out the stars. Her state-issue SUV sat alone in the back parking lot. She stood in darkness adjusting her eyes. This could wait until morning. She pictured her empty motel room and knew she wouldn't sleep. She'd lie awake trying to fix things in her head and end up with nothing to show for it in the morning. She checked she had Lindsay Moore's house keys before striking out across the dark pavement. Beyond the car's front bumper there was a high chain-link fence and a thin line of trees. Through the branches she could see a two-story home. She clicked the remote and headlights flashed as her car doors unlocked. Her eyes swept across the parking lot, searching the shadows. Something was moving toward her, but she couldn't see where it was coming from. Leaves rustled and branches snapped. There was a low growl and a large dog launched itself from the other side of the chain-link fence. Its mouth gaped wide, revealing sharp white teeth that snapped at the empty air between them. Macy jumped into her car and locked the doors. In the upper rooms of the house, lights came on as she backed away. A man threw open a window and shouted down at the dog.

The streets were deserted. She drove three blocks, took a right on Tucker Road, and kept going in a straight line for several miles. There were no streetlights this far out of town. The headlights picked up an occasional driveway and mailbox but little else. She couldn't miss Lindsay's home. It was on fire. Nearby trees swayed dangerously close to the flames. Jessie picked up the radio and talked to dispatch before putting in a call to Aiden. He didn't sound happy to hear from her.

"Do you have any idea what time it is?"

"You need to come meet me. We have a problem."

"Where are you?"

"I'm at 517 Tucker."

"What are you doing all the way out there?"

"At the moment I'm watching Patricia Dune's house burn down."

"I'm on my way."

Macy stared out into the night. The headlights just caught where the road came to a dead end at the Flathead River. There wasn't any passing traffic and the closest neighbor was a quarter mile back in the direction of town. The house could have burned to the ground without anyone noticing. She swung open the car door and stepped outside. The heat was intense. The fire had almost consumed the front porch. Glass shattered as windows exploded. She walked the property's perimeter, looking for a way in. There was only one section that wasn't engulfed in flames. She pried off the window screens and used a rock to break the window. She had to scream to be heard.

"Lindsay, are you in there? Lindsay!"

Smoke was drifting in through the bedroom's open door. She took out her flashlight and swung the beam around the room. The dresser drawers were open and clothing was piled up on the bed. She brushed away the broken glass and leaned in farther.

"Lindsay!"

The hallway was in flames. There was a strong smell of gasoline. It looked like someone had doused the clothes on the bed. Macy wanted to be sure. She stretched out as far as she could, but they were out of reach. She lifted a leg up and fell into the room. It was too dark to see what she'd tripped over. She hit her shoulder hard against the bed-frame and lay gasping for breath. In a matter of seconds the room had filled with smoke. She grabbed some of the clothing off the bed and left the way she came.

Her hands stank of gasoline. She slipped the shirt into an evidence bag and tried to call Ray, but her fingers were shaking too much to work the keypad on her cell phone. She leaned her forehead against the steering wheel and screamed instead. Part of the house's roof collapsed, sending millions of sparks into the sky. Toward Wilmington Creek, she could see flashing lights. Sirens soon filled the night.

Macy sat on the tailgate of the paramedic's rig with her shirt pulled halfway up her back. The paramedic focused in on the task at hand and ignored all attempts at small talk.

"When was your last tetanus shot?"

Macy almost shrugged, but then thought better of it. "I'm not sure. Do I need stitches?"

"No, it's not deep enough, but you've got a three-inch cut. Do you have any idea what you fell on?"

"A bedframe."

"You'll be sore for a couple of days, but should be fine. You may want to take some ibuprofen."

Aiden made his way toward her. "Hey, are you okay?"

"Yes, it's nothing." She glanced over at the house. Despite the amount of water being dumped on it, it was still burning out of control. "This was arson."

"How do you know?"

Macy handed him the evidence bag. "I found this on the bed in the back bedroom. An accelerant was used. I'm pretty sure it's gasoline."

"You were inside?"

"I managed to open a bedroom window. No one answered when I called, but the smell was unmistakable."

"What were you doing out here in the first place?"

"I was looking for Lindsay Moore. She works for the state as a special investigator."

"But this is Patricia Dune's house."

"Lindsay Moore is her real name."

"Is this some kind of joke?"

"I wish that were the case. Lindsay has been up here posing as a Ph.D. student. She was looking for Ethan Green."

"How come you're only telling me about this now?"

"Until a couple of hours ago I had no idea she was up here. Ray Davidson called me. He's worried because she didn't check in when she was supposed to. He sent me over to investigate."

"So he called you in the middle of the night?"

"Like I said, he was worried."

"When did she disappear?"

"As near as he can tell, sometime on Tuesday."

"That's three days. We need to put an APB out on her right away."

She held up a hand. "Didn't I hear you say you found a burnt-up SUV two days ago?"

"Yes, it was up near the site of the Waldo Canyon fire."

"Lindsay drives an SUV."

"Damn, I'll call it in now. We'll get some search teams out there right away." He paused. "Did Ray say why they were suddenly interested in finding Green?"

"An informant has pegged him for the shooting of that highway patrol officer last summer, and the FBI believe he's re-forming his militia." She slid off the tailgate and very gingerly rotated her shoulder. "What about the neighbors? There's not much traffic out here. Maybe someone saw something."

"Tyler Locke owns the next house along."

"Should I read anything into that?"

He frowned. "Keep an open mind. Remember."

"I'm surprised he keeps a house here, given he's gone all the time. Doesn't he live in Georgia when he's not deployed?"

"He inherited the place from his grandmother. As far as I know he plans on coming back to live here once he's discharged from the army."

"Have Tyler or Dylan ever had any involvement with any militia groups?"

"We checked. Neither of them have any known affiliation, but these guys don't exactly publicize their members' names."

"Is it too early to wake Tyler up?"

"All this noise. I'm sure he's up already."

Aiden knocked on the door and stepped well back while he waited for Tyler to answer. The lights were on in the kitchen and they could hear the television through the window screens.

"Who is it?"

"Tyler, it's Aiden. I have Detective Macy Greeley with me. We need to have a quick word."

Tyler appeared in a T-shirt and jeans. An unlit cigarette dangled from his lips. "I just saw you guys on the news." He held open the door to let them in. "Can I offer you a cup of coffee? Sounds like it's been a long night."

"That would be very much appreciated. We're talking to all the neighbors."

Tyler cleared some space on the cluttered kitchen counter and poured coffee into two cups. "That shouldn't take too long. Hardly anybody lives out this way anymore."

Macy cast her eyes over the mess in the living room before surveying the book titles on the shelf next to the television. For the most part they were well-thumbed classics. Given the layer of dust, Macy guessed they'd not recently been touched. The porn DVDs told another story. Half of the boxes were open with discs spilling out.

Tyler handed her a cup of coffee. "I'm not much of a reader. The books belonged to my grandmother."

"I take it the video collection is yours though?"

"It's a hobby."

"Were you acquainted with Patricia Dune?"

"Should I be?"

Aiden stirred milk into his coffee with a spoon he found in the dish drainer.

"She was renting the Anderson property. Tall blond woman in her midthirties. She drove a dark blue SUV."

"I've seen her coming and going, but we never talked." He picked up the coffeepot and swirled the remaining contents before pouring out another cup. "Was she in the house?"

"It's too early to tell."

Macy took a sip of coffee. "Are you here on your own?"

"May I ask why you want to know?"

Aiden shook his head. "We want to know if you were around to hear or see anything. If anyone is with you we'd want to talk to them as well."

"I was up video conferencing with my platoon half the night so I've been awake for hours. I can't say that I noticed anything suspicious."

Macy didn't skip a beat. "When you say half the night, what does that mean exactly?"

Tyler went over to his desk that was set up in the living room and started punching some keys. "It means I was online from one thirty until nearly four."

"Your computer is next to the front window. Did you see any vehicles pass by your house in that time?"

He rubbed his chin. "Aside from all the recent action, the last vehicle I remember drove by at around nine forty-five, heading back toward town."

"Are you sure about the time?"

"I was just setting my alarm so I'd wake up in time to catch my platoon online. They've just returned to Bagram Air Base so it's the first time I've been able to talk to them. John was like a brother. As you can imagine, they're pretty low."

Aiden placed his empty cup in the sink. "There's nothing else in that direction aside from the river, so the car must have come from the Anderson house."

Macy walked to the sliding glass doors overlooking the backyard. Other than a dim light showing in the garage windows, the view was flat and gray. There was a backhoe in the corner of the lot, along with several pallets of cinder blocks There was a deep pit in the center of the yard. She couldn't be sure, but it looked like Tyler was putting in a swimming pool. Beyond a chain-link fence the woods stretched out for miles. She couldn't see a single light.

Tyler stood next to her. "I'm building a nuclear fallout shelter. I tried to do the same in Georgia, but the water table is too high. Ended up putting in a pond instead."

"You live in northern Montana. Is a shelter really necessary?"

"I believe it is."

"Have you ever been involved in any of the militia groups around here?"

"Years ago when I was in high school. Why?"

"Preparing for the end of the world seems to be a preoccupation in many of the groups."

He shrugged. "With all due respect, I've done six tours of duty in some the worst hellholes on the planet. If digging a hole in my backyard makes me feel more secure, that's what I'm going to do."

"You're right," she said, turning away from the window. "I apologize. You should do whatever makes you feel safe."

"I don't need your permission."

A female's voice called out from the darkened hallway leading to the back of the house.

"Tyler? What's going on? Come back to bed."

Macy looked at Tyler. "You've got company?"

He crossed his thick arms. "Sarah Reed. She's been here since eight yesterday evening. I take it you want to speak to her?"

"I'll let you do the honors."

Tyler yelled over the top of Macy's head. "Sarah, what time did you come over last night?"

"Eight."

"Did you see or hear anything suspicious since you've been here?"

"No. Who's asking?"

"Nothing to worry about. Go back to bed." A door slammed and Tyler shrugged. "She's not at her best first thing in the morning."

Aiden put down his coffee cup. "We should get going. It looks like you have your hands full here."

Macy looked Tyler full in the face for the first time. "I hope you were able to give the guys in your platoon some comfort."

"I did what I could. God's hands now."

16

Aiden stepped into the office and closed the door behind him. It was coming up to nine in the morning and neither he nor Macy had slept at all. He disappeared behind the closet door and came out wearing a clean shirt. He buttoned it up while standing in front of her. He wouldn't look her in the eye.

"I have to head over to Waldo Canyon. One of the fire crews we've had helping us with the search for Lindsay Moore found a body."

Macy kept her own eyes on her laptop. "Is this the same place you found the burnt-out SUV a couple days ago?"

"Not exactly, but pretty close."

She checked the time. "I've got a call coming in from a few guys in John Dalton's platoon. When I'm finished I'll head over."

"I take it you're assuming it's Lindsay."

"Is anyone else missing who drives an SUV?"

"You never know. It could be a hiker or maybe someone from a fire crew."

"We both know that's not going to be the case."

"I'll call you later and let you know the best place to meet."

. . .

Liquefied air shimmered above Route 93 and in the distance the black river of road melted into the horizon. To the west, ridgelines burned under the midday sun and wisps of gray smoke bled into the sky. The fire had come right up onto the hard shoulder, leaving finger-shaped scorch marks along the edge of the pavement. Barren trees and blackened undergrowth went on for miles. Macy spotted a mailbox, a driveway, and the remains of a swing set. A home that once stood a quarter mile off the road was burned down to the foundations. Through the charred tree trunks, Macy could make out the dark hearth of a chimney stack.

She picked up the phone and called her mother for the second time in an hour.

"Mom, I'm sorry about having to cut you off earlier. Thanks again for coming up to see me yesterday."

"It was no trouble."

"Anyway, it was a nice surprise. I really appreciated it. And thank you for listening."

"Macy, I've been up half the night thinking about it. This thing with Ray isn't good for you. You have to end it."

Macy popped a couple of aspirin in her mouth and swallowed them down with the last of her Diet Coke.

"He showed up at my motel last night unannounced."

"Please say that you told him to go to hell."

"I tried."

"You need to try harder."

"I know."

"Will you be able to come home this weekend?"

"It doesn't look like it. We've found another body."

"I thought you said Wilmington Creek was a safe place."

"They're having a bad week."

"You're being careful?"

"Always. How's Luke?"

Even though she couldn't see her mother, Macy pictured Ellen moving about the nursery they'd set up in the little room that adjoined Macy's. More than likely, Luke was being carried around. He was a child whose feet rarely touched the ground.

"He's perfect."

"You're not getting overtired?"

"Heavens, no. Anyway, the girls are coming over this weekend. I'll have plenty of help."

"Poker night?"

"Isn't that why God invented Saturday evenings?"

"Watch out for Abby. She cleaned me out last week."

"That's because Abby cheats."

Macy leaned forward and squinted. In the distance a crucifix hovered above the blackened landscape. It wasn't until she was closer that she understood what she was seeing. The lower half of a utility pole had burned away, leaving the top half dangling from the electrical cables lacing the insulators mounted on the cross arms.

Macy pulled into the picnic area and parked in front of a burnt-out block that had once been a visitors' center. "Mom, something's come up. I'll call you back later."

Outside it was one hundred degrees and dead quiet save for the ticking of the motor. The traffic that normally crowded Route 93 had been redirected and the usual high-pitched chorus of cicadas was silent. Unable to take her eyes off the crucifix, she almost stumbled making her way down to what was left of a picnic area. The last time she'd visited the visitors' center, flies had swarmed with every footfall and the smell of decaying bodies had filled the air. After suffocating in the back of an eighteen-wheeler, the bodies of four Eastern European girls had been dumped behind the toilet block. She would never forget the smell. It was her first big case and Ray had been the lead investigator. He had taken Macy under his wing, and her life was never the same again.

Her thin cotton shirt offered no protection from the sun. It felt like she'd light up like touch paper if she stood outside a minute longer. By the time she got back to her car she was dizzy. She sat behind the steering wheel, nursing another Diet Coke she fished out of her ice chest. She rolled the sweating can back and forth across her forehead while the air conditioner hummed on high.

The turnoff for Waldo Canyon was only a few miles farther on. Aiden's patrol car sat off to the side. He tipped his hat back and signaled Macy to follow him. Macy was relieved she was on her own. Sharing a ride would have forced them to talk, and Macy wasn't in the mood. She stared off into the scarred landscape and tried to focus. Ray had called to say he was bringing the medical examiner's report from John Dalton's shooting up to Wilmington Creek so they could discuss the findings in person. He wouldn't tell her over the phone what was going on. *It's gotten very complicated. I think you have to hear this in person.*

Progress was slow. They had to pull over onto the soft shoulder several times to let trucks carrying fire crews trundle past. She watched their weary heads bob up and down with the movement of the open-backed truck. Their faces were too covered with soot to make out their features. When she was in college, Macy had spent a couple summers working on fire crews. Some of the men who worked alongside her had scared her more than the fires they were fighting. She always made sure she was never alone with them. She'd been studying criminal psychology. Back then everyone she met was a potential case study.

The view opened up as they rounded a wide bend. On the higher slopes, blackened tree stumps pierced the landscape like railroad spikes. They turned off the paved road and rattled along a gravel track for a mile before pulling up next to a burnt-out SUV.

Macy didn't waste time with small talk. "Is this Lindsay's SUV?"

"We got a vehicle identification number off it. It's a match. She was last spotted at the diner in Walleye on Tuesday at lunchtime. According to her server, she ate alone."

"Was the wildfire active in this area Tuesday afternoon?"

He wiped his forehead with his sleeve and replaced his hat. "It was moving fast. She really had no business coming up here."

"She could have been meeting someone."

"Possible, but I'm not sure how we would find that out."

All that was left of the SUV was a rib cage of singed metal and shattered glass. Dark puddles of rubber lay beneath the wheel rims. Inside the cab, fragments of charred seat covers stuck to the metal frames. The foam padding had liquefied and pooled on the floor.

"Any sign of a cell phone or laptop?"

"They searched the area and came up with nothing. Had she been in touch recently?"

"Apparently, not since last week."

"You'd have thought your boss would have kept a closer eye on her."

"I have to admit it's not his usual style."

"I don't work for him, so I wouldn't know."

"Aiden, you may not realize it yet, but one way or another, we all work for Ray." She inspected the area around the truck. While some of the trees were burned from root to tip, others were untouched. She even spotted wildflowers growing within a few feet of the SUV's back bumper, and just fifty yards farther on, the trees opened up to a green meadow full of waist-high lupines and yellow arrowleaf. What she was seeing didn't make any sense. "When did the Waldo Canyon fire start?"

"A pilot called it in last Wednesday. The origin was about five miles west, near Prospect Lake."

"Do you see how the area around the truck isn't burned as consistently as the wooded area farther up the slope?"

Aiden turned and spit. "Farther up there's nothing left but blackened stumps."

Macy tried to focus, but the heat was knocking her senseless. "The way the fire traveled through the area around the SUV is confused. Some trees are untouched and others are burnt to the ground.

There are wildflowers growing within a few feet of the back bumper, and yet at the other side of the vehicle everything is gone. If the wildfire traveled through here you'd expect to see damage that was far more uniform. Everything would be burned to a crisp. What I'm seeing here is patterning you'd normally associate with the origin of a fire before it's so hot it's whipping up its own momentum."

"Like I said, the fire didn't pass through here until Tuesday."

"I think the SUV and surrounding area were torched using an accelerant." She pointed to some undergrowth. "That burn pattern is almost perfectly straight. It's as if someone walked along pouring out an accelerant before lighting it."

"I suppose they could have siphoned off gas from the tank."

"I want forensics to have another look." She paused. "Are they still up in the ravine?"

"Yep, they're none too happy. They're cooking in their protective gear. Lindsay's body was airlifted out about an hour ago. It should already be at the medical examiner's office."

Macy flipped through her notebook. "She interviewed you. What did you think? Is it possible she could have stumbled onto something that put her in danger?"

"I got the impression she was going out of her way to be controversial, which makes sense now that I know why she was really here. She certainly wasn't afraid to mix it up with the locals. We met over drinks, but all she ordered was water. She struck me as someone who took life a little too seriously."

Macy poked her head through the shattered truck window. It was impossible to tell whether or not Lindsay had been taken by force. "Was she seeing anybody up here?"

"Not that I know of. Why?"

Macy brushed her hair off her face. A thin film of grit stuck to her skin. "No particular reason. She's always been a bit of an enigma. She never socialized with anyone from the office. I have to admit that it made me curious."

"Well, she got under people's skin, that's for sure. There wasn't anything nice about her approach."

"Nice or not. Nobody deserves to die like that." Macy looked up the slope and frowned. "I suppose we can't go any farther by car."

Aiden grabbed his rucksack. "No, it's all on foot from here. We'll have to be careful. There's still a lot left to burn." He glanced at the pack she was carrying. "You got water?"

"I got water."

Aiden took out a map and spread it across the hood of his vehicle. Someone had penciled in the burn areas of the Waldo Canyon fire. "We're here," he said before tracing a finger along the long line of a stream backtracking from where it spilled into the Flathead River. He stopped his finger on the spot they'd found Lindsay.

"Why would she have run toward a fire when most people want to go the opposite direction?"

"She may have been chased."

They followed the arc of the meadow for a few minutes before entering the woods. Now that the overhead canopy was burned off, Macy could see straight up into the sky. She stayed close behind Aiden. There were no distinct landmarks, but he seemed to know where he was going. He talked about summers spent working for the forestry department back when he was in high school.

"I used to know this area quite well, but it's difficult to make sense of it with all this devastation." He accidentally brushed against the smoldering remains of a fallen tree. The white ash flaked away, revealing red-hot coals. He took a sip of water and indicated that Macy should do the same. "I've never seen it so dry."

Macy nodded in agreement. She could barely breathe, let alone speak. The trail dipped and they had to negotiate a narrow ledge that zigzagged down the steep sides of a ravine. At the base there was a streambed choked with debris. Charred tree stumps and boulders ringed an onyx pool. Macy had already been e-mailed crime scene photos, so she recognized the site. The water was so saturated with ash that nothing was visible aside from Lindsay Moore's face. Her expression was empty. There was no panic, no last agonized scream for help. It looked like she'd simply shut her eyes and died.

Macy and the medical examiner, Ryan Marshall, had been working together for so long he rarely bothered with formalities.

"I'm not sure what happened here. A preliminary examination has revealed a wound in the left shoulder that I'm almost certain is from a gunshot. There are abrasions to her hands, which could be defensive wounds. Ligature marks to her wrists indicate she was tied up at some point. Time of death is almost impossible to assess given the extremes in temperature, but according to Aiden the fire passed through here between five and six Tuesday afternoon."

"Do we have a cause of death?"

"I don't believe the wound to her shoulder was life-threatening. I'm leaning toward smoke inhalation. We'll have to do more tests to be sure."

Aiden looked up at the cliff edge. "She may have lost her way and stepped right over the side of the cliff."

Ryan nodded. "She might have been sheltering in the stream when the fire passed over. She wouldn't have been the first person to try it."

Toward the east Macy could just make out the Flathead Valley. "Did you find her cell phone?"

"We're just about to check the water. We had a couple of guys crawling around on their hands and knees doing a fingertip search near her vehicle. They came up with nothing."

"I want your team to have another look at her vehicle. I think an accelerant was used."

"You're the boss."

"If that were the case, I'd be home with my feet up. Aiden, how hot did you say it's supposed to get today?"

"Somewhere around a hundred and two."

Ryan opened the collar of his protective suit. "It hit a hundred and two in this suit some time ago. We need to get moving or we're going to have a few more fatalities on our hands."

Macy looked down the length of the ravine. "She may have been looking for this ravine. It heads right out into the valley."

"That makes sense."

Macy knelt down next to the water. It was a long drop from the cliff top. "Lindsay would have run if she could. I'm thinking she was hurt in the fall."

Ryan started to slip out of his suit. "We'll know soon enough."

"We have to get hold of her phone records. She must have had a good reason to come out here."

Aiden and Macy hiked out of the ravine in silence. He'd increased his pace and she was having difficulty keeping up. She tried to disguise it, but couldn't keep her breathing even.

She caught up with him as they were heading downhill. "Aiden, I know you're not pleased about finding out about Lindsay this way, but I want to be clear. Until last night I had no idea she was working in Wilmington Creek."

"There's no need for you to apologize. That's Ray's job."

"Then it might be a long wait. He doesn't apologize."

"How long have you known him?"

"Ray? Going on twelve years. He recruited me."

"I should have guessed something was up with Lindsay."

"Why's that?"

"Because I saw them together."

"When was this?"

"Early May. It was late and I pulled him over for speeding. It was a bit of a surprise to find the captain of the state police slumming it this far north. Lindsay was his passenger. He didn't tell me that she was a cop, so naturally I thought it was something else."

"You thought they were having an affair?"

"A married man alone with an attractive woman at that hour. What else was I supposed to think?"

"Well, you were wrong."

Aiden turned and looked her full in the face. "A little piece of advice. You should stop sleeping with your boss."

"That's out of order."

"You're the one that's out of order."

"Were you watching me?"

"You weren't exactly discreet. Your hotel is a block away from my office. Your door opens onto Main Street."

Her mind flashed to the man sitting on the diving board. "And you happened to be sitting outside?"

"Don't be ridiculous. I was dropping off the transcripts from the interviews the team did up at Crawley's place. When I saw you had company, I headed home."

"It's not what you think."

"Is Ray Davidson the guy you were telling me about the other night?"

"Yes."

"Then it's exactly what I think."

"Is our working together going to be a problem?"

"If Lindsay's house hadn't been burned down, would you have told me about her being up here?"

"Of course I would have, but Lindsay had gone off radar so I had to act fast. Ray wanted to know if he should be worried."

"So he sends his girlfriend over to have a snoop around."

"Look, it's one thing to be critical of my private life, but don't you dare tell me how to do my job. I'm damn good at this. I've earned the right to be here. I'm nobody's girlfriend when I'm working."

Aiden dug his hands deep in his pockets. "Hey, I apologize. That was out of order."

"Your problems with Ray aren't recent, are they?"

"They're not problems. I just don't like the guy's style. He's too political for me."

Macy stepped past him. "I never said he was a saint."

"I never said I was either."

"Then let's just drop it. Lindsay was trying to track Ethan Green down and has ended up dead. Like it or not, he's now a suspect."

"Given the history between Green and Jeremy Dalton, it's something to think about."

"Do you know why they fell out? From what Jeremy said, they used to be friends."

"There are rumors, but no one knows for sure. Some people said it was personal, others said it was political. Ethan formed his militia in the midseventies. There should still be a copy of his original manifesto in our files. He opposed government intervention and the private ownership of productive land. Jeremy's family was the largest landowner in the valley. Needless to say, they didn't see eye to eye. But it didn't come to a head until the government laid siege to Randy Weaver's family home up on Ruby Ridge."

"Why was that a point of contention?"

"Jeremy Dalton came out strongly in support of the government's response, while Ethan Green considered it to be a declaration of war."

"Has Jeremy's line softened at all? Ruby Ridge was a gross misuse of authority, and the siege resulted in the deaths of Randy Weaver's son and wife, both of whom were completely innocent. I can't see how anyone can defend how it was handled."

"Waco was just as bad. Nobody seems to have learned anything."

"How many homicides do you have up here in an average year?"

"One, maybe two, but that's in the whole valley."

"What are the odds that these two cases aren't related?"

"Slim to none."

"Maybe Lindsay found Ethan Green after all."

"She sure stirred up some trouble if she did."

"Has his militia disbanded?"

"There was a power struggle and the New Montana Militia reformed under different leadership. Ethan was sidelined. He took a few loyal people with him, but the numbers stayed low. After Oklahoma, membership declined further. It's only been in the last few years that there has been renewed interest in joining these groups."

"So Ethan Green has been mobilizing people?"

"Like I said, last summer he went off the radar completely. Is this informant you've got on the highway patrol officer case reliable?"

"I can't say, as I don't handle him, but I'm making some enquiries. What about that compound Ethan was living in? Is the land still in his name?"

"Barely. He's behind in paying property taxes. I hear it may be going up for auction."

"Have you been out there recently?"

"No, it's been at least a year."

"So what was the other reason?"

"Pardon?"

"You said there may have been a personal reason for Ethan and Jeremy falling out."

"There have always been rumors going around about Annie and Ethan. People say they were having an affair, but then again, they say a lot of things about Annie. She's never been all that popular around here."

Macy raised an eyebrow. "Given that John was worried Jeremy wasn't his real father, that could be significant."

"It certainly puts that text message Annie received from John's phone in a new light."

They stepped out into the meadow and picked their way across the churned-over earth of a recently dug fire line. Even though the sun was in full force it was cooler out in the open. About two hundred yards farther on Macy could see the light reflecting off the wind-shields of their cars. She focused her mind on the last Diet Coke in her cooler. It was the only thing that kept her going.

"You said a fire crew found the body."

"They were assisting us with the search."

"Find out if any of the guys that found Lindsay's body is named

Nick. You never know. The guy that was harassing Lana at The Whitefish was on a fire crew."

"I'll give them a call."

Aiden slipped his phone out of his pocket, but Macy kept walking.

"If it's okay with you, I'm going to go on ahead. I'll pass out if I don't get something cold to drink."

Aiden caught up with her a few minutes later. She already had her engine running and the air conditioner set to the highest level. She handed him a water bottle from the cooler. "Looks like you need this."

"We might have just gotten lucky. Nick Childs was part of the team that found the body. Apparently, he's a dead ringer for the composite sketch. I'm having him and his friend Peter Lane brought in for questioning. I'll send their photos over to Lana and Jean at The Whitefish for confirmation."

"It would be a hell of a break."

"Sometimes they make it easy for us. By the way, what did the guys from John Dalton's platoon have to say?"

"Same story. John was sound. No disputes with anyone. Peacemaker, that kind of thing."

Aiden's phone rang. He put it to his ear and rubbed his eyes.

"Okay. Okay. I hear you. Put an APB out on his vehicle and have a team meet me out at the campsite where he's been staying." He hung up and looked at Macy. "Nick Childs took off about an hour ago, heading south. They ran a check on him. He's a convicted felon. Sexual assault and armed robbery."

"We've got a license number for his vehicle?"

"Yep, we'll find him. His friend Peter Lane is on his way to the station for questioning."

"I'll head over now to question him," said Macy as she climbed into her car. "Call me if anything interesting comes up at the campsite."

17

Macy stopped at a vending machine on the way to the interview room. She'd gone by the hotel on the way into town to have a quick shower. Her hair was still wet so she was cold. It didn't help that the air conditioner was switched to arctic. She punched in the code for a candy bar just as her phone rang. It was Aiden. She went and stood next to a window where there was a better signal. Sun was streaming in through the gaps in the blinds.

"Aiden, you should be able to hear me better now."

"Loud and clear. Nick Childs was picked up a few miles north of Kalispell. They've taken him into custody. He didn't have any fire-arms in his possession."

"He could have dumped the gun anywhere between here and Ka-lispell."

"I'm at the campsite now. He appears to have left in a hurry."

"When can we question him?"

"Once he's processed. They're bringing him up."

"That's very accommodating."

"It must be a slow day."

"Have them check to see if he has a satellite navigation system in his vehicle. If it was switched on it might give us an indication of where he was on the night John was murdered."

"Will do. By the way, it's not a late-model V8. It's a pickup truck."

"Montana's usual F-150?"

"You got it."

"Ray texted me. He'll be here in an hour to discuss the case in person."

"Do you think he wants to apologize?"

"I already told you he doesn't do that. I'm getting the feeling that the crime scene analysis has come up with something unexpected. I called to ask what was going on and was redirected to Ray."

"And just when I thought things had gotten complicated enough."

"They sent me the access codes for Lindsay's case notes. From what I've seen so far it doesn't look like she was even close to finding Ethan Green. She was convinced he was either dead or had moved away. We need further proof if we want to tie him to her death."

"It would be nice if Nick Childs stepped up. What have you found out about him and his friend?"

Macy glanced at her notes. "They're seasonal firefighters. Childs has been doing it for years, but Peter only signed on with the state this summer. Childs was working out at Waldo Canyon the afternoon Lindsay disappeared."

"That could be a coincidence."

"I did a couple summers on fire crews. It would have been difficult for him to slip off unnoticed."

"We'll talk to everyone on his team. What do they do the rest of the year?"

"During the ski season, Nick Childs works down at Big Sky as a lift operator, and Peter Lane is an English teacher at Bozeman High School."

"Have you interviewed Lane yet?"

"I'm just about to. I'll let you know what I find out."

. . .

Peter Lane stood up and wiped his hands on his shorts as Macy entered the interview room. He was only thirty-one, but already going bald. His fingers were wrapped in blister tape.

"Mr. Lane, my name is Detective Macy Greeley."

He gave her a firm handshake. "Pleased to meet you."

Macy clicked on the voice recorder. "I assure you that this is just a formality. Mr. Lane, could you please state your full name and date of birth."

He had a slight stammer. "Am I under . . . arrest?"

"Mr. Lane, I understand you've waived your right to a lawyer? Have you changed your mind?"

"Isn't this about the body we found?"

"It's on my list of things to discuss, but before we can continue I really need you to state your name and date of birth."

Peter leaned over the recorder and spoke slowly. "Peter Lane, born third of June, 1983."

Macy smiled. "That wasn't so difficult, was it?"

"No, ma'am. The woman we found. This is just about her?"

Macy placed a file on the table and took out her notebook. "We believe she died as a direct result of a fire." She took a photo of Lindsay Moore out of the file and slid it across the table. "Out of curiosity, what kind of car do you drive, Mr. Lane?"

Peter Lane stared at the picture. Lindsay wore her full dress uniform and looked directly into the camera. "I have a Volvo station wagon," he said before glancing at Macy. "Who's this?"

"You've never seen her before?"

He shook his head.

"Take your time. I want you to be sure."

"I'm sure. Who is she?"

"She's the woman who died in the Waldo Canyon fire."

His voice went up an octave. "She was a police officer?"

Macy tapped the photo with her index finger. "Lindsay Moore was a special investigator working for the state."

"I had nothing to do with this."

"You just found her?"

"It was actually Nick who found her, not me."

"Why does the report say otherwise?"

"He's got an ex-wife who wants money from him. He was worried his name would end up in the papers."

Macy glanced down at her notes.

"Did you know your friend Nick has been wanted for questioning in relation to a recent murder?"

Peter Lane gave her a blank stare.

Macy settled back in her chair. "A few days ago John Dalton was shot in the alley outside The Whitefish. I believe you're familiar with the establishment. You used to frequent it with Nick Childs."

"Yes, but—"

"And you were both barred from the premises when a woman who worked there made a complaint against you."

"That had nothing to do with me."

"I'm sensing a theme here, Mr. Lane. You seem to be a lot of places you shouldn't be with Nick Childs, and every time something happens it has nothing to do with you. Are you aware that your friend is in police custody in Kalispell?"

Peter Lane shook his head. A rash was spreading upward from the collar of his shirt. Wine-colored blotches blended with the stubble of his beard. He rubbed his face.

"Mr. Childs took off before we had a chance to call you both in for questioning."

"Nick told me he was leaving for a few days, but he didn't say why."

"It certainly makes him look guilty of something. I just need to figure out what."

Peter started picking at the blister tape on his hands.

"Mr. Lane, I'd like to know what made Lana Clark so uncomfortable that she complained to her manager after you two visited her bar. Could you help me with that?"

"I suppose so."

"Would it encourage you to be more cooperative if you knew that Nick Childs has served time for multiple offenses which include aggravated sexual assault and armed robbery?"

"I didn't know."

"You're a high school teacher and a father of two young children. He's not someone you want to be associated with."

His voice rose again. "He kept hinting that he knew Lana from somewhere. She humored him the first few times we came in, but she lost her temper when Nick said she'd never had a problem with getting paid for her services before, so what was the big deal now. I wanted to intervene, but we got kicked out before I had a chance. I gave the place a wide berth after that. I can't speak for Nick."

"Did Nick give you any reason to believe he was telling the truth about Lana's past? Did he mention a specific name or location?"

"The night we got kicked out he asked her if Charlie knew how she really paid her way through school."

"Charlie?"

He shrugged. "He never explained."

"Was he angry about being barred from The Whitefish?"

"Quite the opposite. I was under the impression he thought it was funny."

"Mr. Lane, you seem like a nice man. Given his actions, I'm surprised you remained friends with him."

"Nick really took me under his wing. I'd never been on a fire crew and didn't have a clue what I was doing. I was grateful, but the way he acted that night did put me on edge. I've been trying to distance myself."

Macy picked up Lindsay's photo and slid it back in the file. "Mr. Lane, I really appreciate your cooperating with us today. I may have a few more questions for you so I'd like you to sit tight. Is that okay?"

"Yes, I suppose so. I'm not heading home until tomorrow."

"Can I get you a sandwich or something?"

"Thank you. Anything would be great. I'm not fussy."

Macy shut the door and put in a call to Aiden.

"Lana lied to us. Nick Childs knew her from when she lived in Georgia. The night he got kicked out of The Whitefish, he mentioned Charlie Lott by name."

"Do you suppose what he was saying about her being a prostitute was true too?"

"We need to speak to Lana again."

"Any chance Nick Childs is our murderer?"

"I'm not sure."

"We've been searching the campsite, but nothing has come up. No one noticed that he went missing the afternoon Lindsay disappeared."

"Okay, keep me posted. I'm going to see if Ray has arrived."

Macy found Ray sitting in Aiden's office with his feet propped up on the desk, reading the local paper. She stood watching him for a few seconds before stepping into the room and closing the door.

"Have you been waiting long?"

"Not long at all. I flew in. Given that I only got back to Helena at four in the morning, it seemed the most sensible mode of transport."

"That must make a nice change from driving."

"They told me you were interviewing a potential witness." He brushed a piece of lint from his pant leg. "I figured I'd wait in here."

As she made her way toward her desk he caught her by the wrist and tried to kiss her.

She twisted free. "Ray, you know better."

He laughed. "Sometimes you're such a—"

"Don't even think about finishing that sentence." She sat down and turned on her laptop. In the time she'd been out of the office she'd received 126 emails, and not one of them was from the medical examiner. "Please tell me you managed to get the medical examiner's report and something on ballistics."

He tapped a file on the desk. "I've got it with me."

"And?"

"And I think we should wait for Chief Marsh."

"He's out searching a suspect's campsite. He won't be back for hours."

"I just got off the phone. He's on his way."

Macy handed Ray the composite sketch of Nick Childs. "I've been interviewing Peter Lane. Apparently, Nick Childs knew Lana Clark and her boyfriend Charlie Lott back in Georgia. We have yet to establish whether he was involved with John Dalton's murder."

"He wasn't."

Macy folded her hands in her lap. "You're going to make me wait?"

"I am."

"Are you doing this because I didn't kiss you?"

"I am."

She pointed at his shoes. "If you don't want to come off as a total asshole you may want to take your feet off Aiden's desk."

"Touchy."

"Apparently not as touchy as you'd like me to be."

"Are we going to spend the entire afternoon scoring points off each other?"

"It wouldn't be ideal."

"It's been a long twenty-four hours. I need you to be nice to me."

She glanced at her computer screen. "I remember you telling me that you knew Lindsay's father?"

"Her father and I were very close. He really looked after me when I joined the force. Since he died, Lindsay's pretty much been on her own. She's like family."

"No mother?"

"They don't speak. It was an ugly divorce and Lindsay took her father's side." Ray dropped his feet to the floor and swiveled his chair so he was facing Macy, their knees almost touching. "Her sister sided with their mother when the family broke up. I'm not sure where she is now. I just got off the phone with her mother. For all it's worth, she knows her daughter is dead."

Macy lowered her voice. "Do you have to fly back tonight?"

"The plane takes off in an hour."

"You can make some excuse."

"Sorry, but I can't."

Macy went back to reading her e-mails.

"Macy, don't be upset."

She shook her head. "I'm not upset, Ray. I'm ambivalent."

"That sounds worse."

"That's because it is."

"Don't do this. I was here last night. I only slept a few hours."

"Well, good for you. I didn't sleep at all."

There was a light knock and Ray stood as the door swung open. Aiden placed his backpack on the floor before reaching out to shake Ray's hand. He didn't smile.

"It's been a while."

"Yes, it has. Detective Greeley has been filling me in."

"I'm sorry we didn't have better news."

"It's a tragic loss. Lindsay was a fine police officer."

Aiden glanced over at Macy but she didn't look up from her laptop. "Macy said you had some information on the Dalton case."

"There was a ballistics match with the gun used to kill highway patrol officer Timothy Wallace last summer. Ethan Green was never convicted of that murder, but, as you now know, he's been identified as the shooter by a reliable informant."

Aiden sat down behind his desk. "And here I was hoping Green was rotting in a shallow grave."

"There's more. I got a rush on that 9mm slug the ME found in Lindsay's left shoulder. The techs compared it with what we have in the Dalton case. It was also from the same gun." Ray handed Macy and Aiden copies of the ballistics report. "Ethan Green has been very busy."

Macy raised an eyebrow. "I've been making some calls. I'm not so sure about your informant. I think it's premature to hang all this on Ethan Green."

"Macy, our informant has been working with us for a long time. He's also a source for the FBI. The word is Ethan's re-forming his militia, and he's got something big planned. That's why I sent Lindsay up here in the first place."

Aiden flipped through the report. "Do you think John Dalton's murder was some kind of political statement?"

"Could be."

Macy frowned. "Given the text message that was sent to Annie, I still say this is personal. Did anything come up in the DNA analysis? There was a rumor going around that Annie and Ethan had an affair. She convinced John that Jeremy wasn't his real father. Maybe it was Green."

"The results from the DNA analysis aren't in yet, but they promised to have something to us by tomorrow at the latest."

Macy clicked on a new e-mail from the medical examiner and opened the attached file containing the autopsy results on Lindsay Moore. She had injuries consistent with a fall. Her spine was severed and plant fibers were embedded in the cuts on her hands. The toxicology report came back clean. There was no evidence of sexual assault. She'd died of smoke inhalation.

Ray rubbed his eyes and yawned. "John may not be the only person Annie Dalton's been talking to." He glanced at Aiden. "What about the sister?"

"As far as we know, she hasn't been told anything."

Macy scrolled through the report on the screen in front of her. "She may be busy connecting the dots on her own."

Ray stood up and began pacing what little space there was. "You know, even if the rumors are incorrect, it still makes sense when you think about it. Green didn't have to know why John was snooping around and asking questions about him. He just knew that Lindsay Moore was doing the same thing. He may have gotten paranoid and decided to take them both out."

"So, Ray, where do we go from here?"

"Macy talks to the press this afternoon. We need to get the word out that we're looking for Ethan Green, put an APB out on his vehicle."

"There's been an APB out on his vehicle for more than a year. Not one sighting."

"We'll also have to search his property."

"It's over a hundred acres. We'll need more resources."

Ray picked up his phone. "That won't be a problem."

Macy turned her chair to face them. "Ray, when were you going to tell us that Lindsay was three to four months pregnant?"

He sighed. "I was just about to get to that."

"Was there a boyfriend?"

"Not that I know of."

"Conception took place after she moved here. We could be looking for someone local. How do we know this doesn't have anything to do with her death? Murder is usually personal."

"Her phone records didn't show any unusual activity."

"That's inconclusive. There are many ways to communicate that are difficult to trace. They could have used the Internet."

"You seem to forget that we have a ballistics match with the gun used by Ethan Green to kill a highway patrol officer."

"And you seem to forget that Ethan Green was never convicted of that crime. Your informant has been offered a plea bargain in return for giving evidence. You and I both know that's not good enough. We'll need a lot more before we can pin all this on Ethan Green." Macy snapped her laptop shut and headed for the door. "I'm going to work on a press statement. I'll be in the interview room if you need me."

. . .

Macy had just printed out the first draft of her statement when Ray walked into the room and quietly shut the door behind him. Macy didn't look up from her laptop. She was speed-reading through Lindsay Moore's case notes.

"What's on your mind, Ray?"

"What's with your attitude? I thought we were on the same side."

Macy stared at him for a long moment before speaking. "Excuse me?"

He lowered his voice. "Regardless of what's going on between us, I am your commanding officer. I expect your support. How you behaved back there was unprofessional."

"I'm the lead detective on this case. Whether you agree with it or not, my opinion is valid. You can't just come up here, dump all this on me, and expect me to fall into line."

"I'm not dumping anything on you."

"Ray, I was on the special task force put together to investigate that state trooper's murder. I've not only read the report, I helped write it. I have good reason to doubt the veracity of your informant's testimony. He's up for murder one, and in exchange for information on militia groups he names Ethan Green as the shooter. It happened in the middle of the night out on Route 93 south of Missoula. How could there be any witnesses?"

"It's not just me who thinks this guy's statement is sound. The FBI is on board as well. Our guy was active in the area at the time. His cell phone can be triangulated to within twenty miles of the incident."

"That's hardly surprising, since your informant lives in Missoula. I'm not saying that Ethan Green didn't do it, I'm just doubting that you actually have a witness."

"What's the difference, if we get the right guy in the end?"

"I want to talk to the informant before we go forward with the press conference. I also want the ballistics analysis done again. There's too much riding on this. If we get it wrong, we lose valuable time."

"We're not getting it wrong. I was there when they did the ballistics tests. I personally delivered the slug the ME found in Lindsay's shoulder. You're going to have to trust me on this, Macy. Ethan Green is our man."

"You give me until tomorrow afternoon to do what I need to do, and I'll be much happier making a statement to the press."

Ray placed his hand on the table. "Lindsay was on to something. She called me just last week."

"I've been going through her files, Ray." She turned her laptop around. "It's all there on the mainframe. I was issued the access codes this morning. I've read through everything she's logged over the past few weeks. There's nothing. The day before she died she wrote that she was becoming more convinced that Ethan Green is either dead or has left town."

"So why did she call me and tell me something completely different?"

"Maybe she wanted to extend her time up here. There was a man in her life. Perhaps he was local and she wasn't ready to leave."

Ray looked at his watch. "We're running out of time. I want to catch the six o'clock news."

"I would like to postpone until tomorrow."

"You're willing to risk him getting away or, worse, striking again."

"I don't want to risk compromising the investigation. If we put a name as big as Ethan Green's out there and we get it wrong, we're going to lose the public's confidence. I say we wait."

"Can I see your notes for the press statement?"

Macy handed them over and watched as Ray read through them.

"You may not be willing to stick your neck out, but I am. Ethan Green is the shooter, and the sooner the public gets on board, the better."

Macy threw her pen aside. "I guess it's your show."

"And don't think that I don't know what's really going on here. You promised you would never let our relationship get in the way of doing your job."

"That is completely out of line. I've never done that before, and I'm not doing it now."

Ray started making notes in the margins. "Macy, I've really had enough of your shit for one day. I'm going to do the press conference and then I'm heading home. I think you're overtired. I suggest you get a good night's sleep and call me in the morning."

He left without saying good-bye.

18

Annie waved Jessie into her hospital room, but didn't look up from her book. "About time you showed up."

"I tried to come before, but they wouldn't let me see you."

"Where's my granddaughter? You should have brought her."

"She's staying with Monica and her husband for a couple of days. I needed to get her away from the house. It's been so depressing up at the ranch."

Annie stared at her daughter with a blank expression on her face.

"Monica is my best friend from grade school. We grew up together."

"Did I approve of her?"

"She was your favorite," Jessie lied.

Annie pointed at the paper bag Jessie was carrying. "What have you brought me?"

Jessie placed the bag on the bed and started to empty out the contents. The doctor had taken away the jar of raspberry jam and removed the glass from the framed photo of Tara. Nothing that could be used as a weapon was allowed. Jessie stumbled over her words.

"It's just the few things I managed to get past the doctors. Some cookies you like. A few of your books. One of your journals." She placed the photo of Tara on the bedside table.

"They're worried I'll kill myself." Annie snapped her book shut and set it down on her lap. "I requested a room on the sixth floor with a balcony, but they turned me down."

"Please don't joke about stuff like that."

"Why not? Gallows humor is one of the few pleasures I have left."

"I'm trying to get you out of here."

"Don't bother."

"You're just going to give up?"

Annie pushed a stray lock of hair from her eyes. "Jessie, you really need to start paying attention. Whatever Jeremy might be saying, I'm not like this by choice. Sometimes I think you believe that this is all part of a master plan to make my family miserable."

"Well, it worked."

She waved a hand. "There you go."

"I'm sorry. I just think that maybe early on you could have done more to get help. It's like you cut yourself off from us. We didn't understand what was happening. We just knew you didn't want to be around us anymore."

She smoothed the book cover with her hands. "At some point it became easier to do nothing. Even a cage can be comfortable. Besides, I decided long ago that I'm not wired for happiness . . . whatever that means. Sometimes life breaks you."

"You just have to keep trying."

"And sometimes you have to admit it's hopeless. I was broken all the way down. That's a line from a song, isn't it?" Her fingers fluttered to her lips and she started humming softly.

"Were you ever happy?"

"Do I get points for faking it?"

"I read your journals. The man you had an affair with. You never refer to him by name."

Annie stopped humming. Her gaze sharpened again.

"He is someone I never wanted you to know about."

"You loved him. He made you happy. You say as much in your journals."

"Don't give him too much credit. Not a lot of effort was required. Things with Jeremy were bad to the point of breaking." She shook her head. "I was so soft. So stupid. I loved that man to the point of obsession."

Jessie sat down in the only chair. Her mother had been reading a frayed copy of *The Year of Magical Thinking* by Joan Didion.

"Why did you stay with Jeremy?"

"I didn't feel like I had a choice."

"That's ridiculous. Lots of people get divorced."

"Have you ever heard the expression *too big to fail*? That was Jeremy and me. I'd put all my hopes and money into my marriage. I didn't have a backup plan." Her voice trailed off. "Besides. I was pregnant and that man, the one I was obsessed with, well, he left me without so much as a backward glance. One day was full of promise and the next was empty."

Jessie thought about this for a few seconds before responding.

"Jeremy isn't my father?"

"Jeremy couldn't be anyone's father. He wouldn't admit it, but he was shooting blanks."

Jessie opened her mouth to speak, but her mother cut her off.

"I'm going to tell you the same thing I told John. Don't go looking for your real father. I learned too late that he was cruel." She lowered her voice. "After all these years it still hurts. What does that make me?"

"It makes you human."

"I'll tell you one thing I know. *He* wasn't human. Nobody cuts people cold like that."

"How long did John know about this?"

"For a few months. He told me he decided it wasn't important. He loved Jeremy like a father, and Jeremy loved him like a son." She reached out and took hold of Jessie's black hair. "Your problem is that you always looked too much like your real father. Same dark eyes and that hair. Nobody has hair like that in Jeremy's family." She pressed her fingers to her eyes like she was trying to erase the memory. "Jeremy caught us in bed together. His best man and his wife. There was no going back to the way things were after that."

Jessie stood up very slowly. Her legs were so heavy that she couldn't imagine how she'd make it out of the room.

"I have to go," she said, taking the first tentative step for the door.

"You've been listening, though?" Annie tried to take hold of her hand, but Jessie snatched it away. "You need to speak to the lawyers. Don't let Jeremy railroad you. You own half of everything. You understand? Half."

Jessie didn't want to hear about it. She focused all her energy on making it out of the room.

"I have to go," she said again.

"Don't go looking for your father. He's not the man I thought he was."

Jessie held the door frame and gave her mother one last backward glance.

"I'll visit again soon."

Annie picked up her book and turned to the page she'd been reading. "Next time bring something sharp."

Tyler's face was bright red. "You just don't get it, do you, Jessie? When I heard those sirens at three this morning, I thought they were coming to arrest me. I had a backpack full of explosives sitting in my car, packed and ready to go." He pinched his fingers together so they were almost touching. "I came this close to losing it."

He stood in the middle of his kitchen, holding a green plastic garbage bag. He swept empty bottles and pizza boxes into it before moving to the living room. He bent over the coffee table and chucked in porn magazines, cigarette butts, and more bottles. The smell of stale beer and cigarettes made her feel sick.

Jessie remained on the front porch with the screen door half open, waiting for him to invite her inside. It was late afternoon and the sun was warm on her back. He stepped past her and threw the tied-off bag outside before grabbing another off the kitchen counter. His damp T-shirt stuck to his skin and thick beads of perspiration dripped down the back of his neck. He stunk.

"Close the door, you're letting flies in."

She stepped inside but stayed near the door. She was wary of being around Tyler when he was angry. He reminded her too much of Jeremy.

"Where's Dylan?"

"He's out back playing with his dog." He picked a T-shirt up from the floor and smelled it before chucking it into the hallway. "How much do you know about Dylan's condition?"

She shrugged. "I know he's hurting."

"It's worse than that. He's taking pills for everything—sleeping, waking, pain, anxiety, more pain. He told me he sees dead people sometimes. I'd say our friend Dylan is as fucked up as they come."

"I didn't know it was that bad."

He pointed to his temple. "You need to stop messing with his head. Why are you panicking because someone gave your necklace back? Why can't you just be thankful like a normal person? Ethan is dead. Don't go digging him up if you don't have to."

"Who else would have left it for me? There was no card. Just my name."

"Jessie, please don't waste my time with this shit. I've got real problems to deal with." He jabbed the end of his lit cigarette in her direction. "Ethan didn't kill John. Someone else did. That's the son of a bitch we need to be worrying about right now."

"I thought you were going to blow the cliff this morning."

He grabbed a blanket off the sofa, shook it out, and started folding.

"Jess, I've been questioned twice today and they've set up a road-block just outside my house. There's no way I'm going anywhere with twenty-four pounds of high explosives in my car. It will have to wait."

Tyler picked up the television remote and tuned into the local news station. The post box at the end of his driveway was in the center of the shot. Jessie's beat-up hatchback was parked next to it. The camera swept across the landscape before focusing in on a reporter who looked young enough to be in high school. He pointed out the roadblock the police had erected and summarized what they knew so far before launching into the breaking news.

Tyler hit Pause and called Dylan into the house. "Dylan, get your ass in here. You need to see this."

Dylan stood just inside the screen door. "That guy's right in front of the house. Maybe we should go say hello."

Tyler pointed the remote at the television again. "That's not helpful."

The reporter stared into the camera and delivered his lines.

The body discovered in the area of the Waldo Canyon fire has been formally identified as Lindsay Moore, a special investigator working for the state police in Helena. Sources close to the police department say she was working undercover in Wilmington Creek and posing as Ph.D. student Patricia Dune. Late last night her home on Tucker Road burned to the ground in an apparent arson attack. It was first thought that Lindsay Moore might have been in the house, but fire investigators were quick to confirm that the house was unoccupied at the time of the incident. We're now going live to a press conference outside the Wilmington Creek Police Department, where the lead investigator, Detective Macy Greeley, is talking to reporters.

Jessie sat down on the arm of the sofa. Tara had been going on and on about how wonderful Macy Greeley was. *She showed me her gun. She has a son named Luke.* The cameras were rolling but Macy Greeley was nowhere to be seen. A man wearing a suit came out instead.

The sun was in his eyes. He slipped on a pair of sunglasses and spoke confidently.

"Given the serious nature of the crimes that have been committed here in Wilmington Creek, I've decided to make a personal appeal to the citizens of the Flathead Valley. For those who don't know me, my name is Ray Davidson and I'm the captain of the state police. First and foremost, my thoughts and prayers go out to Lindsay Moore's family, friends, and colleagues. Lindsay was a highly respected police officer who proudly served the state of Montana for more than a decade. We're calling on the local community for help in tracking down her killer."

Tyler folded his arms over his chest. "I told you they don't know jack shit."

"We have been able to link the gun used in the murders of John Dalton and Lindsay Moore to the one used to kill highway patrol officer Timothy Wallace last summer. Although no one has been formally charged, Ethan Green has since been identified as the man who pulled the trigger." He held up a mug shot. "Ethan Green is well known to state law enforcement. He's served time for firearms offenses, burglary, and assault and battery."

Dylan stepped farther into the room and sank down onto the nearest chair. "Holy shit."

"We are asking the public to remain vigilant. Ethan Green is a highly trained survivalist who has intimate knowledge of the wilderness areas in and around the Flathead Valley. Many here in the local community know him personally and are familiar with his efforts to raise private militias. According to our sources at the state level and in the FBI, he is once again active in the militia movement and may be planning a major attack on the federal government. If you have any information, please contact the authorities on the special hotline that has been set up."

Tyler switched off the television. Outside, Dylan's dog yelped and scratched at the screen door, and in the distance a train sounded its whistle as it passed through the Flathead Valley. Tyler went into the kitchen, took a beer out of the refrigerator, and drained it while hanging on the open door.

"Talk about a cluster fuck."

Dylan picked up a lighter and flipped it between his fingers.

"He'll try to pick us off one at a time."

Tyler took long, ferocious drags off a cigarette without bothering to flick away the ash. "Ethan must have been planning John's murder all year. That took some patience." He leveled his gaze on Jessie. "I bet he saves you 'til last. That's what I'd do. I'd take my time with you."

Dylan slid the screen door open and his dog ran into the room with a tennis ball in its mouth. "Tyler, there's no need for that. Jessie's scared enough as it is."

"But I'm right, aren't I? That's what he'll do. Either you or me is next, and then it will be Jessie, saved for last."

Jessie kept her voice low. "Dylan, we need to go to the police."

Tyler stepped out of the kitchen and grabbed hold of her arm. "Do you think I'm deaf, or something? I see what you're trying to do, but Dylan isn't stupid enough to listen to the girl who got us into this mess in the first place."

"It's you and John that fucked up."

Tyler slapped her so hard her head snapped back against a framed photograph of Tyler's grandparents. It fell to the floor and broken glass shot across the room.

"We fucked up? *We* fucked up? What about you? Are you ever going to take responsibility for the shit storm you caused that night?"

Dylan grabbed hold of Tyler's shoulder. "That's enough, Tyler. Let her go."

Tyler shoved her into the wall again. "Dylan, you better keep her in line, or I will." He held a lit cigarette within an inch of Jessie's right eye. "No one is going to the police. We'll deal with this ourselves."

Jessie craned her neck. "Quit telling me what to do. I'm going to the police, Tyler! You hear me?"

Tyler grabbed her by the throat. "You go to the police and you bring us all down."

"Tyler, I told you to let her go! Listen to me."

Jessie started screaming. "I'll tell them it was just me and John. I'll leave you guys out of it."

"The hell you will. You'll cave in like you always do."

Dylan grabbed hold of Tyler's hands and tried to pry them away. "Goddamn it, you're choking her. Stop."

Tyler gave her once last shove and released his hands. Jessie sank to the floor and gasped for air.

"You stupid bitch," said Tyler, stomping across the room and kicking over the coffee table. "You're going to ruin everything."

Jessie spoke in a whisper. "I'm not."

Dylan stood between them. "What the fuck, Tyler? You can't treat her like that."

Tyler slammed his fist into the drywall, leaving a hole. "I need to get out of here." He gave Dylan a quick glance as he headed out the screen door. "Are you coming?"

Dylan tried to look Jessie in the eye but she'd turned away.

"Jessie, I'm going to try to make Tyler see sense. I'll be back in a sec."

Jessie didn't move until she was sure they were both gone. She ran her fingers through her hair. A bump was forming behind her right ear. Her throat was bruised and it hurt to breathe. Using the wall for support, she staggered to her feet and steadied herself. If she started crying now there would be no stopping. Shards of glass cracked underfoot. She reached for the countertop for support and tried to focus her mind on something besides that night at the lake, but nothing would shift the last time she saw Ethan Green's face. She still remembered the moment her fingers closed around that rock. It had felt reassuringly heavy. There was an unopened whiskey bottle on the breakfast bar. She closed her fingers around its neck. It also felt reassuringly heavy. She slipped it in her bag and left the way she'd come.

. . .

Jessie ground her way through the hatchback's gearbox as she headed north toward the Canadian border. The farther she drove, the more the forested hills closed in on her. She pulled off on a dirt road and the car clattered as she made her way east. The track twisted with the changing terrain, and just when she was feeling lost, it came to an abrupt end on the stony beach of a tributary. Before getting out, she checked her phone. There was no signal, so she threw it into her bag and grabbed the whiskey bottle from the cup holder. A third of it was already gone. A cloud of insects trailed behind her as she made her way north along the shore. Her feet sank in the loose gravel. The conversation she'd had with her mother replayed in her head.

He caught us in bed together. His best man and his wife.

Aside from a few rust-colored needles, the tree her mother had described in her journal had been picked clean by pine beetles. Dry limbs twisted outward, their gnarled tips still holding offerings—faded lace panties, keys without chains, crucifixes woven from twigs, and higher up, a pair of sneakers hanging from their laces. Jessie wove the broken necklace around a low branch. The heart-shaped locket spun like a top until she stilled it with her thumb and forefinger. The hot springs were hidden behind a ring of smooth granite boulders. The gray pool didn't seem any more magical than the tree. Jessie took a long swallow from the whiskey bottle before stepping in fully clothed. Steam rose around her. She waded out to the middle and dipped down so that she was sitting with just her head and shoulders exposed. She tilted her head back so her dark hair floated around her face. The smoky haze had thinned. She would see the stars.

Annie had written about coming to these hot springs with a man that Jessie had grown up admiring from afar. There were always stories about him in the papers. To some he was a modern-day folk hero. To others he was a common criminal. The fact that Jeremy hated him only made Jessie like him more. In all these years she'd never suspected that he might be her father. She wondered if Ethan Green knew the truth about their connection—that he'd killed his own son and tried to rape his own daughter.

The morning after it had happened, it didn't hurt as much as it should have, but that was only because she was still drunk. She'd laughed at Dylan. *Come on,* she'd said, confused by the look on his face. *I don't look that bad?* He'd pulled her out of his bed and positioned her in front of a full-length mirror. Jessie was naked aside from a bra and a pair of Dylan's boxer shorts. She put her fingertips to the swollen lips of the battered stranger in the reflection. She'd thought she might be dreaming. Dylan had held up his camera like an apology. *We need evidence in case the police ever tie you to Ethan's death.* She'd nodded in agreement, but in her head she had been picking through all the blind spots from the night before. She'd lost hours, and no amount of sifting could get them back. She remembered waking up in the dirt with Ethan Green lying on top of her. He hadn't looked like he was sleeping. The fact that he was actually dead made no sense at all.

Dylan had taken photographs: close-ups of her raw knuckles and broken fingernails; her bugged-out eye—red and swollen like a ripe fruit; her split lip; the black-and-blue handprints on her thighs; the boot imprint stamped on her belly. She looked down at her bruised body.

Dylan, who did this?

Ethan Green.

I killed him?

Don't you remember?

I'm not sure.

Dylan had put the camera aside and there was no lens to shield her from his gaze.

Jessie, how long do you think you can keep this up before you end up dead? When are you going to realize there are people in this town who love you?

She had waited, reworking his words like she might do a riddle, trying to bend her low opinion of herself around them, trying to make him into the fool. He was talking nonsense. He had reached out to touch her, but stopped before his fingertips found her skin. Then it had hit her. She'd looked up at him. There it was, and it was unconditional. It was the first time she'd ever seen a man cry. She'd run to the bathroom, where she was sick until she was nothing but thin skin stretched over a drum of bones. She had washed her face, gingerly touching her bulging eye and lip. She'd used the toilet and there was a deep, penetrating hurt that burned and left her gasping for breath. Violent cramps had shot across her abdomen. She clutched hold of the sink and cried out for help, but Dylan was gone. She had returned to bed and gripped the pillow tight. She'd wondered how she could die when she already felt dead.

Jessie gazed up at the darkening sky. Tyler's words were still fresh in her head. *Ethan must have been planning John's murder all year. That took some patience.* And then that knowing smile. *I bet he saves you 'til last. That's what I'd do. I'd take my time with you.*

Darkness fell and, as promised, the sky crystalized. Jessie tracked satellites and airplanes making their way through the thick veil of stars. She sipped from the bottle and wished she could fly to the moon. She shook herself awake. If she wasn't careful she could drift away into nothingness and be none the wiser. The whiskey bottle slid from her fingertips and they floated side by side. People would explain it to Tara but she would never understand. Jessie tried to focus. All she needed to do was walk away. The car wasn't far. There was a towel in the back, a sweatshirt too. She'd dry off and drive away. She imagined picking her way along the shore in the pitch-black.

Jessie opened her eyes and coughed up water. She'd fallen asleep. She thought she heard someone calling her name. She might have been dreaming. A beam of light skimmed the top of the boulders surrounding the pool. She sat up and water cascaded from her hair. She searched the darkness. There it was again. The light bobbed up and down along the shoreline and flicked toward the trees. She waited, half submerged. Dylan called for her again and she stood shivering in the rising heat. This time she answered.

19

Nick Childs was only forty-one years of age, but looked much older. His skin was darkened by years in the sun. There were two white blotches on his forehead where the pigment was gone. The Kalispell Police Department had held him overnight, but he was to be released as soon as Macy was through interviewing him.

"Mr. Childs, as you know, you were originally wanted for questioning in connection with the murder of John Dalton. You are no longer a suspect in that crime."

"Does that mean I can finally go?"

"I was hoping you'd be willing to answer a couple of questions first. I'm following up on a witness statement." She pushed Lana's and Charlie's photographs across the table. "I'd like to know how you're familiar with Charlie Lott, if you're aware of his present whereabouts, and if you knew Lana Clark prior to meeting her here in Wilmington Creek."

"I take it Lana hasn't been talking too much."

"I'd like to hear your side of the story."

He picked up Lana's photograph and smirked. "I met Lana about four years ago. I was down in Georgia, visiting some cousins. She was working at a strip club, but she was willing to take it further for the right price. I spent a lot of money on her that summer."

"Do you remember the name of the club?"

"The Night Crawler. It was about thirty miles east of Fort Benning. She said she was doing it to earn money for college. I treated her well. Hell, I even tipped her."

"How did you know Charlie Lott?"

"He came into the club one night. I got the impression from talking to him that he didn't know Lana was doing business on the side. She got real nervous when she saw us sitting together. The next night she was gone. I was pretty surprised when I found her working at The Whitefish and she had all her clothes on."

'Tell me about Charlie."

"Not much to tell. Seemed to be a pretty mellow guy. He was dealing but it was small time. I think he was a musician or something."

"Did Lana ever tell you that Charlie threatened her?"

"I wasn't paying her to talk.'

"Have you had any contact with him since?"

'It was just that one time. I only remember him 'cause the situation struck me as funny. We're drinking beers together and he's got no idea I've been meeting his girlfriend in a motel room five nights running."

Macy peered over the bar at The Whitefish, looking for some sign of life. It was eleven in the morning and the place was deserted. On the drive over, she'd called the manager and had been assured that Lana would be working.

"Hello," she said. "Is anyone here?"

The door to a storeroom opened and Lana stepped out, carrying several boxes stacked on top of one another. She didn't see Macy until she put them down on the counter. She took a little jump back and nearly upset a tray of freshly washed glasses.

"Fuck, you scared me."

Macy didn't apologize. "Lana, we need to talk."

Lana took out a utility knife and sliced open a box containing bags of potato chips. "I already told you everything I know."

"That's not for you to decide." She gestured to the empty tables. "Would you rather do this here, or come down to the station?"

"I thought you were looking for some guy named Ethan Green. As far as I know, I've never met the guy."

"I interviewed Nick Childs this morning."

"What's that got to do with me?"

"Can we sit?"

Lana plucked a glass from the countertop and poured herself a couple of measures of whiskey. "This time I'm going to have that drink."

"Suit yourself."

Macy dropped down in one of the many booths. The table's surface was sticky. She slipped her notebook and pen from her bag and waited patiently for Lana to finish her drink.

"While you're over there taking your time, I'd like a Diet Coke."

She moved glacially. "Ice?"

"Yes, please."

Lana leaned over the table and wiped it down with a wet rag before handing Macy her drink. "I suppose Nick Childs told you all about me."

"He did."

"I knew that little runt was going to ruin my life the moment he showed up here. I didn't just come here to hide. I wanted a fresh start. Wilmington Creek. What are the odds that asshole walks in the door?"

"It does seem ironic. When was this?"

"About two months ago." She sat opposite Macy, swirling the remains of the whiskey. The ice tinkled against the glass. "I told him that I'd put all that behind me, but he threatened to expose me if I didn't cooperate."

"By cooperate, I take it he wanted you to take him on as a client again."

"No, it was worse than that. He wanted it for free. I was so afraid he'd say something. He'd come in with his friend and just sit at the bar watching me. Whenever John was here I made a point of acting like we weren't together. I was already worried that John's family wouldn't think I was good enough, but this was far worse. If Nick Childs talked, I'd have to walk."

"I've met John's family. You had nothing to worry about. They seem to be pretty messed up."

"John was thinking of going into politics. Even if I got rid of Nick Childs, there would be others. I'd be looking over my shoulder for the rest of my life."

"What did you do?"

"I told John I wasn't sure about us and I needed time."

"That's not how you felt though."

"No, I really loved him. Through and through loved him." She pulled a Kleenex out of a pocket and wiped her tears. "I couldn't risk him finding out though. He'd have never understood. I was all set to leave town, but then Jean overheard Nick threatening me and kicked him out of the bar. I was sure he'd come back, but I never saw him again. After a while I began to believe it would be okay. That's when things between me and John started to yo-yo. He didn't trust me any-more and he'd made promises to Tanya. It was a mess. One minute we were together and the next he was telling me it was over."

"You seem a bright girl. You must have known your actions would come back to haunt you."

She pressed the tissue to her eyes. "I needed the money. My mother hasn't been well for a long time. She can't work. There's no insurance. I did it for her. Not for me. For her. I lied and said it was to pay for school, but I didn't see a penny of what I made. I don't know what would have happened if I hadn't taken care of things."

"If that's the case, I'm truly sorry."

"And then I finally have a chance at being happy and, of all people, Nick Childs shows up." She lowered her voice. "I didn't even have that many clients. If I didn't like the look of them I'd steer clear. Nick seemed all right."

"No offense, Lana, but you're a terrible judge of character. Nick is a convicted felon. He's served time for multiple offenses, including aggravated sexual assault and armed robbery."

"Shit."

"That's an understatement."

"What happens now?"

"That really depends on Nick Childs. If he keeps his mouth shut, no one will be the wiser."

"I'm tired of running."

"Are you sure? It's not just Nick you have to worry about. Charlie is still out there somewhere."

"The worst has happened. I'm not afraid anymore."

"All the same. I advise you to continue to take precautions."

"I'm sorry I didn't tell you everything before. I know I've wasted your time."

"I'm going to pretend it never happened."

"Thank you. That means a lot to me." She drained the remainder of the whiskey. "I have to get back to work or Jean will go ape shit."

Macy gathered her things and made her way to the door. "I'll keep an eye out for news about Charlie. I'll let you know if I hear anything."

Being careful to take the route marked out as safe by the fire investigators, Macy picked her way through what was left of Lindsay's home. Water no longer dripped from the exposed rafters. Twenty-four hours after the fire, the house was bone dry. In places the ceiling was reinforced with freshly cut two-by-fours. Other than the linoleum floor, there was little that remained of the kitchen. The officers stationed out front told her Ryan was in the cellar. Macy stuck her head through an opening in the back wall of the kitchen. Acrid dust swirled in the lamplight. The wooden stairs had been replaced with a ladder. She took a deep breath.

"Ryan, are you down there?"

"Yep, watch your step. It's a mess."

Ryan stood alone in the middle of the low-ceilinged room. Cables and lights hung everywhere. Some areas had been completely consumed by the fire, but others were left untouched. Scorch marks ran up the walls, and in places the ceiling was open to the floor above. Shafts of light cut into the room at odd angles. They'd cleared a path through the debris.

"Where's your trusty sidekick, Aiden?"

"He's coordinating the team searching Ethan Green's property. They've been up there since dawn."

"Not your kind of thing?"

"Seems too much like hard work."

"What's the story with Aiden anyway?"

"Why? Are you interested?"

"I might be."

"Ryan, he's been married." She paused. "To a woman."

"Maybe he saw the light."

"I'm telling you, he's not your type."

"You sound like you have inside information."

"I might."

He laughed. "Someday you'll have to tell me everything."

"You'll have to wait until I write my memoir."

"As long as I'm in the acknowledgments."

"Wouldn't dream of leaving you out. Can we get to work now?"

Ryan switched on a flashlight and pointed it to what was left of a storage unit. "Whoever did this knew what they were doing."

"What am I looking at?"

"The landlord is a retired doctor. Instead of destroying old patient records, he kept them here."

"That's pretty creepy, but go on."

"Everything was pulled out and piled up before being doused in gasoline." He poked at a thin sheen of gray residue on the charred remains of a folder. "I'm pretty sure that's candle wax. We've found it in almost every room in the house."

"What's the significance?"

"White utility candles can be bought in almost any hardware or home store. Cut them to the desired size, set them on top of your flammable material, and leave them to do their thing. They burn at a rate of one inch every forty-five minutes, giving the arsonist plenty of time to get away and establish an alibi before the fire starts."

"Neat trick."

"Low-tech and pretty much untraceable."

"Did you find anything else?"

"Nothing you can use. If you hadn't come along when you did, there's a good chance the fire wouldn't have been ruled as arson. Other than what you pulled out the bedroom window, this wax is all we have. And I don't think anyone would have gone looking for it if you hadn't found evidence that an accelerant was used. The accelerant was poured on the soft furnishings, beds and sofas. Whoever did this was careful not to leave any burn patterns on the floors."

"It seems like they were counting on us not finding Lindsay's body up at the canyon. They must have been wanting to destroy physical evidence in the house and her car."

"Looks that way."

"Kind of odd that her killer took such lengths to hide evidence of Lindsay's murder, given how publicly John Dalton was killed."

"Maybe Lindsay wasn't part of his master plan."

"Which would mean there is a master plan. The neighbor, Tyler Locke, said he saw a car drive by his house a little before ten."

"That was probably the arsonist. By the way, I thought we'd decided we were looking for Ethan Green. You seem a little reticent about mentioning him by name."

"I found all of Lindsay's case notes on the mainframe. She didn't seem close to finding Green. In fact, she was growing more convinced that he'd left town or died."

"Are you tracking down everyone she spoke to?"

"So far they're sticking with what they told Lindsay. Nobody has seen Ethan since last summer."

"Have they found anything out on his property?"

"There's no cell phone reception up there, so I have no idea what's going on."

"Could it be that someone in his militia wanted to pick up where Ethan left off? At one point he had a lot of followers. Someone could be using his gun."

"The FBI and Ray think otherwise. They believe Ethan Green is behind all this."

"What's your next move?"

"Since I already drove all the way out here, I'm going to walk over and have another word with Tyler Locke. He may have remembered something else about the car he saw. At the very least, I want to get his thoughts on Ethan Green. Maybe John Dalton had some sort of disagreement with him in the past. John's niece witnessed an argument. She couldn't identify Green from a series of photographs, but she's awfully young to be relied on as a witness."

There was a handwritten note taped to the front door. Tyler was out in the garage. She cupped her eyes with her hands and looked inside the house. Tyler had tidied the place up since she'd last visited. There was a faint smell of cleaning products, and smoke. Through the back windows she could see a mound of rubbish smoldering in the backyard. It glowed like the lit end of a cigarette.

The double doors to the garage were shut, so Macy went around to the side entrance. She ran her eyes along the back fence of the property and peered into the half-dug fallout shelter. She couldn't shake the feeling that she was being watched. At the side door she paused and gazed out across the yard and saw no one. She knocked on the half-open door and stepped inside the garage. Fragmented light filtered through the small windows along the back wall. She tried the light switch, but it wasn't working. Tyler's Suburban was parked inside, facing toward the garage doors. His bald head was leaning against the window on the driver's side. He looked like he was asleep. She took a cautious step forward.

"Tyler Locke, it's Detective Macy Greeley."

Tyler didn't move. She waited.

"I'd like to have a word with you about the car you saw the other night."

Macy removed her gun from its holster and stayed well back as she rounded the vehicle on the driver's side. Thick orange electrical cables stretched from a hole cut through the masonry to the car's side window. Tyler's mouth and nose were covered with wide strips of silver duct tape. His bare head was unnaturally pale.

She ran for the door. Outside, the backyard was bigger than she remembered, the sun hotter. The force of the blast lifted her into the air like a kite before sending her stumbling down the steep sides of the freshly dug hole. She spit up dirt and dust as she struggled to her hands and knees. The Suburban's back bumper had skewered the hard-packed soil just a few feet from her head. It was bent like a frozen smile. She pointed her gun up at the sky, scanning the limited horizon for any sign of a threat, but she was shaking too much to hold the gun steady. She shoved it into its holster and crawled up the earthen slope.

The ringing in her ears was so strong she was thrown off balance. She staggered to her feet and held on to her right arm. A sharp pain ran down its length. All the back windows of the house were shattered, and scattered debris burned on the dead grass and in the trees. The garage was in flames; two of its walls were blown clean away.

Tyler's car was half buried in a deep crater that had been punched into the center of the concrete floor.

Two figures moved through the smoke. Jessie Dalton was the first to emerge. She ran toward Macy.

"Where's Tyler? Is he okay?"

Macy swallowed. Her hearing was starting to come back. She caught some of what Jessie said, and guessed the rest. She tried to piece together the last few minutes. She craned her neck so she could see over Jessie's shoulder. Dylan was pacing back and forth a few feet away from what was left of the garage. His mouth was wide as if from screaming. Macy's voice sounded muted in her head. She had to yell to be heard.

"Tell Dylan to get back."

"You should sit down."

More shouting. The group of officers who had been assigned to Lindsay Moore's home arrived. Ryan was still in his protective overalls. A couple of patrolmen attempted to move Dylan away from the garage, but he started swinging at them. One tried to grab him and he twisted away. He turned to the garage and called Tyler's name. Macy could hear him clearly now.

Jessie started to walk away. "I need to go talk to Dylan."

Everything was starting to spin. Macy dropped to her knees in the dry grass. "That's not a good idea. Stay here."

"He'll listen to me. It will be okay."

Macy fought against being physically sick. "Look at him, Jessie. He doesn't even know where he is right now. Let them do their job."

"They don't know him like I do."

Macy closed her eyes. "Talk to the guy in the white overalls. He'll understand."

Dylan paced back and forth in front of the fire, turning away whenever Jessie tried to speak to him. She waited, hands tucked deep in her pockets. She tried again. She reached for his lower arm, but he threw her off. He stared at what was left of Tyler's car. His face was twisted in pain. He put his hand to his mouth and dipped his head. Jessie started talking and this time he listened. Their heads were bent toward each other as if in prayer. Jessie led him to the front of the house, where he sat in the shade of the porch with his eyes shut tight. Inches apart, Jessie stayed by his side. She seemed to be saying the same thing over and over. Macy was nearby, being tended to by Ryan. As far as she could tell, the two friends never once touched.

20

With a patrol car following close behind, Dylan drove north toward Collier but pulled in at a truck stop a little south of town. It was getting late and the back lot was filling with eighteen-wheelers. Even with his windows closed and the music turned on he could hear the roar of engines. The ground shook as they crawled by. His mother, Sarah, was working behind the counter. He could see her move along the length of the bar, refilling glasses with a tall pitcher of water. When he was younger he'd come and visit her sometimes. She'd make him ice-cream sundaes and brag about him to whoever came in. He came to visit less often after his father moved out. She'd been having an affair with one of the cooks. His name was Parker and he was a pretty nice guy, but it hadn't lasted long enough for Dylan to get used to him hanging around the house, the smell of fried food clinging to his clothes. Other men followed, but it was Tyler who'd stuck it out the longest. Even though he was gone most of the time, she still considered him to be the *one*. Dylan knew the feeling wasn't mutual, but his mother didn't want to hear anything he had to say on the subject. In her eyes, Tyler could do no wrong.

Dylan put his truck in park and cut the engine. He needed to be the one to tell her. If he left it any longer someone else would get to her first or she'd see it on the news. She acted tough, but he knew better. Sarah was worn thin. Her voice was ragged from smoking and her legs ached from a lifetime of working on her feet. She was sixteen when she'd dropped out of high school and gotten a job at the diner. She was eighteen when she'd gone into labor during the breakfast shift. She took two weeks off before heading back. There was no choice. They needed the second paycheck and the health insurance that came with it. She worked days and Dylan's father got a job as a night security guard. There was really no way it was ever going to last. Sarah would not thank Dylan for the news he was about to deliver.

Dylan approached the officers who'd been sent to keep an eye on him and spoke to them through their open window.

"This may take awhile. Do you mind waiting out here?"

They told him to take his time.

The diner's interior hadn't changed much in the past twenty-six years. Only a four-alarm fire could lift the deep fug that had settled into the woodwork. Dylan removed his baseball cap out of habit, and stood in the entrance. It wasn't a place to come for a quiet meal. Growing up he'd often dreamed of taking his mother away from all this, but that was never going to happen. She'd also settled into the woodwork. Work was how she defined herself. She knew everyone and everyone knew her. This was the first place she was ever welcomed with open arms.

Dylan felt calmer than he'd been in days. It was as if he'd been bled dry. There was nothing left of the nervous energy that had been plaguing him. The worst had happened. Tyler and John were dead. It had a strange effect on him. He felt more alive than he had in months. All that adrenaline that was constantly pouring out of him suddenly made sense. He understood perfectly what was required of him. He looked down the length of the diner. It was a full house. His mother was busy. He caught sight of the television screen in the next room. The news was on. He had to act fast.

Someone who looked like they'd had too much to drink brushed past him and he was knocked into the cigarette machine. Several pairs of eyes, including his mother's, turned on him. Sarah nodded toward an empty stool and dropped a menu down on the counter in front of it.

"You're not looking so hot. You better sit down before you fall down."

Dylan eased onto the stool but didn't open the menu. His mother came back by and lifted an eyebrow. "What brings you here?"

"Is there someplace we can talk? Maybe Traci's office."

She rolled her eyes. "It's the dinner rush. Can it wait?"

"No, it can't. We need to talk."

"Give me a sec. I'll see if I can take my break early."

There was a commotion at the far end of the restaurant. Other diners rose from their seats and cheered as two men squared off against each other across a table crowded with empty plates. Dylan looked up at the sound of his name being called. His mother's ex-boyfriend, Parker, slid two plates of food under the warming lamps. He waved to Dylan and smiled. That was another thing Sarah had a talent for. She collected ex-boyfriends. With the exception of Dylan's father, she'd managed to remain friends with every man she'd ever slept with. Dylan looked down the length of the counter for his mother, but she'd gone to break up the fight. Head held high, with her ponytail bouncing up and down, she walked toward the table where the men were now close to exchanging blows. A busboy followed close behind. She'd learned the hard way how to handle situations like this. When Dylan was five, she was hit on the side of the head with a baseball bat. She had only partial hearing in her left ear and was missing two of her back teeth. Since then her diplomacy skills had sharpened. She could read a room better than most. Within seconds the argument was over and the two men were seated again. She cleared the table and made small talk. She left them laughing. With the fight over, the rest of the diners returned to their seats.

Dylan glanced over to the television again. The news cameras were focused on Tyler's house. The burned-out garage was clearly visible. Sarah walked toward him, unaware. She even smiled. Dylan went over to meet her, but a waitress named Tempi stepped between them. She grabbed Sarah by the arm and jerked a thumb toward the television set.

"Sarah, it's Tyler. Something's happened. It's on the news."

Sarah met her son's eyes and froze.

Dylan couldn't speak. He tried to swallow, but his mouth was bone dry. They stared at each other. Sarah was soon surrounded. People were laying hands on her like she was a holy relic. He pushed his way through and held his mother in his arms. She was so birdlike. It had been so long since they'd hugged that he'd forgotten this about her. He remembered what Jessie had kept saying to him earlier. He repeated it word for word.

"I'm here for you. I love you. Don't you ever forget that."

She buried her head in his chest. She was shaking so much he had trouble containing her. He kissed the top of her head and stroked her hair. Everyone in the restaurant was watching them now. Not one person spoke. All that noise had distilled down to his mother's quiet grief.

Dylan sat alone and sweating in his living room. His dog was panting in the corner. It had been pacing the house since he arrived home. He'd taken him outside and doused him with water from the garden hose. The house now stank of wet dog and Sarah's cigarettes. Most of the lights were off and the television was silent. There was a loaded rifle on the table in front of him. He checked his handgun again and set it down on his lap. The last time he'd looked in on his mother, she was sprawled across the bed clinging onto a wad of tissues. He closed and locked her window and left her sleeping in the airless room that always smelled like her favorite perfume. After they'd come home from the diner, they'd talked for the first time in what seemed years. Her popping one cigarette between her lips after another and him popping open beer cans. Sarah was full of regrets. She and Tyler had argued the last time they were together. She hadn't been able to reel him back in the way she usually did. When she left his house she'd had a feeling she'd never see him again.

If I'd known it was going to be the last time I saw him, I would have tried harder. She had started to cry. *I don't even have a picture of the two of us together to remember him by. He didn't really love me that way,* she'd said, tucking her feet under her body as she sat back against the pillows, her eyes drooping with each word. *I was never enough for him. Sometimes I'm sure he thought I was too old.*

Dylan hadn't known how to respond. His feelings about their relationship had always been ambivalent.

I think there was another woman back in Georgia. At least that's the impression I got when I tried to visit him. Did you know about her? He must have told you.

We didn't talk about stuff like that. It would have been awkward.

You're just like your father that way. Never talking. Never asking for anything. That man could give me the silent treatment like it was nobody's business.

Can we not talk about Dad? He's got nothing to do with this.

She'd blinked a few times before focusing in on him again. *I feel so groggy. I can barely keep my eyes open.*

It's the pills I gave you.

Her voice had slurred. *Tyler was trying to make me understand what's been going on with you. He loved you like a brother. Did you know that? It made me jealous. Still does. I just can't believe he's really gone.*

Neither can I.

He said he was coming home for good soon.

Not that soon. One more deployment is what he told me. It was going to be at least another year.

She had yawned. *I suppose we should go see his family tomorrow. His mom hates me.*

Tyler didn't care much for her so I wouldn't let that worry you.

Dylan, you aren't going anywhere, are you? You're going to stick around for a while.

Dylan turned off the light. *I might. I might not.*

I need you here. I'm all alone now.

Dylan leaned his forehead against her door frame and closed his eyes. Sarah had a way of shaping the world to suit her own needs. She wasn't an especially supportive mother. The day his father moved out she'd declared that Dylan was the man of the house and left him to his own devices. As far as he knew he was the only senior at his high school that paid rent. She didn't seem to notice that he'd recently lost the two people that mattered most to him in the world. He tucked his mother into bed and stubbed out her last cigarette before telling her to get some sleep. When she asked him to stay he told her he'd be right next door. When she told him she loved him he closed the door.

There was a single patrol car parked out front. Through the bay window he could just make out the front hood reflecting light from a lone streetlamp. Fifty yards farther on, the tarmac gave way to gravel and Wilmington Creek gave way to the big sky country. He walked over to the back door and peered out in the yard. There was nothing to see. Darkness bled from every shadow. Beyond the back fence was the municipal graveyard. The tombstones on this end were the oldest and jutted from the soil at odd angles.

Headlights trailed across the north-facing wall of the living room and the big engine of a police cruiser rumbled a few seconds longer before going quiet. Dylan hid his guns under the sofa and went to answer the door before Aiden Marsh had a chance to ring the bell.

They sat at the kitchen under a chandelier fashioned from stained glass. Aiden had brought his own coffee and Dylan drank beer out of a pint glass he'd smuggled out of an airport pub in England.

Aiden's uniform was rumpled and covered with dust. There were sweat stains under his arms and at some point he'd spilt something down the front of his shirt. He apologized for his appearance, explaining that he'd spent the day searching Ethan Green's property.

"You were closer to Tyler than anyone."

"Him and John were like brothers to me."

"How are you holding up?"

A shrug. "Would it be wrong to admit that this seems normal?"

"No, it wouldn't be wrong to feel that way, but you do know where you are right now. This isn't normal for Wilmington Creek."

"I'm well aware of where I am. Right. Now."

"That's not what I'm hearing."

Dylan sat back in his chair. "What are you hearing?"

"The officers I spoke to said you became aggressive when they tried to move you away from the garage."

"I've not had to face shit like this since the day I was wounded. I am truly sorry for what I might have said or done."

"They know you're having difficulties."

"That's the problem with living here. Everyone seems to know. It makes me want to get away and make a fresh start."

"I hear demons like to follow a man."

"I hear that too."

"There are people here who care about you. They want to see you through this."

"Like my mom? She doesn't seem to notice that I'm hurting too."

Aiden glanced down the hallway and lowered his voice. "No, like Jessie. I hear she was the one who talked you down."

Dylan took a sip of his beer. His left eye was twitching. He could feel the pulse jumping around inside the lower lid. He was sure Aiden could see it too. He blinked a few times, but it wouldn't go away.

"Maybe I'll just take Jessie with me? She could keep me in line."

"Now you're just talking crap."

"Yeah, I'm good at that sometimes." He rubbed his eye. "I'd start over if I could. I'd rather lose everything I know than walk around with what I've got in my head."

"I'll never understand why you signed up. For John it made perfect sense, and Tyler didn't really have much of a choice, but you never belonged over there."

"I blame it on a total lack of imagination." He pointed an unlit cigarette at Aiden. "The things I saw . . . It was not all right."

Dylan's dog barked and they both looked out the window. Another patrol car had pulled up. The officers chatted through their open windows.

Aiden looked at his watch. "The night shift has arrived."

"I'll be sure to bring them coffee in the morning."

Aiden slid a piece of paper across the table. "This is the statement you gave to the officers at the scene. Is there anything you'd like to add to it?"

Dylan looked it over for a few seconds, his eyes barely glancing at the page. "No, it's all there. Jessie stayed here last night so we were together all day. We were on the way to the ranch when we both got the same text from Tyler telling me to come to his house at sixteen hundred hours."

"Was he usually so specific about the time?"

"No, that was a new one. I just figured he was going a bit commando. We've all been on edge because of what happened to John."

"We found Jessie's car out on Ethan's property. Do you have anything to say about that?"

"She came to believe Ethan Green was her daddy and went to pay her respects. When I found her she was so drunk she could barely walk. Her mother wrote some bullshit about some hot springs in a journal so Jessie went to find them. She figured if they were real then all the other stuff her mother has been saying might be true as well. I don't want to think what might have happened if I hadn't shown up. Annie needs to stop spouting her bullshit."

"You're right that Annie needs to stop. They may have had an affair, but Ethan isn't Jessie's father. DNA doesn't lie. The analysis from the crime scene came back this evening. Jessie and John couldn't be Ethan's children."

"That's really fucked up. Jessie believed it was true." He fingered his phone. "I need to call her."

"I've been trying, but she's not picking up."

"She's pretty upset."

"We all are. I've got a detective in the hospital and half the valley's police force up here investigating crime scenes. Stuff like this doesn't happen in Wilmington Creek."

Dylan played with the lighter, but did not light the cigarette. "Macy Greeley? How is she?"

"They're keeping her in the hospital tonight as a precaution."

"I imagine her ears will be ringing for some time."

"She's okay. No concussion, but she has some bruising from the fall she took."

"Tyler's fallout shelter actually came in handy. Oh, the irony."

"Did he talk to you about what he was doing out there? Aside from that particular project, he seemed fairly sane."

"That's because he was sane." He shook his head. "I humored him. It was a pretty ambitious project for one guy and a backhoe, especially when you consider he was shipping out again soon. What happened, anyway? Did a gas tank explode or something?"

"It wasn't an accident. We found a detonator beyond the fence line. It was set to manual. Detective Greeley saw Tyler. He was sitting in the front seat of his truck and appeared to be unconscious. His mouth was bound with duct tape. Given you'd received a text message asking you to come to the house, it seems probable that you and Jessie were meant to be there when it went off. What I want to know is why Ethan Green is targeting you and your friends."

"You need to talk to Jessie."

"How about you save me the time it takes to drive over there?"

"It's not my story to tell."

"You're lucky I'm too tired to arrest your ass for obstruction."

Dylan held out his arms, wrists facing upward, fists clenched. "I'll go quietly. I'm too tired to resist."

Aiden eased his chair back. "Are you sure Jessie is going to tell me what I need to know?"

"It's about the only thing I am sure of."

Aiden walked into the living room and looked around. "You stay out of trouble tonight. We've got two uniforms stationed out front. I don't want you to take a shot at them if they come around back to check on things."

Dylan tipped another can of beer into the empty pint glass. "I suggest you tell them not to come around back then."

Aiden headed for the door. "Get some sleep. I'll call you in the morning."

Dylan's dog let out a low growl, but stopped short of barking. Dylan shook himself awake. He was slumped down on the sofa with his rifle across his lap. His leg felt like it was on fire. He stretched it out in front of him. The pain was sobering. He focused in on it. He rubbed his eyes and glanced around the room. He stood up with difficulty and walked out onto the back porch, carrying his gun in one hand. His dog came along and stood beside him. There wasn't much to see. The concrete porch was cool on his bare feet. He stepped out on the grass and walked along the length of the house.

His mother's bedroom light was on. She'd opened the window. A slight breeze lifted the curtain fabric. At first he thought she might be talking in her sleep. Her voice was breathy and excited, rising and lowering in pitch and speed. He caught fragments, but they made no sense. She said, *I promise I'll be there* more than once. He thought she might be on the phone to her sister in Boise. Last he heard, his aunt was pregnant with her third child, but still living on her own. She and

Sarah hadn't always gotten along. Dylan lit a cigarette and waited to hear more, but the conversation had ended. He went back inside. There was a missed call from Jessie on his cell phone, but she didn't pick up when he returned the call. He tried Wade's number and got hold of him on the first ring.

"Wade, it's Dylan. How's Jessie? I've got a missed call."

"Far as I know, she's sleeping."

"You got cops keeping an eye on things?"

"There are a couple out front, plus Jeremy has some of our boys patrolling the grounds. You okay over there?"

"Aiden left a couple of hours ago." He peeked out the front window. "There's a patrol car parked out front."

"Fucking Ethan Green. I always hated that asshole. Tyler and me, we had our differences, but I am sorry. No one deserves to go like that."

Dylan found that he couldn't speak.

"Dylan, you still there?"

"Yes."

"I think you should come up here and stay with us for a bit until all this blows over. I've got a spare room."

"I appreciate that."

"You're like family. Jessie needs you around. Would be good for Jeremy too."

"I'll keep that in mind. I've got my mom here. She needs me too."

"Just so long as you're looking after yourself."

"I'm doing my best."

"Well, I better get going. It's going to be another long night."

Dylan said goodnight and hung up. He'd slept for two hours. Anything could have happened. In the kitchen he prepared a fresh pot of coffee. He heard a door creak on its hinges and stepped out into the living room. The light in the hallway was on and the door to the spare bedroom was wide open. He picked up his gun and tucked it in the back of his jeans.

"Mom?"

He heard a loud thump and backed up against the wall. A closet door slid shut.

"Mom, is that you?"

Dylan reached for his gun at the same time his mother stepped out of the spare room. Her face was ragged from crying and she carried an empty suitcase. She stared up at him, her features fiercely lit by the overhead light. She pulled the headphones away from her ears. Her eyes were so alert she looked feverish.

"I'm going to my sister's for a few days," she said, bustling down the hallway toward her room. "I'm too scared to stay in this house another night."

Dylan kept his gun pressed tight against the small of his back so she couldn't see it. He took his finger off the trigger and closed his eyes for a second. His heart was pounding hard in his chest. He would say nothing that would keep her from going. She was right. She wasn't safe in her own home. Seconds later he heard the clatter of metal hangers as she sifted through the clothes in her closet. The opening and shutting of dresser drawers soon followed. He couldn't imagine her lasting long at her sister's place in Boise, but she seemed to be packing like she was planning on going away for some time. He stood in the doorway and watched her move back and forth from suitcase to the dresser. She'd replaced her headphones and was singing. Her voice was the sweetest sound he'd heard in a long time.

21

Aiden stood at the end of Macy's hospital bed with his hat in his hands. She'd been given a private room on the sixth floor, over-looking a rooftop courtyard. Morning sun cut through the haze. The Whitefish Range was visible in the distance.

"I'm happy to see that you're still in one piece."

Macy focused on a fixed point on the opposite wall. The headache wasn't getting any better, but at least the dizziness had passed. "It was a close call." She slipped out of the bed and nearly stumbled, her legs felt so weak. "We have to question everyone again. If Green is really responsible, someone around here must have been in contact with him."

"We've already started. Anything you need?"

Macy turned away from Aiden. "The only thing I *need* is to get out of the hospital gown. Untie me."

"Are you sure you're well enough to leave?"

"One night in Collier County Hospital is more than adequate." She grabbed her T-shirt off the back of a chair but stopped moving when she caught sight of the look on Aiden's face. "What's wrong? Haven't you seen a woman in her underwear before?"

"It looks like someone took a few shots at you with a baseball bat."

"It feels like it too. Nothing is broken though." Macy tried to put on her shirt, but raising her arms hurt too much. "A little help."

"They found the detonator out behind the garage. It was set to manual."

"Meaning whoever it was saw me coming and decided to push the button anyway."

"It looks that way. Your friend Ryan is pretty impressed with the hardware. Military. Very high-tech."

"Candles were used to start the fire at Lindsay's house. Our killer isn't consistently high-tech."

Aiden helped her into her trousers one leg at a time. "Maybe at Lindsay's place he had to use what was on hand but Tyler's murder was planned?"

"And we circle right back to motive again. Which is what exactly?"

"Tyler may have seen something. He was Lindsay's only neighbor."

"Then why not just shoot Tyler? An entire building was blown up. Doesn't that seem like overkill to you? Have you checked out Dylan and Jessie's story? I'm not imagining it, am I? They were there."

"They drove up right after it went off. Tyler sent them a text earlier in the day saying he wanted them to meet him at the house at four. They arrived a few minutes later than planned."

"I doubt Tyler sent that text. I'm guessing that Dylan and Jessie were supposed to be in the garage with Tyler when the bomb went off. We need to figure out why someone wants them dead."

"I went to see Dylan late last night. According to the first responders, he lost it. Jessie managed to talk him down, but it was touch and go."

"I remember that now. She impressed me. How's Dylan doing?"

"Very calm. Almost too calm. He told me this felt normal to him."

"That's messed up."

"We've got a unit watching his house. He's got guns. They weren't where I could see them, but I know they were there."

"Did you ask him why he and his friends are being targeted?"

"He wouldn't say anything. Told me it was Jessie's story to tell."

"Will she talk?"

"He says yes. I got a message as I was driving over here. She's expecting us."

"What about the search of Ethan's property?"

"No sign of Ethan. Vandals have pretty much destroyed the place. Every window is broken. Drug paraphernalia, empty beer bottles, and blocked toilets. Looks like someone was using it as a meth lab at some point. No one has spent the night there in a long time."

"You said his land was over a hundred acres? That's a lot of places to hide."

"Ray was true to his word. We had dog handlers, helicopters, and half of Flathead Valley's finest out there searching the property. The only interesting thing we found was Jessie Dalton's car."

"What was she doing out there?"

"According to Dylan, she went to some hot springs where Annie and Ethan Green used to go. When he finally tracked her down she was so drunk she could barely walk."

"All this time she thought Green was her father?"

"As far as I know she still does. We need to get over there and speak to her."

"The DNA analysis came back?"

"Yes. Green's profile is on the database. If he was any relation to John Dalton, his name would have come up in the report."

Tara Dalton was waiting for them in front of the ranch house. She was sitting on the porch, wearing oversized cowboy boots and a rose-printed dress that was a few sizes too big. She half ran, half stumbled to the patrol car as Aiden pulled into a space between two pickup trucks. Hands on knees and playing at being out of breath, Tara informed them that her mother was in the tack room and that she was to take them to see her. She promptly grabbed them both by the hands and dragged them toward the stables.

"Mommy and Grandpa aren't speaking."

Aiden ruffled Tara's hair. "You don't need to worry. It will get better soon."

Tara looked up at Macy. "Are you still sad about not being with your son?"

"A little, but it's nice to see you again."

"The lady that came to talk to me about Uncle John gave me sticker." Tara pulled at a sticker shaped like a golden star. It was curling up around the edges. "She said I was very brave."

"That's because you were."

"I think my mom needs a star."

Tara let go of their hands and ran up to a chestnut mare with a black mane. Its big head was hanging out the low doors of the stables. Tara stood on a low stool so she could stroke its long nose. It responded by nuzzling at her dress. She giggled.

"Trixie is hungry."

Macy looked around. "You have a lot of horses."

Tara corrected her. "They're quarter horses. I had a pony named Honey but she died."

"I'm sorry."

She shrugged. "Honey was pretty old. It happens."

They found Jessie sitting at a long wooden workbench, sorting through a pile of harnesses. The gloves she wore were stained with the dark wax she was rubbing into the leather. The usual collection of bracelets was roping both her wrists and a bandana was tied in a knot around her throat. It had slipped down, revealing finger-shaped bruises. It didn't look as if she'd slept. Her eyes were swollen and red and her hands trembled. She took off the gloves and kissed the top of her daughter's head. Her voice was hoarse.

"You found them."

Tara rolled her eyes. "I waited forever."

"I need you to do one more thing."

Tara swung from her mother's arm, nearly toppling them both over. "I'm tired."

"Well, this is easy. I want you to pick a DVD for us to watch together. I'll come up to the house when we're through here."

"Will we have lunch? I want peanut butter and jelly on white bread and I want you to cut off the crusts."

"It's a bit early for lunch. I'll make you a snack."

Tara waved back at them as she skipped out into the sunshine, her heels slipping out of her boots with every step.

Jessie brought them into Annie's office. Show ribbons and photos crowded the walls. She saw Macy looking at a picture of her mother.

"That's from before she was ill. Sometimes people forget how strong she used to be."

"It's hard to believe she's the same person."

Jessie fidgeted behind the desk. If she wasn't picking at her nails, she was twisting the ends of her hair. She kept glancing up at the door. Along one wall, documents were placed in neat stacks. Two large sacks were stuffed with garbage.

"I've been tidying up."

Aiden took the chair next to Macy. "Are you going to take over the business?"

"At the moment, I'm just trying to stay out of Jeremy's way. As a rule, he never comes in here."

"How are you holding up? Dylan said you were in a bad way when he found you the other night."

Jessie folded her arms across her chest. Even though it was hot, they were covered in goose bumps. "Dylan's one to talk. He's the one who lost it yesterday."

Macy slipped her notebook out of her bag. "We're making sure Dylan is getting the help he needs."

"Did you know that aside from a little clinic in Kalispell, the clos-est VA hospital is all the way over in Helena?" Jessie pulled her hair back from her face and adjusted the bandana. "He's stoned on meds most of the time. He's got no business driving all that way on his own."

Aiden cleared his throat. "It's going to take time."

"I don't think he believes that anymore."

Macy passed a piece of paper to Jessie. "Amongst other things, we need to talk about what happened yesterday afternoon. This is the state-ment you gave to responding officers. According to this, you were with Dylan when you both received a text from Tyler requesting that you come to his house at four o'clock in the afternoon. The text stated that he had something urgent to discuss regarding your brother's murder."

Jessie stared at the piece of paper.

"Is that correct, Jessie?"

"Yes. We drove over to Tyler's together."

"Why would you think that Tyler had information about your brother's murder?"

"He has friends that work for Alden. I thought maybe he'd heard something."

"We don't believe that the explosion was just meant for Tyler. Whoever set it off was waiting for you and Dylan. They nearly got me instead."

"You really think it was Ethan Green?"

"He's wanted for questioning."

Her voice cracked. "At that press conference that man said he was your prime suspect."

"He is."

"Did you know that he's also my father?"

Macy pulled another sheet of paper out of her file and handed it to Jessie. "That's not true. The DNA analysis from the crime scene came in yesterday. Ethan Green is a convicted felon. We have his

DNA on file. There was no match to John or anything else we found at the crime scene."

"My mother said—"

"It doesn't matter what your mother said. Ethan Green is not your father."

Jessie covered her face in her hands and started crying so hard it sounded like she was choking.

"We're under the impression that John also believed Ethan was his father. We think he may have been looking for him. Did he talk to you about it?"

Jessie grabbed a wad of tissues. "No, not a word."

Aiden leaned forward. "You'd said that you thought John was keeping things from you."

Her chin bobbed up and down.

"I think maybe he was just trying to protect you."

Jessie smoothed her fingertips along the edge of the desk. The rose tattoo on the back of her hand was partially hidden under a bandage. The skin around it was yellowing. "I read my mother's journals. She'd had an affair but never said who the guy was. I checked the employment files in my father's office because I thought it might be someone who used to work at the ranch. I found a file Jeremy was keeping on Ethan Green."

"They used to be friends."

"The year John and I were born, Jeremy paid Ethan thirty thousand dollars to stay away from our family. My mother had been hinting about something for a few days, but only told me Ethan was my father when I visited her a couple of days ago. She said that Jeremy couldn't have children."

Aiden rubbed his face. "I'm sorry, Jessie. I wish we could have gotten this information sooner. It would have saved you a lot of heartbreak."

"It's not your fault." She took a stack of photos from a drawer and pushed them across the table. "Ethan didn't stay away from us like he promised. These are from last summer. Dylan took them."

Macy laid the photos out on the tabletop one by one.

Aiden's voice broke. "Did he do this to you?'

"I'd been at The Whitefish. I was too drunk to drive home and he offered me a lift. We stopped by the mini-market and he bought me a Coke to sober me up. I remember that he insisted that I drink it. I thought he was looking after me, but as usual I got it wrong. Instead of taking me home he drove me out to Darby Lake. I woke up at two in the morning, half dressed, with Ethan lying on top of me. I thought he was dead. There was a big bruise on his forehead."

Macy stared down at an image of Jessie's swollen eye. "Do you remember hitting him?"

"That's one of the few things I do remember clearly from that night. I guess I should have hit him harder."

Aiden kept his voice low. "Jessie, did he rape you?"

"I don't think so. I know he tried." She closed her eyes for a second. "Nothing made sense. I was so panicked I had trouble breathing. I couldn't remember everything properly."

"Why didn't you call the police?"

"Calling John was what I always did when I was in trouble. I thought he'd sort it all out for me, but when he and Tyler got there they had other ideas. They kept saying that no one was going to believe it was an accident and that I'd end up in prison."

"What did they do?"

"John and Tyler dealt with Ethan, and Dylan took me home to his place."

Aiden's voice rose. "How exactly did they *deal* with Ethan?"

"They dumped his body into the deep end of Darby Lake."

Macy sat back in her chair. "It must have come as a bit of a shock to find out that Ethan is our prime suspect."

"We all thought he was dead. His truck is still there. You can see it now because the water is so low." Her voice trailed off. "He got out somehow and now he wants to kill us all."

"We'll know for sure soon enough. There's still a possibility it was an associate of Ethan's who found out what happened."

"None of us told."

"You can't be sure. Someone might have seen you getting into Ethan's truck that night or witnessed something up at the lake. We're interviewing everyone who was close to him."

"After I saw the press conference I wanted to go to the police, but Tyler wouldn't let me. We argued. He thought we should take care of Ethan ourselves." She almost whispered. "If he'd listened to me he'd still be alive."

Macy pointed to the bandana Jessie was wearing. "Jessie, what happened to your neck?"

"It's nothing."

"Did Tyler do that?"

"I don't want to talk about it."

Aiden leaned back in chair and sighed. "Stop being a victim, Jessie. It's never okay for a man to put his hands around a woman's throat."

She brushed away tears. "I'd never seen him so angry. If Dylan hadn't been there I'm not sure what would have happened."

Macy spoke quietly. "May I see?"

Jessie untied the bandana and lifted her chin.

"You should probably have that looked at."

"I don't want Tyler to be remembered for doing something like this. He was a good guy. It's the war. It changed him."

Macy tapped her pen on the table. "Jessie, you covered up a serious crime. There will be consequences. If you can show that you were forced to stay quiet you may have an easier time in the courts."

"I know."

"You really should have reported it. You didn't do anything wrong. You were defending yourself."

"Are you going to arrest me?"

Macy looked at Aiden. "What do you think?"

Aiden glanced down at the photos. "We'll work something out. I'm not going to be the one to put you in a cell for this."

Macy took the binoculars from Aiden and scanned the northern shore of Darby Lake. The area at the base of the cliffs was in shadow. "That's quite a drop. If he was alive when he went over I'd be surprised that he could survive the fall."

"You have to keep in mind that the water level is very low this year. Last summer the lake would have been a good fifteen feet higher."

"When will the divers be here?"

"Any minute now. We're going to need a salvage crew. The only way to get that truck out of the water is with a crane. That will take some doing if it's wedged into the rocks."

Macy sat down at a picnic table in the shade. The temperature had risen along with the humidity. It was stifling. On the news they were starting to talk about rain again.

"I don't think I've ever been this tired."

Aiden kept his eyes on the lake. "You should know that I overheard your argument with Ray Davidson."

"I was worried you might."

"You can't keep letting him treat you that way. You've got to draw the line."

"I don't think I should talk about this with you, or anybody."

"I disagree. I think you should scream about it. And just so you know, I don't have any agenda here."

"I keep hoping there will be a time when I finally give up on him."

"Imagine how good it will feel to walk away."

She shook her head. "I think it's easier when you've been in a relationship that's run its course. You can look back and see everything that went wrong and move on. I've not had that with Ray. It's difficult for me to let go when I don't know where it went wrong. I feel like we have unfinished business, and then there's Luke. He needs a father."

"What Luke needs is a mother who's happy. That's not going to happen until you move on." Aiden's phone buzzed in his hand and he looked at the message. "They're unloading the boats over at the ramp. We should head over there."

It was nearing dusk and clouds of insects danced above the still waters of Darby Lake. A mosquito buzzed near Macy's ear and she brushed it away. The police launches were anchored at the base of the cliffs. Aiden and Macy stood on the bow of the smaller one and watched as the divers prepared to get in the water. Finding the pickup truck had been easy. The cab's roof was less than four feet below the surface. Macy tried to be patient but she couldn't understand why they were bothering with wet suits and air tanks. She swam laps once a week at the gym a couple of blocks from the state police headquarters in Helena. As far as she was concerned, all that was needed to do the job was a waterproof flashlight and a pair of goggles. When at last the divers were ready, they tipped backwards off the side of the boat like they were on a day trip out on the Great Barrier Reef. A couple of minutes later both of them were swimming in her direction. The first one to the boat took his mask off and told her the news.

"There's definitely a body down there. Checked the license plate number as well. It's the vehicle you're looking for."

Macy stared out across the water. Despite what Jessie had told them, she hadn't really expected to find a body. She had a vague sense of unease. In a couple of hours it would be dark. They needed to move fast, but she wasn't sure what the next step should be.

The divers waited for instructions. "What do you want us to do?"

"What can you see? Is there a way of identifying who it is without opening up the car?"

The second diver shook his head. "No way. The head and torso are all tangled up in the air bags. They must have deployed when it hit the water."

"We're losing daylight. Get lights down there if you have to, and start photographing the scene." She turned to Aiden. "How long until Ryan is here? I'm sure he's seen this sort of situation before."

"They're leaving Tyler's place now."

"How soon can we get a crane out here to lift the truck? It would be better if we brought the body up in situ. I don't want to risk losing any evidence."

"I'd say tomorrow afternoon or maybe the day after. It looks like it's pretty wedged in there, so I'm not sure they'll be able to get it out in one piece. It's going to be tricky."

"I'm not sure we can wait that long. Ethan Green is our only suspect. We need to know if it's him that's down there."

"Who else would it be? Everyone else that was there that night is accounted for."

"You've got a point."

"Might have to start looking at Charlie Lott as a suspect again. He still hasn't turned up."

"But it makes no sense that he'd be involved. Aside from John Dalton's death, there's no motive. Besides, how would he have gotten hold of a gun that Ethan Green supposedly used to kill a highway patrol officer?"

Aiden brushed away a mosquito that had settled on his arm. "One of Ethan's followers, then?"

"Someone could have found out what happened and decided to go after them."

"What's the downside to opening up the roof and pulling him out that way?"

"We'd compromise the crime scene. Lose evidence."

"I think I'd better call Ray. He's the one who's been pushing Ethan as a suspect. Who knows? He may want to wait a while longer before being proven wrong."

"He hates when he's wrong."

"At this point I really don't give a shit."

"Anyway, all that aside. We really need to go through all of Ethan's known associates again and decide who to bring in for questioning. Start seeing if we can pull any of these strands together."

22

Aiden took the chair opposite Macy and signaled to the waitress. "Sorry we couldn't have dinner last night. By the time we
wrapped things up at the lake I'd lost the power to speak."

"You and me both."

"I imagine you needed some time to yourself anyway."

"What I needed was sleep."

"Did you get any?"

"Eight hours uninterrupted. I feel like a new woman."

"You look rested."

"Probably helps that I haven't had a drink in three days."

"Three whole days? Is that some sort of record?"

She didn't smile. "It might be."

He thanked the waitress for his coffee and took his first sip, gri-
macing because it was too hot.

Macy poked at her scrambled eggs. "Has Ray been in touch?"

"Not since I broke the news to him about the body we found up at
the lake."

She lowered her voice. "I imagine he's been busy covering his ass."

"As long as it's not at your expense."

"Don't worry, I've been keeping notes. I put my reservations about going ahead with the press conference in an e-mail and sent it to him before he went on air."

"Remind me not to mess with you."

She deadpanned, "Don't mess with me."

"Noted," he said, laughing as he picked up the menu. "What's on the agenda today?"

"Jeremy Dalton called late last night. He wants to come in for an update. He's heard some worrying rumors. I'll meet him over at the station in the next hour."

"Until we officially identify the body we're in a bit of a holding pattern. I've put a team together to interview that amended list of Ethan's associates we made up yesterday, but I'm not all that hopeful. I can't see any of them being loyal enough to do something like this."

"Some heavy equipment passed through town a half hour ago. I imagine it's the crane they'll use to lift the truck."

"I saw it too. It's a beast. The water is pretty shallow at that end so I hope it doesn't run aground."

"You'd think they could pull it out with a helicopter."

"Too close to the cliffs."

Macy placed her napkin on the table. "I thought as a matter of courtesy I'd put in a call to Tyler's commanding officer."

"It's a sad business."

"It's hard to imagine why those boys thought it was a good idea to cover up what happened to Jessie that night."

"They had a lot of experience in combat situations. They probably thought they could handle it on their own."

"But this wasn't combat. Jessie needed the sort of help they couldn't give her. If those pictures are anything to go by, she was in bad shape. She should have gone to the hospital."

"I'm not surprised she's had a relapse. The stuff Annie has been telling them. I hope she can keep it together. She's worked hard to stay

233

clean all this time." He looked around for the waitress. "I'm going to order at the counter to save time. Do you want anything else?"

"Just more coffee when she has a minute." Her phone buzzed and she checked the caller ID. It was Ray and she ignored it. She pulled Charlie Lott's file up on her laptop and scrolled through it, glancing up at Aiden when he returned to the table. "We're running out of suspects."

"Are you looking through Charlie Lott's file again?"

"He was a guitar player who dealt drugs to make ends meet. He didn't know anything about building bombs. Plus he didn't know Lindsay Moore. There's no motive." She sat back in her chair. "I'm troubled that the father of Lindsay's unborn child hasn't come forward. Someone got her pregnant, and she didn't strike me as the type of woman who slept around. It's a shame we didn't get a match on the DNA we took from the fetus."

"That just means the guy isn't in the database. The people we're interviewing again also had direct contact with Lindsay Moore. Something may come up."

"Ethan Green is still the most logical suspect, and he's been dead for a year."

"We're going to have to charge Jessie and Dylan with obstruction."

"They need help, not jail time." She took another stab at her eggs. "Sometimes I wonder why I went into law enforcement in the first place."

"If you want to stay sane you need an exit strategy."

"Do I now?"

"I've got mine all mapped out."

"The cynic in me is picturing a fifth of JD and a loaded gun."

"Christ, you need to take some time off."

"Tell me something I don't know."

"I have some land along the Flathead River and a few investors lined up. We're building a fishing lodge. It should be sweet."

"Sounds idyllic."

Aiden made room for the plate of food the waitress placed in front of him. He picked up a piece of bacon and took a bite. "What about you? Do you have an exit plan?"

"Rewriting it as we speak."

"Just so long as it doesn't involve whiskey and firearms."

She stole a piece of his bacon. "I'll keep you posted."

Despite his size, Jeremy Dalton looked a little lost waiting on the steps outside the police station. Macy shook his hand and guided him through the glass double doors. A couple of the officers stood up as he walked between their desks. He did not meet their eyes.

Macy closed the office door and apologized that Aiden wasn't there to meet with him. "He's heading out to Darby Lake. It's going to be a busy day."

Jeremy took off his hat and tucked his hair behind his ears. "I hear that you're expecting to find Ethan's body."

"That rumor is true."

"Two days ago the captain of the state police announced that Ethan Green was the prime suspect in my son's murder."

Macy hesitated. "It seems he was mistaken."

"I noticed it wasn't you talking to the press."

"I had reservations about going forward with Ethan's name at such an early stage. There wasn't anything in Lindsay Moore's notes that made me believe that Ethan was still active in the area. She was under the impression that he had either died or left the valley sometime last summer. There is still a possibility that someone loyal to Ethan could be involved in your son's murder. We're interviewing everyone who was close to him again."

"What about this Charlie Lott?"

"We're still looking. No one has seen him since he left his grandmother's house in Spokane last month."

"I need to know what happened out at the lake last summer. Dylan's not answering his phone and Jessie and I aren't speaking."

"We're still piecing together the events of the night of July thirteenth. Dylan and Jessie are the only witnesses, and so far their statements match up. We're waiting until we pull the truck from the lake this afternoon before making our findings public."

"I'd rather know everything now."

"I think you're going to find what I'm about to tell you very upsetting."

His small eyes flicked up at her. "My son died this week. I doubt it could get much worse."

"Mr. Dalton, I'm afraid that might not be the case."

"Try me."

"Last summer Ethan picked up Jessie in the parking lot at The Whitefish. It was late and she'd been drinking heavily and decided to sleep it off in her vehicle. He approached her and offered to give her a lift home. He took her to Darby Lake instead."

"That son of a bitch."

"She was physically assaulted, and she's not sure she stopped him before he could take it any further. Other than hitting him on the head with a rock, she remembers very little. She woke up and found him lying on top of her. She believed he was dead. Instead of calling the police she called John. He and Tyler dumped Ethan's body in the lake while Dylan took Jessie home. You should thank Dylan. He was smart enough to take photos of your daughter's injuries."

"Can I see them?"

Macy shook her head. "I wouldn't show them to you if I could."

"Until last summer, John was thinking about staying in the military. His contract was coming up for renewal, but he suddenly changed his mind. Before he left to rejoin his unit he told me he was needed more at home. Now I know why."

"Were you aware that Annie had told John and Jessie that Ethan Green was their father?"

"Are you serious?"

"We're not sure whether John really believed it, but Jessie did. I've informed her that DNA analysis of the crime scene proves otherwise. I assume you're aware that your wife had an affair with Green before they were born."

He stared down at his hands. "Back then Ethan was a heavy drinker. I doubt he remembers much of anything, whereas Annie obsesses on it. She's convinced that it was the best time of her life. I can't believe she'd lie to the kids like that."

"Given her mental state, she may not be aware that she's lying. Have you spoken to Jessie?"

"That may be difficult. We haven't talked much in the past ten years."

"I've seen the family photos up at your house. I get the impression that you used to be close."

"You wouldn't think so from what Annie says. She's been taking medication for bipolar disorder since high school. Sometimes when she was feeling good she'd stop her meds. She'd be euphoric one minute and suicidal the next. I admit that I should have been more patient." He rubbed his hands down his face. "I really tried hanging in there for a long time, but I could only take so much."

"That must have been hard on your children?'

"Jessie couldn't cope. She started staying out later and later and then not coming home at all. I was worried sick. Around the time she was sixteen it spiraled out of control. She was drunk or high or both most of the time. Barely made it to school. I can't tell you how difficult it is to sit back and have your heart broken on a daily basis."

"I hear you cut her off financially at one point."

"Even her therapist said I was out of options. She went missing for nearly four years. We think she was living on the streets in Denver for a while, Reno after that. Tara was two when someone dropped them off at the house in the middle of the night. Jessie was skin, bones, and bruises . . . She covers them up but I know about the cigarette burns and scars on her wrists."

"I figured there was a reason for all the bracelets she wears."

"We had her declared an unfit mother and were awarded sole custody of Tara. That might seem harsh but it's what finally got Jessie into rehab. She couldn't have access to her daughter until she was sober. It was blind luck that Tara turned out normal in the first place; I wasn't going to let Jessie near her again until she got help."

"I hope you find a way to reconnect with her. She needs you more than ever right now."

"Are you going to charge her?"

"It's up to the state attorney."

"These photos Dylan took. Are they compelling?"

"They are. Her phone records give us a time frame. She doesn't remember doing it, but she did text John earlier that night from The Whitefish, asking for a ride. If they'd come forward that night, I doubt she'd have been charged with anything."

"I feel like it's my fault. She knew I'd take Tara away again if I found out she'd been drinking."

"Don't blame yourself. Jessie is an addict, and you are right to put Tara first. I have a hard time understanding why your son and Tyler Locke thought it was a good idea to cover up what happened instead of going to the authorities."

"I hate to accuse those who can't defend themselves, but I doubt very much that it was John's idea. As a rule, he followed Tyler's lead. Tyler was his platoon sergeant, but the lines of authority have been fixed for a long time."

"I don't mean to pry, but you don't seem saddened by Tyler's death. Weren't you close? He worked up at the ranch for quite a few years."

"As close as one could get to him. Tyler had good intentions but he could be prickly at times. I was completely against taking him on, but Annie was determined to make it work."

"His juvenile record is sealed so I'm not sure what he got up to."

"Quite a bit is the answer. Annie caught him breaking into one of our storage units when he was fifteen. He was on the run from one of those youth camps they have during the summer down near Kalispell. Instead of calling the authorities, she made him dinner. I didn't realize he had a criminal record until it was too late to change her mind."

"Did the authorities tell you what he'd done?"

"I found out everything I could but I'm almost certain there was more. He'd stolen a few cars and robbed a liquor store at gunpoint. He'd also done a bit of dealing."

"It couldn't have gone too smoothly."

"I'm convinced he stole money off me on occasion but I don't have any proof. Some of Annie's jewelry went missing and she blamed herself for being absentminded. One of our female employees found his behavior offensive. That sort of thing."

"What do you mean by offensive?"

"Karen Walcott worked in the stables. She came to us a few months after she started, saying Tyler was harassing her. He'd asked her out a few times and didn't seem to want to take no for an answer. She claimed he was stalking her, hanging around her neighborhood late at night, calling her and hanging up, that sort of thing. Annie and I talked to him, but he denied it all."

"What happened?"

"Annie told Karen she was overreacting, so she quit." He paused. "The thing is, I kind of believed her. Tyler could be weird around women. It was around that time that Annie and I started having problems in our marriage again. I didn't want Tyler around anymore. We argued about him a lot."

Macy picked up her pen. "Do you have any idea where Karen is now?"

"I ran into her down at the rodeo in Cheyenne last year but she wasnt too keen to have anything to do with me. I got the impression she's still angry."

"Any idea what she's doing these days?"

"As far as I know she never married. A friend of a friend told me she ran a riding school in Cheyenne."

"I read that you brought charges against Tyler for theft?"

"A sizable quantity of fertilizer went missing. This was following the Oklahoma bombing so we had to report it. There were rumors that Tyler was planning on selling it to some militia group down near Billings, but nothing could be proved. God knows what they would have done if they got their hands on it. After I called the cops Annie didn't speak to me for months."

"You did the right thing."

"I have to admit I was looking for any excuse to get rid of him. John was at an impressionable age and I didn't like how he'd hang on Tyler's every word." He placed his thick hands flat on his lap. "I may have had issues with Tyler in the past, but in the end he made good. He's taken some serious knocks for our country."

"Were there hard feelings?"

"I don't think so. He came to me a few years back and thanked me for all we'd done for him . . . apologized for his behavior. I think he should be commended for turning his life around."

"Maybe you should extend the same generosity to your daughter."

"I'd like to. I'm just worried she'll throw it back in my face."

"She's lost so much. It would surprise me if she wasn't willing to meet you halfway."

"I hear you had a near miss yesterday."

"Thankfully, there was a big hole in the middle of the backyard to jump into."

"Tyler's famous nuclear fallout shelter."

"I was dubious but now I'm now a believer."

They both stood and shook hands.

"Thank you for taking the time to speak to me today."

"I'll let you know what we find today. Unfortunately, it looks like Jessie and Dylan will both need lawyers."

"I'm going to see one now."

. . .

As soon as Jeremy left the office, Macy opened her laptop. Karen Walcott ran a small riding school in the suburbs of Cheyenne. There was a photo of her on the home page of the Web site. She looked like she was in her late thirties. She had a nice smile, pale complexion, and thick dark hair. Macy called the listed number and it went straight to an answering machine. An automated voice informed Macy that Karen Walcott would return the call as soon as possible. Macy explained why she was calling and left her details. The phone rang less than a minute later.

She sounded out of breath. "Detective Greeley, this is Karen Walcott. I'm so sorry I missed your call."

Macy opened her notebook. "That's no problem at all. Thank you for getting back to me so quickly. Do you have time to talk?"

"Yes, of course."

"I understand you made a complaint against Tyler Locke when you were employed by the Daltons. It's been more than ten years, so I understand if you don't remember the details, but I'd be grateful if you could tell me everything you recall."

"Oh, you don't easily forget something like that. May I ask why you're asking after all this time? Has Tyler done the same thing to someone else?"

"That's what I'm trying to figure out."

"I knew I couldn't be the only one. He was so intense. The way he stared at me made my skin crawl."

"I want to know if he did more than stare."

"Mostly he followed me. I could be going to a bar as far away as Butte and he'd somehow manage to find me. The first couple of times I was polite, but then I confronted him at work. He told me I was a stupid bitch and that he wanted nothing to do with me. He was really abusive, but after that he quit following me so I figured it was worth it. A few weeks later I realized he was hanging around my house instead. He'd drive by with the headlights off, but I could see it was him."

"Did you ever think of calling the police?"

"I went to speak to Annie and Jeremy Dalton instead. I'd been working there for a few months by then. Annie and I had become close. I figured she would listen to me. The way she reacted you would have thought I was the one harassing Tyler. I've never felt so betrayed. To his credit, Jeremy tried to get Annie to see things from my point of view, but that woman wouldn't listen. I saw a completely different side to her that day. It wasn't pretty."

"Did you leave town after that?"

"Damn right, I did."

"Did Tyler try to make contact again?"

"There were a few late-night phone calls but thankfully no visits. Even though he never said anything, I knew who it was. He'd done the same thing when I was living in Wilmington Creek. Last year I opened a riding school so I had to put my address online. I've been really anxious but so far he's left me alone. I suppose that just means he moved on to someone else."

"I'm afraid that might be the case."

"Can you tell me what's going on?"

"I have your details. Once I get to the bottom of this I will call and explain everything."

Macy checked the time before venturing into the outer office. A couple of officers were working the phones. Most of the other staff was out at the lake or interviewing potential witnesses. Even by Wilmington Creek standards it was unusually quiet. The officer she'd met when she interviewed Lana put his phone down and waved to get her attention. He handed her a phone message.

"I didn't want to interrupt your meeting with Mr. Dalton. Aiden called. It looks like it will be another couple of hours before they raise the truck."

"Thanks. Anything else come through?"

"So far we've got nothing new from the interviews we've been conducting this morning. Everyone seems to have a solid alibi for the night John was murdered."

Macy headed for the office. "Keep digging. Someone must know something."

She closed the door and checked her phone. There were still no calls from the medical examiner in Helena, but Ray had tried calling her three times. She couldn't be bothered with checking her voicemail. She scrolled down to his number and put the phone to her ear.

"Ray, it's Macy."

"Hey, did you get my messages?"

"Yes, I'm heading out to the lake soon. We should know if it's Ethan Green within a couple of hours."

"I'm not sorry for the way I handled things. I based my decision to go forward with the press conference on the information we had at the time."

Macy scraped her hair away from her face and stared up at the ceiling. "Good thing I wasn't expecting an apology."

"I should have never accused you of putting our personal issues ahead of your job. That was out of order. I can only imagine how hurt you felt."

"Ray, I'd rather not talk about us right now."

"I need to know what you're thinking."

"I'm not thinking anything at the moment. I just want to sort this case out so I can get home to Luke."

"What about your health? I was told you spent the night in the hospital."

"It's just a few bruises. I didn't even have a concussion."

"Are you sure? I don't want you to overdo it."

She raised her voice "Ray, back off. I'm fine."

"I'm just concerned."

"I need to go. I promise we'll talk properly when I'm back in Helena."

"Will you keep me posted on developments?"

"I'll call you later when we know more."

Macy sat drumming her fingers on the desk. Tyler had barely been out of high school when Karen Walcott accused him of stalking her. In between he'd done five tours, and aside from stealing some fertilizer he had a clean record. According to his service record he was with his platoon in Afghanistan during the time Lana was being harassed. She put in a call to his CO in Afghanistan and wasn't surprised that it went straight to voicemail. After leaving him a message, she checked the cover sheet stapled to the front of Tyler's service record. Someone named Stuart Long had sent the e-mail. The address and phone number for the Fort Benning human resources department was listed below his name. While she waited to be put through to Stuart Long, she found the original e-mail on the mainframe and downloaded it to her computer.

"Stuart is in a meeting. Can I help you, ma'am?"

"My name is Detective Macy Greeley. I work as a special investigator for the state of Montana. I'm working on a case that involves an active duty platoon sergeant named Tyler Locke. I'm following up on the service record your office sent us last Wednesday. I need to speak to Mr. Long. I'm worried that the file may be incomplete."

"Are you sure Stuart Long was the individual who sent the file?"

"Absolutely, I have the original e-mail up on my screen right now."

"I'd like you to forward it to me so we can look into it from our end. Service records are normally distributed out of the U.S. Army Personnel Command Center in Kentucky."

"Is it possible Mr. Long's account was hacked?"

"I can't say. I'll know more once we have had a chance to look at the e-mail."

Macy typed in the clerk's e-mail address and hit the Send button. "If there's even a chance that Tyler Locke's service records have been altered, I need you to send me a valid copy right away."

"I'll have to speak to my supervisor. Sorting this out could take some time. Like I said, all requests would normally go through the command center."

"It can't wait. I'm in the middle of a murder investigation. I need to know if Tyler Locke was in Georgia during February of this year."

"I can't promise you anything, but I'll do what I can. We'll certainly get something out to you today."

After hanging up, Macy tried calling the medical examiner's office.

Priscilla's voice was sharp. "Who's this?"

"Priscilla, it's Detective Macy Greeley. You got a second?"

"If this is about your bomb victim it's going to have to wait. We're still sorting body parts. Excuse me." Priscilla covered the mouthpiece and shouted instructions before getting back on the line. "Listen, Macy, I've got two medical school interns puking their guts out. You're going to have to call me back later."

Macy was left listening to a dial tone.

Macy put in a call to Lana Clark but she didn't pick up. Macy looked up the number for The Whitefish and was relieved when the manager answered the phone immediately.

"Jean, this is Detective Macy Greeley. We spoke a few days back. I was wondering if Lana Clark was working today."

"She was supposed to, but she called in sick. Have you tried her at home?"

"There's no answer. Nothing on her cell phone either. Did you actually speak to her, or did she leave a message?"

"Yes, we spoke. It was about an hour ago. It's pretty dead here these days so I was none too bothered."

"How did she sound?"

"She seemed a bit out of it, which is unlike her, but I wouldn't say she was on death's door. I just figured everything that happened here is finally catching up with her. She tried to put on a brave face, but she was very fond of Joan."

"If you hear from her, can you tell her to give me a call immediately?"

"Will do. You guys making any progress? I don't think my customers feel too safe anymore. It's been bad for business."

"We're doing the best we can."

"Why doesn't that fill me with confidence?"

"Have a good day. I'll be in touch."

There was a knock and the same officer she'd spoken to earlier stood at the door. Macy invited him in.

"It's Dean, isn't it?"

"Yes, ma'am. Just wanted to keep you posted. I got another call from Aiden. He thinks you should head up to the lake now. They're making faster progress than predicted. Should have the vehicle out of the water within the next half hour."

"That's great. Thanks for letting me know." She offered him a chair but he remained standing. "Have you been in touch with Lana Clark recently?"

"I saw her a couple nights ago. Why?"

"I'm just concerned. I've been trying to get in touch with her and she's not picking up her cell or her home phone."

"She always has her phone with her."

"You know where she lives?"

"Sure. I've been out there a few times."

"I want you to go check on her."

"Do you think she's in trouble?"

"It's probably nothing."

"I'll head up there now."

Macy stopped him before he left the office. "Call me the second you know something."

"Yes, ma'am. I'm on it."

"Dean," she said, gathering her things. "Take someone with you."

. . .

Macy took the back roads up to Darby Lake. Overhead the sky was a silky gray, and the hay fields flattened out like inland oceans. Solitary houses wavered in the heat. Macy stopped at a four-way intersection and waited for the cross traffic to clear of the cars coming from the direction of Darby Lake. Except for the press, the picnic area was closed until further notice. Macy recognized the officer standing at the roadblock from when she'd worked in Collier. She shook his hand through the open window.

"Hi, Gareth."

"Hey, Macy, how you been?"

She gazed out the windshield. The road ahead buckled like wet floorboards. "I've been better. This heat is getting to me."

"Tell me about it. Another ten minutes of this and I'm going to pass out."

Macy reached over to the passenger seat and fished around in her icebox. "Diet Coke or 7 Up?"

"Either would be great."

She handed him a can. "If it's any consolation, I think they're almost finished at the lake."

He pulled back his hat and wiped the sweat from his brow with his sleeve. "Makes a difference to being up here in winter."

"I can't even imagine it now. All that snow seems like a distant dream."

He held up his drink. "Thanks for this."

"My pleasure. See you soon."

The police had cordoned off the parking lot near the boat ramp. There were a few reporters loitering in the shaded picnic area, but they seemed reluctant to venture across the baking tarmac. Macy pulled up as close as she could to the temporary awning the forensics crew had erected. Ethan's pickup truck glided across the water, riding on the back of a flat-bottomed boat that looked like a small ferry. The boat ramp wasn't steep but the water level had dropped so much that the trailer was out on the rocky beach, its two back wheels submerged in the water as it waited for the truck to arrive. The tow truck driver sat behind the wheel with his engine idling. She could see the crane they'd used to pull the vehicle from the water. It looked like a children's toy sitting at the base of the tall cliffs ringing the escarpment.

Macy found Ryan resting in the shade near the toilet blocks. He looked hungover and she called him on it. He slipped down his sunglasses so he could glare at her.

"I've been stuck in Wilmington Creek all week. Of course I'm hungover."

"Have you spoken to Priscilla today?"

"I heard one of her interns vomited on the evidence."

"You heard wrong. It was two interns."

"You need a pretty strong stomach to deal with what we scraped off the floor of that garage."

"Better you than me. Has she found anything unusual?"

He shrugged. "Considering what we do for a living, that's a pretty open-ended question."

"She's not returning my calls."

"You know the drill. Queen Priscilla will not be rushed."

"How soon do you think we can have the DNA results?"

"That could be another week. Are you having doubts about the identity of the victim?"

"I looked at the preliminary report on the garage. There were two deep freezers."

"One was empty. The other had some ice and a few bags of frozen peas."

"How easy would it be to determine if the remains we found in the garage were previously frozen?"

"There would be ice crystal artifacts in the tissue. A quick check under the microscope is all that's required."

"I need you to call Priscilla and tell her to do it immediately."

"If it wasn't Tyler Locke, who do you think we found in the garage?"

"I'd rather not say until we hear back from her."

Macy headed for the boat ramp, where they were already loading the pickup truck onto a trailer. It took a few tries to get it lined up properly. She stepped away to make room for the tow truck. The front grille of Ethan's pickup was crushed and all the tires were flat, but otherwise it was intact. The paintwork was rusting in places and a brown sludge covered the windows. She could see where the divers had wiped it away to see inside. Rust-colored water dripped from the base of the doors and undercarriage onto the tarp they'd spread across the parking lot beneath the temporary awning.

Aiden came over and stood next to her. "I heard you sent Dean up to Lana Clark's place. Are you going to tell me what's going on?"

"It's just something Jeremy dropped into the conversation this morning. It might be nothing but it got me thinking. A female employee up at the Dalton Ranch accused Tyler of stalking her. It got so bad she quit."

"Why is Jeremy only telling us this now?"

"He didn't realize it was relevant."

"Did you speak to the woman?"

"Karen Walcott still remembers it like it was yesterday. Tyler followed her, drove by her house at night with his headlights off, called her up but never said a word. Sound familiar?"

"Wasn't Tyler in Afghanistan when Lana was being harassed?"

"There's a chance we were sent falsified service records from a hacked Fort Benning e-mail account. They're sending over his records again so we can be sure we have a valid copy."

"I don't wish to point out the obvious, but you're the one who said Tyler was in his garage before it blew up."

"Once I saw the truck was wired up to explode, I got out of there in a hurry. In hindsight, I assumed it was Tyler. I didn't actually get close enough to be sure."

Ryan brushed past Macy, wearing his protective gear. "Priscilla nearly bit my head off, but she's running the tests you asked for."

"Thanks, Ryan. I owe you a drink."

Aiden removed his sunglasses and cleaned them with a tissue. "So who do you think was in the garage?"

"Charlie Lott is my best guess."

Macy stood with the sun on her back and waited for Ryan's team to open the doors to Ethan Green's pickup truck. The driver's side door popped open and Macy stepped away as a crime scene photographer moved in to take pictures. He conferred with Ryan for a couple of minutes before going around to the passenger side. Ryan used a pair of scissors to cut through the wet air bag that was tangled around the upper body. As it peeled away, there was a sucking sound and Ethan's head snapped backwards so that it was hanging out the door. Dark eyes protruded from a pale face and water streamed through long black hair that glistened like an oil slick caught in sunlight. Ryan called Macy and Aiden over for a closer look. Macy watched an air bubble form between Ethan's parted lips. She almost lost her breakfast when it popped. She'd already seen enough.

Aiden was the first to speak. "That's Ethan Green all right."

Ryan adjusted the body's position so he could examine the wound on the forehead. "He's got a contusion here." He pointed with a gloved finger. "You can see here that it was starting to bruise. It doesn't look like a strong enough blow to kill him."

Macy's words were as heavy as boots. She had difficulty lifting them. "Are there any other wounds?"

Ryan tilted the head slightly and teased away a clump of matted hair to reveal the right temple. "There's some more bruising here and the skin is broken."

Ryan peeled back more of the wet remnants of the air bag, inadvertently pulling away Ethan's shirt as well. There was a wound to his chest.

"Here we go," he said. "That's an exit wound. Let's turn him over."

One of Ryan's colleagues came over to help. They carefully rotated Ethan's body. He leaned in, blocking the view.

"It has to be confirmed but I'd say there's a good chance that Ethan Green died as a result of exsanguination. There are two gunshot wounds. One slug went right through, but with any luck the other will help us identify the weapon used." He glanced over at Macy. "I assume you're hoping it's a 9mm."

Aiden took hold of Macy's arm to steady her.

"Are you okay?"

She waved him away but he kept holding on.

"I just need some air." She looked up at Ryan. "Keep this quiet for now. It changes everything."

They walked over to the picnic area and Macy sat in the shade sipping water from a bottle while Aiden paced back and forth in front of her.

Macy glanced over at the truck. "Ethan regained consciousness and was shot with his own gun. Tyler could have taken it home with him. It would explain the tie-in with the highway patrolman's murder. It looks like Ray was right about that after all."

Aiden thought about this for a few seconds. "That makes Tyler the prime suspect in John's murder. We need to confirm that Charlie Lott's body was in Tyler's garage."

She kept her eyes on the ground. It was difficult to find a pine needle amongst the cigarette butts. Someone had been wearing bright pink lipstick.

Her cell phone buzzed and she picked it up. "It's the medical examiner."

Priscilla sounded like she was on a speakerphone. "Macy, I ran the tests you wanted. There are ice crystal artifacts in the tissue I examined."

"You're confident the remains were previously frozen?"

"Yes, I'm one hundred percent sure that's the case. There isn't the damage you'd associate with multiple freezing and thawing cycles over a long period. Further tests may give you a better time frame, but I'd say you're looking at a month, maybe more."

251

"We need to get DNA analysis done right away. I'll call the authorities in Spokane so you have something for comparison."

"Do you have someone specific in mind?"

"Charlie Lott has been missing for nearly a month. I think his body has been stored in one of the freezers in Tyler Locke's garage all this time."

Aiden tried radioing the officer Macy had sent to Lana Clark's home, but there was no answer. He had the same result when he tried his cell phone.

Macy fell in next to Aiden as they headed for his vehicle. "I told Dean not to go alone. Please tell me he listened."

"It seems he didn't." Aiden slammed the door shut and started the car up. "A team is meeting us up there."

"How far to Lana's place?"

"Twenty minutes if we hurry. When's the last time you tried her cell phone?"

"I'll do it again now." Macy left another message on Lana's cell and dialed the home number before giving up. "No one is answering. Can we send a police helicopter?"

"I've got one in the air, but there's no place to touch down. The terrain is too rough." He gripped the steering wheel and floored it once they cleared the gravel parking lot. "I didn't see this coming."

Macy squinted at her phone. It was difficult to read the screen with the vehicle rattling across the uneven road. The file was in her inbox as promised. "I've just received another copy of Tyler's service records."

"And?"

"Just a second." She tried to keep the phone steady. "This is impossible to read with the car bouncing around."

"Can't you just call them?"

"Wait. Here we go. It says here that on January twenty-eighth, Tyler was evacuated from Afghanistan for mental health reasons."

"He's been in Georgia all this time."

"He's not even active duty. He was discharged nearly a month ago."

Macy kept reading. "They're investigating the source of the e-mail but it appears that Tyler created a bogus account using the name of someone who works in their human resources department and sent us a falsified service record."

"It was a pretty risky move on Tyler's part. Someone in my office should have noticed."

"Tyler had to cover his tracks. If we'd known he was in Georgia all this time, he'd have been viewed in an entirely different light. You'd think someone around here would have known he was back in the States."

"John must have. They were in the same platoon."

"Tyler probably asked him to keep it quiet."

Aiden tapped the steering wheel. "I'm no expert on these things, but Tyler seems a little too organized to be suffering from PTSD."

"I hear you. I'm guessing he panicked when he found out John and Lana were dating. Other than getting wounded, the only way he could get back to Fort Benning in a hurry was to pretend to have a mental breakdown."

"I guess that makes sense."

Macy was beginning to feel ill. She spoke slowly and kept her eyes on the road. "He returns to Georgia and finds he can't engage with Lana in a socially acceptable way, so his obsession escalates to the point that he starts stalking her. Maybe he figured if he scared her enough she'd come running to him for help."

"But she came here instead."

"She thought she was safe, but it turns out she moved to her stalker's hometown. I wish Jeremy had told us about Karen Walcott sooner."

"If he didn't take it seriously when it happened, he's not going to give it much thought years later."

Aiden joined Route 93 and increased his speed. "And then there's Lindsay. I'm not sure what Tyler's motive to kill her would have been, but he certainly had opportunity. He was her closest neighbor."

Macy tried Lana's number again. "Still no answer. How much farther?"

"Ten minutes." He passed several eighteen-wheelers that had pulled over to the side. "We have to take a secondary road the rest of the way. It's going to get hairy."

He took a sharp right and his back wheels skidded to the left. The SUV rocked back and forth a couple times. Macy groped around the glove box and pulled out an empty evidence bag.

Aiden glanced over at her. "Shit. Sorry. Are you going to be sick?"

Macy held the bag under her chin. "It's okay. I just can't talk right now."

"I'll open the window."

Macy stuck her head out the window and her ponytail whipped around and hit her in the face. They were climbing out of the valley now. Through the trees she could see sunlight reflecting off water. There was a stream down there somewhere. She turned away and tried to focus on the road twisting out in front of them. They passed a handful of mailboxes on the way up. The houses were lost in the pine trees. There wasn't a single car.

"She lives in the middle of nowhere. You'd think she'd want to be close to people after what happened to her back in Georgia."

"I doubt she has much choice. It's probably all she can afford."

They slowed down before turning left onto a narrow road.

"Almost there." Aiden pointed beyond the passenger-side window. "You can just see it through the trees."

"I'll keep my eyes on the road if that's okay with you."

Aiden drove another fifty yards before parking his vehicle in a turnout. He picked up the radio and requested an ambulance and made sure there were roadblocks in place north and south of the junction on Route 93.

He checked his gun and looked over at Macy. "You feeling better now?"

She lied and said she was fine.

He reached around to the backseat and pulled out two bulletproof vests. "I imagine this is going to be a little large on you."

She pulled it over her head and did up the straps. It felt like she was wearing a sandwich board. They watched the one-story house from where a line of trees opened into a small clearing. Macy recognized Lana's light gray Toyota. Dean's patrol car was parked off to the left with the hazard lights blinking. The rest of the team was still five minutes away, but Aiden didn't think they should wait.

"I think Tyler is long gone."

"I'm worried about Dean and Lana."

"That makes two of us."

"Have you ever been inside this house?"

"A few times in high school. It looks small from the outside but there are a few bedrooms." He craned his neck. "As I recall, there are a couple outbuildings at the rear of the property. One's a garage."

"So there may be another car."

"I'll sweep around to the right and check it first."

"I'll go to the left and meet you around back."

As Macy moved through the trees, mosquitoes and blackflies rose from the dry undergrowth in swarms. She swatted them away. Everything stuck to her. Her shirt and trousers felt heavy. She could hear her heart beating in her head. A branch snapped and she swung her gun in a wide arc, but saw nothing. She took furtive glances at the house and over her shoulder as she made her way. There wasn't a hint of wind. She stepped through an opening in the trees and entered a vegetable garden that had been laid out in careful rows. Everything was dead. Dry husks of corn stalks grew up past her head. The earth was powder dry. She moved through the rows, growing more anxious with each step. At the rear of the garden, a path crisscrossed with animal tracks led deep into the woods. Flies buzzed around a wooden compost bin secured by a heavy metal latch.

Keeping low, Macy came alongside Dean's patrol car and peered in the open window. The keys were still in the ignition. She removed them and put them in her pocket. She peeked in the home's windows as she went around the side to meet Aiden. She caught glimpses of domestic clutter and heard the strains of a sitcom laugh track through the screen windows. Aiden was waiting for her. They spoke in whispers.

"The garage is empty."

"So is Dean's car. His keys were still in the ignition."

They stayed low so they couldn't be seen from the bedroom windows. Aiden checked the sliding door leading into the living room and found it unlocked. Macy kept her eyes on the backyard. The garage doors were wide open, but a small, windowless shed was secured with a padlock. Aiden was breathing heavily next to her. He leaned against the wall and pulled back his hat so he could wipe the sweat from his eyes. His hair was soaked through and matted to his forehead.

"I think we should go in."

"Wait," said Macy, grabbing his arm. "The television has been switched off."

A woman's voice called out from the bedroom window to their right. "Lana, is that you, sweetheart? I thought you said you were going to bring me some lunch."

Macy kept her voice low. "Who's that?"

"I don't know. She sounds older."

"Lana's mom?"

"She didn't say anything about her mom living with her . . ."

"Lana, quit playing games and come give me a hand. I'm thirsty."

Macy touched Aiden's arm. "If Dean was in there, he would have answered."

They slid open the screen door and stepped into a family room paneled with dark wood. A pillow and blanket spilled onto the floor from a brown corduroy sofa. A collection of nail polish bottles covered the coffee table. Bright pink varnish was splattered across the wood surface. It was the same color as the lipstick on the cigarette butts Macy had seen near the picnic table at the lake. Aiden moved into the kitchen. Someone had been preparing a meal. Water had boiled dry in a blackened pan. He turned off the burner.

They checked the bedrooms one by one, easing each door open before moving on to the next. Aiden pointed out snapshots of Lana taped to a mirror.

"This is Lana's room."

There were signs that she'd left in a hurry. A few of the drawers were pulled out and emptied. Clothes hangers were scattered on the floor. In the bathroom at the end of the hallway, the cabinet was open and the shower curtain drawn shut. Macy held her breath as Aiden pulled it open. Aside from a stray bar of soap the bath was empty.

They hovered outside the remaining bedroom listening to a news program that was playing on the television. A female newscaster was taking them live to Darby Lake. Aiden counted to three before turning the handle and sweeping into the room with his gun drawn.

"Police. Keep your hands where I can see them."

At first Macy didn't know what she was looking at. There was too much flesh. The woman on the bed blinked up at them. Thick arms ballooned out from her sides as she tried in vain to raise them. The blankets were kicked off. She wore a nightdress. Her legs had the girth of tree trunks, but her feet were small like a child's. She looked from Aiden to Macy with her mouth drawn open into a bow.

"Where's Lana?"

Aiden ignored the question. "Who else is here?"

Her voice turned shrill. "It's just me and Lana. Where is she?"

Macy checked the en suite bathroom. There was a large walk-in shower and someone had built a pulley system above the toilet. "It's clear," she said, reentering the bedroom.

Aiden went to the window and shifted the curtains. "The team's coming up the drive. I'll go out front and organize a more thorough search."

The woman blinked up at them again. "Why aren't you telling me anything? Where's Lana?"

"Ma'am, my name is Detective Macy Greeley. Could you please identify yourself?"

"Marsha Clark. What's going on?"

"That's what we're trying to figure out. Are you Lana's mother?" Macy noticed an empty water glass on the bedside table and took it to the bathroom for a refill.

Marsha gulped it down. "Yes. I moved up here from Georgia about a month ago. I couldn't live on my own anymore."

"When is the last time you saw Lana?"

"It's been at least an hour. She said she was going to make lunch. I must have dozed off. It's been so hot."

"Has anyone else been living here?"

"No."

"Any visitors?"

"She doesn't seem to have any girlfriends, but I've heard a couple of men in the house." Lana's mother gazed down the length of her body. "She doesn't introduce me to them though."

"Anyone come today?"

"Yes, he was a new one. I heard him and Lana arguing. He tried to come in here but she talked him out of it. I heard her call him Tyler."

"Tyler and Lana seem to have left. Did you overhear anything that might help us find them?"

"Is Lana in trouble? I didn't like the sound of him."

"I need to know if you heard anything. Did he say where he was taking her?"

"Nothing specific. I drifted off. I didn't even know she left."

A team of paramedics appeared at the door and Macy excused herself.

Marsha's voice followed her out of the room. "You'll tell me when you find Lana."

Macy hoped she wasn't right, but she'd had a bad feeling since she'd found Dean's keys in his car. She walked past the officers sweeping through the rooms and caught sight of Aiden directing a team to go search the outbuildings and the woods surrounding the house. Beyond the shaded porch an ambulance sat in the shade of the trees. Closer still, two patrol cars were parked in the front yard. The sun was setting behind the trees but the temperature didn't seem to be dropping. Macy walked across the dry grass toward the vegetable plot. She stopped at the back end of Dean's patrol car and reminded herself that Dean could be anywhere, then popped the trunk. She stared for a second before easing it shut.

Aiden called to her from the porch. "Macy, we found Dean locked in the shed. He's alive."

Macy went around the side of the house to where paramedics were attending to Dean. He'd been wrapped up with half a roll of duct tape. One of his cheeks was grazed and his forehead was bruised and swollen. As soon as they cut the tape away from his mouth he started apologizing.

Aiden told him to worry about saying sorry later. "Do you have any idea where Tyler may have taken Lana?"

He spit up some blood. "No. Tyler comes up to me outside and I'm relieved to see the guy. I tell him everyone thinks he's dead and he hits me with a baseball bat."

Macy knelt down next to him. "I'd say you're lucky."

"It doesn't feel that way at the moment."

The paramedics undid the tape binding Dean's wrists and dropped it into an evidence bag Aiden was holding.

"Did you see the car he was driving?"

"Yeah, I saw it. Late-model blue Chevelle like we've been looking for. There were Idaho plates on it, though."

"What about Lana? Did you see her?" asked Aiden.

"No, sir. I didn't." He pressed his palm to one of his eyes. "I really fucked up, didn't I?"

Macy touched his knee. "I'm not sure you would have done much better if there were two of you. Do you remember the license plate number?"

"At some point, I passed out from the heat. It must be over a hundred and ten in that shed."

"License plate?"

"All I could get was 2CR4."

Aiden walked over and inspected the tire tracks cutting into the dusty soil. "He probably stole the plates off a tourist coming through town."

Macy looked around. "So what now, Aiden?"

"Tyler can't have gotten far in the last hour and a half. That car doesn't have much range on a tank of gas, and going off-road isn't an option. I'm betting that he's still in the valley."

A helicopter circled overhead, kicking up dust. Macy pointed to the sky.

"Make sure those guys know what we're looking for."

He picked up his radio. "I'm on it."

23

They stopped in at a mini-market on the way up to the Dalton Ranch to pick up something to eat. Macy came across Aiden staring longingly at the refrigerated cases stacked with cartons of beer. She nudged him down the aisle toward the coffee dispenser.

"There's plenty of time for that later."

"I feel like I let Lana down."

"You and me both."

"But it's different with you. You didn't know Tyler. You'd think I would have realized."

"I can give you all kinds of reasons why that wasn't going to happen, but no matter what I say, you're going to replay every interaction you've ever had with him."

"I guess I won't be the only one."

"No, I suspect a lot of people around here are going to wake up tomorrow morning feeling like they've been taken for a ride."

The valley spun away, silent and dark outside the car windows. Macy fought the urge to reach over and take Aiden's hand. They were colleagues. It would be inappropriate. She was just being emotional, and her life was complicated enough. Distracted, she fiddled with the air conditioner. Considering the temperature hadn't dipped much below ninety all day, she felt surprisingly chilled. She was beginning to think she might be suffering from heat stroke. She sat back and closed her eyes.

"I had a feeling something wasn't right. I should have thrown everything at it."

Aiden checked the side-view mirror and pulled into the outside lane to overtake a camper van. "You told Dean to bring someone with him and he didn't listen. Did you manage to speak to Tyler's commanding officer?"

"His CO didn't realize Tyler's mental health evacuation was relevant. He thought it was very brave for Tyler to admit he was struggling. As a rule, soldiers of his rank never do. They've had a few guys come forward since he left. I didn't have the heart to tell him that Tyler was probably faking it."

"It looks like Tyler's issues predate his stretch in the army."

"Do you think he tracked down Charlie Lott?"

"It's more likely that Charlie came here looking for Lana and found Tyler instead."

"Every property Tyler's ever been associated with will have to be checked. There's still an APB on Charlie Lott's car, but I think we can assume Tyler's keeping it out of sight, given how unique it is. For all we know he might be driving something else by now. What's your read on his parents? Are they cooperating?"

"Hard to say." He handed her a map. "They're third generation. They marked all the properties that are owned by the extended family. There are twenty-three so far but we're checking to make sure it's accurate."

"I'm beginning to wonder if it was Tyler who got Jessie started on drugs. He has a history of dealing. There's no reason to believe he stopped. She was fourteen when she started using. He was what? Twenty?"

"It's possible."

"Annie seems to have had a real blind spot when it comes to him."

"That text Annie received the night John died is making more sense now."

"Jeremy mentioned that he and Annie argued a lot about Tyler." She paused. "Aiden, do we know what Tyler's movements were on the day Lindsay died?"

"According to his statement, he was out working on the ranch with John on Tuesday afternoon. Dylan spoke to John about it, but we're going to need more than hearsay. We'll have to check and see if anyone at the ranch saw them together."

"I suppose we should swing by and see Dylan on our way back to town."

"No need. He's moved into Wade Larkin's spare room. His mother decided to spend some time with her sister in Boise. They convinced Dylan it wasn't a good idea for him to be on his own."

"Are we sure Sarah is where she's supposed to be? She's been sleeping with Tyler Locke for years. They could be meeting up somewhere."

Aiden's eyes flicked up to the rearview mirror. "We have someone looking into it."

"I keep going back to Lindsay Moore. How is she involved in this? Tyler isn't going around killing just anyone. He left two witnesses up at Lana's house."

"I was wondering about that as well. She was asking a lot of questions about Green. He must have gotten nervous. Until we found Green's body, Tyler had Dylan and Jessie under control."

Macy unwrapped a packet of chewing gum and offered a piece to Aiden. "Has someone warned Bob Crawley that his association with Lana might put him in danger too?"

"We offered him police protection, but he declined."

"I doubt his wife is going to be so forgiving this time. His behavior has put his family in danger. Plus there's the possibility he's been paying Lana for sex. That's bound to come out eventually."

"You think that's really what was going on?"

"You saw the situation with Lana's mother. There's no way Lana is pulling in enough income at The Whitefish to support the two of them."

"You have to wonder why Lana mentioned her relationship with Bob in the first place, then."

"Maybe she thought that if she said it was an affair from the beginning, people might never stop to question whether it might have been something else."

"I suppose you're right. Have you spoken to Ray?"

"Briefly. He was polite, but not to the point of apologizing. He did admit that he'd gotten it wrong, which makes a nice change. Since then he's tried to get in touch a half a dozen times. I've not bothered to return his calls."

"That might come back to bite you on the ass. He's still your boss."

"Given the nature of some of the correspondence, I doubt he'll risk complaining." She paused. "He seems overly concerned that I was taking on too much, considering I'd been caught up in that explosion."

"Aside from what happened out at the lake today, you seem fine."

"That had nothing to do with my health. I'm pretty squeamish around dead bodies. There's always something that gets to me."

"You could always become a traffic cop." He grinned.

"Don't laugh. I'm sure Ray is contemplating it."

"He wouldn't dare."

"We'll see." She paused. "At any rate, I think I'm going to take some time off after this. I have a lot of vacation days built up."

"You should come up to the Flathead Valley. It's a nice place if you're not working."

"So I hear."

He gave her a quick glance. "It was just a thought. Feel free to ignore it."

"Aiden," said Macy. "It is a nice thought, but it's probably not a good idea."

"Like I said, it was just a thought."

They turned onto the long drive leading up to the Dalton's ranch house. Every light was on. They drove past a pickup truck parked on the side of the main access road. A man with a rifle waved them through.

"It seems like Jeremy isn't taking any chances."

"There are too many guns around. It's making me nervous."

"There have always been too many guns around. Does Jessie know yet that she didn't kill Ethan?"

"I don't think so. Ryan seems to have kept that quiet."

"I hope Jessie and Dylan know where Tyler's taken Lana."

"I wouldn't hold my breath. Tyler seems to have thought this through. I doubt he'd have told them anything."

Aiden parked near a patrol car that was stationed out front and had a quick word with the officers on duty before heading to the front door. Jeremy stood behind the screen with his thick arms folded around his chest.

"You're high if you think I'm going to let you arrest my daughter for murdering that lowlife."

Aiden shoved his hands deep in his pockets. "Jeremy, we're not here to arrest anyone."

Jeremy Dalton didn't budge.

Macy peered into the front window. "Mr. Dalton, is Jessie on the premises?" Macy hadn't seen his daughter's car in the driveway. It had dawned on her that Jeremy had the resources to hide her from the authorities. For all they knew, Jessie was already on her way to Canada.

"She's here but you're not speaking to her."

"That's not what we agreed to on the phone." Aiden caught sight of a Cadillac parked under the trees. "I see you've called your lawyer."

"If it was your daughter, you'd do the same thing."

Macy looked up at Jeremy. "Mr. Dalton, as far as I can tell, Jessie didn't kill Ethan Green. The most I could get her on is obstruction, and compared to the shit storm brewing out here, that's the least of my priorities."

Jeremy stepped out onto the front porch and the screen door snapped shut behind him. "What are you talking about? I heard you found Ethan's body."

"You heard correctly, and once I'm in a room with Jessie and Dylan, I'll tell you everything else you need to know."

They gathered in the formal dining room. There was an imposing cupboard made of dark-stained wood along one wall. It was full of cut-glass crystal and delicate teacups that looked as if they'd never been used. The room felt incongruous to the rest of the house, which was a warren of intersecting rooms that lacked any sort of order. This was the type of room you came to only when summoned. Macy took a sip of the iced tea she'd been served and looked around the table. Aiden sat on her left; Jeremy was at the head of the table, his back to a bay window overlooking the front yard. Jessie and Dylan flanked a long-faced lawyer named Frank Hobbs. Aside from the lawyer, no one looked as if they'd slept for some time. The door opened and Wade Larkin stepped in. He took the seat opposite Jeremy and apologized for delaying them.

Macy kept her eyes on Jessie. "Jessie, in your original statement you said that you struck Ethan Green in the head several times with a rock. We found bruising on his forehead to suggest this was the case, but the bruising also indicates that Ethan Green was still alive. We don't believe your actions killed him. It is more probable that he lost consciousness for a period of time."

"Did he drown?"

"Ethan Green was shot twice with the same gun that was used to kill highway patrol officer Timothy Wallace last summer. We believe that Tyler used that same weapon to murder your brother and wound Lindsay Moore."

Jessie started to say something again, but this time the lawyer put his hand up to stop her. "Not another word."

"We now know that Tyler didn't die in that explosion. We're waiting for confirmation, but it was probably Charlie Lott's remains that were found in the garage. There is evidence to suggest his body had been kept in one of Tyler's deep freezers for the past month." Macy glanced over at Dylan. "It was Tyler who was stalking Lana Clark back in Georgia, not Charlie Lott, as was previously believed."

Dylan interrupted her. "That can't be right. Tyler wasn't at Fort Benning. He was in Afghanistan."

"Again, Tyler covered his tracks. He created an e-mail account and sent us falsified service records. We've since learned the truth. In late January, Tyler was evacuated from Afghanistan for mental health reasons. He was stationed at Fort Benning until he was discharged from military service four weeks ago. Given that they served in the same platoon, we're assuming that John was aware of this, but kept it quiet."

Jessie ignored her lawyer. "You're wrong. Tyler wouldn't have killed John. They were like brothers."

"I know this is hard to take in all at once, but he's fooled everyone. Earlier today he assaulted a patrol officer and abducted Lana Clark. There's a statewide manhunt being organized as we speak. He's a very dangerous man. That bomb was probably meant to kill the two of you. I just happened to get to Tyler's house first."

"Tyler is an explosives expert," said Dylan. "If he wanted you dead, you'd be dead."

Frank Hobbs looked up from his notes. "Is the state planning on bringing charges against my clients?"

Macy put an evidence bag on the table. Inside was a crumpled Ziploc baggie containing several capsules. "Jessie, are you familiar with Rohypnol?"

Jessie picked up the bag and turned it over in her hands. "They're roofies."

"Have you ever taken them before?"

"I'm not sure."

"You're aware that 'roofies' is the street name for Rohypnol, also commonly known as a date rape drug?"

"So I've heard."

"In your statement you said that you drank a Coke that Ethan Green bought you at a convenience store and that later you were dizzy, had difficulty breathing, and that you suffered memory loss. All these are symptoms of someone who has ingested Rohypnol. We found this bag of tablets in the front pocket of Ethan's jeans. He could have slipped some into your drink. It's pretty much tasteless, so you would have been completely unaware you were being drugged."

Aiden continued, "Ethan Green has been wanted for questioning related to an event that occurred in Collier the evening before he picked you up at The Whitefish. A tox screen revealed there was Rohypnol in the victim's system, and she identified Ethan Green as her assailant. The authorities have been looking for him ever since."

Macy looked up at the lawyer. "It's up to the district attorney as to whether Jessie and Dylan are charged with obstruction, but given the extenuating circumstances and the threats Jessie received from Tyler, I somehow doubt she'll bother. Right now my main priorities are finding Tyler and getting Lana home safe and sound." She unfolded the map and placed it on the table. "This has already been marked with properties known to be associated with Tyler's family. We're pretty confident he's stayed in the valley, but the area is vast. There are a lot of abandoned properties, hunting and fishing lodges, and many people live off the grid. If you have any idea where he might be, you need to tell us now."

Dylan circled a large area south of Darby Lake. "Tyler didn't say exactly where it was, but he mentioned a house he's been looking after that's down in this area. It belongs to some friend of his who's been living off the grid."

"Did he mention a name?"

"All I know is that his first name is Lacey and that he's down on the Mexico-Arizona border for the next few weeks training with a militia group."

Wade spoke for the first time. "That would be the Minute Men."

Jeremy leaned in so he could get a better look at the map. "I've heard of Lacey. He's ex-military."

Aiden frowned. "We're looking at an area that's twenty to thirty square miles. We'll check all the access roads first. There's no way Charlie Lott's car could handle the terrain. We find the car, and we know we're on to something."

Wade pushed his chair from the table. "Aiden, I've got some friends down in Arizona. I'm going to make some calls."

"Thanks, Wade. Let us know if you find anything."

Macy put the evidence bag away. "Dylan, I need to ask you about your mother, Sarah."

Dylan glanced down at his phone. "She left for her sister's in Boise early this morning."

"I imagine she was pretty upset. That's a long drive. Have you spoken to her?"

"No, but that's not unusual." He pressed some keys on his phone.

"You're worried about her, aren't you?"

"Yes, ma'am."

"How was she with Tyler? Would she help him if he asked?"

"I'm afraid she would."

"You need to let us know the minute you hear from her."

"She was on the phone with someone last night. I thought it was my aunt, but I could have been mistaken. They don't get along too well. It would be weird for my mom to reach out to her now."

"Do you think it was Tyler?"

"Hard to say. She started packing right after she hung up."

"What type of car does your mother drive?"

"She's got a pickup truck just like mine. It's dark green though."

Macy glanced over at Jessie. She still wore a bandana around her neck. She looked as if she was holding her breath.

"Jessie, I know you're tired, but I have one more question and we'll be going."

Frank Hobbs folded his hands together. "I think my client has been helpful enough for one evening."

Jessie puffed out her cheeks. "Frank, it's okay for her to ask. I already know I don't have to answer."

"Jessie, there's something that's been bothering me since I learned Tyler served time as a juvenile for dealing drugs. Was he the one who got you started?"

She hesitated and Frank spoke again. "Detective Greeley, I fail to see how this is relevant."

Jessie glanced up at her father. "I know it sounds stupid, but it made me feel special when he singled me out."

"How old were you?"

"Thirteen."

"Did your brother know?"

She looked down at her hands. "No, it was our secret."

"Were there other secrets? Did Tyler ever tell you anything that might help us find him?"

"He knew a lot of people around here who lived on the fringe. He'd take me to meth labs, abandoned houses in the hills. He knew a lot of guys in the militias. There were always guns around."

Macy pushed the map in Jessie's direction. "I need you to try to remember where some of these places are."

Jessie picked up a pen. "It's been a long time. They might not be there anymore."

"That's okay. You let us worry about that."

"There was that place north of Collier that they found last year."

Macy bit her lip. "You were there?"

"Yes, ma'am."

The pen hovered over the map. "This may take a while."

Macy sipped at her iced tea. It had gone tepid. "This is important. Take your time."

. . .

Macy climbed into Aiden's car and pulled her seat belt on. He'd been waiting with the engine idling while she had a few last words with Jeremy and the lawyer.

"Well," he said, pulling out of the parking space. "That went better than expected."

"I don't like lawyers."

"Isn't Ray Davidson a lawyer?"

"There you go."

"Just so you know, I've been on the phone with him. His plane landed a half hour ago. He's expecting us at the station."

"Did you put an APB out on Sarah Reed's car?"

"Yep. I still can't believe she'd be so stupid."

"Love seems to have that effect on people. He probably fed her some line that he was being set up, and she bought it." She turned on the light and held up the map. In all, Jessie had marked the location of half a dozen meth labs and three militia compounds. "This should keep us busy for a while."

"I'll do a cross-check. I'm pretty sure most of those labs are shut down. Meth isn't as much of a problem as it was a few years back."

"I need to pick up my car. It's still out at Darby Lake."

"We'll swing by on the way into town."

Macy leaned against the window and closed her eyes. "I guess the one good thing that's come out of this is that Jessie and Jeremy seem to be talking."

"Is that what you were discussing?"

"Jeremy feels awful knowing he let Tyler near his kids."

"I wonder why Tyler didn't try giving drugs to John."

"Jessie must have been the easier mark. You wonder how she's still standing after everything she's been through."

"How are you feeling?"

"Barely standing. I'm exhausted. I feel pretty beat up."

"After we pick up your car, you should head straight back to your hotel. Given what you've been through in the past three days, it's perfectly understandable. We're organizing a team to search the access roads south of the lake. They'll head out sometime tonight with dog handlers. There's not much more that you can do today."

Macy stared out the windshield. Beyond the reach of the headlights the world was black. She closed her eyes and slept.

The hot water burned into Macy's bruised shoulder blades. She placed her palms flat against the bathroom tiles and focused in on the pain. Somewhere along the way, recounting Ray's many transgressions had become her daily mantra. She'd been wrong. Nothing was worth this much misery. She shut off the taps and opened her eyes. The bathroom was so hot she felt light-headed. She held on to the rail attached to the wall and waited for the dizziness to pass. The overhead fan was on and pipes clicked and hissed in the walls. She pulled the curtain open and took care stepping out of the shower. Her reflection in the mirror was so steamed over she could have been a stranger approaching in the fog. Using a towel, she wiped a small window of steam away so she could see her face. Her eyes were swollen but clear. She wrapped up and opened the door.

Ray was sitting on her bed with his legs stretched out and the top button of his shirt undone. His tie hung loose at his throat. He looked up from his cell phone and ran his eyes over her. He didn't smile. Macy pulled the towel up farther and secured it tightly. She didn't smile either.

"How did you get in?" she said, glancing at the door.

"Are you really going to do this?"

"Do what?"

"This little performance of yours."

"It's not a performance, Ray. I am well and truly pissed off." She pointed at the door. "Get out of my room."

"You've got to be fucking kidding me."

"Ray, go."

"I'm not going anywhere until we've talked. Your behavior has been completely unprofessional. You've ignored my messages and phone calls. We're in the middle of a major investigation."

"An investigation you nearly screwed up."

"I made the right call at the time."

"No, Ray. *I* made the right call. And since you brought up all these phone calls and messages, since when is '*Macy, we really need to talk about our relationship*' a work matter? Leave me alone. You're married. We have no relationship."

"I'm separated."

"Being separated isn't a state of mind, Ray. It's a physical act. Move out and I'll consider you separated. Get divorced and I'll consider you available." She steadied her voice. "Not that it matters anymore. Whatever this has been, it's over now."

"We have a child together."

"No, we have a child apart."

"He's my son. He needs me."

"You have three daughters you don't spend any time with. You're always parading their problems in front of me as excuses for your behavior. They're the ones who need you. Luke doesn't even know you exist."

"What brought this on? We were fine a couple of days ago."

"You were fine, but I wasn't. All these delays and second chances. You pushed me away one too many times. And it doesn't help that you went and pulled that shit with me about the press conference. It's one thing to mess with my personal life, but it's another thing to mess with my career. The things you said were completely unacceptable." She hesitated. "You think you have all the power here, but you don't. I know things about you."

"Don't threaten me."

"What do you think you're doing right now? You break into my hotel room while I'm in the shower." She pointed at the door again. "I told you to leave and you didn't. Whose behavior is more threatening?"

He held open his arms. "Come here."

"What part of what I just said made you think I want to be anywhere near you? It's over."

"You're going to regret this."

"Excuse me?"

He sighed. "Macy, you're going to regret not giving me another chance. We were so close to getting everything we wanted."

"That's not how I saw it. If anything, you've become more distant over the past few months. I was lonely enough before. I didn't realize it could actually get worse."

He stood up and straightened his tie. "Your problem has always been that you're too needy."

"I'm going to pretend I didn't hear that."

He moved in close and stood over her. He was six inches taller and twice as wide. She kept her eyes on the knot in his tie and waited for him to back down. He ran his fingertips over her bare shoulders. She didn't move. He held his lips to her damp hair for a few seconds before whispering in her ear.

"This isn't over."

"As far as I'm concerned this never began. Get out, Ray."

He threw a key card on the bed and walked out the door without closing it behind him.

Macy packed in a hurry. She'd seen Ray intimidate witnesses, but never expected to be on the receiving end. She kept glancing at the door. The security chain was on, but that wasn't enough. Ray's room was a few doors away. More distance was required. She didn't want to be in the same town, let alone the same motel. She sat on the edge of the bed with her laptop perched on her knees. There was a motel on the road leading to the Dalton Ranch. As she recalled, the Vacancy sign had been lit. She was just about to call them when she saw an incoming text message from Aiden, asking if she was still awake. Instead of sending him a reply she dialed his number.

"Aiden, it's me."

"Sorry if I woke you."

"Not at all. What's up?"

"Wade Larkin's contact came through. We've got a name."

Macy checked the time. It was 11:21. "Are you in the office?"

"No, I came home for a quick shower."

"I'll come over."

"Are you sure?"

"I was just about to leave anyway."

"What's going on?"

"Remind me of your address."

"It's 23 Sutter Street."

"I'll be there in five."

Aiden's one-story home was two blocks from Main Street. There was a single tree centered in a crusty-looking front yard and a low hedge running below the front porch Macy parked on the hard shoulder across the road and sat staring out at the dark windows. The curtains were drawn and the only visible light was above the door. A patrol car was backed into the driveway facing toward her. She picked up her bag and slid out of the cab.

He answered the door in jeans and a T-shirt. His feet were bare and his hair was still soaked through. He apologized for the mess and invited her in.

She ran her eyes over the sparsely furnished front room. "I wouldn't call this messy."

There was a single black-and-white photo of a landscape hanging over a leather sofa. The kitchen counters were bare, but case notes were spread out on the dining room table. In the center was a topographical map. She moved toward the table and looked down at it. An area south of Darby Lake had been highlighted with yellow marker. Several roads were marked with different-colored pens. Aiden stood so close their arms were touching. She could feel his breath on her neck. He traced a line between Route 93 and Lacey Truman's property.

"Truman has a forty-three-acre plot that borders the state park. The only access is via a logging road."

"Do we know anything else?" she said, leaning in for a closer look. "It would be helpful if we had the layout of the property."

"The owner has a deep mistrust of the authorities. Jeremy Dalton is handling the negotiations. Last I heard, they were offering him money."

She turned and caught him watching her.

"Do we have a file on him?"

"He's never had any trouble with the law. I checked out his Web site. It's the usual antigovernment stuff but it's well written, which makes a change. He has a lot of combat experience and hires himself out to various groups as a consultant. Runs training programs in disaster preparedness, war games, that sort of thing. He's also a card-carrying member of Mensa."

"Let's hope he's smart enough to cooperate," she said, pulling her hair into a ponytail. It was starting to stick to the back of her neck. "How does Tyler know him?"

"They served together in Iraq."

"Anything come back from the other properties?"

"We're checking them all. Two of the meth labs were still active. The compounds are proving trickier to approach. We're using known contacts to negotiate access. The last thing we want is to pick a fight with these guys if we don't have to."

Macy tapped the map with a pen. "He'd be pretty hemmed in if he chose to take a stand at Lacey Truman's house. It looks like it's built into the ridge."

"He'll count on us not knowing about it."

"Don't be too sure. Underestimating Tyler is what got us into trouble in the first place. Has anyone managed to speak to Sarah Reed?"

"She's not picking up her cell phone, and Dylan's aunt hasn't heard from her in months. We're checking Sarah's phone records." He gestured toward the kitchen. "Do you want some coffee? I could make a fresh pot."

His arm was against hers again. She was trying to decide if he was doing it on purpose.

"I don't know. I feel like maybe I should leave."

He tilted his head. "You just got here."

She slid her fingertips across the back of his hand. A lattice of veins wove their way up the length of his bare arm. He had a tattoo of a Celtic cross on his bicep. She couldn't raise her voice above a whisper.

"I don't know what this is."

"That makes two of us."

She kissed him softly on the lips and curved her body to meet his. Beneath his thin shirt, his back was warm and smooth. Drops of water fell from his wet hair and ran down her cheeks, pooling in the hollows, leaving tracks across her skin. His lips lingered at her throat and his fingertips grazed her neck. He pulled off her shirt and dipped down to kiss the soft skin above her breasts. She didn't see the empty walls and untouched moving boxes as he carried her through the house. The bedroom was dimly lit and the bed unmade. They fell into it together and peeled off layers until there was nothing left but flesh. Moonlight bled through the blinds. A fan hummed in the corner. The digital clock read 11:33 P.M.

24

Jessie stared up into the twist of tree limbs. Jagged patches of starlit sky filtered through the leaves. The grass was cool on her back. Through the screen door she could hear Jeremy and Wade taking turns talking on the speakerphone in the kitchen. The man on the other end of the line sounded like his voice had been mined in a gravel pit. Lacey Truman took some convincing. It was only after Jeremy offered him money that he started to cooperate. They'd been haggling over a number ever since. Ray Davidson was with them, but she had yet to hear him utter a single word. He was communicating with handwritten notes so Lacey wouldn't know law enforcement was monitoring the call. Jeremy's voice rose and fell depending on progress. The volume swelled whenever he started to lose patience. Earlier he'd stomped out onto the porch and smoked a cigarette he bummed out of Jessie's pack with a promise that he'd buy her more if she promised not to tell Natalie.

You okay? he had asked.

She'd raised her hand to shade her eyes from the porch light. *I'm not sure.*

I meant what I said earlier. I want us to make a fresh start.

I know you do.

I'm afraid though. I don't want things to ever go back to the way they were.

I'm not going to lie to you. Sometimes I want to go back. Especially now.

You know no good will come of it.

I was thinking that maybe I need to go to that rehab center you sent me to a few years ago. Just for a while, until everything calms down.

If that's what you want to do, I'll make the arrangements.

Wade had called Jeremy back into the kitchen. He'd stubbed out his cigarette with the heel of his boot before heading in.

Jessie, maybe you should go to bed. Some rest will do you good.

That's not a good idea. It's better to be down here with everyone else.

When did you last check on Tara?

A half hour ago. She was sound asleep.

Now she heard footsteps coming along the porch. A figure moved through the shadows. A firm step followed by a slightly hesitant footfall. She could see the glow of his cigarette. Dylan had started smoking again too. He settled into one of the rattan chairs and rested his bad leg on a low table. For a while neither of them spoke.

She rolled over onto her belly and looked up at him. He had a beer in one hand and his cigarette in the other. His eyes were shut. She threw a pebble and it hit the wall next to his head.

"Did you know?"

He opened his eyes and took another pull on his cigarette before stuffing it into the neck of his beer bottle. Apparently, he'd had enough of both. He spoke through a cloud of smoke.

"I swear I didn't."

She sat up and wrapped her arms around her knees. "All this time I thought I killed Ethan, and John didn't say a word. He must have known what it was doing to me."

"I suspect Tyler kept him quiet."

"Could they have it wrong about him?"

"I don't see how. There are witnesses. He's got Lana."

"I mean the part about killing John." Her voice cracked. "Tyler loved John."

"Apparently, he loved Lana even more."

"That's too twisted to be called love."

"Tyler isn't who I thought he was."

"I could say the same for my brother. He should have told us the truth."

"I'm trying to imagine what kind of leverage Tyler may have had and I'm coming up with nothing. Something must have happened over in Afghanistan."

"How come you didn't know Tyler was back in Georgia all this time?"

"I'm not really in touch with anyone. I don't check my e-mail. I don't return calls."

"How's that working out for you?"

"It's not."

"So do you think Sarah is with Tyler?"

"I hope not, but given how she felt about him . . ."

"It wasn't mutual."

"She didn't care. She just wanted to be with him."

"She's so beautiful. She could have anybody."

"Is the stuff that matters ever really just about that?"

"I suppose not. Will you stay with us for a while?"

He grimaced as he shifted his weight. "We'll see. It makes sense for now."

"I'm going back into rehab for a bit. It would be nice if you were here with Tara," she said, fumbling with the thin plastic wrapping on a fresh pack of cigarettes. "Lately, I feel like I'm slipping all the time."

"We're a couple of head cases, aren't we?"

"That's probably why we get along."

"Just so you know, I might be going away for a couple of months as well. The VA wants to send me to a place out in California where they're developing a new treatment for PTSD. I read the brochure. Seems like a bunch of hippie shit to me, but what the hell."

She broke off a dandelion and twirled it in her fingertips. "Maybe you'll get to wear flowers in your hair while you practice yoga."

"More likely it will be a bunch of vets screaming at each other in a locked room while a counselor hides under the table."

"I've been in that room. Just substitute addicts for vets."

"It's going to be hard to face all that again."

"Will you go anyway?"

"I think I better. I know I'm lucky to be offered a place. Feeling this way forever isn't an option."

"If you ever want to talk, I'm always here."

"We could share war stories."

"At least you remember yours."

"No offense, but it seems like you did a lot of things that are best forgotten."

"It would be nice to know who Tara's father is. I probably slept with him to get drugs, but you never know. Maybe it was more than that."

"Well, at least your war stories involve getting laid."

"Is that your idea of looking on the bright side?"

"Yep. That's all I got." He smiled.

"Do you really think Tyler is heading to Lacey Truman's property?"

He hesitated before answering. "Hard to say. He told me about it, so—"

"What do you mean by so?"

"He's relying on me to keep my mouth shut. I can't believe he thinks I'd cover for him after everything he's done."

"Warped sense of loyalty."

"Maybe."

"They seem to be looking all over the valley for him."

"I hope they find him. I want to look that fucker in the eye again. He's got a lot of explaining to do."

"He's killed a cop. They are bringing in SWAT teams and half the state's law enforcement to hunt him down. There's a lot of people who want him dead."

"The thing about the cop doesn't make sense, though. As far as I know, he was with John the afternoon she went missing. In fact I'm sure of it, 'cause John talked to me later that night. He had no reason to lie."

"He wasn't lying. I saw them together. They were repairing some fencing out on the eastern boundary."

"I don't suppose you've said anything to the police."

"I'm not doing Tyler any favors. He's got too much to answer for."

He hesitated. "Did he really get you started?"

She tapped her cigarette onto the rim of a clay pot. "He was the first of my many dealers."

"All those times you went off with him. I thought there was something going on between you two for a while."

"It was never like that." She looked up at the night sky and caught sight of a shooting star. "I hope Lana's okay."

Dylan cocked his head toward the kitchen door. "It's gone quiet in there. Do you think they finally struck a deal?"

"Last I heard, they were offering him thirty grand for the layout of his property."

"Christ, that's a lot of money."

"That guy who gave the press conference showed up an hour ago."

"That would be Ray Davidson. I think he's the captain of the state police."

"I heard him on the phone as he was walking up to the house. I think he was arguing with his wife."

"I imagine he doesn't make it home for dinner too often."

"He looks familiar to me. I can't place him though."

"Probably from the news."

"Maybe." She rolled over on her side. "Do you remember the necklace I told you about? Do you suppose Tyler left it for me?"

'It had to be him."

'But why would he do that? It makes no sense."

'Maybe it was his way of saying sorry."

She shivered. "We never really knew him."

'Up until a couple hours ago I was mourning his death. I keep forgetting I'm supposed to hate him now."

"I know what you mean."

He yawned. "I think it's been three days since I slept."

"Go to bed. I'm fine out here on my own."

He set his mouth into a hard line and pushed up from the chair. "If you hear anything, come get me."

"I'm too tired to walk all the way over to Wade's. Remember to leave your phone on."

Jessie moved onto the chair Dylan had vacated and wrapped up in a blanket that was thrown over the back. The conversation with Lacey Truman had finished and the men in the kitchen were waiting for a computer file he was sending them with the layout of the property. The house was built into the ridge and there was a bomb shelter built beneath it. The food stockpiled there could easily last a month. Lacey had advised against going in heavy-handed. *Tyler won't be intimidated by a show of force. He's seen it all.* The area was crisscrossed with dozens of trails and animal tracks, and the only access road was fully visible from the house. They would have to go in on foot if they were going to surprise him.

The door opened and Ray Davidson stepped outside. He took a quick look around but didn't seem to notice that Jessie was staring right at him with an unlit cigarette in her hand. She watched him carefully. There was something familiar about his profile. He walked out onto the lawn and stared out into the distance. Several times he picked up his phone. He appeared to be scrolling through his messages. He sent a couple off, his fingers fluttering over the keys. He drifted along the fence before turning back to the house and sitting on a bench under the trees. A couple of minutes later, he picked up the phone and put it to his ear. Although he was keeping his voice down, he was so close Jessie could hear everything he said.

"Macy," he said, taking a quick look around. "Will you please pick up the goddamn phone and tell me where you are? I'm sorry about earlier. I don't want to lose you and our son."

He hung up and keyed in another number. This time he didn't bother to speak softly.

"Hi, sweetheart. Sorry about earlier. Are the girls okay?" He listened. "Look, I know we've been having a rough time but things will get better now, you'll see . . . I love you too. We'll talk again tomorrow."

Jessie struck the match just as he stepped onto the porch. It flared against the tip of her cigarette. He stood a few feet away, looking down at her.

"I know you from somewhere," she said, pointing the smoldering cigarette at him. "Do you live around here?"

"No. You must be mistaken."

"That's weird. You look familiar."

"I'm on the news sometimes," he said, turning to go. "Maybe that's it."

She took a long drag. "So, where *do* you live?"

"Down in Helena."

"With your wife and daughters?"

"Yes."

"Sounds like you have the perfect lie."

"Excuse me?"

"I said it sounds like you have the perfect life." She tilted her head toward the kitchen door. "The computer file you were waiting for has arrived."

"You were listening?"

She took a long draw and looked him in the eye.

"I heard everything."

25

Macy checked into her new motel at around one in the morning, but was already on the road again by five. She'd not seen any of her fellow guests. The parking lot was full of minivans with Canadian plates and homemade signs saying *Yellowstone or Bust*. It looked like an entire group was heading south in tandem. She checked the time. There was an operations briefing scheduled for six at the local elementary school's auditorium. She'd be able to grab some breakfast if she hurried. She glanced at her reflection in the rearview mirror. There was no disguising the fact that she'd barely slept. She took a deep breath and concentrated on the coming day. Despite her efforts, Ray was foremost in her thoughts. It was only a matter of time before they were in the same room again. She had to figure out a way of negotiating their personal situation without jeopardizing her career. She stopped at the first of Wilmington Creek's three traffic lights and waited for the signal to change. The main road through town was lined with patrol cars and SWAT team vehicles. They'd yet to locate Charlie Lott's vehicle, but that hadn't stopped Ray from gathering the troops.

Macy parked in a free space in front of The Whitefish where a young officer stood looking down at the cards and flowers that had been left in tribute to John Dalton. The paper had faded and the moldering mound smelled of sweet decay. Some of the candles were still lit, but most were only a pool of hard wax on the pavement. She crossed the street and ducked into the Wilmington Creek Bar and Grill. Considering the early hour, it was very busy. Aiden wasn't there, but Ray was sitting at a table near the door with three senior police officers she recognized. It was impossible to pretend she didn't see him. He waved her over and offered her the empty chair to his left. They were discussing strategy. A detailed map of the terrain surrounding Lacey Truman's property was spread out in front of them. His home and all the access points had been highlighted.

"Where's Alden Marsh?" she asked, leaning back so the waitress could pour coffee into a clean mug that had suddenly appeared.

"You just missed him," said Ray, gesturing to her place at the table. "There's been a development. We found Charlie Lott's car a couple miles south of the access road. Looks like he and Lana spent the night in it. There's a trailhead within walking distance. Fresh tracks indicate they don't have too much of a head start."

Ray pointed to the spot on the map where the car was found.

An officer named Howard Reynolds yawned into his closed fist. "Macy, after what happened to you it's good to see you up and about. Ray was just telling us how you decided that it was best that you sit today's operation out. It's a shame, but he said you were adamant."

Macy concentrated on the map, tracing her eyes across the pathways and focusing in on every contour. There was a rushing noise in her ears. She imagined this was what it sounded like when someone's blood boiled. Her expression didn't change though. The years of being Ray's subordinate kicked in instinctively. She was grateful. No matter how loud she wanted to scream, she wouldn't question his authority in front of a group of senior police officers. This wasn't the time or the place. She swallowed. Out of the corner of her eye she caught sight of Ray raising his freshly poured cup of coffee to his lips. It took all her self-control not to throw it in his face. She saw herself point at the map. Her voice sounded wooden.

"Tell me again where you found the car?"

Howard's stubby finger followed the thin thread of a tertiary road to where it forked and then headed south. "It was parked here."

"Was it hidden?"

"It was parked off the road. That's all I know so far."

"And how far is that from the property?"

Ray spoke this time. "It's a seven-mile hike in, but it's over fairly rough terrain." He sighed like he meant it. "We'll miss you today, but you made the right call. It's going to be pretty hard going."

Macy followed a trail that wove through the landscape toward the house on the ridge. It crossed a stream before heading uphill. "What's this cross marked here?"

Howard talked through a mouthful of scrambled eggs. "That's where the dogs lost Lana's scent."

A waitress handed Macy a menu, but she shook her head. She'd lost her appetite. "Why do you suppose that happened?"

Ray started to get up and the others at the table followed his lead.

Howard put his crumpled napkin next to his plate. "We can't really say. Sometimes it happens."

"And sometimes suspects double back."

"They thought of that, but came up with nothing. A team is heading up to the property now, so we'll know for sure soon enough."

"Not necessarily. The compound is pretty well fortified. It may be a while before you can establish whether he's there."

Ray grumbled. "He's got a hostage and he's highly visible. There aren't many places he can go."

"You're forgetting about Sarah Reed. She might be helping him." Macy addressed Howard. "Can I keep this?"

"I don't see why not. We have lots of copies."

"We're heading over to the operations briefing," said Ray. "You should come along in case there are any questions. You've had direct contact with Tyler Locke."

Macy picked up the map. Her hands were starting to shake. She turned away and grabbed her bag.

"I've just got to stop by Alden's office first. I want to get my notes."

Howard gave her a pat on the back. "You've done fantastic work getting us this far. We'll bring it home for you."

Keeping her eyes low, Macy darted down the covered walkway. All around her, SWAT team members were clinking about in their heavy gear. Farther on, local law enforcement loitered around their vehicles, talking in low voices, some smoking cigarettes, most drinking from takeaway coffee cups the size of Big Gulps. The sun was just coming up as she opened the front doors to the police station and headed past the empty desks in the main room. She slammed Aiden's office door behind her and threw her bag on the nearest chair. A larger version of the same map they'd been looking at in the restaurant was tacked to the wall above Aiden's desk. She focused in on the point where the dog handlers had lost Lana Clark's scent. The door opened and she was relieved to hear Aiden's voice.

"Hey," he said, catching hold of her arm as she started to move away. "Everything okay? Ray said you were unwell."

She didn't look at him. "There's nothing wrong with my health, Aiden."

"Then why are you staying behind today?"

"That was Ray's decision, not mine. Last night I told him it was over between us. This morning he effectively took me off the case."

"He can't do that."

"He just did."

"Does that mean you're heading back to Helena?"

"I don't know. I don't like leaving things unfinished."

"What are you going to do about Ray?"

"I'm not sure what I can do without ruining my career. He's a pow-erful man and I was stupid to get involved with him. And don't even get me started on the way he's handling this." She glanced up at the map. "As far as I can tell, they're about to create a hostage situation that we won't be able to get out of. Tyler isn't the type to negotiate."

"The owner has a month of supplies stockpiled up there. This could go on for a long time." He reached for the door handle. "We'd better get moving. The briefing starts in a couple of minutes."

"I'm not going. I can't be in the same room as Ray right now. I might say or do something I'll regret later on."

"I'll tell them you aren't feeling well. Given what he's telling every-one, no one will question it."

"Thank you."

"You'll stick around?"

She kept her eyes on the map. "I might go for a drive."

The door to the office closed and Macy stepped around the desk so she could study the map more closely. Unlike the printout, this one comprised the whole western area of the valley south of Darby Lake. She traced her finger along the highlighted path, from where they'd lost Lana's scent to where they'd found Charlie Lott's car. It was a distance of three miles and crossed a stream at about the midpoint. The stream originated in the higher elevations and flowed east to-ward the valley floor, eventually following the course of a well-marked trail. She tracked its progress to where it met the Flathead River. Ty-ler and Lana would have had to cover a distance of approximately six miles to get there. She checked the time. It was coming up on twenty to six. She gathered her things and made sure her gun was loaded before stepping outside. Aside from a sleepy-eyed receptionist, the office was completely empty.

. . .

Macy drove past the patrol cars and SWAT vans parked along Main Street. At the elementary school, the last of the patrol officers were entering the auditorium.

Her eyes flicked up to the rearview mirror. Aiden had seen her. He'd been talking to Ray. Even from a distance Macy could tell it was a tense exchange. Seconds later her phone rang.

Aiden's voice was muffled. "Where are you going?"

"The dog handlers lost Lana's scent. It's a long shot, but it's possible Tyler doubled back and followed a stream heading east. A trail leads straight to the Flathead River."

"He'd need someone to help him."

Macy checked the wing mirror. "That's where Sarah Reed comes in."

"I want you to call me if you see anything suspicious."

"Will do."

"I don't like the idea of you heading down there on your own."

"Don't worry, it's probably nothing."

"You thought that about Karen Walcott and look what happened."

Macy turned south onto Route 93 and increased her speed.

"Keep this to yourself, okay? I don't want to turn this into a circus."

"I suppose you'd like to show Ray up."

"To tell you the truth, I think that would just make matters worse. In a way, I'm hoping I'm wrong about this."

Macy crossed over railway tracks before coming to a narrow bridge that sat low over the Flathead River. To the north the shoreline was choked with rock and dotted with wildflowers. The view was hazy in the morning light. A thin mist hovered inches above the water and birds flitted above the deeper pools. The dirt road swung sharply to the north and she was instantly swallowed up by the quiet cool of a densely wooded area. Macy rolled down her window and cut her speed. The smell of fresh pine mingled with wood smoke. Shadowy pathways branched out in all directions. The truck bounced along for another few minutes before the trees suddenly vanished. The western slope was flattened out and the plant life was sparse. It looked as if there'd been a landslide at some point. She stopped at the trailhead and pulled out her binoculars. The path snaked upward in a series of tight switchbacks. There was no movement whatsoever, and she'd not seen a single car since leaving Route 93. She turned around where the track widened, and parked so she had a clear view of the area. She stepped outside. Other than birdsong and the flowing water it was silent.

If Tyler had decided to bring Lana here, there was no way of knowing how long they'd take to make the journey. It was seven miles. Depending on how much Lana slowed him down, that could take all day or less than a couple of hours. The ground near the trailhead was hard packed and dusty. There were traces of tire tracks everywhere, but it was impossible to tell if they were recent. Macy stepped down onto the boulders that lined the river. The water level was low enough that it could be traversed safely on foot. She climbed down onto the wash of bleached stone and walked to where the span was at its most narrow. There was a single footprint in the wet sand. She squatted down low. The heel was deep and rounded at the back. It could have been made by a cowboy boot.

The land on the opposite side of the river rose to the reinforced embankment that supported the railway line. From there it was only a matter of a few feet of open ground before you reached a densely planted stand of pine trees. Macy could see nothing in the deep shadows. It would be easy to conceal a car in there. She pulled out the map again. The area could be reached on a farm track that ran in a straight line from the secondary road she took from Route 93.

Macy followed the gravel farm track until it gave way to a deep-rutted road leading into the center of a stand of pine trees that covered at least three acres. A vehicle that had passed through recently had flattened the vegetation. She walked slowly with her weapon drawn. From a small clearing, the opposite shore of the Flathead River was almost visible through the trees. Some bark was scraped from a tree trunk. There were green flecks of paint embedded in the wood. She glanced back toward the river. She could have sworn she saw something move.

Macy kept low as she made her way west. The undergrowth was so thick it was difficult to find a path. Fallen branches crackled underfoot and above her restless birds flitted through the canopy. She found Sarah Reed standing on the edge of the railroad tracks. Her back was to Macy and she wore a long white wedding dress. Her arms hung limp at her sides and she was holding a gun in her right hand. There was an open suitcase on the ground next to her.

Macy brushed away a cloud of gnats. "Sarah Reed. My name is Detective Macy Greeley. I want you to drop your weapon and keep your hands where we can see them."

Sarah didn't move.

"Sarah, nod if you can hear me."

She nodded.

"Drop the gun, Sarah."

Sarah's shoulders were shaking. She may have been crying.

"Sarah, did you come here to meet Tyler Locke?"

Sarah's words escaped with a sob. "He lied to me."

Macy fought the urge to lower her weapon. "He lied to everyone."

"He was just going to leave me here."

"Was Lana Clark with him?"

"She hates him. Even I could see that."

"Sarah, you need to put your weapon down. I will shoot you if I have to."

She glanced down at the gun in her hand and stared at it like she was noticing it for the first time. "He didn't think I'd do it. Said I was a stupid bitch. Always had been." She was laughing and crying at the same time. "So I shot him."

"Do you know where is he now?"

"He left me here."

The ground started to tremble. At first it was so slight that Macy thought she was imagining it, but then a metallic shudder ran through the steel rails. A train was approaching from the north, and it was coming fast.

Sarah raised her eyes. She was shivering in her long dress. There were brambles caught in the lace. Her feet were bare.

A warning whistle blew.

"Sarah, I want you to come over here where it's safer."

The gun slipped from Sarah's hand and tumbled down the gravel embankment. She turned to face Macy with her arms half raised, but she didn't move away from the tracks. A fan of fine wrinkles fishtailed her eyes. The DMV photo they had pulled didn't do her justice. She may have been an older woman, but Sarah Reed was fiercely attractive. There was a second high-pitched whistle, louder and more frantic than the first.

Macy had to raise her voice to be heard. "Please, Sarah, step away from the tracks."

The earth shuddered. The metal rails ticked and hissed. Brakes screamed. Sarah jumped just as the train blew past. Macy stared at the spot where Sarah had once stood. Despite her best efforts to hold it in, Macy started crying.

The last train carriage was at least fifty yards to the south. It had taken a long time to stop. Aside from the crackle of her police radio the woods were quiet. Macy had difficulty making herself understood. Instead of slowing down and speaking clearly, she raised her voice. The woman working dispatch told her to take her time.

"Tyler Locke is driving a green F-150 pickup truck registered to Sarah Reed. He was last seen in the company of Lana Clark, twelve miles south of Wilmington Creek near the Devil's Canyon trailhead. He might have a gunshot wound."

She requested assistance. "No, an ambulance will not be necessary."

Macy walked along the empty tracks until she reached the northern edge of the stand of trees. The air was so clear she could see all the way to Canada. She took a deep breath. Tyler Locke could be anywhere. She didn't like the odds. She turned around and started heading back to the train. The driver was walking toward her. His shoulders were slumped and a baseball cap shaded his face. He wore heavy work gloves and inspected the track as he made his way north. He was twenty feet from where Sarah had stood when he stopped and stared out in the direction of the river. His shoulders slumped further. He looked like he was carrying the weight of the world.

Macy pulled up in front of the truck stop's diner and cut the engine. The parking area was almost empty. Three mobile homes sat on a patch of bare earth at the far end of the lot. One was now a burnt-out shell and another one's middle had caved in. The third home appeared to be occupied. Every so often the curtains shifted. Macy felt as if she was being watched. As a professional courtesy, she'd put in a call to Ray. She'd been relieved when he didn't pick up. According to his personal assistant, he was already on his way back to Helena. She had to admit that it was unsettling to be cut loose so suddenly.

Macy couldn't stop thinking about Sarah Reed. She blew her nose and tilted up her sunglasses so she could look in the mirror. It was obvious she'd been crying. She rooted around the glove compartment for a bottle of eyedrops, but came up with a wreath-shaped Christmas ornament she'd been given by someone at the office. There was a picture of Luke in the center. She slipped it into her bag. She had to stay focused. The sooner she found Tyler, the sooner she could go home.

Her cell phone rang and she put Aiden on speakerphone. Macy had been relieved when he'd insisted on going on his own to speak to Dylan. She pictured Sarah's white satin dress crumpled, torn, and covered in blood on the opposite side of the tracks. Her body had flown all the way to the river's edge. She was lying on her front. It looked as if she'd crawled there. Macy couldn't help but feel she'd failed them both.

"Hey Aiden, how are you holding up?"

"I'm on my way to see Dylan now."

"I am sorry."

"Me too."

"I let his therapist know what happened."

"That was probably wise. I've arranged for Jessie to meet me there, and for a family support officer to see him as well. Have you had a chance to interview Sarah's colleagues?"

"I just pulled up at the diner."

"You'll have to get started without me."

"Ray is on his way back to Helena."

"Have you spoken to him?"

"He didn't answer my call."

"He's telling everyone that you discussed your plans with him before heading out this morning." He paused. "I don't think anyone's buying it."

"Howard Reynolds called to compliment me on my swift recovery. I'm pretty sure he realized something wasn't right about what went down at breakfast. He told me to give him a call later."

"What are you going to say?"

"I don't know. It's tricky. I really don't want to speak ill of Ray professionally."

"I don't think you have to. It's obvious to everyone that's paying attention that he's made some bad calls over the past few days."

"Ray doesn't usually get involved on an operational level. I really don't know why he's been all over this case."

"Could it have something to do with what's going on between the two of you?"

"God, I hope not. He's a professional. He wouldn't let our situation affect his judgment."

"That's not how it looks from the outside."

"I think you're connecting dots that aren't there."

"Anyway, he's gone now. You can breathe again."

"And Wilmington Creek can go back to being the sleepy ranching community it's always been."

"Traffic has definitely thinned, but I don't think anyone will rest easy until Tyler is in custody."

"We need to take a look at Sarah's financial records. It's likely she withdrew a lot of cash in the last couple of days."

"I'll get on it."

"Did you get warrants to search those three remaining properties Jessie told us about?"

"It wasn't necessary. The owners are cooperating. Wade came through for us again."

"Now there's an interesting character. The state should put him on payroll."

"Or put him on a watch list. He knows a lot of people he shouldn't." He paused. "Macy?"

"Aiden?"

"Are we okay?"

Macy ran her fingers along the grooves in the steering wheel. It felt like the curvature of a spine. Last night was when they should have made time for talking. Now it was too late to know in advance what each other's expectations were. She had a feeling Aiden wanted more. She wasn't sure how she felt. Somewhere in between cautious and interested was the best she could do.

"Define okay."

"I just hope there's no weirdness about us."

"I can't speak for you, but I'm good. Anyway, last night was good."

"Last night was damn good." He lowered his voice. "I just thought maybe we should talk about it."

"Aiden."

"Macy."

"Don't worry. We're okay. I want to see you again. I like you."

"That's nice to hear."

"It's just that I don't need to talk things through. If it's working I don't like to mess with it."

"Okay."

"Most men find it refreshing."

"Maybe I'm not like most men."

"You're sensitive. I'll keep that in mind."

Aiden burst out laughing. "Okay, I can see where this is going."

"I wish I had your confidence."

"Call me if anything comes up."

"Don't worry, I will."

Macy pocketed the phone and grabbed her bag. She'd called ahead to let Sarah's boss know she was coming. Macy went inside the diner and asked to speak to Traci. The waitress behind the counter handed her a cup of coffee and directed her to a small office in the back. Traci was in her midthirties, which was surprising because her voice was already very rough. She stood up and shook Macy's hand before swinging the door shut. Macy took a seat and pulled out her notebook.

"You're younger than I expected."

Traci dropped into the chair behind the desk. "My mother gave up managing the day-to-day stuff just last year. I've been here a long time though. Started working during my sophomore year of high school."

"I take it you've known Sarah for quite a while then."

"Most of my life."

"When did you last speak to her?"

"I think it was the day after—well, it was the day after we all thought Tyler died. She wanted to take some time off, which was understandable."

"I'm sorry, but I have some very sad news. Sarah died early this morning. She was struck by a train. It was suicide."

Traci covered her mouth.

"I found Sarah at an isolated location along the Flathead River. We suspect Tyler lured her there because he needed a car and cash." Macy's voice broke. "I tried to talk to her, but she wouldn't listen. I imagine she thought she didn't have a choice."

"Tyler just took her car and left her there?"

"It appears so. He had Lana Clark with him."

Traci sat back in her chair. "You know Sarah fell in love with that asshole after just one date. My mom and I tried to get her to see sense but she wouldn't listen. Tyler was the one. She was obsessed with him. She didn't seem to care that he didn't feel the same way. She was convinced he'd come around."

"I want to speak to her coworkers. I need to figure out where Sarah has been the last couple of days. Tyler may have taken Lana there." She paused. "Maybe there was someplace they used to go together?"

Traci stood up and moved toward the door. "I'm pretty sure there was a cabin somewhere, but Tempi will know the details. It was remote. Maybe somewhere northeast of here."

"Where's Tempi? I need to speak to her."

"She was working behind the counter when you came in. I'll go get her."

Tempi talked through a wad of Kleenex that she kept pressed to her face like a mask.

"Sarah called me yesterday. She told me not to worry if she wasn't in touch. She said she needed to get away for a while."

"What time was this?"

"It must have been around five."

"Did she say anything else?"

"Nothing specific. She seemed really calm, which was odd considering everything that's happened. I thought that maybe she was in shock."

"Did she ever tell you about a cabin she'd go to with Tyler?"

Tempi pulled another tissue from the box on the desk and blew. "There was an old guy that used to come in the diner just to talk to Sarah. Never ate much, but he'd go on and on about his life and how he had this place where he used to take his family. Sarah would refill his coffee cup and listen. He seemed harmless. Just needed the company, I suppose. Anyway, about five years ago an envelope arrives for Sarah. Inside there's a map and a key. He knew how much she liked hunting. He said she could use his cabin anytime she liked. Weird thing was we never saw him again."

"Did you get a name?"

"Lou Bartlett."

"Was he local?"

"I assumed he lived somewhere nearby because he was always coming in. I thought the cabin was kind of isolated, but Sarah loved it up there."

"You've been to see it?"

"Yes, I thought it was better if I went with her that first time. You get all kinds of weird guys coming through town. I wanted to make sure it was okay."

"Tempi, this is important. You need to tell me exactly where that cabin is."

Aiden pulled into the truck stop parking lot just as Macy stepped out of the diner. She grabbed her gear from the back of her vehicle and jumped into his. He had an ordinance survey map spread out on the seat between them.

"Lou Bartlett's property is on the land registry. The coordinates they gave me should put it right about here." He bent forward and marked a spot on the map.

Macy traced her eyes over the roads leading up to the property. "That matches up with what I've been told."

"Good. Let's get going."

She pulled on her seat belt. "Do you think we should call for backup?"

"We already have teams checking those three other properties. Let's make sure he's there before calling for support."

Macy lowered her voice. "How did Dylan take the news?"

"A little too well for my liking. He seems numb. I couldn't get any reaction out of him."

"That's just a front. Does he have any idea where his mother has been the last couple of days?"

"I'm not sure he even knew where he's been. He really wasn't up to answering any questions. He's with Jessie. I'm not sure how much help she'll be though. The family support officer is on her way."

Macy slipped on a pair of sunglasses. "You know, I've been thinking a lot about Tyler's commanding officer and the guys I interviewed from his platoon. Not one of them mentioned Tyler's mental health evacuation. They only spoke about Tyler in relation to John. Nothing more, nothing less."

"It's not surprising. There's a lot of stigma associated with mental illness."

"That needs to change."

"Well, good luck with that."

As the patrol car sped north on Route 93, Aiden glanced over at the map.

"Can you check? I think the turnoff is only a couple miles further on."

His phone rang and he put it on speaker. Jessie Dalton's voice filled the SUV. She sounded out of breath.

"Aiden, Dylan went after Tyler. I couldn't stop him."

"Did he say where he was going?"

"Some cabin his mother uses. He's going to do something crazy."

"We're heading up there now. Hang tight. I'll call you when I have news."

Aiden took a sharp turn and headed east toward the Whitefish Range.

'This might be a good time to call for backup." Macy picked up the police radio and glanced over at Aiden. "This isn't going to end well."

Aiden increased his speed. "That's hardly surprising given how it began."

26

D ylan's pickup truck rattled along the gravel track, kicking up so much dust it was difficult to see what was coming up behind. He turned onto a paved road and hit eighty miles an hour on a straightaway heading east. The loose suspension bounced across the solid waves of asphalt. He checked the rearview mirror. Jessie's hatchback had vanished from sight. To her credit she'd kept up for longer than he thought possible. He should have taken her car keys away before he left the house, but he hadn't been thinking clearly.

He'd been sorting through his mother's unopened mail when Aiden had pulled up in his patrol car with Jessie following close behind. Dylan had stepped out onto the front porch to greet them but had been uneasy at the way Jessie walked with her eyes down and her hands thrust deep into her pockets. He'd led them into the sitting room, but had not sat. He'd stood staring out at the gravestones beyond the back fence. His dog had gotten loose and had been running around the cemetery with his nose to the ground, trying to sniff something out. Dylan had slid the door open and called his dog home.

Aiden, I know you aren't here to keep me company, so let's just get this over with.

His mother had died in an *instant*. That was the word that Aiden had used. *Instant*. Dylan had fought the desire to laugh. There was nothing instantaneous about his mother's death. He'd seen that train coming for years.

Aiden had left with a promise to check in on him later, but Jessie had remained where she'd been sitting since she'd slunk into the house. She'd watched Dylan's every move. The only thing she'd managed to say so far had been *sorry*. He was thankful for her silence.

Normally prone to fidget, he couldn't do much more than stand in the middle of the kitchen and stare at the walls. For the first time since he'd moved back home he had noticed that they'd changed color. They were blue. He could have sworn they were supposed to be yellow. He didn't understand. His mother had always hated the color blue.

I knew about the wedding dress, he'd said. *Mom had it hidden in a cupboard along with a bunch of bridal magazines. I think she's been planning on marrying Tyler for years.*

Do you think he ever asked her?

Maybe. It would explain why she had it with her.

Your poor mother.

He was so manipulative. He'd let her get close then push her away. She came off all tough, but she really didn't stand a chance. I should have tried harder to stop it.

How were you going to do that? Near as I can tell, there was no talking sense to her.

I could have gone straight to Tyler. He'd shrugged. *Maybe he would have listened.*

And maybe he would have laughed in your face.

I wonder where he is.

I hope he bleeds to death.

That would be too good for him.

Do you think your mother found someplace for them to stay?

Dylan had pulled open the junk drawer where Sarah kept all her spare keys in a cigar tin. The ones to Lou Bartlett's cabin had been missing. Jessie had come into the kitchen and stood next to him.

You should call Aiden.

Let Aiden figure it out himself.

Jessie had wanted to come but he wouldn't let her get in his truck. Given all he'd lost, he'd figured he'd earned the right to deal with Tyler on his own. He'd crossed over Route 93 about eight miles north of Wilmington Creek and headed toward the Whitefish Range. The road had started to climb immediately. Now the sun-bleached tarmac slipped by in a rush, and sky and land bled together in a wash of color that fragmented around the edges. The road rose and dipped and the wheels briefly lost their grip. The truck came down hard and a sharp pain kicked up through his leg. He pushed down on the gas pedal and snapped round a corner like a whip. The back end scraped the guardrail, letting out a metallic scream so sharp he thought he saw sparks jump from the steering wheel. He downshifted, picked up speed, and flew across another rise. He was getting close now. He rounded a curve and took in the view. Jagged peaks erupted from the landscape. Below, rocks tumbled down to the lowlands where a stream threaded through the needle of a deep gorge.

For most of the way, the driveway wasn't visible from the cabin. At the final turn, pine trees ringed a large mass of boulders. After that the land opened up into a high mountain meadow. Dylan didn't even try to hide his car. He pulled up within sight of the cabin, blocking the drive at the narrowest point. His mother's pickup truck was parked out front with the driver's side door hanging open.

"Tyler," he called. "You in there?"

Dylan stood watching the house. The shutters were closed tight and the front door was shut. Around the side there was some washing hanging out to dry. Stark white sheets fluttered in the breeze. Using his mother's truck as cover, he made his way to the porch, poking his head inside one of the vehicle's open windows as he passed. Blood had seeped into the creases of the driver's seat. It was tacky to the touch. Keeping low, he stepped onto the small porch. A blood trail stopped at the base of the closed door. He moved to one side and banged on the wooden slats with his fist.

"Tyler, it's Dylan. Open the door."

Dylan leaned in and listened. The thick outer walls were constructed from the heavy trunks of pine trees. He could hear nothing beyond his own breathing. He tried again.

"Tyler, it's just me out here. Open the door."

There was the sharp sound of a metal latch being slid back. The hinges groaned as the door drew open a foot. Lana stared out at him, her hair loose and sticking to her damp forehead. Her eyes were raw, but alert. Tyler stood behind her with one hand gripped tight around her neck. Dylan looked past Lana and addressed Tyler directly.

"If I managed to find you, the cops can't be far behind."

"Go home, Dylan."

The whites of Tyler's eyes caught what little light there was. They were glazed over and webbed with fine broken veins. Lana was crying. Fat tears rolled down her cheeks unchecked. Dylan kept his eyes on Tyler.

"I'm not going anywhere without Lana."

Tyler twisted Lana's long hair in his fist and pulled her head back. He rested his right arm on her shoulder and aimed a gun in Dylan's face.

"How about I just shoot you now?"

Dylan leaned in so the barrel was inches from his forehead.

"Let's see if you're man enough to do it while I'm looking right at you."

"Fuck you, Dylan."

"What? Did you think I was going to turn around and make it easy for you?"

Tyler tightened his grip on the gun.

"That's how you managed it with John. How did that make you feel? You're the one that's always going on about honor."

Tyler pressed the gun against Dylan's forehead. "Shut up."

Dylan didn't move. "And now you've dragged Lana up here so you can play happy families. This isn't how it works. You love someone. They love you back. You can't make that shit up."

Tyler raised his voice. "Lana, open the door." He shoved her forward. "I said open the door."

He kept his gun aimed at Dylan as they stepped out on the porch. Lana wore no shoes and her skin was so flushed she looked feverish. She misjudged the step and nearly toppled over, crying out when Tyler tightened his grip on her hair. He was bare-chested and bleeding heavily from a wound to his stomach. The gauze was soaked through with blood. Dark stains seeped into the waistline of his jeans and spread down his thigh.

Dylan glanced at the bandages wrapped around Tyler's torso.

"Looks like my mother should have aimed a little higher."

The sun was high in the sky, casting a harsh light that caught hold of everything. Perspiration was streaming down Tyler's forehead and chest. He moved with difficulty, his lips twisting into a grimace as he pulled Lana to him. He'd taken hold of her neck again.

Dylan took a few steps back and they followed him farther out into the open.

"Let Lana go so we can talk this through."

"Dylan, I want you to get in your truck and get the hell out of here."

"And do what? John and my mom are dead, and you might as well be. I loved you like a brother, Tyler." He spread his arms. "Do you have any idea what you've done?"

"Sarah's dead?"

Dylan practically spit. "You don't have the right to feel bad about my mother. Not after the way you treated her."

"When I left she was alive. It had nothing to do with me."

"She jumped in front of a train. It had everything to do with you."

Tyler had no answer.

'She was wearing a wedding dress. Did you promise to marry her?" He took a step closer so the gun's barrel was pressed to his chest. "Is that why she had it with her? Were you going to be my daddy?"

"I don't want to hurt you."

"Then let Lana go."

'I can't."

'Why's that? Does she love you?"

"Yes."

"She hates you."

"That's not true. Tell him, Lana. Tell him what you said earlier."

Lana started to speak but stopped. Her mouth snapped into a stubborn line. Tyler shook her so hard that she nearly fell to her knees.

"Tell him."

She kept her mouth shut.

"If you have to hold a gun to Lana's head to get her to say she loves you, it doesn't count."

Dylan took a step to the right and Tyler circled around with him. Dylan now had a clear view of the driveway. There was the slightest sway of the trees ringing the boulders and a flash as something reflective caught the light. He steadied his voice.

"You do know they're coming for you? You killed a cop. You're going to prison."

Tyler's hand was shaking so much he could barely hold the gun steady.

"I didn't kill that cop."

"No one is going to believe you."

"I won't go to jail."

"Are you hoping someone will take you out of your misery, or will you do it yourself?"

Lana closed her eyes. She was muttering prayers under her breath. She was limp in Tyler's grip, so close to collapse it appeared that he was all that was propping her up.

Dylan scanned the terrain beyond Tyler's wide shoulders. He wasn't imagining things. They weren't alone. Someone was moving amongst the rocks to the left of his truck.

"What do you say? Are you ready to take one for the team? Should we pray for your soul?"

Tyler started crying. "I want you to tell Jeremy that I'm sorry."

"If I really believed that, I'd call him right now." He caught Tyler's eye. "I'm asking you as a friend. Let Lana go. It will just be you and me. You know me. You trust me. We can talk this through."

"No."

"There's still time to make this right. You let Lana go and it shows you're sorry." His voice cracked. "Don't you see that?"

"Come on," he said, jabbing the gun into Lana's ribs. "I've had enough of this bullshit. We're going back inside."

Lana knocked Tyler's hand away and started swinging her arms wildly.

"Let go of me. I hate you. You hear me, Tyler? I hate you."

Tyler tried to keep hold of her, but she twisted from his arms and stumbled away, falling to her knees and crawling. Dylan jumped on Tyler before he had a chance to shoot. There was a sickening crunch as Tyler head-butted Dylan square in the face. The cartilage in Dylan's nose splintered and blood poured down his chin. Locked in each other's arms, they hit the ground fighting.

The gun went off in that same instant.

A crack.

A scream.

And all that pain that followed.

Dylan lay on his back, gasping for air. His ears were ringing and the acrid taste of sick pooled in the back of his throat. He reached over and wrenched the pistol from Tyler's hand. As he pressed it to Tyler's head, he squeezed his eyes shut and felt for the trigger. The metal crescent curved around his finger like a ring. It was a perfect fit.

"Do it," said Tyler.

Dylan tossed the gun to one side and said, "Do it yourself."

There were voices. Footfalls. Shouts. The static of a police radio. Dylan stared up into the cloudless sky, catching hold of that blue he loved so much.

Macy Greeley knelt next to him, long wisps of red hair escaping a ponytail. Her skin glowed white. She put an ice-cold hand to his cheek.

"Dylan, can you hear me? Help is on the way."

She shouted instructions into a police radio she held in one hand while applying pressure to his wounded chest with the other. Blood gushed up between her fingers. It sprayed a fine arc of arterial red across her white T-shirt. He lay back and searched the sky for another hint of that blue. A helicopter hovered overhead, blocking out the mid-day sun.

"Hang in there."

He gazed up into her pale face. She had freckles. They reminded him of summer. He closed his eyes.

It was going to be okay.

He was safe.

This time he was really going home.

27

The heat wave broke a little after midnight. Lightning strikes rattled the windows, waking Luke from what had already been a fractious sleep. He spent the rest of the night in Macy's bed, his nose on her shoulder, his arms and legs flung wide. When the alarm went off, she untangled herself from the sheets, got dressed, and went downstairs to make breakfast. Her mother, Ellen, was standing at the back door looking out into the garden. She'd pulled her nightgown tight around. It was a hard rain. It overwhelmed the gutters and ran off the roof in a cascade. Ellen wiped away condensation from the glass.

"There was a hailstorm during the night. My flower beds are destroyed."

"I heard. It sounded like golf balls were landing on the roof."

"I'm not sure I'm happy that you're taking Luke with you to Lindsay Moore's funeral. Are you sure it's a good idea?"

"The funeral was private. This is just the service. Besides, it will give people something positive to focus on. From what I understand, Lindsay hasn't much in the way of family. A lot of people are bringing their kids."

"I suppose Ray will be there with his family in tow."

"It won't be a problem."

Macy went into the kitchen, poured a cup of coffee, and started preparing breakfast. "Mom," she said, changing the subject. "About this friend who's coming for dinner."

"Aiden Marsh?"

She looked up from the bagel she was slicing in half. "Oh, I forgot I told you his name."

"He's very handsome. My girlfriends approve."

"How do your girlfriends know what he looks like?"

Her mother sipped her coffee. "We Googled him. You didn't tell me he was the chief of police. That certainly livened things up at lunch on Wednesday."

Macy went over and wrapped her arms around her mother. Together they watched it rain.

"I have to remember not to give you names."

"Will you promise not to rush into anything? You've got a lot of healing to do. Your relationship with Ray destroyed your confidence."

"I don't think I have much choice. Aiden lives up in Wilmington Creek and I live here. Anyway, this feels different. I like him, but I don't need to be with him. If I didn't hear from him again it would be fine."

"Does he know about Ray?"

"Yes, and before you ask, he also knows Ray is Luke's father."

"What about at work? Do you think Ray is going to give you any trouble? He's your boss. He could make your life miserable."

"It's because he's my boss that he wouldn't dare do anything. I could file a complaint, and he knows it. Anyway, after how everything went down, I'm pretty untouchable. He ended up looking kind of foolish."

"One of your better results. Is there any news on Dylan Reed? You said you were going to make a call last night."

"I left a message with his doctors, but they haven't gotten back to me. As far as I know, he hasn't woken up yet."

"A lot of people are praying for him. And what about Lana Clark? I imagine she'll be having nightmares her entire life."

"I think she's finally taking things into her own hands. I heard she's been offered a book deal."

The doorbell rang.

"This is early for a Saturday morning."

"It might be a delivery. I'll get it."

Macy looked through the peephole. A hooded rain jacket framed Jessie Dalton's pale face. Macy released the security chain and opened the door. They stared at each other across the threshold. Jessie's jacket was sodden. A brand-new pickup truck was parked at the curb. Macy recognized the Dalton Ranch logo on the door.

"Jessie, how did you know where I lived?"

She pulled the hood back. "I came to your office yesterday to talk to you."

"Did you follow me home?"

"I wanted to see you at work, but I lost my nerve."

Macy looked out at the truck again. "Did you sleep in your car?"

She nodded. "It's important. Can I come in?"

Macy called to Ellen before opening the door further. "Mom, can you go check on Luke?"

"Who is it?"

Macy gestured for Jessie to come in. "Jessie Dalton, this is my mother, Ellen. Ellen, Jessie."

Ellen came forward and took Jessie's hand. "You're so cold. I'll put on another pot of coffee before I go upstairs."

Macy led Jessie to the living room. If it were possible, Jessie looked even thinner. She seemed to disappear between all the pillows lined up on the sofa. Macy pulled up a chair and sat across from her.

"How is Dylan? Has he woken up?"

She brightened. "For a few minutes yesterday. I've been with him all this time. I needed to be there when he opened his eyes."

"Did he say anything?"

"No, he's really weak. He recognized me though. He held my hand."

"That's a good sign." Macy picked a stray feather from a pillow. "He's lucky to be alive."

"I don't believe living was ever in his plans."

"You're going to have your hands full looking after him."

"I know."

"Are you in Helena to visit your mom?"

"That was the intention. I need to talk to her about the stuff she's been saying. It may not make a difference but it will make me feel better." She glanced at the family photos stacked three deep on the bookshelf. "Tyler's lawyer called. He wants to know if I saw Tyler up at the ranch the afternoon Lindsay Moore died."

"You have yet to give a statement to the police on that matter. Is there a reason you're hesitating?"

"I can't make up my mind whether I should lie. I figure Tyler should get whatever he deserves and more. If he gets sent down for killing a cop I figure they'll make his life miserable."

"That's probably true."

"I knew John was out repairing a fence on the eastern boundary that day so I rode out to meet him. I came over a rise and saw the two of them working together. They were digging new postholes. Tyler had his shirt off. All those tattoos and that bare head. Even from a distance I recognized him. He doesn't know that I saw him. If I wanted to, I could keep quiet about it."

"Why have you decided to speak out?"

"He couldn't have killed Lindsay Moore. It doesn't seem right that someone else gets away with it."

"It does raise a lot of questions. There was a ballistics match. You see the confusion."

"I read in the papers that she was pregnant."

"Yes, somewhere between three and four months."

"I think I know who the father might be."

Ellen stood in the door with a tray of coffee cups and pastries. "Sorry to interrupt," she said, placing the tray on the coffee table and giving Jessie a pointed look. "You'll eat something." She touched Macy on the top of the head. "Luke is having his breakfast."

"Thank you, Mom. Could you please close the door?"

Macy turned around to find that Jessie was staring directly at her.

"You seem nice," said Jessie. "I don't want to hurt you."

Macy tilted her head. "I don't see how you could."

"The night Ray Davidson was up at the ranch, I overheard him talking on his phone. He was leaving you a message. He was upset because he thought he was losing you and his son."

"It's been a trying time for all of us. I've decided it is best to move on. He wasn't good for me."

"I don't think he was good for Lindsay Moore either."

Macy put down her cup. "What are you trying to say?"

"I saw them together."

"That's not unexpected. She worked for him."

"It wasn't like that. They were a couple."

Macy felt a fluttering in her chest. She cleared her throat. "Go on."

"Do you know a bar called the Whispering Pines?"

"I've seen it. As I recall, it's down near Walleye Junction. Right off Route 93."

"That's the one. A few of us met for drinks there to celebrate my girlfriend's birthday. Monica and me went out back to smoke a cigarette, and they were out there too. I think they must have been drunk, otherwise they would have been more discreet."

"They were having sex?"

"No, but they were all over each other. He had her backed up against the side of a car."

'And you're sure it was them?"

"When they were inside the bar I recognized Lindsay from seeing her around town. I didn't realize it was Ray Davidson until I spoke to him up at the house."

"Do you know the exact date?"

"Monica's birthday is May third."

"Sugar."

"Pardon?"

Macy felt dizzy. She waved a hand. "I'm trying not to say shit so often because of my son . . ." Her voice trailed off. Aiden had said that he'd pulled Ray over for speeding sometime in early May. Lindsay was in the passenger seat. He'd also thought they were a couple. She needed to find out the exact date.

Jessie's voice sounded far away. "What are you going to do?"

"That's a very good question. You're absolutely sure it was them?"

"I wasn't the only one who saw them together. Monica said she'd back me up."

Macy walked to the window and gazed out at the driving rain. She could hear Luke in the next room, giggling over his breakfast. She pictured Ray kissing his son's forehead and smoothing his dark hair. They were so similar.

"Ray Davidson killed her, didn't he? That baby she was carrying was his."

"I'm afraid you're probably right."

Macy returned to her seat and took Jessie's hands. They were warm now. "You have to be absolutely sure. Ray's lawyers will try to discredit you. They'll drag your entire history out in the open."

"I could say the same thing about you. Everyone will know you were together, that he's Luke's father."

"That can't be a factor in your decision to give evidence."

"I've spoken to Jeremy. He said he'd support me whatever decision I made."

"That's good to hear. I have a feeling you're going to need him." Macy glanced up at a photo of Luke. He'd lost a half sister or brother. "Lindsay's funeral is on Tuesday."

"Is she being cremated?"

"It's what she wanted, but given how she died, her mother decided it would be in bad taste."

"So there's still evidence."

"There's always been plenty of evidence. It just appears that Ray has been manipulating it behind the scenes."

There was a knock and the door opened. Ellen stood with Luke in her arms. "Sorry, sweetheart. He wants to see you and won't take no for an answer."

Macy took Luke onto her lap.

"I'm going to be in the kitchen if you need me."

Macy thanked her mother before turning to Jessie again. "You'll need to make a formal statement. Your lawyer can liaise directly with the state attorney to make the arrangements. Given my personal involvement, I'll need to remove myself from the investigation."

"Will you be fired?"

"No, but I might have to take a leave of absence."

"It doesn't seem right that you're the one who's being punished."

"It will be okay. I've been wanting to take some time off anyway."

Jessie held on to Luke's outstretched hand. "Hey, little guy. Did you know that you have a very brave mommy?"

Macy pressed her lips against Luke's hair. "I'd say the same thing to your daughter if she were here right now."

Howard Reynolds gave Macy a sharp look. "Are you sure you're up to this?"

She gazed out across the park. Ray had arrived early. He was sitting by himself on a bench with his feet planted wide. She'd not seen him since Lindsay's memorial service. She'd ducked out before he finished speaking, and his last words still haunted her.

It is my greatest regret that I wasn't able to protect Lindsay. I fear I will go to my grave knowing I failed her. . . .

Macy had called Aiden as soon as Jessie left her house. He confirmed that he'd pulled Ray's car over on the third of May. The meeting she'd had with Howard Reynolds lasted longer. They'd sat in his home office for over three hours. He wanted more proof, but agreed to help Macy put an internal investigation together. The days ticked by. Lindsay's DNA was found on a bullet fragment in a bag containing evidence from the highway patrol officer's shooting. It wasn't even a 9mm bullet as previously thought. Lindsay had been shot with a .22 caliber weapon. According to the logbook, Ray had accessed the case evidence the same day her body was transported to Helena. He'd also removed his DNA profile from the state database around the same time. They ran further tests and found a match within seconds. Ray had fathered Lindsay's unborn child.

Howard was speaking again. "We have enough evidence. You really don't have to put yourself through this."

"We both know it's not as easy as that. We have no murder weapon and no witnesses. I need to get him to admit it on tape."

She started walking toward Ray. The air was cool, but the sun burned hot on her back. Above the city the sky was a brilliant blue. She wore a light jacket and flat shoes. They crunched on the gravel. Her arms swung robotically by her sides. She couldn't even walk properly. She had no idea how she'd manage this.

Ray looked up and for a split second he was Luke. The similarity was striking. She hesitated. She could turn and walk away. Howard was right. According to the state attorney, they already had enough evidence to charge him. He might not be convicted for murdering Lindsay, but there was a long list of other crimes that would stick.

He approached her with his arms outstretched. She stood very still while he gave her a long hug. She'd been prepared for him to be

Karin Salvalaggio

the man who'd threatened her in her motel room and murdered the woman carrying his child. It was shocking that he could be so many things all at once. He smiled.

"Thank you for coming," he said. "I'm sorry for how I've behaved. I've really missed you."

She let herself be led. The flat of his hand pressed against the base of her spine. It was as if a million synapses had been set in motion all at once. She couldn't remember what she was supposed to say, what she was supposed to make him say.

Ray didn't stop at the bench.

"Let's walk," he said.

Macy had been told to stay within sight of the surveillance van. Her voice sounded wooden.

"Let's sit," she said.

He brushed off the bench with a newspaper someone had left behind. Wilmington Creek was still making headlines. After weeks of uncertainty, Dylan Reed was expected to make a full recovery. There was a photo of him sitting up in a hospital bed looking like a reluctant celebrity.

"It's nice that it isn't so hot anymore," she said, relieved to be sitting. She'd felt unsteady on her feet, even a little dizzy. This was better. Now she only had to think about what to say. She kept her hands on her lap. She was hoping not to have to touch him again. "I saw you with Jessica at the memorial service. Does that mean you're back together?"

"You must know by now that it's all an act."

"I want to believe you."

"Macy, you're the one person I can be honest with. I think that's why I've missed you so much."

She smoothed her palms against her jeans. "It's very important that you're honest with me now."

He put his hand to his chest. "I'll get down to my knees and swear on the Bible if that's what it takes. My wife and I are getting divorced."

318

'Ray," she said, her voice rising slightly. "This isn't about you and your wife."

He started to speak but she put a hand up. If she didn't say it now she never would. She picked a point in the middle distance and focused on it.

"This is about you and Lindsay Moore. I know you were having an affair."

"Don't be ridiculous."

She took his hand. It was warm and familiar. She remembered how she used to trace her fingers across the grooves in his palm. *Did you know that you have a long lifeline?*

"Ray, please. There's still a chance for us to get past this, but I need you to be honest." She couldn't meet his eye. "I'm worried how this will look if it gets out."

He cleared his throat several times. "I've been under a lot of stress. Leaving my marriage is more difficult than I thought it would be."

"Sometimes I think I put too much pressure on you."

"It's not your fault. I swear I never meant to drag it out like this."

"I know you didn't."

"Lindsay was there when everything else got too complicated. It seemed to be such a simple choice at the time."

"So it's true?"

He nodded.

"How long were you seeing her for?"

"It wasn't like that," he said, squeezing her hand. "We'd agreed it was just supposed to be the one night, but she became more and more convinced that there was more to it than just sex. I tried everything. Even physically distancing myself." He paused. "It's why I sent her to Wilmington Creek."

There were real tears in Macy's eyes. "Ray, I know you're a good man, but I'm scared other people won't understand you the way I do. You realize how it's going to look if this gets out. Lindsay was three months pregnant when she died. People will think you're the father."

Ray started to say something then stopped.

She looked at him but he looked away. "Ray?"

"Believe me. I know how it looks."

"I need you to deny it."

"I can't."

"Jesus, Ray, how could you be so irresponsible?"

"She told me she was on the pill."

Macy took a second to calm her nerves. He'd admitted to the affair. He'd admitted to being the father. She was almost done. She slowed down.

"Then you must have slept with her again after she moved up to Wilmington Creek."

"It was only to buy time." He dragged his fingers through his hair. "It was the biggest mistake of my life."

"But we tested a DNA sample from the fetus. Your name didn't come up as a match."

"I removed my profile from the database."

"So you're safe. No one has to know."

He smoothed his fingertips along her wrist. "If the authorities find out about the affair they'll check again. How did you know about me and Lindsay?"

"Someone who saw you together has come forward. I think I put them off making a formal statement, but they could change their mind."

"Who?"

Macy hesitated. He wouldn't trust her if she didn't give him a name.

"Jessie Dalton."

"She's an ex–drug addict. She's not a credible witness."

"There are plenty of people who want your job, Ray. You know they'd press for a full investigation." She put her head on his shoulder. "If I'm going to help you, you need to tell me everything. You have to trust me now."

He held his lips to her forehead. "Lindsay threatened to go public."

"You would have lost everything."

"She'd call the house in the middle of the night and hang up. It was only a matter of time before she spoke to my wife. I drove up to Wilmington Creek because I was hoping to make her understand, but she wasn't like you. There was no reasoning with her."

Macy flinched. Her body stiffened as he wrapped his arms around her. She couldn't think straight. She pictured words in her head. She read them aloud one by one and prayed she was making sense.

"What happened, Ray?"

"The same thing that happened every time I tried to reason with her. She became hysterical. Claimed she was carrying my baby." He turned to look at Macy. "It's important that you understand. I really thought she was lying."

"There were ligature marks on her wrists."

"I had to restrain her until she calmed down."

"How did she end up in Waldo Canyon?"

"When she left the house I followed her. She'd threatened to drive all the way to Helena to speak to my wife in person. I think she was trying to lose me on the back roads south of town. There was smoke everywhere. At a certain point she got out of the car and started running."

Macy's voice cracked. "Is that when you shot her?"

"I had to stop her."

"Where's the gun?"

"I dumped it in the Flathead River."

Macy closed her eyes for a few seconds. All she saw was Lindsay floating alone in that black pool. "I suppose you were hoping her body was never found."

"That was the idea."

"You got lucky. If she hadn't fallen from that cliff she might have made it out of those woods alive."

Macy risked a quick glance over to where the surveillance van was parked. Two police cars had pulled up behind it. Several officers were moving toward them. Ray squeezed her hand. He hadn't seen them.

"Macy, I swear I'd take it all back if I could."

"I know you would." Macy removed her hands from his grasp and stood with difficulty. "I have to go."

"What's going on?"

She kept her voice steady. "You need to do the right thing. This is going to be hell for everyone, especially your children. Dragging our private lives through the courts will just make it worse."

He finally noticed the advancing officers. One of them held an arrest warrant.

"Are you wearing a wire?"

"Try to think about what I just said."

"I trusted you."

She started up the path she'd followed earlier, nodding to the arresting officers as they passed her going the opposite direction. Seconds later she heard them order Ray to put his hands where they could be seen. She didn't turn around to see what happened next, but that didn't stop her from imagining every little detail. Howard was waiting for her at the van. He handed her a handkerchief. Aside from his embroidered initials it was pure white. She handed it back.

"I'm fine," she said. "Did we get everything we needed?"

"And then some." He glanced over her shoulder. "I didn't really believe it until I heard him say it with his own mouth. All these years and it turns out I didn't know him at all."

"I know what you mean. Do you need me to stick around?"

"No, you've done your bit. It's up to the lawyers now. Do you think he'll take your advice?"

"I don't know. I hope so."

"So I'll see you on Monday?"

She puffed out her cheeks. "I think it would be a good idea if I took some time off."

"Going someplace special?"

"I don't know. I haven't planned anything yet."

"There's no hurry," he said, patting her on the back. "Your job will still be here when you get back."

It was after midnight and everyone in the house was asleep. Macy crept downstairs and opened the front door as quietly as she could. Aiden looked beat from the long drive. He held her close and kissed the top of her head.

"You okay?" he asked.

"I'm better now."

"It's been a long few weeks."

"It has. Are you tired or hungry?"

"Tired."

She took his hand and led him up the stairs. "When do you have to go back?"

"Not sure. I have to ask my boss."

"He's a friend of mine. If you like I'll put in a good word for you."

"That's very kind. I'll let him know."

She closed the bedroom door and they kissed for a long time.

"Come here," he said, pulling her down onto the bed and holding her tight in his arms. "You have no idea how worried I was about you today."

She managed to smile. "It's okay. I'm fine."

He lifted her chin so he could look her in the eye. "There's no way you're fine, so stop pretending. You probably just had one of the hardest days of your life."

She buried her head in his shoulder. "If I start crying I don't think I'll be able to stop."

"I wouldn't worry about that," he said, reaching over to shut off the bedside lamp. "We all stop eventually. It just takes some of us longer than others."

Macy shut her eyes and listened to the dull drumbeat of Aiden's heart. Against her better judgment she'd turned to have one last look at Ray before driving away. Flanked by officers, he'd been in handcuffs. She'd expected him to look diminished, but he hadn't magically shrunk down to a manageable size. If anything, he seemed to have grown in stature. There was so much unfinished business between them. She just knew he was going to haunt her for years to come.

Aiden wiped the tears from her cheeks. "Try to sleep," he said, pressing his lips into her hair.

"You'll be here in the morning?"

"You must have said something really nice to my boss. He says I can stay until the middle of the week."

"I told you he was a good friend."

"Try to sleep now."

Macy closed her eyes and focused on her breathing. She counted in her head. Her eyes fluttered open then shut again. Her whole body shuddered. She finally let go. She finally slept.